Orhan Pamuk

Silent House

Orhan Pamuk won the Nobel Prize for Literature in 2006. His novel *My Name Is Red* won the 2003 IMPAC Dublin Literary Award. His work has been translated into more than sixty languages.

INTERNATIONAL

Silent House

Silent House

ORHAN PAMUK

Translated from the Turkish
by Robert Finn

Vintage International
Vintage Books
A Division of Random House, Inc.
New York

FIRST VINTAGE INTERNATIONAL EDITION, JULY 2013

Translation copyright © 2012 by Orhan Pamuk

The Library of Congress has cataloged the Knopf edition as follows:
Pamuk, Orhan.
[Sessiz ev. English]
Silent house / by Orhan Pamuk ; [translated by Robert Finn].
p. cm.
1. Turkey—Fiction. I. Finn, Robert P. II. Title.
PL248.P34S4713 2012
894'.3533—dc 2012005468

Vintage ISBN: 978-0-307-74483-8

Book design by Cassandra J. Pappas

www.vintagebooks.com

Printed in the United States of America
10 9 8 7 6 5 4 3 2 1

CONTENTS

Silent House

I

Recep Goes to the Movies

❖

"Dinner is nearly ready, Madam," I said. "Please come to the table." She said nothing, just stood there, planted on her cane. I went over, took her by the arm, and brought her to the table. She just muttered a little. I went down to the kitchen, got her tray, and put it in front of her. She looked at it but didn't touch the food. I got out her napkin, stretched it out under her huge ears, and knotted it.

"Well, what did you make tonight?" she said. "Let's see what you put together."

"Baked eggplant," I said. "You requested it yesterday, right?"

She looked at me.

I slid the plate in front of her. She pushed the food around with her fork, complaining to herself. After picking at it a little, she began to eat.

"Madam, don't forget your salad," I said before going inside and sitting down to my own eggplant.

A little later, she called out, "Salt. Recep, where's the salt?" I went back out and saw it was right in front of her.

"Here it is!"

"Well, this is a new one," she said. "Why do you go inside when I'm eating?"

I didn't answer.

"They're coming tomorrow, aren't they?"

"They're coming, Madam, they're coming," I said. "Weren't you going to put some salt on that?"

"You mind your own business!" she said. "Are they coming?"

"Tomorrow afternoon," I said. "They called, you know."

"What else have you got?"

I took the uneaten eggplant back, ladled a good portion of beans onto a fresh plate, and brought it out to her. When she'd lost interest in the beans and started stirring them around, I returned to the kitchen and sat down to resume my supper. A little later she called out again, this time for pepper, but I pretended not to hear her. When she cried *Fruit!* I went in and pushed the fruit bowl in front of her. Her thin, bony hand began to wander over the fruit like a drowsy spider. Finally it stopped.

"All rotten! Where'd you find these? Lying on the ground under the trees?"

"They're not rotten, Madam," I said. "They're just ripe. These are the best peaches. I got them from the fruit seller. You know there are no peach trees around here anymore."

Pretending she hadn't heard me she chose one of the peaches. I went inside and was just finishing my beans when she shouted, "Untie me! Recep, where are you? Let me out of this!"

I ran in and as I undid her napkin I saw that she had left half the peach.

"Let me at least give you some apricots, Madam. Otherwise you'll wake me up in the middle of the night and tell me you're hungry."

"I've never been so hungry that I've had to eat things that have fallen off the trees, thank you."

As she wiped her mouth she wrinkled her face, then pretended to pray for a while before getting up.

"Take me upstairs!"

She leaned on me and we made our way, stopping on the ninth step to catch our breath.

"Have you made up their rooms?" she said, gasping.

"I made them up."

"Okay, then let's go," she said, leaning on me all the more.

We continued to the top step. "Eighteen, nineteen, thank God," she said, and went into her room.

"Let's turn on your light," I said. "I am going to be at the movies."

"The movies!" she said. "A grown man. Well, don't stay out late."

I went down, finished my beans, and washed the dishes. I already had my tie on under my apron. So I had only to get my jacket, check for my wallet, and be gone.

The wind blew cool from the sea, and it was pleasant. The leaves of the fig tree were rustling. I shut the garden gate and walked down toward the beach. Where our garden wall ended, the pavement and the new concrete houses began. They were on their balconies, in their little narrow gardens, watching, families listening to the news on TV, the women at their charcoal grills. They didn't see me. Meat on the grills and smoke. Families, lives; I wonder what it's like. When winter comes, though, there'll be nobody around. Then I'll be frightened just to hear my own footsteps in the empty streets. I felt myself shivering and put on my jacket and turned the corner.

It was funny to think how they all sat down to eat their dinner and watch TV at the same time! As I was walking around in the back streets, a car pulled up at the end of one of those that opened onto the square, and a tired husband back from Istanbul got out. He went into the house with his bag, looking upset to be getting home so late for his dinner in front of the television. When I got down to the shore again, I heard Ismail's voice: "National lottery, six days left!"

He didn't see me; I didn't say anything either. He was bobbing up and down as he walked among the tables in the restaurant. One table called him over, and he went, bending down to present a fistful of lottery tickets to a girl in a white dress with a ribbon in her hair. The girl picked carefully as her mother and father smiled with pleasure. I turned away, saying I was not going to look anymore. If I had called out, if Ismail had seen me, he would have quickly limped over to me. He would have said, Brother, why don't you ever stop by? Your house is so far away, Ismail, I would have said, and it's up high on the hill. Yes, you're right, he would have said. When Doğan Bey gave us that money, brother, if I had bought property here instead of on the hill, oh Recep, if I had bought on the shore instead of up there because it was near the train station, I'd be a millionaire, he would have said, always in those words. His pretty wife would say nothing, only look at you. Why should I go? True, sometimes I want to, sometimes on winter nights when I have no one to talk to, I feel the urge and I do go, but it's always the same words.

The casinos on the shore were empty. The televisions were on. The tea men had lined up hundreds of empty tea glasses in rows they all sparkled nice and clean under the powerful lights. They were waiting for the news to finish and the crowds to pour out into the streets. The cats were crouched under the empty chairs. I walked on.

Rowboats were pulled up close to the wall on the other side of the breakwater. There was nobody on the dirty little beach. Seaweed that had landed on the shore and dried out, bottles, pieces of plastic . . . They said they were going to knock down Ibrahim the coffee man's house, the coffeehouses, too. I suddenly got excited when I saw the light in the windows of the coffeehouse. Maybe there'd be somebody there. Somebody who didn't play cards—we'd talk. He'd ask, How are you. I'd tell him, he'd listen, and How are you; he'd tell and I'd listen. Raising our voices to be heard above the television and the general din. Friendship. Maybe we'd even go to the movies together.

But as soon as I walked into the coffeehouse I lost my good spirits, because those two punks were there again. They were glad when they saw me, and they looked at each other and laughed. But I don't see you, I'm looking at my watch. I'm looking for a friend. Nevzat was sitting over there on the left, watching the card players. I got a chair and joined him. I was happy.

"So," I said. "How are you?"

He didn't say anything.

I looked at the television a little bit; it was the end of the news. I looked at the cards being passed around and at Nevzat looking at them. I wanted them all to finish their hand, and they did, but still they didn't talk to me; they just talked and laughed among themselves. Then they resumed their game and got wrapped up in it before stopping again. Finally, as they were dealing out the cards for another hand, I figured I'd better say something.

"Nevzat, that milk you gave us this morning was very good."

He nodded without turning his head from the cards.

"Plenty of fat in it; it's good."

He nodded again. I looked at my watch. It was five to nine. I looked at the television and lost track of things; much later I realized that the young men were snickering. When I saw the newspaper in their hands, I thought in fear, Oh God, not another picture. Because they kept looking at me and then the newspaper, laughing in a nasty way. Pay no attention, Recep! But I thought about it anyway: sometimes they put a picture in the papers, they have no feelings. They write something terrible underneath, just as when they print a picture of a naked lady or a bear giving birth in the zoo. In a panic, I turned to Nevzat and said, without thinking:

"How are you?"

He turned to me for a second, muttering something, but I couldn't think of anything more to say because my mind was on the picture. So I gave up and began to watch the two young guys on the sly. When we came eye to eye, they began to smirk even more. I turned away. A king fell on the table. The players all cursed, some of them happy and some of them disappointed. Then a new game began; the cards and the good mood changed hands. Was there a face card? I had a sudden thought.

"Cemil," I called out. "A tea over here!"

So I had found something to keep me busy for a little while, but it didn't last very long. I kept thinking about what the young men were laughing about in the newspaper. When I looked again, they had given it to Cemil and were pointing out the picture. When Cemil saw my discomfort, he let them have it: "Hoodlums!"

Well, everything was out in the open. I couldn't pretend I hadn't noticed anymore. I should have left a long time ago. The young guys were laughing openly.

"What is going on, Cemil?" I said. "What is in that paper?"

"Nothing!" he said.

I tried to hold myself back, but I didn't have the strength because I was overwhelmed with curiosity. I got up from the chair like someone in a trance, took a few slow steps over to Cemil, passing the young men who had fallen silent.

"Give me that paper!"

He made as if to withhold the paper as he spoke softly. "Who knows if it's even real? I've never heard of such a thing." Then staring fiercely at the young men, he said, "Shameless!" before finally surrendering the newspaper.

Like a hungry wolf I grabbed it from his hand and opened it, my heart was pounding as I looked at the page he had pointed to, but there was no picture.

"Down there!" said Cemil growing nervous.

My eyes moved quickly over the "History Corner."

" 'Üsküdar's historical treasures,' " I began to read aloud, " 'Yahya Kemal, the poet, and Üsküdar . . . " Then below headlines "General Mehmet" . . . "the Greek Mosque" . . . "Şemsi Pasha Mosque and Library" . . . Finally I followed Cemil's fingertip down to the bottom and I saw:

"The Dwarves' House in Üsküdar!"

I felt the blood rush to my face as I read the item in one breath.

" 'Along with these, there was at one time a dwarves' house in Üsküdar. This house, which was built for dwarves, not for ordinary people, was perfectly complete. Except its rooms, doors, windows, and stairs were made for dwarves, and a regular person had to bend himself in half to get in. According to research done by the art historian Dr. Süheyl Enver, this house was built by Handan Sultan, spouse of Sultan Mehmet III, and mother of Sultan Ahmet I. This lady loved her dwarves so much, this excessive affection occupies a special place in the history of the Harem. Handan Sultan wanted her dear friends to live together undisturbed in peace after she died, so she put the palace carpenter Ramazan Usta to work. It is said that the perfection of the ironwork and woodwork made this little house a work of art. However, we must admit that we do not know for certain whether such a strange and interesting building actually existed, as it is not mentioned by the historian Evliya Çelebi, who wandered through Üsküdar in the same years. Even if there had really been such a place, this curious house must have disappeared in the famous fire that terrorized Üsküdar in 1642.' "

"Just forget it, Recep," Cemil said as I stood there trembling. "Why do you pay attention to these punks?"

I had a terrible compulsion to read the newspaper again, but I didn't have the strength. Drenched in sweat, I felt as if I couldn't breathe. The paper slipped out of my hand and fell to the floor.

"Have a seat," said Cemil. "Take it easy. You're upset, don't over-react." Then he said again, "Punks!" talking to the young men who were watching with malicious interest as I swayed on my feet.

"Yes," I said, "I am upset." I was quiet for a minute and collected myself and then, mustering all my strength, I spoke again. "Not because I'm a dwarf, am I upset," I said. "What's really upsetting is that people can be nasty enough to make fun of a fifty-five-year-old dwarf."

There was a silence. The card players must have heard, too. Nevzat and I came eye to eye. The young men were looking down; they were at least a bit ashamed. My head was now spinning; the television was droning away.

"Punks," repeated Cemil, now with less feeling.

And then, as I was weaving my way to the door, "Hey, Recep, where are you going?"

I didn't answer. I managed in a couple of faltering steps to leave the bright lights of the coffeehouse behind me. I was outside again, in the cool dark night.

I was in no condition to continue, but I forced myself to take a few more steps before sitting down on one of the posts near the jetty. I breathed deeply in the clean air; my heart was still beating fast. What should I do? The lights of the casinos and restaurants were gleaming in the distance. They had strung colored lights in the trees, and underneath those lights people were eating, talking with one another: my God!

The door of the coffeehouse opened, and I heard Cemil call out: "Recep, Recep, where are you?"

I didn't make a sound. He didn't see me and went inside.

A long time afterward, I heard the rumbling of the train to Ankara. It must have been about ten past nine, and I was thinking like this: They were all just words, weren't they? A cloud of sound that disappeared the moment it came out? I felt a little better, but I didn't want to go home. There was nothing else to do: I'd still go to the movies. I'd stopped sweating; my heart had slowed down; I was better. I took a deep breath and walked on.

In the coffeehouse, I thought, they've forgotten me and those words now, and the television is still droning. If Cemil hasn't thrown them out, the young men are looking for somebody else to make fun of. So, here I am on the street again, the crowd's out, they've finished their food, and now they're taking a little stroll to digest before they sit down in front of the TV again or go to the nightclubs. They eat ice cream, talk, and greet one another. The women and their husbands who come back from Istanbul in the evenings and their children always chewing on something; they recognize one another and say hello. I passed by the restaurants again. Ismail wasn't there. Maybe he sold out the tickets he had in his hand and was climbing the hill up to his house again. If I had planned to go see him instead of a movie, we might have talked. But we always say the same things.

The avenue was pretty crowded. Cars waiting in front of the ice-cream shop and groups of three or four walking together tied up the traffic. I looked presentable in my tie and jacket but I can't stand crowds like that; I turned off into a side street. The kids were playing hide-and-seek between the cars on the narrow streets in the blue light coming from the televisions. When I was little I used to think that I would be good at this game, but I never had the courage to join in with them like Ismail. But if I had played I would have hidden myself best of all, maybe here, in the ruins of the caravanserai that my mother said had had plague or, for example, in the village, in the haystack, and if I never came out, then who would they have made fun of, I wondered, but my mother would have looked for me, she would have said, Ismail, where's your brother? And Ismail would have pulled on his nose and said, How would I know, as I stayed hidden listening to them, whispering, I live in secret, all by myself, Mother, where no one can see me, only my mother would then start to cry so much that I'd come out, saying, Look, here I am, I'm not hiding anymore, see, I'm not hiding anymore, Mother, and my mother would have said, Why were you hiding, my son, and I would have thought, Maybe she's right, what use is hiding, what's to be gained living in secret? I would have forgotten for a moment.

I saw them as they moved quickly down the avenue. Sıtkı Bey, grown up and married, with his wife, and he even had a kid as tall as I was. He recognized me, smiled, and paused.

"Hello, Recep Efendi," he said. "How are you?"

I always waited for them to talk first.

"Hello, Sıtkı Bey," I said. "I'm fine, thank you."

I shook hands with him. Not with his wife. The children were staring in fear and curiosity.

"Sweetie, Recep Bey's been living here in Cennethisar longer than just about anybody else."

His wife nodded with a smile. I was happy, proud of being one of the old-timers here.

"How's Grandma?"

"Oh," I said, "Madam always complains, but she's fine."

"How many years has it been?" he said. "Where is Faruk?"

"They're coming tomorrow," I said.

He started explaining to his wife that Faruk Bey was his child-hood friend. Then without shaking hands, just nodding, we said good-bye and parted. Now he was talking to his wife about his child-hood and about me, how I took them to the well when they were lit-tle and showed them how to fish for mullet, and then the kid would finally ask his question: "Daddy, why is that man so small?" I used to say: Because my mother gave birth before she got married. But Sıtkı Bey got married, Faruk Bey got married, and they had no kids at all. But because my mother had done just the opposite, Madam sent her, along with us, to the village. Before she sent us, there were words and she threatened us all with her cane, and my mother pleaded, Don't do that, Madam, what fault of the children's is it? Sometimes, I think I heard those words, on that terrible day . . .

In the well-lit street of the movie theater, I heard the music they play before the film starts. I looked at still shots from the film that was showing: *Let's Meet in Paradise*. It's an old film: in one scene, Hülya Koçyiğit and Ediz Hun are in each other's arms, then Ediz is in prison, then Hülya is singing a song, but you'd never be able to tell what order these things happened in until you'd seen the film. This probably occurred to them when they put the pictures up; it gets people interested. I went to the ticket window, One please. The woman pulled off a ticket and rose a little from her seat so as to hold it out to me

"Is the film any good?" I asked.

She hadn't seen it. Sometimes, out of the blue, I just want to talk to someone like this. I took my seat and waited.

When first they meet, the girl is a singer and doesn't like him, but the next day, when the guy saves her from those villains, she likes him and then realizes she loves him, but her father is against their getting married. Then the guy goes to prison. I didn't go out with the crowd at the intermission. When it started again, the girl marries the son of the nightclub owner, but they don't have any kids and they don't do anything about it either. Eventually, the husband runs off after a bad woman and Ediz escapes from prison. In a house near the Istanbul Bridge, he meets Hülya Koçyiğit, who sings a song. The song left me in a strange mood. At the end, she wants to free herself from the lousy husband, and since he's met his own punishment anyway, we figure out that they are going to get married. Her father is looking at them warmly from behind as they are walking arm in arm on the road, walking, getting smaller and smaller and THE END.

After the lights came up, and everybody was filing out, buzzing about the film, I wanted to talk about it with someone, too. It was ten after eleven. Madam would be waiting, but I didn't want to return home.

I walked toward the beach over to the hill. Maybe Kemal Bey, the pharmacist, would be on duty and not feeling sleepy. I'll barge in, we'll talk, I'll tell him things, he'll listen to me, lost in thought, staring into the lights of the food stand across the way at the kids shouting at one another and racing their cars. When I saw that the pharmacy lights were on, I was happy. He hadn't gone to bed. I opened the door and the bell rang. Oh God, it wasn't Kemal Bey but his wife.

"Hello," I said and paused. "I need an aspirin."

"A box or one tablet," said the wife.

"Two tablets. I have a headache. I'm a little bored ... Kemal Bey ... ," I said, but she wasn't listening. She had her scissors out and was cutting the individual aspirin packets.

"Did Kemal Bey already go out for the morning fish?" I said.

"Kemal's asleep upstairs."

I looked at the ceiling for a minute and considered that, just two inches above it, my friend lay sleeping. If he happened to stir, I would tell him about my evening. He might have something to say about those kids at the coffeehouse, but then again he might not, he might simply stare out in that bewildered way, so thoughtful, as I talked, as we talked. I took the change his wife set out with her little white hands. Then I looked around and saw lying there right on the couch one of those photo novels for all to see. Nice lady! I said good night and left without troubling her further; the bell jingled again. The streets were emptier, and the children playing hide-and-seek had gone home.

As I latched the garden gate behind me, I saw Madam's light through the shutters: she could never sleep before I went to bed. I went in through the kitchen door and locked it behind me, too, and as I slowly climbed up the stairs I wondered, Were there steps in the dwarves' house in Üsküdar? Which paper was it, I would go and get from the store tomorrow, Do you have yesterday's *Tercüman,* our Faruk Bey is looking for it, I'd say. He's a historian, he is interested in the 'History Corner . . .'

"I'm here, Madam," I said, finding her lying in bed.

"Well done," she said. "You finally managed to find your way home."

"The film was over late, what was I supposed to do?"

"Did you make sure of the doors?"

"I closed them," I said. "Do you want anything before I'm sound asleep in bed?"

"They are coming tomorrow, aren't they?"

"Yes," I said. "I've made up their beds and prepared their rooms."

"Okay," she said. "Close my door tight."

Downstairs, I went right to bed and to sleep.

2

Grandmother Waits in Bed

❧

I listen to him going down the stairs one by one. What does he do in the streets until all hours? I wonder. Don't think about it, Fatma, you'll only get disgusted. But still, I wonder. Did he shut the doors tight, that sneaky dwarf? He couldn't care less! He'll get right into bed to prove he's a born servant, snore all night long. Sleep that untroubled, carefree sleep of a servant, and leave me to the night. I think that sleep will come for me, too, and I'll forget, but I wait all alone and I realize that I'm waiting in vain.

Selâhattin used to say that sleep is a chemical phenomenon, one day they'll discover its formula just as they discovered that H_2O is the formula for water. Oh, not our fools, of course, unfortunately it'll be the Europeans again who find it, and then no one will have to put on funny pajamas and sleep between these useless sheets and under ridiculous flowered quilts and lie there until morning just because he's tired. At that time, all we'll have to do is to put three drops from a bottle into a glass of water every evening and then drink it, and it will make us as fit and fresh as if we had just woken up in the morning from a deep sleep. Think of all the things we could do with those extra hours, Fatma, think of it!

I don't have to think about it, Selâhattin, I know. I stare at the ceiling, I stare and stare and wait for some thought to carry me away, but it doesn't happen. If I could drink wine or *rakı,* maybe I could sleep like you, but I don't want that kind of ugly sleep. You used to drink two bottles: I drink to clear my mind and relieve my exhaustion from working on the encyclopedia, Fatma, it's not for pleasure. Then you would doze off, snoring with your mouth open until the smell of *rakı* would drive me away in disgust. Cold woman, poor thing, you're like ice, you have no spirit! If you had a glass now and again, you'd understand! Come on, have a drink, Fatma, I'm ordering you, don't you believe you have to do what your husband tells you. Of course, you believe it, that's what they taught you, well, then, I'm ordering you: Drink, let the sin be mine, come on, drink, Fatma, set your mind free. It's your husband who wants it, come on, oh God! She's making me beg. I'm sick of this loneliness, please, Fatma, have one drink, or you'll be disobeying your husband.

No, I wouldn't fall for a lie in the form of a serpent. I never drank, except once. I was overcome with curiosity. When nobody at all was around. A taste like salt, lemon, and poison on the tip of my tongue. At that moment I was terrified. I was sorry. I rinsed my mouth out right away, I emptied out the glass and rinsed it over and over and I began to feel I would be dizzy. I sat down so I wouldn't fall on the floor, my God, I was afraid I would become an alcoholic like him, too, but nothing happened. Then I understood and relaxed. The devil couldn't get near me.

I'm staring at the ceiling. I still can't get to sleep, might as well get up. I get up, open the shutter quietly, because the mosquitoes don't bother me. I peek out the shutters a little; the wind has died down, a still night. Even the fig tree isn't rustling. Recep's light is off. Just as I figured: right to sleep, since he has nothing to think about, the dwarf. Cook the food, do my little handful of laundry and the shopping, and even then he gets rotten peaches, and afterward, he prowls around the streets for hours.

I can't see the sea, but I think of how far it extends and how much farther it could go. The big, wide world! Noisy motorboats and those rowboats you get into with nothing on, but they smell nice, I like them. I hear the cricket. It's only moved a foot in a week. Then again, I haven't moved even that much. I used to think the world was a beautiful place; I was a child, a fool. I close the shutters and fasten the bolt: let the world stay out there.

I sit down on the chair slowly, looking at the tabletop. Things in silence. A half-full pitcher, the water in it standing motionless. When I want to drink I remove the glass cover, fill it, listening to and watching the water flow; the glass tinkles; the water runs; cool air rises; it's unique; it fascinates me. I'm fascinated, but I don't drink. Not yet. You have to be careful using up the things that make the time pass. I look at my hairbrush and see my hairs caught in it. I pick it up and begin to clean it out. The weak thin hairs of my ninety years. They're falling out one by one. Time, I whisper, what they call our years; we shed them that way, too. I stop and set the brush down. It lies there like an insect on its back, revolting me. If I leave everything this way and nobody touches it for a thousand years, that's how it will stay for a thousand years. Things on top of a table, a key or a water pitcher. How strange; everything in its place, without moving! Then my thoughts would freeze too, colorless and odorless and just sitting there, like a piece of ice.

But tomorrow they'll come and I'll think again. Hello, hello, how are you, they'll kiss my hand, many happy returns, how are you, Grandmother, how are you, how are you, Grandmother? I'll take a look at them. Don't all talk at once, come here and let me have a look at you, come close, tell me, what have you been doing? I know I'll be asking to be fooled, and I'll listen blankly to a few lines of deception! Well, is that all, haven't you anything more to say to your grandmother? They'll look at one another, talk among themselves, I'll hear and understand. Then they'll start to shout. Don't shout, don't shout, thank God my ears can still hear. Excuse me, Grandmother, it's just that our other grandmother doesn't hear well. I'm not your mother's mother, I'm your father's mother. Excuse me, Granny, excuse me! All right, all right, tell me something, that other grandmother of yours, what's she like? They'll suddenly get confused and become quiet. What is our other grandmother like? Then I'll realize that they haven't learned how to see or understand yet, that's all right, I'll ask them again but just as I'm about to ask them, I see that they've forgotten all about it. They're not interested in me or my room or what I'm asking, but in their own thoughts, as I am in mine even now.

I reach out and pick an apricot from the plate. I eat it, waiting. It does no good. Here I am, in the midst of things, not thoughts. I look at the table. It's five to twelve. Next to the clock is the bottle of cologne, next to that the newspaper, and then my handkerchief. They stay that way. I look at them, my eyes travel across them and examine the surfaces to see if they have something more to say to me, but they have reminded me of so much already that they have nothing left to say. Just a bottle of cologne, a newspaper, a hand-kerchief, a key, and a clock; it ticks and no one, not even Selâhattin, knows what time is. One moment and then another right behind it, each smaller and smaller, my thoughts going from here to there, but don't get stuck in one of those thoughts, wiggle away, jump outside, quick come over here, outside of time and this room. I eat another apricot, but I don't go outside: I look at the things even more, and it seems I try to busy myself until I am fed up with the same old things. If I weren't there, if no one were there, these things would stay this way forever and then no one could possibly think he didn't know what life was. No one!

No, I am not distracted by these things. I got up from the chair, went to the bathroom, washed my face, and I went back, ignoring the spiderweb that hung down from the corner where it was. When you turn the switch, the lamp hanging from the ceiling goes off, only the one by the head of my bed stays on, and I get into bed. It's warm out, but I can't do without a quilt, what could I do, something to snuggle up in, get under, and hide inside. I put my head down on the pillow, I wait and I know that sleep will not come right away. The weak light of the lamp strikes the ceiling; I listen to the cricket. Hot summer nights!

But it seems the summers used to be hotter. We drank lemonade and had sherbet. Not in the street, though, not from the men in white aprons; my mother would say, We'll make it at home, where it's clean, Fatma, as we were coming back from the market, nothing new in the shops. We would wait for my father in the evening, he would come and talk and we would listen; he smelled of tobacco and coughed when he spoke. Once he said, Fatma, there's a doctor who wants you. I said nothing! I was quiet, and my father didn't say anything, but the next day again, and I was only fifteen years old, my mother said, "Look, Fatma, they say he's a doctor," and I thought: How strange, I wonder when he could have seen me. I was afraid and didn't ask, but I thought again, Doctor? Egghead? Then my father added: They say he has a good future, Fatma, I asked all around, hardworking and maybe a little greedy, but an honorable and clever man, think on it. I was silent. It was very hot, we were having sherbet. Well, I don't know. Finally, I said, "All right," and then my father made me stand in front of him: My girl, you're going forth from your father's house, get that through your head. He was telling me not to ask too many questions; curiosity is for cats, okay, Father, I know. And let me tell you again, my girl, don't do that with your hand, look, and stop biting your fingernails, how old are you now. Okay, Daddy, I won't ask, yes, but: I didn't ask.

I didn't ask. It had been four years, and we still didn't have a child. Fault of the air in Istanbul, I later understood. One summer evening, Selâhattin came straight to me instead of going to his library and he said, "We're not going to live in Istanbul anymore, Fatma!" I didn't ask, "Why, Selâhattin?" but he told me anyway, jumping around like a gangly kid. We're not going to live in Istanbul anymore, Fatma, because Talat Pasha called me today and this is what he said:

Dr. Selâhattin, you will no longer live in Istanbul, and you will have nothing to do with politics! That's what he said to me, the son of a bitch. You've done what I said not to do, you think you're such a hero, the Pasha said, well, I guess you wouldn't like it if I sent you off with the others on the first ship to the prison in Sinop, but what should I do, you've been a lot of trouble, you've got yourself involved in the party, but you seem like a sensible man, be reasonable, you're married, a doctor, you've got a good profession, you can make enough money to live comfortably anywhere in the world, how's your French, my friend? Goddamn him! Do you understand, Fatma, these Union- ists are going off the deep end, they can't stand freedom, how are they different from Abdülhamit? Okay, Talat Pasha, if I accept your invitation and pack up my things right away, don't think that it's because I'm afraid of the dungeon in Sinop: no! It's because I know I can still give you the answer you deserve from Paris, but not from the corner of a dungeon. We're going to Paris, Fatma, sell one of your diamonds or rings. If you don't want to, okay, I still have some property left from my father, or we can go to Salonica instead of Europe, why should we leave the country, we'll go to Damascus, look at Dr. Reza, he went to Alexandria and writes that he's earning a lot there, where are my letters, I can't find them, didn't I tell you not to touch things on my desk, and God, there's Berlin, too, but did you ever hear of Geneva, they've become worse than Abdülhamit, well, don't just stand there staring at me dumbfounded, get the bags and trunks ready, a freedom fighter's wife has to be strong, doesn't she, there's nothing to fear. I was silent, didn't say a thing, you know best, and I listened as Selâhattin, talking all the while, told me what they were able to do to Abdülhamit from Paris, how he was going to take care of this lot from Paris, too, how the day would come when we would come back in victory by train from Paris! Then he said, no, not Damascus, he said Izmir, and in the evening he was saying Trebizond would do, We have to sell whatever we have, Fatma, are you ready for sacrifice? I want to give all my strength to the struggle, that's why, don't say anything in front of the maids and servants, Fatma, the walls have ears, but Mr. Talat, you didn't even have to tell me to go: I wouldn't stay in this whorehouse called Istanbul a moment longer anyway, but, Fatma, where should we go, say something, I was silent and thinking, He's really just a child. Yes, the devil could only fool a child that much, I realized I had married a child who could be led astray by three books. Later, in the middle of the night, I came out of my room, it was hot, I said, Let me get something to drink, I saw a light in his room and I went there, quietly opened the door, and there was Selâhattin with his elbows on the table and his head in his hands, crying. A harsh light fell on his face from the lamp that was almost burned out. The skull he always kept on his desk was staring at him as he wept. I pulled the door shut quietly, I went to the kitchen and drank a glass of water, and I thought, Well, he's a child, a child.

I get out of the bed slowly and sit at the table and stare at the water pitcher. How does the water manage to stay in there without moving, I wonder, as though astonished at this, as though a pitcher of water is something miraculous. Once I placed a glass over a bee and imprisoned it. When I was bored I would get out of bed and look at it. It wandered around in the glass for two days until it understood that there was no way out and then it decided that there was nothing to do but sit in a corner motionless and wait and wait, not knowing what it was waiting for. When I got tired of it, fed up, really, I opened the shutters before sliding the glass over to the edge of the table and lifting it up so the bee could fly away, but the stupid creature didn't fly away! It just stayed there on the tabletop. I called Recep and told him to swat it with something. But ripping off a piece of newspaper, he carefully picked up the bee and let it go out the window. He couldn't bring himself to do it. He's just like them.

I fill the glass with water. I drink it little by little. Finished! What should I do now? I get back into bed, prop my head against the pillow, and think about when this house was built. Selâhattin used to take me by the hand and show me around: Here's where my examining room will be, here's the dining room, here's the European kitchen; I'm having a separate room built for each of the kids, because every-

one should be able to shut himself up and develop his own personality, yes, Fatma, I want three kids. And see, I'm not having bars put
on the window—what an ugly idea! Are women birds or animals?
We're all free, if you want you can up and leave me, we're putting in
shutters and we're going to have windows just as Europeans do, and
don't say over there and over here anymore, Fatma, that extension
isn't a window seat, it's called a balcony. It's a window that opens
onto freedom, isn't it a beautiful view? Istanbul must be over there,
underneath those clouds, Fatma, fifty kilometers, it's a good thing
we got off the train at Gebze, time passes quickly, and I don't think
they'll be able to put up with this idiot government much longer,
maybe even before the house is finished the Unionists will fall and
we'll go right back to Istanbul, Fatma.

Later, the house was finished, and my son Doğan was born, and
another war had broken out, but the idiot Unionist government was
still in power and Selâhattin was telling me, Why don't you go to
Istanbul, Fatma. Talat didn't exile you, just me, why don't you go,
you'll see your mother, see your father. You'll go see Şukru Pasha's
daughters, do some shopping, get some new things to wear, and at
least you can dress up and show your mother all that stuff you've
made bent over the sewing machine here, pumping away at the pedal
from morning till late at night, ruining those beautiful eyes of yours.
Fatma, why don't you go? But I said, No, we'll go together, Selâhattin, when they're thrown out, we'll go together, but they never were.
Then one day I saw it in the paper—Selâhattin's papers came three
days late, but he no longer jumped on them right away as he used to.
He didn't even pay attention to the war news from Palestine, Galicia,
and Gallipoli, and some days, when he'd forgotten even to scan the
headlines after dinner, I would read the paper first. When I learned
that the Unionists had been overthrown, I left the news like a beautiful ripe fruit on his plate. When he lifted his head up from that
wretched encyclopedia of his and came downstairs for lunch, he saw
the newspaper and could not fail to notice the news, because it was
in huge letters. He read it without saying a thing. I didn't ask, but I

knew he didn't write a single word of his encyclopedia all afternoon, because the sound of his footsteps overhead did not cease until evening. When Selâhattin didn't say anything at supper either, I softly said, Did you see, Selâhattin, they've been thrown out? Oh yes, he said, the government's fallen, hasn't it? The Unionists have sunk the Ottoman Empire and run off, and we've lost the war, too! He couldn't look me in the eye, and we both fell silent. Later, as we were getting up from the table, he said, as though confessing some shameful sin he wanted to forget, Well, I suppose we'll go back to Istanbul but only when the encyclopedia is finished, because that mundane little comedy called politics in Istanbul is nothing compared with the momentous work of this encyclopedia of everything, what I'm doing here is much greater and more profound, a scientific marvel whose influence will endure centuries from now. I have no right to leave this job half done, Fatma, I'm going right upstairs, he said, and off he went, and until he learned he was going to die, after which he would suffer unbelievable torments for another four months, until the blood rushed out of his mouth and he finally expired, he wrote that awful encyclopedia for another thirty years, and because of that, and it's the only thing I have to thank you for, Selâhattin, I would remain here in Cennethisar for seventy years and avoid the sin of your "Istanbul of the Future" and the atheist's state, I've avoided it, haven't I, Fatma, so sleep in peace.

But I can't sleep and I listen to the train passing in the distance, its whistle and then its engine as it rattles on and on. I used to love this sound. I used to think how, far away, there were innocent countries, lands, houses, gardens; I was a child, easily fooled. There goes another train! I can't feel anymore. Don't think, where! My pillow's warm from my cheek; I turn it over. When I put my head on it, it is cool behind my ears. On winter nights it used to be cold, but nobody snuggled with anybody. Selâhattin kept snoring and I used to go into the next room and sit in the dark, disgusted at the stench of wine welling up out of his mouth. Once I went into the room across the hall, saying to myself, let's take a look at these papers, let me see what

he's writing from morning to night: he had written a part of an article about gorillas being the grandfathers of men; he wrote in those
days that the incredible advances of the sciences in the West had
now made God's existence a ridiculous question to be cast aside; he'd
written that the East's continued slumber in the deep and despicable
darkness of the Middle Ages had not led us, a handful of intellectu-
als, toward despair but, on the contrary, toward a great enthusiasm
for work, because what was obvious was that we were not obliged
to take all this knowledge and transport it from there to here, but to
discover it all over again, to close the gap of centuries between East
and West in a shorter time. Now, he wrote, as I complete the sev-
enth year of this glorious work, I see the masses stupefied by fear of
God—My God, Fatma! Don't read any more, but still I was reading;
he wrote, I'm obliged to articulate a number of things that would be
absurdly plain in any advanced nation, just to rouse this mound of
sloths, and, he wrote, At least if I had a friend to discuss all of this
with, but not only am I without even a single friend, I'm finally at
the point of abandoning all hope in this cold woman; from now on,
Selâhattin, you're all alone, and he wrote out, too, all his little tasks
on a piece of paper, he overwrote the map in Polikowsky's book to
make a chart of the migratory routes of storks and other birds; he
recorded three simple fables for proving to the feebleminded that
God doesn't exist, but no, I couldn't read any more, that's enough,
Fatma, I let those sinful papers drop and ran out of the icy room,
never to reenter that cursed chamber until that cold snowy day after
he'd died. Still, Selâhattin had figured it out the very next day: You
went into my room when I was sleeping last night, Fatma? You went
into my room and mixed up my papers? I kept silent. You mixed
them up, left them out of order, even dropped some on the floor, but
it doesn't matter, Fatma, you're welcome to read as much as you like,
read! I kept silent. You read them, didn't you? Good! You did the
right thing, Fatma, what do you think? I still kept silent. You always
knew I wanted you to, didn't you, Fatma? Read them, reading's the
best thing, read and learn, because there's so much to do, you know. I

kept silent. Read them and wake up and one day you'll see how much there is to do in life, Fatma, how many things!

Actually, no, there aren't so many things. I would know: it's been ninety years. Possessions, yes, roomfuls, I can look and see, from there to there, and a little time, endless drips falling from an unstoppable faucet. Just then is in my body and head now, just then is now, the eye closes and opens, the shutter is pushed and shuts, night and day, and then another new morning, but I'm not fooled. I still wait. They'll come tomorrow. Hello, hello! Many happy returns. They'll kiss my hand and laugh. The hair on their heads looks funny when they bend down to kiss my hand. How are you, how are you, Grandmother? What can someone like me say? I'm alive, I'm waiting. Tombs, dead people. Come on, sleep, come.

I turn over in the bed. Now I don't hear the cricket anymore. The bee is gone, too. How long until morning? Crows, magpies, on the roofs in the morning . . . sometimes I wake up early and hear them. Is it true that magpies are thieves? The jewels of queens and princesses, a magpie grabs them, and everybody takes off after it. I wonder how a bird can fly with all that weight. How do creatures fly? Balloons, zeppelins, and that man Selâhattin wrote about. How does Lindbergh fly? If he happened to have two bottles instead of one, he would forget that I don't listen and tell me about it after dinner. Today I wrote about planes, birds, and flying, Fatma, I'm just about to finish the article on air, listen. The air is not empty, Fatma, there are particles in it, and just as a floating boat displaces its weight in the water, no, I don't understand how balloons and zeppelins fly, but Selâhattin was completely animated, telling me about every fact of science, and as always he was shouting by the time he got to his conclusion: Yes, that's what we need, to know this and everything else; an encyclopedia; if we knew the natural and social sciences God would die and we, but by now I was not listening anymore! If he'd finished a second bottle I wouldn't be listening to his raving; No, there is no God, Fatma, there's science now. Your God is dead, you silly woman! Then, when he had nothing else to believe in except his self-love and his self-loathing, he'd be overcome by sickening lust and run over to the hut in the garden. Don't think about it, Fatma. Just a servant . . . Don't give it a thought. Both of them cripples! Think about something else! Beautiful mornings, the old gardens, horse-drawn carriages. . . . Let me just go to sleep.

When my hand reaches out like a careful cat the bedside lamp goes out. Silent darkness! Though I know there's a dim light coming through the shutters. I can't see my things anymore, they're free of my glances, all silent and unto themselves, they think that even without me they can stay where they are, motionless, but I know you; you're there, my furniture, you're there, next to me, as though you know I'm here. Once in a while, one of them creaks, I know the sound, it's no stranger, I want to make a noise, too, and I think: This thing we're in called emptiness is so strange! The clock ticks and divides it. Sharp and decisive. One thought, then another. Then it's morning, and they've come. Hello, hello! I slept, I woke up, it's time and I've had a good sleep. They're here, Madam, they're here! While I'm waiting, another train whistle. Where to? Good-bye! Where to, Fatma, where? We're going, Mother, we're banned from Istanbul. Did you take your rings? I have them! Your sewing machine? That too. Your diamonds, your pearls? You'll need them all your life, Fatma. Come back soon, though! Don't cry, Mother. They put the trunks and things on the train. I haven't even had a child yet, and we're taking a trip. My husband and I, we're exiled to who knows what distant lands, we're getting on the train, you're looking at us, I'm waving; Good-bye, Father; good-bye, Mother; look, I'm going, I'm going far, far away.

3

Hasan and Friends Take Up a Collection

Yes?" said the grocer. "What do you want?"

"The nationalist youth are sponsoring a night," said Mustafa. "We're giving out invitations."

I took the invitations out of my bag.

"I don't go to things like that," said the grocer. "I don't have time."

"You know, couldn't you just take one or two to help out the nationalist youth?" said Mustafa.

"I just got some last week," said the merchant.

"Did you get them from us?" said Mustafa. "We weren't even here last week."

"But if you helped the Communists that's different," said Serdar.

"No," said the grocer. "They don't come here."

"Why not?" said Serdar. "Because they don't feel like it, I guess?"

"I don't know," said the grocer. "Leave me alone. I don't have anything to do with this kind of stuff."

"I'll tell you why they don't come, uncle," said Serdar. "They can't come because they're afraid of us. If it wasn't for us the Communists would have this place shaken down for protection money like Tuzla."

"God forbid!"

"Yeah, you know what they did to the people in Tuzla, don't you? First they take out their windows really nice . . . "

I turned and looked at the window: clean, wide, sparkling glass. "Then, if you still don't pay should I say what they do next?" said Serdar.

I was thinking of graves. If all Communists act like this, the graveyards in Russia must be full to overflowing. The grocer must have got it in the end: he put his hand on his waist and glared red faced at us.

"So, uncle," said Mustafa. "We don't have a lot of time. How many do you want?"

I took out the tickets so he could see them.

"He'll take ten," said Serdar.

"I just got some last week," said the grocer.

"Okay, fine," said Serdar. "Let's not waste our time, guys. I guess this is the only shop in the whole market, the only one who's not afraid to have his window taken out. Hasan, what's the number . . . "

I went outside, looked at the number over the door, and went back in. The vegetable man's face reddened even more.

"Look, uncle," said Mustafa. "We don't mean any disrespect. You're as old as my grandfather, we're not Communists." He turned to me. "Give him five, that's enough this time."

When I held out five tickets, the grocer took them by the edge, as if picking up something disgusting. Then, with great concentration, he began to read what was on the tickets.

"We can give you a receipt, you want one?"

I laughed.

"Don't be disrespectful," said Mustafa.

"I already have five of these tickets," said the merchant. He dug around frantically in the dusty darkness of a drawer, then triumphantly pulled them out to show us. "They're the same, see?"

"Yes," said Mustafa. "The other guys may have given them to you by mistake. But you have to get them from us."

"Besides, is it going to kill you to take five more, uncle?" said Serdar.

The old cheapskate pretended he didn't hear and pointed to a corner of the ticket with his finger.

"This date's already passed," he said. "It was supposed to be two months ago. Look, it says May 1980 here."

"Uncle, do you intend to go to this event?" said Mustafa.

"How can I go tonight to something that was two months ago?" said the grocer.

In the end, I almost lost my patience over five tickets. They taught us nothing in school. Being patient only loses a person time in life, it's no good for anything else. If they asked us to write a composition on this subject, I'd have found so much to write that even the Turkish literature teachers who always had it in for me would have been forced to pass me. Good thing Serdar was just as furious as I was. He lurched over and grabbed the pen from behind the old cheapskate's ear, scaring him half to death, and wrote something on the tickets before shoving them back at him with the pen.

"Satisfied, uncle?" he said. "We made the night two months later. Now five hundred liras please!"

Finally he took out the money and gave it to us. That's the way it is: only the idiot Turkish-language teachers in our school think you can sweet-talk the snake out of its hole. I was so ticked off, I said, Let me hurt this old cheapskate, let me take care of him. As we were going out, I stopped and pulled out one of the peaches from the very bottom of the mound he had arranged by the front door. But he was lucky, and they didn't all come tumbling down. I put the peach in my bag before we moved on to the barber's.

The barber was washing somebody's head under the faucet. He looked at us in the mirror.

"I'll take two, guys," he said, without letting go of the head in his hands.

"If you want, you could have ten, brother," said Mustafa. "You could sell them here."

"Leave two, that's enough," said the barber. "Aren't you from the Association?"

Two! I suddenly lost it. "No, not just two, you'll take ten," I said and counted out ten tickets and held them out.

Even Serdar was surprised. Well, gentlemen, now you see, if I lose my temper this is what I'm like. But the barber didn't take the tickets.

"How old are you?" he said.

The soapy head in his hand was now staring at me in the mirror, too.

"You're not taking them?" I said.

"Maybe we make it eighteen," said Serdar.

"Who sent you from the Association?" he said. "You're awfully excitable."

I couldn't think of anything to say and looked at Mustafa.

"Don't mind it, brother," said Mustafa. "He's still new. He doesn't know you."

"It's obvious that he's new. Guys, leave me two tickets."

He took two hundred liras out of his pocket. The other guys immediately warmed up to him, practically kissed his hand, and immediately forgot all about me. So if you know the guys in the Association it means you're the king around here? I pulled out two tickets and held them out. But he didn't turn and take them.

"Leave them over there!"

I put them down. I was about to say something, but I didn't.

"See you, guys!" he said and then, pointing to me with the top of the shampoo bottle in his hand, "Is this one in school, working?"

"He's been left behind from sophomore year."

"What does your father do?"

I kept quiet.

"His father sells lottery tickets," said Mustafa.

"Watch out for this little fox!" said the barber. "He's a real live one. Okay, I'll see you."

Our guys all laughed. I said, Let me say something, and I was just about to say it—Make sure you take good care of your helper here, okay?—but I didn't. I left without looking at the helper's face. Serdar and Mustafa were laughing between themselves, but I wasn't listening, I was ticked off. Then Serdar said something to Mustafa like this:

"He's just remembered he's a barber; forget about it."

I didn't say anything. My job was to carry the bag and when necessary to take out the tickets and pass them out. I'm only here with you because they called us from Cennethisar and gave us this job and I have nothing to say to you who are on the side of the shopkeepers and make fun of me and laugh and call me names, so I'm just keeping quiet. We went into a pharmacy and I was silent, we went into a butcher's and I was silent, same in the grocer's, and after that, at the hardware shop and the coffee seller's and the café, I was just as silent, not saying anything even when we reached the end of the market. When we came out of the last store Mustafa stuck his hands in his pocket.

"We each deserve a helping of meatballs after this," he said. But still, I was silent, keeping it to myself that they didn't give us that money so we could eat meatballs.

"Yeah," said Serdar. "We each deserve a helping after this."

But when we sat down in the meatball shop they ordered two helpings each. If they were having two each, I wasn't going to have just one. While we waited for the meatballs, Mustafa took out the money and counted it: seventeen thousand liras. Then he said to Serdar:

"Why does he have that look on his face?"

"He's mad we called him a fox," said Serdar.

"Idiot!" said Mustafa. But I didn't pay attention because I was looking at a calendar on the wall. Then the meatballs came. We ate with them talking and me not talking. They wanted dessert, too. I ordered a *revani;* it was good.

Mustafa took out his gun and began to play with it under the table.

"Give it to me!" said Serdar.

He played with it, too. They didn't give it to me and shared a laugh about that before Mustafa stuck it in his waistband, paid the bill, and we got up to leave.

We walked through the market afraid of no one, entered the building where the office was, and went upstairs without saying a word. When we went to the Association, as usual, I felt afraid. I get all stupidly excited as if I'm cheating on a test and the teacher's seen me and knows why I look so nervous.

"This is the whole market, right?" he said.

"Yes, brother," said Mustafa. "All the places you said."

"You have it all with you?"

"Yes," said Mustafa. He took out the gun and the money.

"I'll just take the tool," he said. "Turn over the money to Mr. Zekeriya."

Mustafa gave him the gun. The good-looking guy went inside. Mustafa went too. We waited. For a while, I thought: What are we waiting for; I forgot that we were waiting for Mr. Zekeriya so it was like we were waiting for nothing. Then somebody our age came and offered us cigarettes. I said, I don't smoke, but I took one. He took out a lighter shaped like a locomotive and gave us a light.

"Are you with the Young Nationalists from Cennethisar?"

"Yes," I said.

"What's it like around there?"

I thought about what he meant. The cigarette had a weird taste. I felt like an old man.

"The upper neighborhood is ours," said Serdar.

"I know," he said. "I'm asking about the seashore. Where the Tuzla Communists are."

"Nothing," I blurted out. "There's nothing in Cennethisar on the seashore. It's all rich society people."

He looked at me and laughed. I laughed too.

"So what?" he said. "You never know!"

When he laughed at the mention of "society people," what did he mean? Serdar got up too and went inside somewhere, as if he intended that everyone coming and going should see me out there all alone and would figure out that I was new. I smoked cigarettes and looked at the ceiling, as if thinking important thoughts, things so important that it would be obvious to people going in and out as soon as they saw me: The problems of our movement! There was a book like that I'd read. As I thought that, Mustafa came out of the room and hugged somebody and just then everybody pulled back: Mr. Zekeriya had arrived. He took a good look at me on his way into the room, and I got up, but not all the way. Then they called in Mustafa. When he went inside I wondered what they would talk about, and when they came out again this time I stood up.

"Good!" said Mr. Zekeriya to our Mustafa. "We'll get word to you when we need to. Good work!"

He looked at me for a second and I thought he was going to say something to me but he didn't: he just abruptly sneezed and went upstairs again; to the party headquarters, as they say. Then Mustafa talked in whispers to a kid who had just been talking to me. First I thought they were talking about me, but that was crazy, they were talking about politics . . . I looked away so they wouldn't think I was listening and curious.

Then Mustafa said, "Okay, guys, we're going."

I left the bag. We went to the station without talking, like men satisfied they had done a good job. Then I wondered why Mustafa wasn't talking. I wasn't annoyed with him anymore. How did he like the way I did my part? I wondered. Sitting on the bench waiting for the train I thought about this, then when I saw a lottery shop I thought of my father, even though I didn't want to think about my father now, but I thought about him anyway and I muttered what I wanted to say to him: The most important thing in life isn't a high school diploma, Dad.

When we boarded the train, Serdar and Mustafa were whispering to each other again. They say something or tell some kind of joke and make me look like an idiot. Then I try to think of a comeback, but I can't find one right away and while I'm trying to think of it they see the concentration on my face and laugh even harder, then I get mad and can't help myself and curse, and they laugh harder still, and then I realize that I look even more like an idiot now. When that happens I want to be by myself, when a person is by himself he can relax and think about all the great things he could say and do. Sometimes they make jokes that I don't understand; they wink at each other, like they did just before when they said that word: fox! What kind of animal is that, anyway? There was girl in elementary school, she brought her encyclopedia to school, an animal encyclopedia, you'd say tiger, open it, and look at the *T*s. If I had that encyclopedia I'd open it, and look up "fox," but that girl wouldn't let me see it. No, you'll get it dirty! Okay, bitch, then why did you bring it to school? That girl went to Istanbul, of course, because her father was rich, they said. And she had a friend, with a blue ribbon in her hair . . .

I drifted off . . . When the train came to Tuzla I was excited, but not scared. The Communists could get on at any moment. Serdar and Mustafa had stopped talking; they looked pissed off. Nothing happened. As the train moved on, I could read what the Communists had written on the walls: TUZLA WILL BE THE GRAVE OF THE FASCISTS! The people they called the fascists were us. I cursed a little. Then the train came to our station and we got off. We walked without talking and came to the stop.

"Guys, I have things to do," said Mustafa. "Take care!" We watched him as he disappeared among the minibuses.

"I don't want to go home and study in this heat," I said to Serdar.

"Yeah," said Serdar. "It is hot."

"I can't think straight anyway," I said. I paused for a minute. "Come on, Serdar," I said. "Let's walk over to the coffeehouse."

"No. I'm going to the store. I have work."

If your father has a store, then you automatically have a job as well. But I'm still in school, I didn't drop out like you. But the strange thing is I'm the one they tease the most. I'm positive Serdar is going to the coffeehouse this evening to tell everyone about "the fox." Well, don't worry about it, Hasan. I didn't; I started to climb up the hill.

As I watched the trucks and cars going quickly by to catch the car ferry at Cennethisar or Darıca, I enjoyed feeling as though I were alone, and I yearned to have an adventure. There are lots of things that do happen in life and lots that could, but you're just left waiting for them. It seemed to me that those things I wanted were coming very slowly, and when they did happen it wasn't the way I'd wanted and planned; they'd all taken too long, as if to annoy me, and then suddenly you'd look, and they'd have already passed. Like those cars going by. They started to irritate me, especially since I was watching to see if one of them might stop and save me the bother of having to climb the hill in this heat, but nobody cares in this world. I started to eat my peach, but it didn't make things any better.

If only it were winter, I'd want to walk all by myself on the beach right now, go in the open door without worrying about anybody else. The waves would come and crash on the beach, and every once in a while I would scramble and run back to keep my shoes from getting wet as I walked along and thought about my life, how I would absolutely be an important person one day, how not only all those guys but the girls too would look at me differently then. I wouldn't need anybody else if it were winter. But there's school in the winter, goddamn it, and those crappy teachers . . .

Then I saw the white Anadol coupe going up the hill. As it slowly got closer I realized that they were in it, but instead of waving to them I turned and hid my face. They went right by without realizing it was me. As they passed I thought for a moment maybe I was mistaken, because Nilgün wasn't that pretty when we were little! But who else could the driver be except that fatso Faruk. Then I figured out where I'd go instead of home: I'd go down the hill, linger around their door, maybe I'd see my uncle the dwarf, and he'd ask me in, and if I wasn't too embarrassed I'd go inside, I'd say hello, maybe I'd even kiss their grandmother's hand, then I'd say, did you recognize me, I'm all grown up. Sure, they'd say, we recognized you, we were really good friends when we were little, weren't we, we'd talk and talk, we were friends when we were little, we'd talk and maybe I'd forget about this foul mood I'm in.

4

Faruk at the Wheel

❦

As the Anadol slowly made its way up the hill I asked:
"Did you all recognize him?"

"Who?" said Nilgün.

"The one in blue walking on the side of the road. He knew us right off."

"The tall one?" said Nilgün. She turned around and looked back, but we were far away by now. "Who was it?"

"Hasan!"

"Hasan who?" said Nilgün, at a loss.

"Recep's nephew."

"He's gotten so big!" said Nilgün, surprised. "I didn't recognize him."

"Shame on you!" said Metin. "Your childhood friend."

"Well, why didn't you recognize him then?" said Nilgün.

"I didn't even see him. But as soon as Faruk said something I knew who it was."

"Good for you!" said Nilgün. "You're so smart!"

"You mean that I've completely changed this past year, that's what you mean," said Metin. "But you're the one who's forgotten her own past."

"You're talking nonsense."

"All those books you read make you forget everything!" said Metin.

"Don't be a smart aleck!" said Nilgün.

They stopped talking. Then there was a long silence. We went up the hill where ugly new concrete buildings were being built every year, passing between the gradually disappearing vineyards, cherry orchards, and fig trees.

The portable radio was playing some random "light Western pop." When we saw the sea and Cennethisar in the distance, I sensed from the silence something of the excitement we'd felt as kids, but it didn't last. We went downhill without saying a word, and made our way through the noisy sunburned crowds in their shorts and bathing suits. As Metin was opening the garden gate, Nilgün said, "Honk the horn, Faruk."

I put the car in the garden and looked glumly over the house, which seemed older and emptier each time I came. The paint on the woodwork was all peeling, the vines had crept from the side wall to the front, the shadow of the fig tree fell on Grandmother's closed shutters, and the wrought iron on the downstairs windows was completely rusted. I had a strange feeling: it was as if there were terrible things in this house that I had never apprehended before owing to familiarity but that I was now recognizing with surprise and anxiety. I peered into Grandmother and Recep's damp, deadly interior darkness, which was visible between the decrepit wings of the big front door they'd left open for us.

"Come on, get out, Faruk, what are you sitting there for?" said Nilgün.

Walking straight toward the house, she saw Recep's little figure pop out of the small kitchen door and waddle eagerly toward us. They exchanged hugs and kisses. I turned off the radio that nobody was listening to and got out into the silent garden. Recep was in that jacket he always wore to hide his age and that same weird tie of his. We embraced and kissed as well.

"I was worried," said Recep. "You're late!"

"How are you?"

"Oh," he said, bashful about being asked, "I'm good. I made your beds and prepared your rooms. Madam is waiting. Have you put on some weight, Faruk Bey?"

"How's Grandmother?"

"Fine . . . as long as she can complain . . . Let me take your bags."

"We'll get them later."

We followed Recep upstairs. As I was reminded of the dusty light inside the house that seeped through the shutters and the smell of mildew, I felt somehow happy. When we came to Grandmother's door, Recep stopped for a minute, caught his breath, then, with his eyes gleaming calculated cheerfulness, he called out:

"They're here, Madam, they've arrived!"

"Where are they?" said the irritated old grandmother voice. "Why didn't you tell me, where are they?"

She was lying under a blue flowered quilt, leaning back on three pillows propped one behind the other, in the bed whose brass knobs I used to tap to make them ring when I was a child. One by one, we kissed her hand, which was white and soft, the familiar moles and spots on its wrinkled skin like old friends. The room, Grandmother, and the hand all had the same smell.

"God give you long life!"

"How are you, Grandma?"

"Terrible," said Grandmother, but we didn't say anything. Her lips twitched a little, as if she were a shy young girl or pretending to be. Then she said, "Okay, now, what have you got to say for yourselves?"

As we three siblings looked at one another there was a long silence. The room smelled of mildew, furniture wax, old soap, maybe mint candy, a little lavender, cologne, and dust.

"Well, don't you have anything to say to me?"

"We came here by car, Grandmother," said Metin. "It's exactly fifty minutes from Istanbul."

He says this every time, and every time Grandmother's stubborn face seems distracted for a moment before resuming its expectant expression.

"How long did it used to take you, Grandmother?" said Nilgün, as if she didn't know.

"I just came once!" said Grandmother with triumphant pride. She took a breath and added: "And today I'll ask the questions, not you!" She seemed to like this phrase she used habitually but then struggled for a moment, unable to think of anything as clever as she wanted.

"So how are you?"

"We're fine, Grandmother!"

As if she'd suffered some defeat, her face turned furious. And I remembered being afraid of that face when I was little.

"Recep, put a pillow behind my back!"

"You have all the pillows behind you, Madam."

"Should I get you another one, Grandmother?" said Nilgün.

"So, tell me, what are you up to?"

"Grandma, Nilgün's started at university," I said.

"I know how to talk, too, Faruk, don't worry," said Nilgün. "I'm studying sociology, Grandmother, I've just finished the first year."

"And you?"

"I'll finish high school next year," said Metin.

"After that?"

"After that, I'll go to America!" said Metin.

"What's over there?" said Grandmother.

"Rich people and smart people!" said Nilgün.

"University!" said Metin.

"Don't all talk at once!" said Grandmother. "How about you?"

I didn't tell her that I went back and forth between home and my department carrying a huge heavy bag of books, that I sat around bored in an empty house at night before eating and then fell asleep in front of the television. I didn't tell her that only yesterday morning on my way to the university I was already longing to have a drink, that I was afraid of losing my faith in what they call history, that I missed my wife.

"He's been made an associate professor, Grandmother," said Nilgün.

"Grandmother, you look really well," I said out of desperation.

"What's your wife doing?" said Grandmother.

"I told you the last time, Grandmother," I said. "We got divorced."

"I know, I know!" she said. "What's she doing now?"

"She remarried."

"You got their rooms ready, right?" said Grandmother.

"I did," said Recep.

"Don't you have anything else to say?"

"Grandmother, Istanbul has become very crowded," said Nilgün.

"It's crowded here, too," said Recep.

"Go sit over there, Recep," I said.

"Grandmother, this house has gotten really old and rickety," said Metin.

"I'm not well," said Grandmother.

"It's really falling apart, Grandmother. Let's get it knocked down, have an apartment built, you'll be so much more comfortable—"

"Quiet!" said Nilgün. "She's not listening to you. This isn't the time for it."

There was a silence. I felt as if I could hear the furniture expanding and creaking in the hot airless room. There was a dim, almost distilled light coming in the windows.

"Aren't you going to say anything?" said Grandmother.

"Grandmother, we saw Hasan on the road!" said Nilgün. "He's grown up, he's become enormous."

Grandmother's lips quivered strangely.

"What are they doing, Recep?" asked Nilgün.

"Nothing!" said Recep. "They live in the house on the hill. Hasan's in high school . . . "

"What are you telling them?" shouted Grandmother. "Who are you talking about?"

"What's Ismail doing?" asked Nilgün.

"Nothing," said Recep. "He sells lottery tickets."

"What's he telling you?" Grandmother shouted again. "Talk to me, not him! You get out of here, Recep, go down to your kitchen!"

"He's not a problem, Grandmother," said Nilgün. "Let him stay."

"He's fooled you right off, hasn't he?" said Grandmother. "What did you tell them? Have you made them feel sorry for you already?"

"I haven't said anything, Madam," said Recep as he left.

"Everything's become very expensive, Grandmother," Nilgün said.

There was another silence.

"Okay, Grandmother," I said. "We'd better go settle into our rooms."

"You just came," said Grandmother. "Where are you off to?"

"Nowhere," I said. "We're here for a whole week."

"So you have nothing nice to tell me," said Grandmother, almost smiling with some strange air of triumph.

"Tomorrow we'll go to the cemetery," I said.

Recep installed us one by one into our rooms and opened the shutters. For me he'd made up the one overlooking the well again. It smelled of mildew, linens, and childhood.

"I hung your towel here," he said, showing me.

I lit up a cigarette, and we looked out the open window together.

"Recep, how is Cennethisar this summer?"

"Bad," he said. "It's not like it used to be. People have become bad, really nasty!" he said.

He turned and looked me in the face, expecting understanding. Between the trees the sea was visible in the distance, and we could hear the buzz coming from the beach. Metin joined us:

"Faruk, could you give me the car keys?"

"Where are you going?"

"I'm getting my bag out and then I'm leaving."

"If you bring our bags upstairs, I'll let you have the car until tomorrow morning," I said.

"Don't worry, Faruk Bey, I'll take care of the bags," said Recep.

"Aren't you going to the archives now in search of the plague?" said Metin.

"What are you going to look for?" said Recep.

"The plague I'll look for tomorrow," I said.

"Are you going to start drinking right away?" said Metin.

"What's my drinking to you?" I said, but I wasn't mad.

"Right," said Metin, as he took the car keys and left.

Without thinking about anything I walked out behind Metin and went down the steps to the opening of the narrow passage. Recep was behind me.

"Is the key for the laundry still here?" I said. I slid my hand along the top of the door frame and found the dusty key.

"Madam doesn't know," said Recep. "Don't tell her."

I had to push hard to force the door open. Something must have fallen behind it: a skull covered with dust stuck between the door and the trunk. I picked it up and blew on it, then trying to look cheerful I showed it to him.

"Do you remember this?"

"Sir?"

"I guess you never come in here."

I left the dusty skull on a little table that was covered with papers.

I was playing with a glass pipe I had taken into my hand as a child would, before setting it down on one of the pans of a rusty pair of scales. Standing silent in the doorway, Recep looked fearfully at the things I was touching: hundreds of little vials, pieces of broken glass, trunks, pieces of bone thrown into a box, old newspapers, rusty scissors, tweezers, French books of anatomy and medicine, boxes full of paper, pictures of birds and airplanes tacked to a board, eyeglass lenses, a circle divided into seven colors, chains, the sewing machine whose pedal I used to push pretending to be a driver when I was little, screwdrivers, bugs and lizards pinned to boards, hundreds of empty bottles with MONOPOLIES ADMINISTRATION written on them, all kinds of powders in labeled pharmacy bottles, and even mushrooms, in a flowerpot . . .

"Are those mushrooms, Faruk Bey?" said Recep.

"Yes, take them if you can use them."

He didn't enter, probably because he was afraid; so I went over and gave them to him. Then I found the brass sign indicating in the old Ottoman letters and in Ottoman time that Dr. Selâhattin accepted visitors every day from two to six and in the afternoon from eight to twelve. For a moment I felt like taking it back to Istanbul, not just because I thought it was charming but as a memento of him. Immediately, however, I was overcome by a strange disgust and fear of the past, and so I tossed the sign back on the heap of dusty things. After locking the door, I went over to the kitchen with Recep. On the staircase, Metin was carrying the bags upstairs, grumbling.

5

Metin Wastes No Time

❖

After I'd brought Faruk and Nilgün's suitcases upstairs, I stripped down, put my bathing suit on under my summer clothes, grabbed my wallet, for once full of money, went downstairs, and took off in the old broken-down Anadol, headed for Vedat's. When I got there, there was no sign of life except for the maid working in the kitchen. So I went around to the back through the garden, and pushing a little on the window, I spotted old Vedat lying in his bed. I sprang like a cat into the room and smashed his head into the pillow.

"Hey, you stupid animal," he shouted. "What's the idea? You think this is a joke?"

Pleased with myself, I only smiled smugly as I sized up the room. Everything was the same as last year, even the gross picture of the naked woman on the wall.

"Come on," I said. "Up and at 'em!"

"What are we going to do at this hour?"

"What does anybody do in the afternoon?"

"Nothing!"

"Isn't anybody around?"

"Everybody's around, and there are even a few new ones."

"Where do you hang out?"

"At Ceylan's. They just got here!"

"Okay. Come on. Let's go over there."

"Ceylan won't be up yet."

"Well, then, let's go swimming someplace else," I said. "I haven't been even once so far this year, because I've been wasting all my time teaching English and math to the retarded sons of cloth manufacturers and iron merchants."

"So you're not interested in Ceylan?"

"Get up, let's at least go to Turgay's."

"You know, they offered him a spot on the youth basketball team?"

"I don't care, I gave up basketball."

"Leaves you more time to brownnose your teachers, right?"

Looking at Vedat's tanned, fit, relaxed body I thought: Yeah, I work hard at my classes, if I'm not first in class I get really frustrated, but I don't care what you call it; my father doesn't have a set of looms for me to take over in ten years, a thread factory, an iron depot and a foundry, or even a small contract in Libya, not even an import-export office, my poor dad; he resigned his post as a district administrator and he's got nothing to show for it but a grave we visit once a year so Grandmother doesn't cry in the house, we go so she can do her bawling there.

Vedat had no intention of stirring from the bed where he lay facedown, but at least he dragged his mouth over to the edge of the pillow to speak: he said that Mehmet had brought a nurse back with him from England, who was staying with his family now, although they slept in separate rooms and even though she was not a girl, as he called her, but actually a thirty-year-old woman, she got along well enough with the girls in our group.

"Turan, as you know, is doing his military duty."

How was I supposed to know, I said to myself, I don't spend the winters with Ankara and Istanbul society, I spend them going

between the dorm and my aunt's house and trying to make a little money teaching mathematics, English, and poker to dopey rich
kids like you. But I didn't say anything, and Vedat continued, saying
that Turan's father felt his son wasn't amounting to much and so,
instead of pulling some strings, he decided the life of a private would
straighten Turan out, but when I asked whether he had straightened
out, Vedat said very seriously that he didn't know, only that Turan
had come home on a fifteen-day leave and started going after Hülya,
at which point I was getting lost in my own thoughts, until Vedat,
changing the subject, said, Oh yeah, there's a new guy around, and
I figured out right away that he was okay with Vedat, because he
said this Fikret was "totally cool" and "our kind of guy," not really
explaining why until a little later he started to tell me about how
much horsepower the guy's fiberglass boat had, at which point I got
really fed up and just stopped listening. When he realized this we
were quiet for a while.

"What's your sister doing?" he finally said.

"She's become a typical leftie, always saying 'I can't believe how
blind I was,' just like the rest of them."

"That's a shame, sorry to hear it. Selcuk's sister's like that too," he
said, almost in a whisper. "Even worse, it looks like she's in love with
one of them! What about your sister?"

He could see I was annoyed and realized I didn't like the subject.

"How's your brother doing?"

"All he does is drink and get fat. He's a hopeless slob! But he and
my sister get along just fine. I don't care, they can do whatever they
want, but since one of them is so ideological that she hates money,
and the other is such a slob he wouldn't even lift a finger to earn any,
I'm the one who has to deal with practical matters. That weird, awful
house is still sitting on that plot of land for nothing."

"Aren't your grandmother and that, you know, the guy who works
there, aren't they living in the house?"

"They are. But why can't they live in an apartment of a building we could build there. Then I wouldn't have to spend the whole

winter telling rich retards about the length of the hypotenuse and its relation to the radius of a circle, know what I mean?"

"I see your point," he said. Vedat seemed a little uncomfortable, and I was afraid that he would think I was some kind of enemy of the rich.

He got up from the bed he hadn't budged from until now, naked except for a little bathing suit, a nice tan on his handsome, smooth body. He yawned in an easy way, no pains, no cares.

"Funda will want to come! But she's still asleep."

He went to wake up his sister. A little while later he came back and furiously lit a cigarette as though his life were completely full of problems and he couldn't do without one.

"You still don't smoke?"

"No."

There was a silence. I thought about Funda sleepily scratching herself in her bed. We talked a little about stupid things, like whether the sea was hot or cold. Then Funda came in the door.

"Vedat, where are my sandals?"

Last year this Funda was a little girl, this year she had long, beautiful legs and a little bikini.

"Hello, Metin!"

"Hello."

"How are things? . . . Vedat, I asked you, where are my sandals?"

The brother and sister immediately started to argue: One said he wasn't the keeper of the other's things, the other asked how her straw hat had turned up in his closet the other day, and so it continued, back and forth, until Funda left, slamming the door. When she came back a little later, it was as if nothing were wrong, but then they started up again over who would look for the car key in their mother's room. Finally Vedat went.

"Well, Funda," I said, tense just to be there, "what else is new?"

"What could be new! It's totally boring!"

We pressed on, talking for a while: I asked what year she had just completed—freshman year: she was doing two years' "prep," no, not in the German or Austrian high school, in the Italian one. So then I murmured these words to her: "Equipment electrique, Brevete type, Ansaldo San Giorgio Genova . . . " Funda asked me if I'd read them on some present someone brought me from Italy. I didn't tell her that they were from the incomprehensible metal plates found above the doors on all the trolleys in Istanbul and that everyone in the city who used the trolleys wound up memorizing them to keep from dying of boredom; I got a feeling somehow that she would look down on me if I told her I rode the trolley. Then we were silent. I thought a little about the horrible creature they called their mother who slept until noon, reeked of creams and perfumes, who talked about playing cards to pass the time, and who passed the time by playing cards. Then Vedat came back, swinging the car keys on his finger.

We took the car that had been baking in the sun two hundred meters to Ceylan's. I wanted to say something because I was afraid of seeming too excited.

"They changed this place a lot."

We walked across the flagstones set a step apart in the lawn. A gardener was watering it in the heat. Finally I saw the girls, and trying to act natural, I said to Vedat and Funda, "Hey, do you ever play poker?"

"Huh?"

We came down the steps. The girls looked good lying there. Realizing they'd seen me, I thought with satisfaction: That money I won playing poker bought me the shirt from Ismet's and these Levi's I have over my bathing suit, and in my pants pocket I still have twelve thousand liras I earned in a month giving private lessons to idiots! Still trying to make conversation, I said:

"Do you play cards?"

"What cards?" Funda said to one of them, "Let me introduce you to Metin!"

But I already knew Zeynep.

"Hello, Zeynep, how're things?"

"Good."

"This is Fahrunnisa, but don't call her that, or she'll get mad. She goes by Fafa!"

Fafa was not a pretty girl anyway. We shook hands.

"And this is Ceylan!"

I shook Ceylan's taut, light hand. I wanted to look somewhere else. I thought I might be in love, but it was a silly, childish thought. Looking at the sea I tried to believe that I wasn't nervous but calm and, that way, to calm myself. The others forgot about me and started to talk among themselves.

"Waterskiing is hard, too."

"If I could just get up on my feet."

"Well, at least it's not as dangerous as skiing on the snow."

"Your bathing suit has to be snug."

"It hurts your arms though."

"When Fikret gets here we'll give it a try."

I was bored, I shuffled, I coughed.

"Would you sit down!" said Vedat.

I thought I was looking intriguingly serious.

"Sit!" said Ceylan.

She was pretty enough that I again thought that I could fall in love with her, then a little later, I thought I believed what I had thought.

"There's a chaise longue over there," said Ceylan, pointing with the tip of her nose.

Walking over to the chaise longue I saw it: horrifying furniture inside the open door of the concrete house; in American films, rich unhappy couples sit on furniture like this, drinking whiskey and shouting at each other as they argue about their troubled marriages. The smell of furniture, wealth, and luxury wafting out of the house seemed almost to challenge me—What are you doing here?—but I gave it some thought and I relaxed: I'm smarter than all of them! I looked at the gardener still watering the lawn, I picked up the chaise, went back with it, and sat down beside them listening to the chitchat while trying to decide whether I was in love or not.

Fafa was dishing some dirt about our classmates, and Ceylan, also in our class, kept saying, tell them about this, and, oh, tell them about that, so that by the time the stories had ended I'd been roasted by the sun, and to top it off, I still hadn't made up my mind. Then, not wanting to seem like some kind of boor who didn't enjoy a joke, I decided to tell them some similarly retarded stories of mine, so I described in detail how we stole the exam questions from the principal's office, but I left out how much money we made selling them to some stupid rich kids, some of whom had to pay a second time to get the answers, too, because I figured they would take it the wrong way, my having to do little jobs like that because I didn't have a rich father to give me an Omega wristwatch for my birthday or some other bogus occasion, it would seem crude to them, even though their fathers were up to pretty much the same kind of thing from morning till night. The terrible racket of a motorboat pulling up shattered the relaxed atmosphere. They all turned their heads and looked. I deduced it was Fikret. He came in at high speed as though he were going to crash into the quay, then suddenly stopped, raising a big spray of water before jumping ashore with some difficulty.

"What's up, guys?" he said, shooting me a glance.

"Let me introduce you," said Vedat. "Metin, Fikret!"

"Guys, what do you want to drink?" said Ceylan.

Everybody said Coca-Cola.

Fikret didn't even answer but just pursed his lips and waved away the offer, as if to suggest he had too much on his mind even to enjoy a Coke.

I looked over but couldn't figure out whether Ceylan felt sorry for him or not. But I understood something else: I've been wise to this game the Fikrets play for years. If you're ugly and stupid and you want girls to look at you, you better at least come off really deep, and it doesn't hurt to have a boat that sounds really fast and a car that goes even faster. Ceylan brought the drinks. They sat for a long time talking, glasses in hand.

"Anyone want to listen to some music?"

"Where are we going tonight?"

"Hey, didn't you say you had an Elvis album?"

"I do. Where is that 'Best of Elvis'?"

It all must have been too exhausting to consider, or maybe it was the sun, but they fell silent for a while until they piped up again, but then they stopped before they spoke again and stopped once more; during that last lull, some awful music blared out from an invisible speaker and I thought it was time for me to say something.

"This is really banal music!" I said. "In America they only listen to stuff like this in long elevator rides."

"Long elevator rides?"

Yes, Ceylan, and as I spoke, I watched you looking at me pretending that you weren't, because, yes, I probably believed I was in love now, so though I was embarrassed, I explained it to you, Ceylan. I said how important to the lives of New Yorkers these elevator rides were, how the Empire State Building was exactly twelve hundred and fifty feet and one hundred two stories high, and how there was a fifty-mile view from it, but I didn't mention that I hadn't been to New York and seen that view yet, only that according to the 1957 edition of the *Encyclopaedia Britannica* in our school library the population of the city was 7,891,957, while, according to the same edition, it had been 7,454,995 in 1940.

"Ugh!" said Fafa. "You memorized it like a little brownnoser?"

When you laughed at her, too, Ceylan, I had to prove that I wasn't somebody who memorized things just to brownnose, and so to give an idea how smart I am, I announced that, for example, I could multiply any pair of two-digit numbers in my head.

"Yes," said Vedat. "This guy has an awesome brain, the whole school knows it!"

"Seventeen times nineteen?" said Ceylan.

"Eight hundred thirty-three!" I said.

"Seventy times fourteen?"

"One thousand eight!"

"How do we know it's right?" said Ceylan.

I was excited, but I just smiled at her.

"I'm getting a pen and paper," said Ceylan.

Because you couldn't stand that irritating smile on my face, Ceylan, you jumped up from your seat and ran inside among that awful furniture returning a little later with a notepad from some Swiss hotel and a silver fountain pen and an angry look on your face.

"Thirty-three times twenty-seven equals?" "Eight hundred ninety-one." "Seventeen times twenty-seven equals?" "Five hundred thirteen." "Eighty-one times seventy-nine equals?" "Six thousand three hundred thirty-nine!" "Seventeen times nineteen equals?" "Three hundred twenty-three!" "No, three hundred seventy-three!" "Please multiply it again, Ceylan," "Okay, three hundred twenty-three!" "Ninety-nine times ninety-nine equals?" "That's the easiest: nine thousand eight hundred one!"

"You really memorized them all, like a brownnoser!"

I just smiled and thought how those cheesy books that say all love begins as hatred were right.

Afterward, Ceylan went waterskiing on Fikret's boat, and I immersed myself in thought about the phenomenon of competition, realizing right away that I would probably be at it until the middle of the night, because Goddamn it: I believed I was in love now.

6

Recep Serves Breakfast

❧

I woke up, put on my jacket and tie, and went outside. It was a beautiful morning, still and bright! There were crows and sparrows in
the trees. I looked at the shutters, all shut; they were still sleeping,
they got to bed late last night. Faruk Bey drank, and Nilgün watched
him. Madam shouted something from upstairs once in a while. I
hadn't even heard Metin come in. I worked the pump slowly, not to
disturb them by its creaking; I splashed the cold morning water on
my face, then I went inside, slicing myself two pieces of bread in the
kitchen, which I took out to the chicken coop. As the chickens flut-
tered around clucking, I broke two eggs carefully at one end, drank
the liquid inside, and ate my bread. Leaving the coop door open, I
was bringing the other eggs back to the kitchen when I received a
surprise: Nilgün was awake; she was going somewhere with her bag.
When she saw me she smiled.

"Good morning, Recep."

"Where are you going at this hour?"

"To the sea. It's crowded later. I'll just take a dip. Are the eggs
from the coop?"

"Yes," I said, somehow feeling guilty. "Do you want breakfast?"

"I do," said Nilgün, laughing, and left.

I watched her from behind. A cautious, fussy, wary cat. Sandals on her feet, legs bare. When she was little, her legs were like sticks. I went inside and put on water for the tea. Her mother had been the same. Now she was in the graveyard. We'll go and we'll pray. Did she remember her mother? She wouldn't, she was only three. Doğan Bey was a district administrator in the east; he sent them here the last two summers. Your mother would sit in the garden with Metin on her lap and you at her side, the sun would be on her pale face all day long, but she'd go back to Kemah as white as she came. I used to say to her, Would you like some cherry juice, *küçükhanım,* Thank you, Recep, she'd say, put it over there, little Metin on her lap; I'd put it down, two hours later I'd look, and she'd only have had two sips from the big glass. Then Faruk would come in, fat and sweaty. Mom, I'm thirsty, he'd say, and down the whole thing in one gulp. Good for you! I got out the tablecloth and was spreading it on the table when the smell hit me: Faruk Bey spilled *rakı* on the table last night. I went and got a cloth to wipe it. By now the water had boiled; I brewed the tea. There was milk left over from last night. I'll go to Nevzat tomorrow. I thought of having a coffee, but I held back and gave myself over to work. While I was setting the table Faruk came downstairs. His heavy steps made the boards squeak, just like his grandfather's. He yawned and muttered something.

"I made tea," I said. "Sit and I'll bring you your breakfast."

He plopped onto the chair from which he'd been drinking last night.

"Do you want milk, too?" I said. "We have some good, rich milk."

"Okay, bring it!" he said. "It'll be good for my stomach."

I went to the kitchen. His stomach. Those poisonous liquids he kept drinking would burn a hole through it in the end. If you drink again, Madam said, you'll die. Did you hear what the doctor said? Doğan Bey looked down, thinking, then he said something like:

If my mind can't function I'm better off dying, Mother, I can't live without thinking, but Madam said, this isn't thinking, my boy, it's just depression, but they had stopped listening to each other by that point. Then Doğan Bey died, writing all those letters. Blood was coming out of his mouth, just like his father, it must have been from his stomach, Madam was sobbing, calling for me, as though I could do something. Before he died I took off his bloody shirt, put a freshly ironed one on him, and he was gone. We'll go to the cemetery. I boiled the milk and poured it nicely into a glass. The belly is a dark world that only the Prophet Jonah knows. When I think of that dark pit my hair stands on end. But it was as though I didn't have a stomach; because I know my limits, I'm not like them. When I brought the milk, I saw that Nilgün had arrived, so quick! Her wet hair was beautiful.

"Should I give you your breakfast?" I said.

"Isn't Grandmother coming down to breakfast?" said Nilgün.

"She's coming down," I said. "She comes down mornings and evenings."

"Why doesn't she come down for lunch?"

"She doesn't like the noise from the beach," I said. "I bring a tray up to her at midday."

"Let's wait for Grandmother," said Nilgün. "When does she wake up?"

"She's been awake for a long time," I said. I looked at my watch: eight thirty.

"Hey, Recep!" said Nilgün. "I got the paper from the grocer. I'll get it in the morning from now on."

"Whatever you wish," I said, going upstairs.

"What's the point?" Faruk said. "What do you gain by reading how many people killed how many other people, how many were nationalist, how many were Marxist, how many of them weren't on either side?"

I headed upstairs. You have no ideas, Recep! Death! I think about the hereafter, and I'm afraid, because a person is naturally curious. The source of all knowledge is curiosity, said Selâhattin Bey, you understand, Recep? Upstairs, I tapped on the door.

"Who's there?" she said.

"It's me, Madam."

She had opened the closet and was rooting through it. She made as if to close the door.

"What is it?" she said. "What are they shouting about downstairs?"

"They're waiting for you to come for breakfast."

"Is that why they're yelling at one another?"

The old smell from the closet spread out in the room. As I smelled it, I was remembering.

"No," I said, "they're only kidding around."

"At the table, first thing in the morning?"

"If you're concerned, I'll say something, Madam," I said. "But Faruk isn't drinking. People don't drink at this hour."

"Don't cover for them!" she said. "And don't lie to me! I can tell right away."

"I'm not lying," I said. "They're waiting for you to come for breakfast." She was still looking inside the closet. "Shall I bring you down?"

"No!"

"Will you eat in bed? I can bring up the tray."

"Bring it up," she said. "Tell them to be ready."

"They are ready."

"Fine. Close the door."

Every year before visiting the graveyard she rummaged through the closet as if she were going to find something she'd never seen or worn before, but in the end she wound up wearing that same awful heavy coat. I went to the kitchen to fetch her some bread.

"So what's the count?" Faruk was saying to Nilgün. "How many killed yesterday in street shootings?"

"Total of seventeen," Nilgün read aloud, then remarked, "Half of them right-wingers and half leftists, I guess."

"Your grandmother says she's not coming down to breakfast," I said. "I'll go ahead and serve yours."

"Why isn't she coming down?"

"I don't know," I said. "She's going through her closet . . . Nilgün Hanım, you're sitting in a wet bathing suit, you'll catch a cold. Go up and change and then read the paper . . ."

"Look, she didn't even hear you," said Faruk. "She's mesmerized reading about the dying and the dead. She's still young enough to believe the papers."

Nilgün looked up and gave me a smile as I went down to the kitchen. I turned the bread over and prepared Madam's tray. Madam reads the paper to see if anyone she knows has died, not some young agitator ripped to pierces from bullets and bombs, but some old person who's died in bed. Sometimes she would get annoyed, complaining that ever since Atatürk made everyone take a new name it was chaos, because she couldn't keep track of the families she knew. Sometimes she would clip the death announcements just to make fun of the infernal, made-up surname—What does that name even mean? My father was the one who'd given us our family name and it was Karatash—Blackstone. It was very clear what it meant. But it was true, a name like theirs, Darvinoğlu, who could understand it? I tapped on the door and went in. Madam was still scouring the closet.

"Leave it there," she said.

"Eat it right away!" I said. "Don't let the milk get cold."

"Okay, okay!" she said. "Now shut the door!"

When I remembered the bread, I ran downstairs. At least it hadn't burned. I put Nilgün Hanım's egg and the other breakfasts on the tray and carried it up from the kitchen.

"Sorry it took so long," I said.

"Isn't Metin coming to breakfast?" said Faruk Bey.

Running upstairs again, I began to open his shutters, which woke him in a foul mood. He was still grumbling as I went downstairs to pour out the tea, but by the time I'd brought it out Metin had come down and taken his place.

"Your breakfast will be ready in a moment," I said.

"What time did you get home last night?" said Faruk Bey.

"I forget!" said Metin, wearing only a bathing suit and a shirt.

"Did you leave gas in the car?" said Faruk Bey.

"Don't worry, Faruk!" said Metin. "We drove around in some other people's cars. It's not as if I'm dying to be seen in an Anadol around here."

"What's that supposed to mean?" said Nilgün.

"Just read your newspaper!" said Metin. "I'm talking to my brother."

I went back in to get the tea and more bread to toast.

"Would you like milk as well, Metin Bey?" I said.

"All your friends asked about you," said Metin. "Used to be you were so close, you couldn't stand to be away from them, now you look down on them because you've read a few books."

"I don't look down on them. I just don't want to see them."

"You could at least say hello."

"Would you like milk as well, Metin Bey?" I said.

"Just because you're political doesn't mean you can't be interested in people, too."

"What is that supposed to mean?" said Nilgün.

"Well," said Metin, "I have a sister who's been brainwashed, but I see her every day."

"That's just stupid!"

"Did you want milk as well, Metin Bey?"

"Guys, don't start," said Faruk Bey.

"No, I don't want milk," said Metin.

I rushed to the kitchen and turned over the bread. They brainwashed her! Was that good? There's no hope for us until they clean out all the filth in their brains, those empty beliefs and lies, Selâhattin Bey used to say, and that's why I've been writing all these years, Fatma, that's why. I got myself a glass of milk and drank half. When the bread was toasted I brought it out.

"When Grandmother prays in the cemetery, you do likewise, okay?" Faruk Bey was saying.

"I've forgotten the prayers that Auntie taught me," said Nilgün.

"That didn't take long," said Metin.

"Metin, I've forgotten them, too," said Faruk Bey. "Just hold your hands the way she does so she doesn't get upset, is all I'm saying."

"Don't worry, I'll do it," said Metin. "I don't mind things like that."

"You do it, too, okay, Nilgün?" said Faruk Bey. "Put something on your head as well."

"Fine," said Nilgün.

"It won't destroy your political beliefs?" said Metin.

I left and went upstairs. Madam had finished her breakfast and was back at the closet.

"What?" she said. "What do you want?"

"Do you want a glass of milk?"

"No, I don't."

I was picking up her tray when she slammed the closet door and yelled, "And stay out of my closet!"

"I'm nowhere near it, Madam!" I said. "As you can see, I'm just getting the tray."

"What are they doing downstairs?"

"They're getting ready."

"I still haven't decided . . . ," she said and seeming suddenly embarrassed began to root around in the closet again.

"Madam!" I said. "If we don't set off soon we'll get caught in the heat."

"Okay, okay. Make sure the door is closed."

I went downstairs and put on water to heat for washing up the dishes. As I drank the other half of my milk and waited for the water to warm up, I thought about the cemetery, and I felt a bit emotional, a little strange; I thought about the clothes and the equipment in the laundry room as well. A person feels like crying sometimes, in a cemetery. I went out, Metin Bey wanted tea, which I brought. Faruk Bey, smoking a cigarette, was looking at the garden. The two were silent. I went in and finished washing up. When I went in again Metin Bey had returned from getting dressed, so I went back, took off my apron, checked my jacket and tie, combed my hair, and smiled at myself in the mirror the way I did after the barber combed my hair. I went outside.

"We're ready," they said.

Upstairs, Madam had finally gotten dressed, the same terrible black coat, of course, her skirts touching the floor, since Madam was getting a little shorter each year, and the tips of her weird pointy boots stuck out like the identical noses of two curious foxes. She was putting a scarf on her head. She looked embarrassed to see me, and we were silent for a minute.

"Won't you be too warm in this heat?" I said.

"Is everybody ready?"

"They are."

She was looking around the room for something and, seeing that the closet was closed, seemed to look for something else, before looking at the closet again.

"Take me down, then."

She saw me pulling the door open but had to give it a tug with her own hand, too. At the top of the stairs she leaned on me rather than on her cane. We went down very slowly, and when the others had gathered outside, we all worked at getting Madam into the car.

"Did you make sure the doors are closed?" she said.

"Yes, Madam," I said, but then I went back in and this time slammed them so she could be assured.

7

Grandmother Offers Her Prayers

My God, suddenly, so strange, when the car started to move, I got so excited, just as I did when as a girl I'd gotten into a horse-drawn carriage, but then I thought of you, all you poor souls in the cemetery, and I thought I would cry, but not yet, Fatma, because looking out the windows as the car passed through the gate into the streets, I saw Recep in the house, was he going to stay there all by himself, I began to wonder, but the car stopped and we waited a little till the dwarf got in on the other side and crawled into the back.

"You shut the doors tight, didn't you, Recep?"

"Yes, Faruk Bey."

I sighed and leaned all the way back in my seat.

"Grandmother, you heard, didn't you, Recep shut the doors tight. So don't let it be like last year, constantly saying that they were left open . . ."

I started to think about them and, of course, I remembered they were talking about how you had hung a brass sign on the garden gate, Selâhattin, that said DOCTOR SELÂHATTIN, these are my hours and I won't take money from the poor, Fatma, you said, I want to be in touch with the people, of course we don't have many patients yet, it's not a big city, we're all the way out on the shore after all, really nobody else except a few miserable villagers in those days, now when I lifted my head—My God, look at the apartment buildings, the shops, the crowds, these half-naked people on the beach, don't look, Fatma, what's all that noise, all of them falling on top of one another, look, the hell you dreamed of has come to earth, Selâhattin, you won, if this is what you wanted, of course, look at the crowd, maybe this was it.

"Grandmother looks really interested in everything, doesn't she?"

No, I wasn't looking at anything, but your shameless grandchildren, Selâhattin.

"Should we go the long way around and give you a little tour, Grandmother?"

They must think your innocent wife is like you, yes, well, what can the poor kids do, brought up as they were, because you made your son just like yourself, Selâhattin, Doğan didn't have any interest in his children either, Mother, their aunts can take care of them now, I can't do it; if the aunts take care of them, then this is how they turn out, believing their grandmother is keen to see all the ugliness on the way to the cemetery, well, I'm not even looking, I bend my head down and open my purse, I inhale the smell of old age that rises up, and in the alligator darkness my little dry hand fishes for my handkerchief and I dab my poor dry eyes, because my thoughts are of them, only of them.

"What's the matter, Grandmother, don't cry!"

They don't know how much I love all of you, how I can hardly bear to think that you're dead on this sunny day; I dab my eyes a little again, poor me, and okay, that's enough now, Fatma, I should know how to bear up, since I've spent my whole life in pain, there, it's over now, nothing's the matter, I lift up my head, I'm looking at everything—apartment buildings, walls, plastic signs, posters, shop-windows, colors—but right away I start to hate it, my God, what ugliness: Don't look anymore, Fatma.

"Grandmother, what did it used to be like around here?"

I'm lost in my own thoughts and sorrows and I don't hear what you're saying, so how can I tell you that this used to be one garden after another, what beautiful gardens, where are they now, there was no one around and in those years, before the devil took your grandfather, early in the evenings, he'd say, Fatma, let's go for a walk, I'm just stewing in here, we never go anywhere, this encyclopedia is exhausting me, I don't want to be like some Eastern despot saying I don't have any time, I want to make my wife happy, let's at least walk a little in the garden, and we can talk, I'll tell you about what I read today, I think about the necessity of science and how we're so backward because we lack it, I truly understand now our need for a Renaissance, for a scientific awakening, there's an awesome job before me that must be done, and so I'm actually grateful to Talat Pasha for exiling me to this lonely corner, where I can read and think about these things, because if it weren't for this emptiness and all the time in the world, I could never have come to these conclusions, would never have realized the importance of my historic task, Fatma, anyway, all of Rousseau's thoughts were the visions of a solitary wanderer in the countryside, surrounded by nature, but here the two of us are together.

"Marlboros here, get your Marlboros!"

Lifting my head, I got a fright, he almost stuck his arm inside the car, Careful, little boy, you'll be crushed, and soon we'd left all the concrete behind, finally, thank God, we were among the gardens, spread out . . .

"Really hot, isn't it, Faruk?"

. . . on both sides of the road going up the hill, where Selâhattin and I used to walk in those early years and, along the way, one or two miserable villagers would stop us and say hello, because they hadn't yet grown afraid of him. Doctor, my wife is very sick, would you come, please God, because he hadn't yet gone raving mad, the poor things, Fatma, I feel sorry for them, I don't charge them anything, what can I do, but when we needed money they didn't come anyway,

then it was my rings, my diamonds, did I shut the closet door, I panicked, yes, I did.

"Grandma, are you okay?"

They don't give a soul a moment's peace with these ridiculous
questions; I dab my eyes with my handkerchief: How can a person be
okay when she is going to the graves of her husband and son, all I—

"Look, Grandmother, we're going by Ismail's house. There!"

feel is sorrow, but listen to what they're saying, my God, here's
the house of the cripple, your bastard, but I'm not looking, do they
know that, I

"Recep, how is Ismail?"

know and listen

"Fine. Selling lottery tickets."

carefully, no, you don't hear, Fatma, I

"How's his foot?"

just have to save myself and my husband and my son from sin,
does

"Same as always, Faruk Bey. He limps."

anyone know I had anything to do with this, did he

"How's Hasan?"

go and tell them, that dwarf, knowing they're so interested in
equality, like their father and grandfather . . .

"His marks are terrible. He failed English and mathematics. And
he has no job."

Let's see, they'll say, well, Grandmother, then that makes them
our uncles, we had no idea, for shame, Fatma, don't think about it,
is that why you've come here today—but we still aren't there, I start
to put my handkerchief to my eyes, imagine, on this sad day for me
they're sitting in the car chatting about this and that, as though we
were out for a ride, a long time ago, about the only time we ever
did, we had gotten a one-horse cart, and Selâhattin and I went up
the hill *tiki-taka, tiki-taka:* What a good idea, Fatma, I never seem
to find time for things like this because I'm always working on the
encyclopedia, if only we had brought a bottle of wine along and some

hard-boiled eggs, we could go and sit somewhere in the country, but just to get some fresh air, some nature, not to stuff ourselves for no reason, the way the Turks do, doesn't the sea look beautiful from here, in Europe they call this a picnic, they do everything in moderation, Fatma, God willing we'll be like that one day, our sons won't see it but maybe our grandchildren, both boys and girls, God willing,

"We're here, Grandmother, we're here, look!"

in those days when science is ascendant our grandchildren will live happily in our nation that will be no different from the European nations, my grandchildren, they'll come to my grave, yours, too . . . and when the motor stops my heart jumps, it's so quiet here, the crickets in the heat, death at the age of ninety, they get out and open the door.

"Give me your hand, Grandmother."

This plastic thing is harder to get out of than a horse-drawn carriage. God help us, if I fall I'll die on the spot and they'll bury me at once, maybe they'd like that,

"Easy does it, take my arm, lean on me, Grandmother!"

or maybe they'll be sad, forgive me, why am I even thinking like that now? I get out, we walk among the gravestones with one of them on each arm, moving slowly, God, forgive me, these gravestones just give me the creeps,

"Are you okay, Grandmother?"

slowly in the heat, with nobody, this burnt smell of the dried weeds, me, too, one day, I'd be

"Where was it?"

among them, the graves—But don't think of that now, Fatma,

"It's this way, Faruk Bey!"

look, he's still talking, the dwarf, to prove he knows where they are buried better than his own grandchildren, because I'm his son, too, is that what you mean, but when the others see their father's and real mother's

"Here it is!"

grave . . .

"We're here Grandmother!"

My heart, I'm going to cry now, yes, you're here, you poor things, let go of my arms, leave me alone with them, I wipe my eyes and when I see you all here, my Lord, why didn't you take me, too, as though, for shame, I know anyway, I never once gave in to the devil, but I didn't come here to accuse you, I'm going to cry now... I wiped my nose and when I held my breath for a second I heard the crickets and put my handkerchief in my pocket. I lifted up my hands and prayed and prayed to God that you might rest in peace, and when my prayer was done, I lifted my head and saw that at least they had lifted up their hands in prayer, too, good, Nilgün had covered her head nicely, but I hated the way that dwarf liked to show off— God, please forgive him, but I can't stand to see someone so proud of being a bastard, as though he loves you more than any of the rest of us, Selâhattin, who do you think you are fooling, I wish I had brought my cane, where did I leave it, did they close the doors, but I didn't come here to think about this, I came to think about you, here under this lonely gravestone, oh, did you ever think that one day I would come here and read on a stone placed on top of you:

DOCTOR SELÂHATTIN DARVINOĞLU
1881–1942
MAY HIS SOUL REST IN PEACE

I just read it, oh, Selâhattin, and you stopped believing anyway, and that's why your soul is suffering the torments of hell, dear God, I don't want to think about it, but is it my fault, how many times did I tell him to say he was sorry, and didn't you make fun of me: Foolish woman, stupid woman, they brainwashed you just like everybody else, there is no God, no hereafter, the other world is a terrible lie they made up to keep us in line in this world, there's no proof of God except that scholastic nonsense, there are only phenomena, and we can know them and the relationships among them, and so my duty is to explain to the whole East that there is no God, are you listening, Fatma, for shame, don't think of it, I want to think of you as in those early days, when you still hadn't given in to the devil, not just in death and fond memories, but you really were a child, though, as my father said, you had a brilliant future, didn't she just sit there quietly in his office, she did, otherwise God knows what he might have done to those poor sick people, even totally uncovered European ladies with painted faces would come and shut themselves up in there, and their husbands came, too, I would be uncomfortable in the next room, don't think of that, Fatma, yes, yes, maybe everything happened because of them, just when we had settled in, and we had one or two regular customers, patients, that is, because they were hard to come by, and about that I think you were right, Selâhattin, a bunch of sleepyheads from some remote village that nobody cared about, who spent their time dozing with the fishermen in the corners of a coffeehouse at some abandoned dock on the seashore, who never got sick in this clean air, who wouldn't know it if they had, and who wouldn't come if they did know it, who would come anyway, a few families, a few stupid villagers, but in spite of this you became known and people came all the way from Izmit, the most from Gebze, some came by boat from Tuzla, and just as he started to make money, he began to abuse his patients, God, I was listening from the next room: What did you put on this cut, First we put tobacco, doctor, then we bound it in dried dung, Those are just old folk remedies, there's something called science now, well, what's the matter with this child, He's had a fever for five days, doctor, Why didn't you bring him earlier, Didn't you see the windstorm on the sea, doctor, Well, you almost killed the kid, What can we do if it's God's will, What God, there is no God, God is dead—My God, ask forgiveness, Selâhattin, What forgiveness, foolish woman, don't you talk nonsense, too, like those stupid villagers, I'm ashamed of you, I'm going to make all these people grow up but I can't even put two thoughts in my own wife's head, you're such an idiot, at least realize how stupid you are and believe in me; But you're going to lose all your patients, Selâhattin, when I say that, I listen from the next room, he's so stubborn he loses control, listen to the poor woman who's come all this way with her husband to get some medicine: She should uncover herself, he says, irritating me, you're her husband, you stupid villager, you tell her, she won't uncover herself, fine, I'm not examining her, get out, I'm not going to give in to your primitive idiocies, Please, doctor, give us some medicine, No, if your wife doesn't uncover herself there's no medicine or anything else, no, get out, they misled you all with this lie of God, for shame . . . If only you could keep it to yourself, Selâhattin, or at least not talk to them like that, no I'm not afraid of anyone, but look, who knows what they're saying behind my back, they say this doctor is an atheist, don't go to him, he's the devil himself, didn't you see the skull on his desk, his office is filled with books, he has strange charms for casting spells, lenses that can turn a flea into a camel, pipes with smoke coming out the end, there are dead turtles pinned to boards there, don't go, who in their right mind would submit to this godless man if they didn't have to, this guy could, God forbid, make a healthy person sick, anybody who crosses his threshold runs into an evil spirit, not long ago he told a patient who had come all the way from Yarımca, You look like a sensible person, I like you, take these papers and read them in your village coffeehouse, I've written about what you have to do to fight typhus and tuberculosis, he said, I also wrote that there's no God, go and maybe at least your village will wake up, he said, anyway if I could send someone sensible like you to every village to gather the villagers together every evening in the coffeehouse and read an article from my encyclopedia for an hour, this country would be liberated, but first, oh, I have to finish the encyclopedia and it keeps dragging on, damn it, and there's no money, Fatma, your diamonds, your rings, your jewelry box, did they close the gate tight, they didn't, of course, because patients no longer came aside from a few hopeless cases no longer afraid of anything, and some other poor souls who regretted it as soon as they entered the garden but who were afraid to turn back and anger the devil, but you paid no attention, Selâhattin, maybe because of my diamonds, The patients don't come anymore, and it's good that they don't, because when I see these fools I get irritated and depressed, it's so hard to believe that these animals will ever make something of themselves, the other day while we were talking I asked one of them what is the sum of the interior angles of a triangle and, of course, I knew, the poor villager who had never heard of a triangle in his life wouldn't know the answer, but I got a pencil and paper and explained it to him, let me see how good they are at mathematics, I said, but it's not the fault of these poor things, Fatma, the government never reached them to give them a good education, my God, I spent forever explaining, trying to make him understand, but the poor fool just sat there looking blankly at me, scared as well, oh, you foolish woman, just the way you're look-ing at me now, as though you'd just seen the devil, poor creature, I'm your husband, you know, and, yes, you are a devil, Selâhattin, look now, you're in hell, with the demons in the fires of hell, the burning cauldrons, or is death the way you said it was, I've discovered death, Fatma, he said, listen to me, this is more important than anything else, it's so terrible now, death—I couldn't bear it, thinking about him there in the grave, I was afraid and

"Are you all right, Grandmother?"

I got dizzy all of a sudden, I thought I would fall down, but don't worry, Selâhattin, even if you don't want me to

"Why don't you sit down for a minute over there and relax, Grandmother!"

I'll pray for your soul, be quiet, they were quiet, and I heard a car going by on the road, then the crickets and it was over, amen, and I took out my handkerchief and dabbed my eyes and then I went over, you're the one who's always really in my mind, son, but first let me get your father out of that place, I said, my poor, dumb, unlucky boy,

DISTRICT ADMINISTRATOR DOĞAN DARVINOĞLU

1915–1967

MAY HE REST IN PEACE

okay, I'm praying, my hopeless, unfortunate, bitter, unhappy, orphan boy, I'm praying for you, amen, you're here, too, oh my God, for a moment I felt as if you hadn't died, and where was my handkerchief, by the time I reached it, I'd begun to sob,

"Grandmother, Grandmother, don't cry!"

trembling, if they hadn't come over to me I think I would have thrown myself down on the earth, dear God, how unlucky I was, that I should be coming here to my own son's grave, what have I done for you to punish me like this, forgive me, but I did what I could, would I ever have wanted it to be like this, son, my Doğan, didn't I tell you so many, so many times that the best thing you can do in life is not to turn out like your father, didn't I send you away to boarding schools so you wouldn't see him and take him as your model, my boy, and even when we didn't have money anymore, in those days, I never let on to you that the only things keeping us going were the diamonds, jewels, and rings in the box that your dear grandfather and grand-mother gave me as a dowry, and I sent you to the finest schools, you'd come late on Saturday afternoons, your drunken father wouldn't go to the station to pick you up, not only failing to earn a penny himself but trying his best to squeeze money out of me so he could print those crazy writings that were just all curses from beginning to end, but, at least on cold winter nights, I could say to myself that my son is studying in a French school, and then one day I looked and, ah, instead of becoming an engineer or a businessman like the others, you signed up there, Are you going to be a politician, I know, if you want you could even become prime minister, but isn't it a shame that someone like you . . . Mother, this country can only be straightened out through politics, Is it up to you, my brainless son, to straighten it out, but by the time I said that, in those days when he came for his vacation exhausted and worried, dear God, I'm so unlucky he's learned to pace anxiously back and forth, exactly like his father, and look, you're already smoking at your age, what's all this melancholy, son, and when you said for the sake of the country, didn't I fill your pockets with money thinking maybe you'd straighten out, go to Istanbul and enjoy yourself, take out some girls, and don't think about all this, just relax, and without letting your father know, didn't I give you my pink pearls and tell you to take them to Istanbul and sell them and enjoy yourself, and then with that insignificant colorless little girl, how would I know that you would just marry her right off and bring her home, didn't I tell you to experience life, at least stick to the job, maybe they'd make you a minister, don't settle for being a district administrator, look, it's almost your turn to be a governor, son, didn't I tell you, No, Mother, I can't take it anymore, they're all disgusting, horrible, Oh, my poor boy, why don't you just go back and forth to work like everybody else, but I know I said one day, I was angry, It's because you're lazy and cowardly, just like your father, you don't have the courage to live and be among other people, it's easier to vilify them and hate them, No, Mother, you don't know, they're all disgusting, I can't even take being a district administrator anymore, they do all these things to the miserable villagers, to the poor wretches, they oppress them, and my wife is dead, let their aunts take care of the kids, I'm going to resign and come here to live, please don't bother me, I've been thinking about this for years, me in this quiet corner,

"Come on, Grandmother, it's getting really hot."

I want to sit by myself and write the truth, No, I won't allow it,

"Wait a little bit, Metin Bey . . . "

you can't stay here, you have to go out and be part of life, Recep, don't give him anything to eat, he's a grown man, he should go out and earn his own living, Please, Mother, you'll humiliate me

"Someone should clean off the tops of those graves."

in front of everyone my age, Be quiet, have you no respect, can't I spend a little time alone with your father, I see the animal filth, too, who would have thought everything would come to this, but I said to him then, Are you drinking, I said, you were silent son, why, you're still a young man, I'll get you married again, okay, what will you do here from morning till night, in this place with no one around, you're silent, aren't you, oh my Lord, I know, you'll sit down like your father and start to write nonsense, you're silent, aren't you, oh, son, how can I teach you that you are not responsible for all the crimes and sins and injustice in this world, I'm just a poor ignorant woman, and look, now I have no one, they make fun of me, if you could see the miserable life I've had, son, how unlucky I've been, how much I cry . . . I clutched my handkerchief and crumpled it up,

"Enough, Grandmother, enough, don't cry anymore. We'll come again . . ."

my God, I'm so unlucky, they want to take me away, leave me in peace with my son and my departed husband, I want to be alone with them—I want to lie down on the grave, but I don't, No, Fatma, look, your grandchildren feel sorry for you, they see now how unlucky and miserable I am, they're right, and in this heat, well, I'm saying the Fatiha prayer one last time at least but when I saw that ugly dwarf standing there staring in stupid arrogance, they don't leave you alone for a second, the devil is everywhere, as though he's lying in ambush behind the wall, goading us to annoy one another, okay once more

"Grandmother, you don't look well, let's go now."

Fatiha, when I lift my hands they leave me alone and they lift their hands, too, we pray and pray for the last time, the cars are going by, it's so hot, it's a good thing I didn't put on a sweater underneath, I left it in the closet at the last minute, I locked it in the empty house, God protect us that there be no thief, a person gets so distracted, forgive me, amen, now we're

"Lean on me, Grandmother!"

going, good-bye, oh, you're there too, who has a brain left to think with,

GÜL DARVINOĞLU

1922–1964

MAY SHE REST IN PEACE

but they're making me go and I don't have the strength to stand on my feet and say another prayer in this heat anyway, when I pray for them it was the same as if I prayed for you, little, pale, dull girl, but Doğan liked you, he brought you and made you kiss my hand, then he came to my room quietly at night, How are you, Mother, What can I say, son, this weak, pale little girl, I said, I understood right away you wouldn't live long, having three kids was enough for you, you were worn out, poor thing, you ate from the side of your plate like a cat, one or two mouthfuls, I'd say, can I give you another spoonful, your eyes would widen in hopelessness: this dull little wife, what sin could she have had anyway that she would need my prayer; look, I'm going because they've taken me by the arm and

"Are you okay, Grandmother?"

thank God we're going home now.

8

Hasan Procrastinates

❖

Just as they were leaving, Grandmother wanted to say one more prayer, and this time only Nilgün lifted her hands to pray with her; Faruk had pulled out a handkerchief the size of a sheet and was mopping his sweat, Uncle Recep was holding Grandmother's for her, and Metin had stuck his hands in the back pockets of his blue jeans, not even pretending to pray anymore. They quickly finished mumbling through the prayer and as Grandmother started swaying to the left and to the right they took her again by the arms and were leading her off. When they turned their backs to me I lifted my head straight up and from behind the wall and the bushes, and I could see quite easily; it was a funny scene: as they went off, with the fatso giant called Faruk on one side and the dwarf who's my uncle on the other, their grandmother looked like a scary puppet in clothes too big for her, that strange frightening coat like a black blanket. Still I didn't laugh and maybe because we were in the cemetery I shivered and I looked at you, Nilgün, and that scarf that looked so nice on you, then I looked at your skinny legs. It was so strange: you've grown up, you're a beautiful girl, but your legs are still like sticks.

Later after you got in the car and left, I came out from where I hid so you wouldn't get the wrong idea and I went over to look at those silent graves for myself: that's your grandfather and that's your mother and father but I only remember your father. When we were playing in the garden, once in a while he would stick his head out the shutters of the room and see us together, but he never said anything about me playing with you. I said the Fatiha prayer for him and stayed there for a while, not doing anything except cooking in the sun and listening to the crickets, and I thought strange things, strange dark things, I shivered, my thoughts got all mixed up, as if I'd smoked a cigarette. Then I left the cemetery, and I was going back to where I left my mathematics open on the table. Because an hour ago when I was sitting at the table, just as I looked out the window, you were going up the hill in your white Anadol and I realized, because your grandmother was with you, where you must be going and then, while I was thinking about the cemetery and the dead, it became even more impossible for me to follow that stupid annoying math and so I said, Why not just go and check them out, I'll relax after I see what they're up to in the cemetery, then I'll come back and work, I said, so I hopped out the window to keep my mother from getting upset over nothing, ran up here, and saw you and now it's back to the math problem I left.

The dusty road ended, and the asphalt began. Cars were going by, and once or twice I signaled, but people with cars no longer have consciences: they go downhill at top speed, without even seeing me. Then I came to Tahsin's. He and his mother were picking fruit in the back while his father sat at the stand selling cherries, but it was as if he couldn't see me, maybe because I wasn't driving a luxury car at a hundred kilometers an hour and suddenly braking so I could jump out and buy five kilos of cherries at eighty liras a kilo, he didn't even lift his head and look at me. Yes, I would say that I'm the only one left who can't think about something besides money, but when I saw Halil's garbage truck I was happy. They were going downhill, I put up my hand for them to stop, and I got on.

"What's your dad doing?" he said.

"The lottery," I said. "What else? He works the trains in the mornings."

"You?"

"I'm still in school," I said. "How fast can this thing go?"

"Eighty!" he said. "What are you doing here anyway?"

"I was feeling fed up," I said. "I took a walk."

"If you're already fed up at this age . . . ," they said, laughing, and braking in front of my house.

"No," I said. "I'm going all the way down."

"What's there?"

"I have a friend there, you don't know them."

As we passed the house, I looked at my open window. I'll be back, I thought, before my father gets home at noon. I got out of the truck as soon as we came into the neighborhood at the bottom of the hill. I walked quickly so that Halil's guys wouldn't think I was some kind of useless bum. I went all the way out to the breakwater and sat down a little and looked at the sea, since I was dripping sweat from the heat. A motorboat pulled up at high speed, dropped off a girl on the dock before zooming off again. Looking at that girl, I thought of you, Nilgün. I saw how you lifted up your hands in prayer just a little while ago: It was weird. Just like you were actually talking with Him. It says in the book, there are angels. Then I thought: There's the devil, too. And other things. I thought about them as though I wanted to be scared, to shiver and feel guilty so I'd run home up the hill, do my math, but I'd be sitting down soon enough anyway, so why not wander around for a while?

When I got to the beach and heard all that noise that just stuns you and saw that mass of flesh, I thought again about guilt, sin, and the devil. A quivering mass of flesh: once in a while a bright beach ball would waft slowly up, as though it wanted to escape all this guilt and sin, but then it would fall down and get lost in the mass of flesh again; the women wouldn't let it go. I looked some more through the wire fence covered with ivy at the crowd and the women. It's strange, sometimes I feel like doing something bad, then I feel ashamed, it's as if I want to hurt them a little so they'll notice me: that way, I would have punished them and nobody would give in to the devil and maybe they would only be afraid of me then. It's a feeling like this: we're in power and they're behaving properly because of it. I got embarrassed to have these thoughts, and to forget my embarrassment I thought of you, Nilgün. You're innocent. I was saying to myself, I'll look at the crowd for a little while longer, then go back to the math book, when the guy who takes care of the beach said,

"What are you hanging around here for?"

"Is it forbidden?" I said.

"If you're going in, go over there and get a ticket!" he said. "If you have a bathing suit and money . . . "

"Take it easy," I said. "I'm going."

If you have money, if you have money, how much is it: this was what they prayed now instead of the Fatiha: You're all so disgusting, sometimes I feel completely alone: Half of them disgusting, half of them idiots. When you think of it you become afraid of the crowd, but thank God our guys are here, when I'm with them I don't get confused; I know then what's a crime and what's a sin, I can tell the difference between good and evil and I'm not afraid: I understand very well what has to be done. Then I thought of how our guys kept teasing me in the coffeehouse last night, calling me the Fox, and I got angry. Fine. I can do those things that have to be done all by myself, gentlemen, I can walk that road alone, because I know. I believe and trust in myself.

I kept on walking and reached your house, Nilgün, without even noticing, I realized it when I saw that old wall covered with moss. The garden gate was closed. I went over and sat down under the chestnut tree on the other side of the road, looked at the windows and doors, and wondered what you were doing inside. Maybe you were eating something, maybe you still had that scarf on your head, maybe you were taking an afternoon nap. I picked up a stick and absentmindedly drew your picture in the sand collected on the side of the road. Your face is prettier when you're asleep. When I look at it, I forget all about sin and guilt, and those sinful guilty rashes that I sometimes feel like I'm covered with up to my throat, and I think, What could I have done wrong, I'm not one of them, I believe I'm like you. Then I think: If I sneak into the garden and over by where the tree sticks out and climb up the wall and slip into your room through the open window like a cat and kiss you on your cheek: Who are you? Don't you recognize me, we played hide-and-seek, I love you, I love you more than all those fine fellows you know could ever possibly love you! Then I lost my temper: I wiped out the face I had drawn on the sand with my foot and just when I got up sick of all these stupid imaginings, I saw:

Nilgün coming out of the house and walking toward the gate.

They get everything wrong, they see everything as bad. I quickly moved off, turning my back to the gate. After I heard your voice I turned around: you had come out of the gate and going where, I wondered. So I followed you.

She had a funny way of walking: like a man. If I ran up and put my hand on your shoulder: Don't you recognize me, Nilgün, I'm Hasan, you know, we used to play in your garden when we were kids, Metin was there, too, later we went fishing.

She didn't look back when she turned the corner, just kept on walking: Are you going to the beach, are you going to join them, too? I was annoyed, but I kept following her. She was moving quickly on her stick legs, What's the hurry, or is somebody waiting for you?

She didn't stop at the beach but kept on going uphill. I could guess now who was waiting for her. Maybe you'll get in his car, maybe he has a boat: wondering which one he was, I kept following you, because I knew you were no different from the others.

She vanished into the grocery store. There was a kid selling ice cream in front of the store; since I knew the little guy, I waited a bit at a distance so he wouldn't get the wrong idea. I don't like sucking up to rich people.

A little later Nilgün came out, but instead of continuing on, she started walking the way she had come, straight toward me. I quickly turned and bent down, making as if to tie my shoelace. She came closer and closer with her package in hand, and when she looked at me, I was embarrassed.

"Hello," I said as I got up.

"Hello, Hasan," she said. "How are you?" She paused. "We saw you yesterday on the road. My brother recognized you. You've grown up, you've really changed. What are you doing?" She paused again. "You still live up above there, your uncle said, your father's in the lottery." She was quiet again. "Well, what are you up to, tell me, what year are you in?"

"Me?" I said. "I'm taking this year off," I finally managed to say.

"What?"

"Are you going to the beach, Nilgün?"

"No," she said, "I'm coming from the grocery. We took my grandmother to the cemetery. She was a little affected by the heat, I think. I got some cologne."

"So you're not going to the beach," I said.

"It's really crowded," she said. "I'll go early in the morning, when nobody's there."

We were silent for a bit. Then she smiled and I laughed and noticed how her face looked different from what I'd imagined looking at it from a distance. Also, I was sweating like a jerk. She said it was the heat. I was quiet. She took a step.

"Well, okay," she said. "Say hello to your father, okay?"

She put out her hand and we shook. Her hand was soft and light. I was embarrassed because mine was sweaty.

"Bye!" I said.

I didn't watch her go on her way. I walked off like someone who had something important to do.

9

Faruk Sees Stories in the Archives

✿

After we got back from the cemetery, Grandmother ate dinner with us downstairs, then began to feel unwell. Nilgün and I were laughing, and she gave us a really dirty look before her head slumped down on her chest. We took her by the arm, brought her upstairs to bed, and put some of the cologne Nilgün had bought on her wrists and temples. Then I went to my room to have my first after-dinner cigarette. After we realized that there was nothing seriously wrong with Grandmother, I got into the Anadol, which in the sun had gotten hot as an oven. Instead of the main road, I took the Darıca road, which had been carefully asphalted very recently. I remembered some of the cherry and fig trees. Recep and I used to come around here as kids, supposedly to hunt crows, or just for a walk. That structure I'd been imagining was a caravanserai must be farther down. There were new neighborhoods on the hills, and more being built. But I didn't see anything new in Darıca: just that ten-year-old statue of Atatürk!

In Gebze I went straight to the district office. The district administrator had changed. Two years ago there was a man at this table who was tired of life; now there was a young fellow who gestured with his arms when he spoke. Winning him over hadn't even required showing him, as I'd planned to, my thesis, recently published by the faculty, or informing him that I had already done research in the district archives many times before or that my late father had been a district administrator. No, he simply sent me off right away with a man whom he summoned. The man and I looked for Riza, whom I knew from my earlier visit, but as he had apparently stepped away to visit the dispensary, I decided to walk around in the market until he came back.

I followed a tight passage overhung with berry bushes, going downhill into the market. The streets were empty, except for a dog wandering on the pavement and a man mounting an Aygaz propane tank at the blacksmith's. I turned without looking into the stationer's window, before walking on, sheltering in the narrow shadows of the shop fronts until the mosque appeared. After backtracking a bit, I sat under the plane tree in the little square, had a tea to stay alert, and, trying to ignore the heat, half listened to the sound of the radio coming from the coffeehouse, pleased that no one was paying any attention to me.

When I got back to the district office Riza had returned and expressed pleasure to see me. While he sought out the key, I had to write out a request. We went downstairs together. When he opened the door, I instantly recalled the smell of mildew, dust, and damp. We chatted a little as he dusted the old table and chair before leaving me to my work.

There wasn't actually very much in the Gebze archives. What there was dated from a short time that very few people knew or cared about, when the town had been the local seat. The great majority of documents from that period had been sent to Izmit, then called Iznikmit. Left behind were forgotten decrees, deed registries, court records, all in boxes and registers piled up on top of one another, collecting dust.

Thirty years ago, a devoted high school history teacher animated by the bureaucratic nationalism peculiar to those years had tried to put the Ottoman documents in some kind of order but gave up. Two years ago, I decided to take up where he'd left off, but I was defeated in a week. To be an archivist requires an even more humble and generous spirit than to be a historian. In our day, those willing to get a little ink on their fingers and possessed of the necessary humility are few and far between. The devoted teacher had no such humility and immediately got the idea of doing a book to profit from his hours in the archives. In the days when I was fighting incessantly with Selma, I remember enjoying a beer while reading this book in which the teacher recounted his own life and that of his friends as well as those of the famous people and historic buildings of Gebze. When I mentioned this book to some of my colleagues on the faculty, they all gave the same response: No, it was impossible that documents for such an undertaking could exist in Gebze! I was silent while they proved to me that there couldn't even be archives in Gebze.

It was more pleasurable to work in a place that the experts said didn't exist than to scrounge with my jealous colleagues in the archives of the prime minister's office. I enjoyed the smell and feel of the yellowed, mildewed, wrinkled pieces of paper. As I read them, I felt as though I could see the people who had written them and those whose lives were somehow affected by these documents. Perhaps I had come to the archives just for this pleasure, and not to follow the trail of the plague that I thought I had picked up last year. As one reads through the faded piles of papers, they gradually begin to separate from one another. Just as, after a long sea journey, an all-oppressing fog suddenly lifts to reveal with astonishing clarity every tree, stone, and bird on a stretch of shore, so, too, as I read on, from individual pages, the millions of lives and stories jumbled together suddenly took discrete form in my mind. Then I became quite happy, deciding that this is history, this colorful vital thing that is coming alive in my mind. If I had to say what it is more exactly, I couldn't. A little later, anyway, it disappears, leaving only a strange taste behind.

While reading a court record I thought, Maybe I can recapture this sensation by transcribing what I'm reading. I started to write in my notebook. Someone named Celal claims that Mehmet has cussed at him: "You son of a bitch!" But Mehmet denied it before the judge. Celal, who testifies, "He did say it," has two witnesses, Hasan and Kasım. The judge calls Mehmet to deny it under oath, but Mehmet can't. The date was erased, I couldn't write it down. Then I read of somebody called Hamza who appointed a certain Abdi as his executor, and I wrote that down. I also made a note that a Russian slave named Dimitri had been caught. The owner was one Veli Bey from Tuzla, and they decided to return Dimitri to him. I read about what happened to the shepherd Yusuf who was imprisoned after losing a cow. He had neither sold nor slaughtered the cow. He just lost it. His brother Ramazan posted bail and Yusuf was released. Then I read a decree. For some reason, it was ordered that some ships laden with wheat should go directly to Istanbul without docking in Gebze, Tuzla, or Eskihisar. Someone called Ibrahim had said, "If I don't go to Istanbul, let my wife be considered a divorced woman," and when he didn't go to Istanbul, it was so argued. Ibrahim later attested that he hadn't gone to Istanbul but that he would, though he hadn't specified a time in his oath. Looking over the amounts in *akçe* in the ledger entries, I tried to figure out some of the rents that had been paid to the comptroller, but I couldn't determine an exact figure. At the same time, I copied down in my notebook the annual income from a large number of mills, orchards, gardens, and olive groves, feeling I could actually see them, though I was probably just fooling myself.

When I went outside for a cigarette in the corridor, I realized that instead of following up on the plague that I had come across last year, I could actually pursue any story I wanted. What kind of story should it be? From the window at the end of the corridor, I could see the wall of a house behind the district office building; a truck standing in front of the wall made you wonder what was going on in there. I snuffed my cigarette butt in the sand of the red fire bucket and went back inside.

A complaint had been lodged by someone named Ethem against a certain Kasım. While Ethem was not at home, Kasım had gone to his house and spoken roughly with his family. Kasım did not deny having gone but said he had just been by to eat *gözleme* and take his portion of oil. Another pair was involved in a case because one had yanked the other's beard. I wrote down the names of two women, Kevser and Kezban, who were engaging in prostitution; the plaintiffs wanted them removed from the neighborhood. Then I read Ali's testimony that Kevser had engaged in this kind of activity before. A certain Satilmış was owed a debt of twenty-two gold pieces by Kalender, but Kalender denied the debt.

I wrote down these things as well: A boy named Muharrem had left home to go read the Koran, when his father, Resul, caught him with a young man, also named Resul. Claiming that Resul had seduced his son, the father demanded an investigation. Resul said that Muharrem had come to him of his own will, that the two had gone together to the mill, whereupon Muharrem had gone off to gather figs and lost himself in the gardens. After I put the date in my notebook, I thought about what it must have been like, some four hundred years ago, to be the figs in a boy's fancy or to be Resul imagining the boy imagining the figs. Then I read and wrote down the orders to capture a cavalry soldier who had turned to banditry, to close all taverns immediately and bring wine drinkers to justice: thefts, business disagreements, outlaws, marriages, and divorces . . . What use could these stories be? I was so engrossed I didn't even think about going out into the corridor to smoke a cigarette. Ignoring the fact that the stories had to have some use, I was copying a huge mass of figures and words related to meat when my eye happened on an investigation of a dead body found in the stone quarries. The workers were interrogated, pressed one by one to explain what they had been doing that day. For the first time I felt I could really envision that twenty-third of Recep 1028 (which the West had lived as the sixth of July 1619), and I was quite pleased. I thought a cigarette might complement my good mood, but I held myself back and copied everything I had read exactly into my notebook. By the time I was done, the sun was lower in the sky and now visible at the edge of the basement window. I would have gladly agreed to spend my whole life in that cool basement if only three square meals could be brought at appropriate intervals, as well as a pack of cigarettes and in the evening a little *rakı* left by the door. There were enough stories among those pieces of paper to last a lifetime, and these stories would lift the fog obscuring the patch of earth I had alighted on. Just the thought swelled my confidence in myself and in my work. Then like a good and responsible student, I counted up the number of pages I had written: exactly nine! I decided that I deserved to go home and have a drink.

10

Metin Socializes

❧

We were sitting on Ceylan's dock; I was about to dive into the water, but, damn it, still listening to everything they were saying.

"What should we do tonight?" said Gülnur.

"Let's do something different," said Fafa.

"Yeah! Let's go to Suadiye."

"What's there?" said Turgay.

"Music!" shouted Gülnur.

"There's music here too."

I dove in and thought about how next year at this time I would be in New York, I thought about my poor mother and father in the grave, and I imagined the freedom along the city's avenues, the blacks who would play jazz for me on the street corners, those subway stations where no one pays any attention to anyone else, the endless labyrinth of the tunnels under the streets, and it lifted my spirits, but then I thought about how if I couldn't get the money on account of my brother and sister I wouldn't be able to go, and I got peeved, but now at least I'm thinking about you, Ceylan: the way you sit on the dock, the way you stretch out your legs, and about how I love you and how I'm going to make you love me.

I poked my head up out of the water and looked back. I had gone really far from the shore, and I was overcome by a strange fear: they were there, but I was in a scary liquid that had no beginning or end, full of salt and seaweed. All of a sudden I panicked and swam as though a shark were chasing me. I bounded out of the water and went over and sat beside Ceylan.

Just to say something, I said, "The water's really nice."

"But you came right out," said Ceylan.

I turned and listened to Fikret, who was explaining one of the problems that only special people have: in this case, how his father had suffered a heart attack this winter and all the responsibility had fallen on Fikret, even though he's only eighteen, until his older brother could come back from Germany, how he had managed all the work and the men and everything. When he said that his father might die at any moment, just trying to prove that very soon he might be even more important, I said that my father had died a long time ago and we had gone to his grave this morning.

"Hey, guys! You're getting me all depressed," said Ceylan. She got up and walked away.

"Let's do something!"

Fafa lifted her head up from a magazine, "What?"

"We could go over around Hisar!" said Zeynep.

"We were just there yesterday," said Vedat.

"Let's go fishing then," said Ceylan.

Turan was trying to open a tube of suntan lotion.

"It's a little hot," said Fikret.

"I'm going crazy!" said Ceylan, annoyed and hopeless.

"Can't do anything with you people!" said Gülnur.

Ceylan asked, "Well, how about it?"

Nobody said anything.

After a long silence, the cap from Turan's tube of sun cream fell down and rolled over like a marble before stopping next to Ceylan's foot. Ceylan kicked it, and it fell into the sea.

"It's not mine, it's Hülya's," said Turan.

"I'll buy her a new one," said Ceylan, coming over to sit by me.

I thought about whether I loved Ceylan or not; I believed I did: vacant, foolish thoughts under the stupefying sun. Turan had gotten up and was staring at the sea from where the cap had fallen in.

"No!" said Ceylan as she jumped to her feet. "You will not go after that, Turan!"

"Okay, then you get it."

"I'll get it," I said. "I just got out of the water." I got up and went over.

"You're a good kid, Metin," said Ceylan.

"Get it then," said Turan, pointing as though he were giving an order.

"Maybe I'm not going to get it," I said. "The water's cold." Fafa laughed as I turned around and sat down again.

"Hülya," said Turan, "I'll get you a new tube."

"No, I said I would," said Ceylan.

"It was finished anyway," said Hülya.

"I'll get it anyway. What kind was it?" said Ceylan. Then, without waiting for an answer, she said in a begging voice, "Come on, guys, let's do something."

At that point Mehmet said that Mary wanted to go across to the island and at once everyone felt that sense of inferiority, the need to please the European, and so we piled into the boats. Ceylan and I got into the same one.

Then she ran to the house and came back with two bottles and shouted: "Gin!"

When somebody else yelled out "Music," Cuneyt ran off, too, and brought that awful stereo and the speakers from the house. The motors roared to life and the boats flew off, and the bows heaved upward before settling down to an even keel. Half a minute later in the middle of the open sea I was thinking: If something breaks or gets scratched or worn out, they don't even care, their boats do forty miles an hour and I'm a bundle of nerves, but, Ceylan, I still love you.

The boats pulled up to the island as though they would crash on the rocks, but the pilots suddenly cut the speed, turned, and stopped. You couldn't see anything but the top of the lighthouse on the other side of the island. A gray dog came out from somewhere, then a black one and another gray one; they ran down to the shore and jumped on the rocks, barking right at us. The bottle of gin was passing from hand to hand, since we had nothing to drink it with; they gave it to me, and I drank from the mouth of the bottle, too.

"The dogs are rabid!" said Gülnur.

"Floor it, Fikret, let's see what they do!" said Ceylan.

When Fikret gave it gas, the dogs turned just as the boats had done and began a crazy run around the island. Everybody in the boats was shouting, singing songs, to provoke the dogs, and the more they were provoked, the wilder they became, they yelped and howled and barked, and I was thinking, this is not the brightest idea for entertainment I have ever seen, but it was still more fun than my aunt's hot, deadly house, better than the small dusty rooms with lace crochet spread on top of the radios.

"Music! Turn it all the way up and let's see what they do!"

With the music blaring we went around the little island two more times. We were going for a third circuit when something in the wake of the boat caught my eye: Ceylan's happy face suddenly appeared, bobbing away far off in the foamy water. I jumped in without thinking, as if diving into a scary dream.

The moment I hit the water I had a sinking feeling. It was as though Ceylan and I were going to die here and no one in the boats would notice. When I lifted my head from the water and looked, I was flabbergasted. One of the boats had stopped, gone over to Ceylan, and they were lifting her out. After they'd pulled Ceylan out, they came over to get me.

"Who pushed you?" said Fikret.

"Nobody pushed him," said Gülnur. "He jumped in."

"Well, then who pushed me?" said Ceylan.

I was trying to pull myself onboard, gripping the oar that Turgay held out to me, but just as I was about to get in the boat, he let go of the oar and I fell into the water again. When I lifted my head out of the water no one was paying any attention to me, but I managed to get back in the boat, completely out of breath.

"Goddamn you, none of you know how to have fun," said Gülnur.

"We'll throw you to the dogs!" said Fikret.

"If you know, teach us," said Turgay.

"Idiots!" shouted Gülnur.

A dog who was watching them jumped onto the nearest rock and howled.

"Crazy!" said Ceylan, looking back at the dog that looked mesmerized as it flashed its sharp gleaming white teeth. "Get a little closer to the dog, Fikret."

"Why?"

"Just do it."

"What are you looking at?" Fikret slowly drew closer to the dog. "Is it a male or a female?" He stopped the motor.

"It's bad luck!" shouted Ceylan, in a weird way.

Suddenly I wanted to throw my arms around her, but instead I just looked at her, wondering what it would take to make her love me. I was becoming increasingly convinced that I was just a no-good lowlife, but at the same time I was feeling pretty good about myself, empty pride being the best antidote for worthlessness, to the point that I wanted to do something to make everyone pay attention to me, though unfortunately I couldn't find either the courage or an excuse to do anything. It was like a straitjacket of poverty they had put on me. A few were dancing around and shouting while in the bow of the other boat two of them were wrestling, each trying to throw the other into the water. Then that boat came near and they started throwing buckets of water at us. We threw water back at them, and there was some dueling with the oars as swords for a while, causing some in our boat to fall in the water. By then the gin bottles were empty. So Fikret grabbed one of them and threw it at the dog, but he missed and the bottle smashed on the rocks.

"What's going on?" shouted Ceylan.

"It's okay, now, it's okay, we're going back," said Fikret.

He started up the motor, but by the time we'd collected the ones who had fallen into the water, the other boat had caught up, and they threw another bucket of water on us.

"Okay, wise guys," said Fikret, "let's see what you can do, come on, we'll race!"

Side by side, the two boats went at the same speed for a while, but then Gülnur gave a shout, and it became obvious that the other boat was going to pass us, which made Fikret curse and order everybody toward the prow so we could gain speed. When the others passed us anyway and started to do a victory dance, Fikret balled up a towel and threw it at them. Of course he missed, but we turned right around and got there in time, but since nobody bothered to reach out and grab it, we rolled like an iron right over it, and the towel disappeared. The other boat, with everybody still howling, started chasing the car ferry that goes from Yalova to Darıca and, when they caught up with it, circled it twice, shouting taunts at the crew, before coming back toward us for a game of bumper cars. When our two boats started to cruise among the swimming heads near the beach without cutting speed, I got nervous, and as the swimmers shouted and tried to get out of the way, I murmured, "What if there's an accident?"

"What are you, a teacher?" shouted Fafa. "You're a high school teacher, huh?"

"Is he a teacher?" said Gülnur.

"I hate teachers!" said Fafa.

"Me too!" said Cuneyt.

"He didn't drink anything," said Turan. "That's the problem. Too many multiplication tables."

"I drank more than you did," I said pathetically, but since I noticed Ceylan wasn't looking I didn't care.

Later, after we'd returned to Ceylan's dock and tied up, I saw a woman about forty-five wearing a robe on the dock: it was her mother.

"You kids are soaking wet," she said. "What were you up to? Baby, where's your towel?"

"I lost it, Mom," said Ceylan.

"How did you do that? You'll catch an awful cold," her mother said.

Ceylan made some gesture to say she didn't care and then said, "Oh, Mom, this is Metin. They live in that old house. The strange silent house."

"Which old house?" said her mother.

We shook hands, she asked what my father did, I explained the situation and also told her that I was going to go to America for university studies.

"We're going to buy a house in America," Ceylan's mother said. "Who can say what's going to happen here. Where's the best place in America?"

I gave her some geographic information, I spoke about the climatic conditions, the population, and cited some statistics, but I couldn't tell whether she was listening because she wasn't looking at me. Then as we were talking a little about the street killings and the leftist gangs and the nationalist thugs in Turkey, Ceylan interrupted.

"Mom, has he got you trapped now listening to his boring knowledge?"

"You're so rude!" said her mother. But then she went off without listening to the rest of what I had to say.

I went over and stretched out on a chaise longue and watched Ceylan and the others diving in and getting out and diving in again. When everyone was reclining on the chairs and on the concrete, giving in to that unbelievable torpor under the sun, I fantasized about a clock left out there on the pier among our idle naked legs: as it exposes its face to the motionless sun it mixes up its hands until it has to confess that it can no longer measure time, and the thoughts of the clock are no different from the thoughts of someone who has no thoughts at all trying to understand what his thoughts are.

11

Grandmother Takes Out
the Silver Candy Bowl

Somebody knocked. I closed my eyes and kept quiet, but the door opened anyway.

"Grandma, are you okay?" said Nilgün.

I didn't respond. I wanted them to look at my pale face and still body and realize that I was in the throes of agony.

"You look better, Grandmother, you have some color in your face."

I thought: They'll never understand and they'll keep smiling, with their plastic cologne bottles and fake good cheer, and I will remain all alone with my pains, my past, and my thoughts. All right, leave me to my nice thoughts.

"Feeling better, Grandmother?"

But they won't leave me. And I don't speak.

"You had a good sleep. Do you want anything?"

"Lemonade!" I said all of a sudden, and when Nilgün had left I carried on with my nice, pure thoughts. I still felt warm after waking up from that cozy sleep, warmth on my cheeks and in my mind.

I thought about the dream, the images in the dream, how I was very small, I had left Istanbul and was on a train, and as the train moved, I could see gardens, one within another, lovely old gardens. Soon Istanbul was far away, and we were in those gardens within gardens within gardens. Then I thought about the first days: the horse-drawn cart, the well bucket with the squeaky pulley, the sewing machine, the peaceful moments as the pedal of the machine creaked, then times we spent laughing together, the sun, the colors, the sudden feeling of fun, the fullness of that moment, Selâhattin, I thought about those first days: getting off in Gebze when we got sick . . . tossing and turning in those rooms at the inn in Gebze, the first time we came to Cennethisar because we thought the air was better. . . . A dock abandoned after the railroad was finished, a few old houses, a few old chicken coops, but the air is wonderful isn't it, Fatma? No need to go any farther! Let's settle down here! We'll be near your mother and father in Istanbul, so they won't worry, and we'll be ready to go right back as soon as the government is toppled. Let's get a house built here!

We used to go for long walks together in those days: There are so many things to do in life, Fatma, Selâhattin would say, come, let me show you a little of the world, how's the kid in your tummy, is it kicking, I know it will be a boy and I'm going to name him Doğan (Birth), so that he'll always remind us of the new world that is dawning, so he lives in security and prosperity and believes that his strength is a match for the world! Take care of your health, Fatma, let's both of us do that, let's live for a long time, isn't the world an extraordinary place, those plants, those brave trees that grow up all by themselves: it's impossible not to be amazed by nature, let's live like Rousseau in the lap of nature and keep far away from those self-proclaimed monarchs and the pashas who suck up to them, let's examine everything all over again with our own minds. Just to think of all these things is so wonderful! Are you tired, dear, take my arm and look at the beauty of the earth and sky, I'm so happy to have escaped all the hypocrisy of Istanbul that I almost feel like writing Talat a thank-you letter! Forget about those people in Istanbul, let them rot for their crimes and the torture that they take such pleasure in inflicting on one another! We'll establish a brand-new world here, thinking and living things that are fresh, simple, happy, and free: a world of freedom such as the East has never seen, a paradise of logic on the face of the earth, I swear, Fatma, it will happen, and we'll do it better than the West, we've seen their mistakes, and we won't repeat them, and if we, or even our sons, don't get to see it, our grandchildren certainly will, I swear, a paradise of logic on this earth! And we absolutely must give the child in your womb a good education, I'll never ever make him cry, he must never feel fear, I will never teach this child the Eastern melancholy, the weeping, pessimism, the defeat of our terrible Oriental fatalism; we'll work on his education together, we'll bring him up free, you understand what this means, don't you, good for you, Fatma, I'm so proud of you, I respect you, you know, I think of you as a free and independent person; I don't think of you the way others think of their wives, as a concubine, an odalisque, a slave: you're my equal, my dear, do you understand? But let's go back now, yes, life's as beautiful as a dream. But there's work to be done so others can see the dream, we're going back.

"Grandma, don't you want your lemonade?"

I lifted up my head from the pillow and looked. "Leave it there," I said, and as she put it down, "Why didn't Recep bring it? Did you make it?"

"I made it," said Nilgün. "Recep's hands were greasy, he's cooking."

I feel sorry for you, dear girl, but what can I do, because the dwarf has already pulled the wool over your eyes, he does that, he's sneaky. I thought: How he got in among them, how he turned their thoughts around, how he drowned them in that evil feeling of shame and guilt with his disgusting, ugly presence, how he fooled them the way he fooled my Doğan. Did he tell them? My head fell exhausted on the pillow, and I thought, Poor me, of that terrible and pathetic thing that kept me from sleeping at night.

I thought about how it must have been as he spoke: Yes, Madam, I am telling them, he would say, I'm telling your grandchildren one by one what you did to me and my poor mother and my brother, let them hear and know all about it, because now, as my departed father—Quiet, dwarf, *no*—as the departed Selâhattin Bey, wrote so beautifully, there's no God now, thank goodness, there's science, we can know everything, we must know everything, they should know, they do know, because I told them, and now they say, Poor Recep, you mean our grandmother mistreated you and still does, we're so sorry, we feel so guilty, so don't trouble yourself washing your greasy hands just to make lemonade; don't work, just sit there and relax, this house belongs to you too, they say, because Recep told them. But did he tell them: Children, can you imagine why your father, Doğan Bey, would have wanted to sell your grandmother's last diamonds and give the money to us, did he tell them that? Just the thought of it and I felt as if I were drowning. My head popped up from the pillow, full of hate!

"Where is he?"

"Who, Grandmother?"

"Recep! Where?"

"Downstairs, I already said, Grandmother. He's cooking."

"What has he said to you?"

"Nothing, Grandmother!" said Nilgün.

No, he wouldn't tell them, he wouldn't dare, Fatma, don't be afraid, he's sneaky, but he's also a coward. I took the lemonade that was next to me and drank it. But then I thought of the closet again.

"What are you doing here?" I said abruptly.

"I'm sitting here with you, Grandmother," said Nilgün. "I missed it here this last year."

"Fine," I said. "Sit! But don't get up now."

I slowly got up, and taking the keys from under my pillow and my cane from the edge of the bedside, off I went.

"Where are you going, Grandmother?" said Nilgün. "Can I help?"

I didn't answer. When I got to the closet I stopped and rested. As I put the key in the lock I looked back: yes, Nilgün was still sitting there. I opened the closet and checked right away: I had gotten all upset for nothing, the box was still there, it was completely empty, but at least it was there still. Then I thought of something as I was closing the door. I took the silver candy bowl from the bottom of the bottom drawer, locked the closet, and brought it over to Nilgün.

"Oh, Grandma, you got up just for me, that was so much trouble."

"Take a red one, too!"

"What a beautiful silver bowl!" she said.

"Don't touch it!"

I went back to my bed, Let me think of something else, I said, but nothing came to mind: I lost myself in thoughts of one of those days when I couldn't leave the closet for a minute: "Look, aren't you being rude, Fatma," he said, that day, "the man came all the way from Istanbul to see us, and you won't even leave your room, and he's so refined, he's like a European. If you're doing this because he's Jewish that's even worse, Fatma, after the Dreyfus affair all of Europe knows how wrong it is to for you to think this way. Then Selâhattin went downstairs, and I looked out from between the shutters.

"Grandmother, isn't the lemonade sweet enough?"

I looked at them from between the shutters: a scrawny old thing who looked even smaller next to Selâhattin, a jeweler from Kapalıçarşı!

But Selâhattin was talking to him as though he were a scholar instead of a little trader; I could overhear: Well, Avram Efendi, what's going on in Istanbul, are people happy with the proclamation of the republic? According to Selâhattin the jeweler said: Business is off, sir, off! And instead of replying, Selâhattin said, "No, really? Business, too? But the republic was supposed to be good for business just as for everything else. Business was going to save us. And not just our people, business will wake up the whole East; first we have to learn how to make money, how to keep accounts and records: this is what they call mathematics, then, when trade and mathematics and money all come together they'll set up factories. And then we, too, will learn not just to make money like them but to think like them as well! What do you think, to live like them do we first have to learn to think like them or is it sufficient to learn first how to make money like them?" The jeweler said, "Who is the 'they' you're talking about?" And Selâhattin said, "Who else, my friend, the Europeans, the Westerners," and he asked, "Don't we have anyone at all who's both a Muslim and a rich businessman? Who's that Işıkçı Cevdet Bey, have you ever heard of him?" The jeweler: "I've heard it said he made a lot of money during the war." And Selâhattin asked, "Well, what else is going on in Istanbul, do you have connections with Babıali, what are those idiots saying, who are they pushing forward as new writers or new poets, do you know any of them?" And then the jeweler said, "I don't really know. Why don't you go and have a look for yourself!" Then I heard Selâhattin shouting, "No, I won't go there! Let them talk to the devil, damn them. They won't produce anything after this. Look at that Abdullah Cevdet, his last book was such a piece of trash, he stole everything from Delahaye but wrote it up as though it were his own, and on top of everything, it was all jumbled, since he didn't understand a thing. Anyway, it's impossible to say anything about religion and industry anymore without reading Bourguignon. He and Ziya Bey always take stuff from other writers and without understanding a thing: besides, Ziya's French is minimal and he can't understand what he's reading, I said to myself, I should write a piece and humiliate them, but who would understand, and would it be worth eating into the time I must devote to my encyclopedia just to be a scribbler of such trivial things. I say leave them, let them devour one another in Istanbul."

I lifted my head from the pillow and took a sip of the lemonade set next to me.

Then Selâhattin said to the jeweler, "Go and tell them that that's what I think of them," to which the jeweler replied, "But I don't even know them, sir, people like that, they never come by my shop," which prompted Selâhattin to start shouting, "I know, I know!" and cut him off, "you don't even have to say anything. Anyway, when I've finished my forty-eight-volume encyclopedia of all the basic principles and ideas, everything that must be said in the East will have been said once and for all: I'll fill that unbelievable gulf in thought in one fell swoop, they'll all be astonished, the newsboys on Galata Bridge will sell my encyclopedia, Bank's Avenue will be turned upside down, they'll go after one another in Sirkeci, some readers will commit suicide, and, above all, the people will understand me, the nation will understand! And that's when I'll return to Istanbul, in the middle of that great awakening, I'll come back!" said Selâhattin, and the jeweler said, "Yes, mister, you stay here meanwhile, Istanbul's no fun anymore, and neither is the Kapalıçarşi. Everyone's trying to gouge the other man's eyes out. One jeweler will try to drive down the price of another's merchandise. But you can trust me. As I said, business is slow, but I figured let me at least go and take a look at the stuff. If you don't mind it's getting late, so perhaps you should show me that diamond. And how about the earrings you mentioned in your letter, what are they like?" Then there was a silence; I listened to the silence with my heart pounding; I had the key in my hand.

"Grandmother, maybe it's too sweet?"

I took another swallow and turned away toward the pillow. "It's just right!" I said. "Congratulations, and good health to you."

"I made it very sweet."

Then I heard the jeweler's nasty cough and Selâhattin saying in a whiny voice: But aren't you staying for dinner, Avram Efendi? When the jeweler mentioned the earrings once more, Selâhattin ran upstairs to my room: Fatma, he said, come on, come downstairs, we're sitting down to eat, it's very rude! But he knew I wouldn't come down. A little later he went down with my Doğan, and then the jeweler said "What a polite boy!" and asked after his mother, and Selâhattin said that I was ill, and as I listened to the three of them eating whatever that whore was serving them, I was filled with disgust. Then he started to tell the jeweler about his encyclopedia.

"Grandmother, what are you thinking, aren't you going to say?"

The encyclopedia: the natural sciences, all the sciences, science and Allah, the West and the Renaissance, night and day, fire and water, the East and time and death and life. Life! Life!

"What time is it now?" I asked.

It's the thing that divides everything as it ticks away: time: I think of it and my hair stands on end.

"It's almost six thirty, Grandmother," said Nilgün. Then she came over to my table and asked, "How old is this clock, Grandmother?"

I didn't recall what else they were saying at the table: something that revolted me and made me want to forget, because in the end, this is what the jeweler said: The dinner was wonderful. But this woman of yours who cooked it is even better. Who is she? And Selâhattin, in his cups, said something like: She's a poor village woman! She's not from around here. When her husband went off to the military he left her here with some distant relative, but that poor fellow's boat sank, and he drowned. Anyway, Fatma was getting worn out, we were looking for a servant, so we put her in the little room downstairs, we couldn't let her starve to death. She's hardworking. But it was too small for her. So I built a shack. Her husband never came back from the military. He was either hanged for desertion, or else he died as a martyr. I really admire her: this woman has both my people's good looks and their willingness to work. I've learned a lot of things from her for my encyclopedia article on the economic life of the village. Please have another glass! I had to close my door to save myself from hearing more!

"Whose clock was this, Grandmother? You told us last year."

"It was my mother's," I said, and when Nilgün laughed, I realized that talking was a waste of breath.

Later, my poor Doğan, who had been forced to have dinner with a Jew and a drunk, came upstairs to me, and before I hugged and kissed him I made him wash his hands, after which I put him down for his afternoon nap. Selâhattin was still droning on downstairs, but it didn't last much longer. The jeweler said he had to go. Selâhattin came upstairs: "The fellow's going, Fatma. Before he does, he wants to see one of your jewels!" I was silent. "You know as well as I do that the man came from Istanbul because I wrote to him about your things, Fatma, we can't send him back empty-handed." I remained mum.

"Grandmother, this picture on the wall, that's your grandfather's picture, isn't it?"

When I still wouldn't speak: Fine, Fatma, he said, half in tears, you know, patients don't come to the waiting room anymore, it's not my fault, I'm not ashamed to tell you, because there is just no end to the stupidity in this damn country; my income is now zero, and if we don't take this opportunity to sell the jeweler something from that box of yours that's full to the brim anyhow . . . have you considered how we'll manage all winter long, no, what am I saying, how we'll manage for the rest of our lives? For ten years I've sold whatever I had to sell, Fatma, you know how much money I've spent on this house, the lot in Saraçhane went three years ago, we got through the last two years thanks to the sale of the shop in Kapalıçarşı, the house in Vefa, you know, Fatma, my no-good cousins refused to sell when I wanted to, and then they wouldn't send me my share of the rent, it's time you realized how we've got by for the last two years; they make fun of me in Gebze: those barbaric excuses for traders there, do you know how cheap I sold them my old jackets, my silver pen set, the only thing I had from my mother, my book trunk and gloves, the mother-of-pearl *tesbih* from my father, and that ridiculous riding coat that would just thrill the fops in Beyoğlu? But I can do no more, and I have no intention of selling my books, the equipment for my experiments, or my medical instruments. I'm saying it plain: I have no intention of casting aside eleven years of work and slinking back to Istanbul without finishing my encyclopedia, which, in one blow, will shake the foundations of everything, of the whole life of the East. The man is waiting downstairs, Fatma! Just take out one little piece from the box. Not just to get rid of this fellow, but so that the East, which has been slumbering for centuries, will wake up and so our Doğan doesn't pass this winter half starving and freezing in the cold, come on, Fatma, open the closet!

"Grandmother, do you know, when I was little I used to be afraid of Grandfather's picture?"

With Selâhattin standing there two feet away from me I finally opened the closet.

"You were afraid?" I said. "What about Grandfather were you afraid of?"

"It's a very dark picture, Grandmother!" said Nilgün. "I was afraid of his beard, of the way he looked out."

Then I took the box out from the recesses of the closet and opened it and spent a long time unable to decide which piece I was going to give up: rings, bracelets, diamond pins, my enamel watch, pearl necklaces, diamond brooches, diamond rings, diamonds. My God!

"You're not mad that I said I was afraid of Grandfather's picture, are you, Grandmother?"

Then with his eyes gleaming as he clutched the single earring I gave him from the ruby pair, muttering curses as I parted with it, Selâhattin ran out; as soon as I heard him bound down the stairs, I knew that he would be swindled: it didn't take long. As he walked toward the garden gate, the jeweler, with that strange bag in his hand and that strange hat on his head, was saying, Whenever you'd like to do some more business, just send me another letter, and I'll be happy to come out here.

He came every time: a year later, with the same strange bag in his hand and strange hat on his head, to get the other ruby earring of the pair. By the time he visited eight months later to get the first of my diamond bracelets, Muslims were required to wear that same hat instead of the fez. The year he came for the second diamond bracelet wouldn't be called 1345 anymore but 1926, by the Christian calendar. When he arrived to get the other bracelet he had the same bag in his hand, but he wasn't asking about the beautiful serving woman anymore. Maybe, I thought, it was because you had to go to a civil court for a divorce now, whereas before it was enough for a husband just to say it three times. On that occasion and for a number of years afterward Selâhattin had to cook the food they ate together himself. As always I wouldn't budge from my room, and I wondered whether by now he had told the jeweler everything. We had gotten rid of the servant and his bastards and would have the house to ourselves until Doğan went to the village and found them, one of them a dwarf, the other a cripple. Those were the best years. In the evening, Selâhattin would lose himself in the newspaper. Once, I was afraid the newspaper had written all about his crime and sin and the punishment I had imposed, but when I looked I saw nothing except pictures of Muslims wearing Christian hats. Another time, when Avram had come, the newspaper had, in addition to the Christian hats on the Muslim heads, Christian letters under the pictures. This was in the time that Selâhattin said, "My whole encyclopedia has been turned upside down in a day," and it was also when he sold my diamond necklace.

"What are you thinking, Grandmother, are you okay?"

The time after that I had removed the diamond ring from the box. When I gave up the emerald ring my grandmother had added to my dowry, it was snowing, and the jeweler had walked to the house from the station in the blizzard, complaining that dogs had attacked him along the way. But I knew he had said it only in the hope of making us take less. His next visit, I remember, was in the fall, because it was then that Doğan had brought me to tears by telling us he was going to study politics at Mülkiye for university. When the jeweler came six months after that, my ruby ring and necklace set went off with him. At the time, Selâhattin still hadn't gone to Gebze to register a family name, even though everyone was meant to do so without delay. Six months later, when he finally made the effort, he said he'd gotten into an argument with the registry clerk. When I read the family name he'd chosen, written on a piece of paper they proudly put in front of me, I didn't wonder: it seemed a mockery that made my hair stand on end. I was disgusted to think how this ugly name, Darvinoğlu (son of Darvin), would one day be carved on my tombstone. A year later when the jeweler came in summer and carried off my rose diamond ring and rose earrings, without telling Selâhattin I gave my pink pearls to Doğan. The poor boy was out of sorts and would pace the floor glumly, back and forth. I told him to sell the pearls and enjoy himself in Istanbul, but he did no such thing, which must have only made it easier to accuse me when he went off and found the bastards in the village after their mother had died, to resettle them back down in our house.

"What are you thinking, Grandmother? Are you thinking of them again?"

When the jeweler next came, he looked older. Selâhattin realized that the box was about empty, but he took one of my pins and declared that the encyclopedia was nearly finished. He was drunk all day long by then, and though I didn't go out of my room, I knew that, because of his drinking, my pin had gone for half of what it was worth, as would my topaz brooch the following year. As for the sums he spent on books, these were never halved. When Selâhattin, who had completely given himself over to the devil by now, next called the old jeweler, war had broken out again. After that Avram would come two more times: the first for my ruby star-and-crescent pin, the second for my diamond pin that said THIS TOO SHALL PASS in the old letters. And so did Selâhattin sell off his good luck with his own hands: a little later, after what he said was an incredible discovery, just as he was thinking of calling the jeweler again, Selâhattin died. When my poor innocent Doğan took the last two diamond solitaire rings I had carefully hidden and gave them to the bastards he had brought back into the house, my box was finally empty. And so it has remained, sitting there at the bottom of my closet.

"What are you thinking, Grandmother, won't you say!"

"Nothing," I said vacantly. "I'm thinking about nothing."

12

Hasan Is Vexed by Mathematics

C oming home in the evening after wandering the streets all day
was like going back to school after the summer vacation. As
everybody went home one by one, I stayed at the coffeehouse until it
closed, hoping somebody would show up with something to do, but
nobody did anything except call me Fox for the umpteenth time, and
so I decided, forget it, I'll go home and study math!

I was walking up the hill, not paying attention to anybody. I
actually liked the dark: nothing but the sound of the crickets, I listened, and I could see my future in the darkness: trips to far-off
countries, bloody wars, the rattle of machine guns, the intoxication
of combat, historical films with galley slaves pulling the oars, whips
to silence the howls of sinners, disciplined armies, factories, and
prostitutes, yes, I will be a great man, I was thinking, and before I
knew it, I was at the top of the hill.

Suddenly something touched a nerve. The lights of our house! I
stopped and looked; our house was like a tomb with a light burning
in it. Nothing moving in the windows. I crawled up close: my mother
wasn't there, she had gone to bed; my father was stretched out asleep

on the couch, waiting for me, let him wait, I'll slip in quietly and go to bed. But when I looked, I saw my window was closed. Okay! When I made some noise trying the other window, my father woke up. Instead of going and opening the door he opened the window.

"Where were you?" he shouted.

I didn't say anything, just listened to the crickets. We were both silent for a bit.

"Come on, get in here, come on!" said my father. "Don't just stand out there."

I came in through the window. My father just stood there in front of me, giving me his look. Then he started again: Son, son, why don't you study, son, son, what are you doing out in the street all day long, and so on. Suddenly I thought: Why does my mother put up with this whiny guy? I'll go wake my mother and have a talk with her, and the two of us will leave this guy's house. Then I thought about how upset my father would get and I got stressed. You're right, it's my fault, I did spend the whole day wandering in the street, but don't worry, Dad, tomorrow you'll see how I can work. If I'd actually said that, he wouldn't have believed me anyway. In the end he stopped talking and was just looking at me, angry, and since he seemed like he was about to cry, I went straight to my room and sat down at my table, as if to say, look, I'm studying math, don't be upset, Dad, okay? Finally, I had to close the door. But my lamp was on, let him see the light from under the door, see, I'm working. He was still muttering to himself.

A little later, I could no longer hear my father's voice, and I was curious, so I slowly opened the door and looked: gone to bed. They want me to be working while they have a nice sleep. Okay, since a lycée diploma's so important, I'll work. I'll work all night without sleeping, see, I'll work so much that my mother will be upset in the morning, but I know that there are much more important things in life. If you like I'll tell you, Mother: Communists, Christians, Zionists, you know what I mean, Masons, who are infiltrating this country—do you know what Carter and the pope talked about with Brezhnev? If I told them they wouldn't listen, if they listened they wouldn't understand . . . So anyway, I said, let me start on his math before I get myself all worked up.

I opened the book, but I got stuck because of that goddamned logarithm. Yes, we write it "log" and we say that a log(AB) = AlogB. This is the first rule, but there are others. The book calls them theorems. First I copied them all nicely in my notebook. Afterward it felt good to look at how I'd written it all out neatly. I've written four pages, I know how to work. So that's all there is to this stuff they call logarithms. Let me do a problem, too, now, I said. Take this logarithm, it says:

$$\text{Log}^6 \sqrt{\frac{ax - b}{ax + c}}$$

Okay, I'll take it. Then I looked at what I'd written in my notebook again, a long time went by, but I still couldn't figure out what I was supposed to divide or multiply by what and what I was supposed to reduce with what. I read it again, I just about memorized it, how did they solve the model problem, I looked at that, too, but the weird symbols still weren't speaking to me. I was really *annoyed,* so I got up. If I had a cigarette right now, I'd smoke it. I sat down again and picked up my pen and tried again, but my hand just made doodles on the page. Nilgün, look at what I wrote on the edge of the page a little later:

To you my heart does not incline
You've made my mind decline

Then I worked a little more, but it was no use. I thought a little more about it: What good is it to know the relationships between all these logs and square roots. Let's say that one day I'm doing government business or I'm so rich that I can only calculate how much money I have by using these logarithms and square roots: on that day, would I be so stupid as not to even think of hiring some little accountant to do these calculations for me?

I put the math aside and opened up the English, but I was already in a bad mood: I thought, God, give that Mr. and Mrs. Brown what they deserve; the same pictures, the same cold smug faces on people who know everything and do everything correctly, these are the English, they have ironed jackets and ties, their streets are perfectly clean. One sits and the others stand and meanwhile they keep on putting a matchbox that doesn't even look like one of ours on, under, in, and next to a desk. I had to memorize when it was *on* or *in* or *under* or—what was the other one—otherwise the lottery agent snoring away in the other room would beat himself up, because his son wasn't studying. I covered them with my hand and memorized them, staring at the ceiling, I memorized them and then, when I couldn't take it, I grabbed the book and threw it at the wall. Damn it to hell! I got up from the table and looked out the window. I'm not the kind of person who's just going to put up with stuff like this. I felt a little better as I looked out from the corner of the garden at the dark sea and at that lighthouse on the island with the dogs, the one that blinks on and off all alone in the darkness. The lights from the neighborhood down below were out; there were only the streetlamps and the lights of the glass factory that made deep rumbling noises, and then a red light from a silent ship. The garden smelled of scorched plants, there was a faint smell of earth and of summer, and it was silent, except for the crickets, bold crickets who reminded us of their existence in the pitch-black darkness of the cherry orchards, the far hills, lonely corners, in the coolness of olive groves, and under the trees. I thought I might have also heard the frogs from the muddy water over by the Yelkenkaya road. I'm going to do a lot of things in life! I thought of it: wars, victories, the fear of defeat and the hope for glory, the kindness I would show the poor things and others whom I would save on that road we would take in this heartless world. The lights in the neighborhood below were dim: they were all sleeping, all asleep, having their dumb, meaningless pathetic dreams while up here, awake above them all, it's just me. I love to live and I hate sleeping: there are so many things to do.

I stepped away from the window, and realizing that I wasn't going to study anymore, I lay down without taking my clothes off. I'll get up and start again in the morning. I told myself, actually, over the last ten days I've done enough English and math. I also said that soon the birds will start singing in the trees, and you'll go to the beach because you think no one's there, Nilgün. But I'll come, too. Who could stop me? At first I thought I wouldn't be able to sleep and that my heart would strangle me again, but then I realized that I was falling asleep after all.

When I woke up the sun was on my arm, and my shirt and pants were damp with sweat. I got right up and looked: my mother and father weren't up yet. I went into the kitchen. As I was eating bread and cheese my mother came in:

"Where were you?"

"Where was I supposed to be, I was here," I said. "I studied all night."

"Are you hungry?" she said. "I'll make some tea, you want some, son?"

"No," I said. "I'm going."

"Where are you off to at this time of day, with no sleep?"

"I'm going for a walk," I said. "It'll do me good. After that I'll come back and study again." Just as I was going out, I could see she was starting to feel sorry for me. So I said, "Hey, Mom, can you give me fifty liras?"

She looked a little hesitant before she said, "So. What are you going to do with the money this time? Okay, never mind! Just don't tell your father!"

She went inside and came back: two twenties and a tenner. I thanked her and went to my room, put my bathing suit on under my pants, then went out the window so I wouldn't wake up my father. I turned and looked back, and my mother was looking at me from the other window. Don't worry, Mom, I know what I'm going to be in life.

I walked down the asphalt way. Cars passed me, going uphill quickly. Guys with ties, their jackets hanging inside the car, as if they couldn't see me as they raced off to Istanbul at one hundred kilometers an hour to make deals and cheat one another. I don't care about you either, gentlemen, with your ties and cuckold's horns!

There was nobody on the beach yet. Since even the ticket seller and the watchman hadn't arrived, I went in for free, and carefully, so as not to get sand in my sneakers, I walked all the way over to the rocks where the beach ended and the wall of a house began, planting myself where the wall didn't get the sun. I would see Nilgün from here when she came in the gate. I could see the bottom of the calm sea: there were wrasse fish riding and turning in amid the seaweed. The careful gray mullet dashed away at the slightest movement. I held my breath.

A long while later, someone with a mask and flippers aimed his gun in the water, going after the mullet. I get so annoyed with these jerks going after the mullet. Then the water cleared again and I saw the mullet and the rockfish. After that, the sun began to beat down on me.

When I was little, and there were no other houses around here except for their strange silent house and our house on the hill, Metin, Nilgün, and I would come here and I would go into the water halfway up to my knees and we'd wait, trying to catch wrasse or blenny fish. But all we ever caught was a rockfish: Throw it away, said Metin, but it had eaten my bait, I'm not going to just throw it away, I'll put it in my box, and Metin would mock me! I'm not cheap, I would say. Maybe Nilgün would hear me and maybe she wouldn't. I'm not cheap, I would say, but I am going to make that rockfish pay for the bait. Metin put a screw nut on the end of his rod instead of a lead weight and said, look at that, Nilgün, he's so cheap, he's keeping it! Guys, Nilgün would say, just throw those fish back in the sea again, okay? It's a shame. I know it's hard to be friendly with them. But you can make soup from rockfish, you just put in some potatoes and onions.

Later I watched a crab. Crabs are always concentrating and thoughtful, because they're always up to something. Why are you waving your leg and your claw around like that, now, little guy? It was like all these crabs knew more than I did. They're all old know-it-alls, from birth. Even the soft little baby ones with the pure-white bellies are all like old men.

Then the surface of the water shimmered and you couldn't see the bottom, until the crowd slowly started to go in and out and it got really cloudy. I took a look over at the gate and I saw you, Nilgün, coming in with your bag. You came over toward this side of the beach and you walked straight toward me.

She came closer and closer and then she stopped and took off the yellow dress she had on and just as I was saying, oh, a blue bikini, she had spread her towel on the ground and stretched out on it, suddenly disappearing from view. When she took a book out of her bag and started to read, I could see her hand holding the book in the air and her head.

I was sweating. A long time went by, and she was still reading. Then I splashed some water on my face to cool off. Another long period of time went by and she was still reading.

What if I just go and say, Hi, Nilgün, I thought I'd go for swim this morning, how are you doing? She'll get mad, I thought, remembering that she was a year older than me. Better go away now, some other time.

Then Nilgün got up and walked toward the sea. She is beautiful, I thought before she dove in. She swam smoothly, moving away from the shore without looking back at the things she'd left on the beach. Don't worry, Nilgün, I'm watching your stuff, I said, as she kept swimming out, not bothering to look behind. It looked as if anybody who wanted to could go rifle through her things, but with me keeping an eye out, nothing would happen to them.

Nobody noticed when I got up and went over to Nilgün's things.

It was okay. Nilgün was my friend. I bent down and looked at the cover of the book lying on top of her bag: there was a Christian grave and two weeping old people and it said *Fathers and Sons*. Underneath the book was her yellow dress, I wondered, What's in her bag? Careful so nobody would see me, I went through it quickly: a tube of suntan lotion, matches, a key warmed by the sun, another book, a wallet, hair clips, a little green comb, sunglasses, a towel, a packet of Samsun cigarettes, and another small bottle. I looked out and Nilgün was still swimming far off. I was leaving everything just as I'd found it when I suddenly put the small green comb in my pocket. Nobody saw.

I went over to the rocks again and waited. Nilgün came out of the water, quickly walked over pigeon-toed, and wrapped herself in her towel, as though she were a little girl instead of a smart young woman a year older than me. Then she dried off, looked in her bag for something, and, not finding it, quickly put on her yellow dress and left.

I was taken aback for a minute, thinking she had done it to get away from me. I ran after her and saw she was going home. I ran ahead and got out in front of her, and she suddenly turned, which took me by surprise, because now it seem she was the one following me. I turned right, stopping in front of the shop and hiding behind a car tying my shoelaces as I looked: she went into the shop.

I positioned myself on the other side of the road so we would happen to run into each other as we went home. I thought, I'll take it out of my pocket and show it to her: Nilgün, is this your comb? I would say. Yes, where did you find it? she would say. You must have dropped it, I would say. How did you know it was mine, she would say. No, I won't say that. You dropped it on the road, I saw you drop it, and I picked it up, I would say. I was waiting under the tree. I was very sweaty.

A little later she came out of the shop, coming straight toward me. Good: I was walking straight toward the shop. I wasn't looking at her face, I was looking down, at the shoelaces I had just tied. Suddenly I lifted my head.

"Hello!" I said. She's so beautiful, I thought.

"Hello," she said. She didn't even smile.

I stopped, but she didn't stop.

"Are you going home, Nilgün?" I said. My voice came out funny.

"Yes," she said and walked off without saying anything else.

"Bye!" I shouted after her. Then I shouted again, "Say hello to Uncle Recep!"

I was embarrassed. She didn't even turn around and say, fine. I just stood there looking at her from behind. Why did she do that? Maybe she understood everything, but what was there to understand? If you meet an old childhood friend on the street, wouldn't you say hello? Weird! I walked along, thinking. Like they say, people have really changed, people resent even having to say hello these days. I thought about how I had fifty liras in my pocket, and then I thought, she must have gotten home by now: what was she thinking? I said, Let me telephone her and tell her everything, so she will just say hello to me, the way she used to, I don't want anything else from you. I walked along thinking and thinking about what I would say. I'd say, I love you, too, so what? I thought of other things. The disgusting people in the street going to the beach. This world is really screwed up!

I went to the post office to look at the directory. They were listed as DARVINOĞLU, SELÂHATTIN FAMILY, SHORE AVENUE NO. 12. I wrote down the phone number so I wouldn't misremember it. I paid ten liras for a token, went to the booth, and dialed the number, but when I got to the last digit, instead of 7, my finger dialed 9. I didn't hang up either. The wrong number rang, and when I still didn't hang up, the ten-lira token clattered down into the box and the line connected.

"Hello!" said a strange woman's voice.

"Hello, who do I have?" I said.

"Ferhat Bey's house," she said. "Who are you?"

"A friend!" I said. "I want to talk a little."

"Go ahead," said the voice. She was curious. "About what?"

"Something important!" I said, trying to think of what I would say. My ten liras were gone anyway.

"Who is this?" she said.

"I'll tell Ferhat Bey!" I said. "Just give me your husband."

"Ferhat?" she said. "Who are you?"

"Just you give him to me!" I said. I looked through the window of the booth; the clerk was busy; he was handing stamps to someone.

"Who are you?" she was still saying.

"I love you," I said. "I love you!"

"What? Who are you?"

"Damn society whore! The Communists are taking over the country and you're still lying half naked on the beach . . . "

She hung up. I hung up, too, slowly. I looked and the clerk was giving the change for the stamps. I calmly walked outside. He didn't even look at me. Well, at least I can't complain that I wasted my ten liras. As I left the post office, I thought: I still have forty liras; if a person can have this much fun with ten he can have four times as much fun with forty. That's what they call mathematics, and because they decided I don't understand it they're leaving me back for a year. Very well, gentlemen, I know how to wait. Just hope you don't regret it in the end.

13

Recep Picks Up Some Milk
and Some Other Things

When Nilgün Hanım came home from the beach Faruk Bey was waiting for her. They sat down and I gave them their breakfast. One of them was mostly reading her newspaper, while the other seemed to be dozing off, but all the same they had a nice chat and shared a few laughs. Then Faruk Bey got his huge briefcase and went off to the archives in Gebze, and Nilgün planted herself in the garden by the henhouse to read a book. Metin was still sleeping. I went upstairs before clearing off the breakfast table.

"I'm going down to the market, Madam," I said. "Do you want anything?"

"Market?" she said. "Is there a market here?"

"Well, they opened shops here years ago," I said. "You know that. What would you like?"

"I don't want a thing from them!" she said.

"What shall we give you for lunch?"

"I don't know," she said. "Make something edible!"

I went downstairs, took off my apron, gathered the empty bottles and the mushrooms, and headed off. She never says what's edible, only what's inedible. I have to judge by experience when I'm figuring out what to make, but fortunately it's been forty years, so I have some idea of what she will eat! I noticed I was sweating and realized it had become warm. The streets had started to fill up, but there were still people going off to work in Istanbul.

I climbed uphill, where there were fewer houses and the gardens and the cherry trees started. The birds were still in the trees. I was in a good mood, but I didn't take the long way. I went on the dirt road, and a little later I saw their house with the television antenna on top. Nevzat's wife and Aunt Cennet were milking the cows. I always enjoy watching them do it, especially in winter, when the milk steams. Nevzat was there as well. He was bent over his motorcycle that he had leaned against the other wall of the house.

"Hello," I said to him.

"Hello," he said, but he didn't turn and look. He had stuck his finger into some part of the motorcycle and was fiddling with it.

We were quiet for a bit. Then, to say something, I said, "Is it broken?"

"No way!" he said. "How could this thing break?"

He was proud of his motorcycle, which he had bought years ago with money he made doing people's gardens and delivering their milk. But the roar drove the whole neighborhood crazy. So I told him not to bother delivering milk to us; I would come and pick it up. It would also give us a chance to talk.

"You brought two bottles."

"Yes," I said. "Faruk Bey and his family are here."

"Fine, put them there."

I set them down, and he brought the funnel and the measure. First, he put it in the measure, then poured the milk through the funnel into the bottle.

"You haven't been by the coffeehouse for two days," he said.

I didn't say anything.

"Listen," he said. "Don't pay any attention to those bums. They have no class."

I thought about that.

Then he said, "But I wonder: Is what the newspaper wrote true? Was there really such a house for dwarves?"

They had all read the paper.

"Where did you go that night anyway?"

"To the movies."

"What was playing?" he said. "Anything good?"

By the time I was finished telling him, he was about to cork the bottles, which were now both full.

"You can't find corks," he said. "They've gotten expensive. They put plastic on cheap wine now. I tell people, Don't lose the cork. If you lose it, it's ten liras. We're not the Pinar Milk Company here. If you don't mind your kids drinking milk with chemicals in it, you can get it from them. You want ours? Save the cork."

He always said the same things. I was just about to pull the corks Faruk Bey gave me out of my pocket, when, for some reason, I changed my mind. Let him enjoy himself, I thought.

"Everything's become very expensive," I said.

"Really!" he said, and carried on about high prices and the good old days; I got bored and didn't pay attention. After he'd filled up all his bottles and loaded them into the motorcycle basket, he said, "I'm going to deliver these. If you'd like, I could drop you off at home." He kicked the pedal and started the motorcycle with a roar. "Come on!" he yelled.

"No," I called out. "I'll walk."

"Suit yourself!" he said, and zoomed away.

I watched the dust he kicked up until he got up onto the asphalt. It was why I was embarrassed to get on with him. As I went on my way, carrying my milk bottles in the string bag, I looked aback. Nevzat's wife and Aunt Cennet were still milking. Aunt Cennet had seen the plague, my mother used to say, the days of the plague, she would tell about it and I would get scared. As the gardens and the crickets ended, the part crowded with houses began. Places that hadn't changed for years. Eventually, they started coming in September for the hunt, with their well-fed vicious dogs that sprang out of their cars like mad curs: Don't go near them, kids, they'll shoot! A lizard in the base of a crack in the wall! I watched till it scurried off! Do you know why the lizard leaves behind his tail, son, Selâhattin Bey had said, according to what principle? I would be quiet and look at him fearfully: he was a tired, worn-out, decrepit father. Wait, let me write it down and give it to you. And he wrote out "Charles Darwin" on a scrap of paper and handed it to me; I have it still, that scrap. In his last days he gave me another piece of paper: This is a list of what we're missing and what we have in excess, son, I'm leaving this just to you, maybe one day you'll understand. I took the paper and looked. It was in the old letters. He looked closely at me with his bloodshot eyes: he had been working the whole day in his room on the encyclopedia, he was tired. And he used to drink in the evenings. Once a week, he would overdo it and fly off the handle. Sometimes, he would wander around drunk for a few days until he passed out in some corner of the garden or in his room or at the seashore. Those days, Madam would close herself up in her room as though she was never going to come out . . . When I got to the butcher's, it was crowded, but the beautiful dark lady wasn't there.

"You'll have to wait a little, Recep," said Mahmut, the butcher.

The bottles had tired me out, so it was good to sit down . . . Later, when I found him where he'd passed out, I would hurry to wake him, so that Madam wouldn't see him and start bawling again and so that he wouldn't stay out there in the cold: Sir, why are you lying here, it's going to rain, you'll catch your death, go home, lie down in your room, I would say. He would grumble and curse in his old man's way: Damn country! All for nothing! If I had been able to finish those volumes, if I had at least sent that article to Stepan a long time back, what time is it, a whole nation is sleeping, the whole East is asleep, no, it's not for nothing, but I'm just not up to it, oh, if I'd only had the kind of woman I needed, when did your mother die, Recep, son? Finally he'd get up and take my arm, and I'd cart him off, as he muttered all the way: When do you think they'll wake up from their stupid sleep, the peaceful sleep of fools. They've immersed themselves in the idiotic comfort of lies, snoozing away in the simpleton's joy of believing the world really is the way it's presented in the superstitious stories and myths crammed in their heads. I'll take a stick and beat them over the head until they wake up! Idiots, forget these lies, wake up, and look around you! By the time we got to his room, he'd be leaning on me all the more. The door of Madam's room would slowly open from inside, and her curious eyes full of disgust would appear and then disappear in the darkness. He would say, oh, you foolish woman, you poor foolish timid woman, I've never been anything but repulsed by you, put me in my bed, Recep, have coffee ready when I wake up, I want to start to work right away, I have to hurry, they've changed the alphabet, the whole plan of my encyclopedia has been upended, fifteen years and still no end in sight, he would say, and then drift off to sleep, still talking to himself. I'd watch for a little to see how he slept, then silently leave the room.

When I realized that one of the children of one of the women waiting for their orders was staring at me, I got annoyed. Let me think about something else, I said, but finally I couldn't stand it, I rose and picked up my bottles.

"I'll be back later," I said.

I headed for the grocer's. Children's curiosity is unbearable. I was curious when I was little, too. I used to think it was because my mother had me before she was married, but that idea came to me later, after she had said that my father wasn't my real father.

"Uncle Recep!" someone said. "Didn't you see me?"

It was Hasan.

"I swear I didn't see you," I said. "I was thinking about something. What are you doing around here?"

"Nothing," he said.

"Go on, go home and study your lessons, Hasan," I said. "What are you going to do around here? You have no business around here."

"What's that supposed to mean?"

"Don't misunderstand, son," I said. "I just mean you should be studying."

"I can't study in the morning, uncle," he said. "It's too hot. I study in the evenings."

"Study in the evenings and in the mornings, too," I said. "You want to get an education, don't you?"

"Of course I do," he said. "It's not as hard as you think to study. I'll do fine."

"May it please God!" I said. "Okay, go on home now."

"Have Faruk Bey and his family come yet?" he said. "I saw the white Anadol. How are they? Did Nilgün and Metin come, too?"

"They did," I said. "They're fine."

"Say hello to Nilgün and Metin," he said. "Anyway I just saw her. We used to be friends a long time ago."

"I'll tell them," I said. "Now, go on home."

"Okay, I'm going," he said. "But I want to ask you something, Uncle Recep. Can you give me fifty liras? I have to get a notebook, and they are really expensive."

"Are you smoking?" I said.

"I'm telling you my notebook is all used up . . . "

I put the bottles down, took out a twenty, and gave it to him.

"This isn't enough," he said.

"Come on, come on," I said. "Before I get annoyed."

"Okay," he said. "I'll get a lead pencil, at least." Just as he was going, he stopped. "Don't tell my father, okay? He gets all upset over nothing."

"Do not upset your father."

There was nobody in the shop, but Nazmi, the grocer, was busy writing in his account book. Then he looked up, and we talked a little. He asked about the visitors. I said they were fine. And Faruk

Bey, too? Why should I tell him he drinks, he knows that already, since Faruk Bey has been coming every evening to get bottle after bottle. The others? They've grown up, you know. Yes, I see the girl, he said, what was her name? Nilgün. She comes in the morning and gets the paper. She's all grown up, yes. But it's really the other one who's grown, I said. Yes, that Metin. He had seen him, too, and told me his impressions of the boy: so there you are; what we call conversation and friendship. We tell each other things that we already know, and it makes me feel good; I know they're just empty words, but it's a distraction, at least, and I still get a kick out of it. He weighed my things and wrapped them up. Write the charges down on a piece of paper, I said. Back at the house I note them all in a ledger, and at the end of the month—in the winter, every two or three months—I show it to Faruk Bey. I say, so much for this, so much for that, take a look in case I've made a mistake in the addition. He doesn't look. Fine, Recep, he says, thank you, these are the household expenses, here's your monthly salary, pulling out damp crumpled bills from his wallet that smells of leather. I put them in my pocket without counting them and then quickly want to change the subject.

Nazmi wrote the bill on a slip of paper and I paid him. As I was leaving the shop, he suddenly said, "You know Rasim?"

"Rasim the fisherman?"

"Yes," he said. "He died yesterday."

He was just looking at me, but I didn't say anything. I took my change, the string bag, and the packages.

"They say it was his heart," he said. "They'll bury him at noon, the day after tomorrow, when his sons come."

Well, there you have it, everything's beyond the power of our speech and our words.

14

Faruk Remembers the Pleasure
of Reading

❦

It was nine thirty when I got to Gebze, and already there was not a trace of the morning coolness. I made straight for the district governor's office, wrote out a request, and signed it. When a clerk put a number on my request without reading it, I imagined another historian three hundred years later finding it amid the ruins and trying to figure out what it was. The historian's profession is a strange one.

Strange, yes, but one that requires patience. In this way, feeling proud of my patience, I started to work with confidence. The story of two shopkeepers who killed each other in a fight immediately gripped my interest. Long after the funeral rites had been held and those two had been buried, their relatives were accusing one another in court. Witnesses testified in detail how the two of them had come at each other with knives in the middle of the market on the seventeenth of Cemaziulevvel 998. After transcribing it, I checked my conversion guide and found it would have been March 24, 1590, by the Christian calendar. So the altercation took place in the winter! All the while I'd had before my eyes the vision of a fiery hot summer day. Maybe it was a sunny March day. Then I read the record of a suit lodged by someone seeking to return an Arab slave he had purchased for six thousand *akçe* only to discover that the slave had an abscess on his foot. The purchaser wrote in clearly angry terms how he had been fooled by the words of the seller and how deep the wound was on the slave's foot. Then I read the things written concerning a man who'd become a powerful landowner and who had business with Istanbul. Elsewhere in the court records it was revealed that twenty years earlier, when still a watchman on the dock, the same man had been convicted of malfeasance. I tried to work out from the decrees the exact nature of the fraud perpetrated in Gebze by this man, whose name was Budak, momentarily diverting myself from trying to track down the plague. I figured out that he had registered a parcel of land that didn't exist and paid taxes on the nonexistent land for two years before exchanging it for a vineyard, and he even managed to worm his way out of trouble by pulling the wool over the new owner's eyes. Or at least that version, which to my mind seemed just right for this Budak character, wasn't disproved by the court records. It was no small feat whipping up this story on very limited evidence. I also had Budak getting involved in winemaking with the grapes from his new vineyard and selling his product illicitly out of a stable belonging to someone else. I took pleasure in reading how, when accused by some men he had ill used in business, he turned around and accused them even more vehemently. Later I learned that he had built a small mosque in Gebze. Just then, I was astonished to remember that my history teacher had devoted several pages in his history of Gebze to this man and that mosque. The Budak in his mind was completely different from the one in mine, his portraying a respectable, established Ottoman gentleman whose picture deserved inclusion in high school history books, while my Budak was at best a clever swindler and a parvenu. Just as I began to wonder whether the truth wasn't in fact more complicated than either story, Riza announced that it was time for the noon break.

Outside, I went through the passage with the berry bushes to the old market to avoid the heat on the new avenue. I walked uphill, all the way to the new mosque. The courtyard was deserted; there were hammering noises coming from the body shop next door. Not yet feeling hungry enough to eat, I turned around and walked over to the coffeehouse. As I passed the opening of one of the side streets, I could swear I heard one of the kids calling out "Fatso." I didn't turn around to see whether the others were laughing or not.

I sat down, asked for tea, and lit up a cigarette. There must be more to history, I thought, than just copying things down and linking a string of events together to make a story. Maybe it was like this: looking for the causes of a series of events, we look to other events to compare them with, and those events in turn must be explained by comparison with other events still, and on and on until we find that our entire lives wouldn't suffice to get to the bottom of so many facts. We have to leave off the task somewhere, expecting others to continue from where we left off, but no sooner do they begin than they decide all our explanations are wrong. And so there always remains important work to be done.

I was bored by these reflections. I lit into the kid who still hadn't brought my tea. Then to console myself, I thought: You're just tormenting yourself, don't you see that your thoughts about what historians do are themselves but another story? In someone else's telling, historians could be said to do something completely different. They may accuse us of harboring ideologies and filling the heads of our contemporaries with more or less false notions about themselves and their world, but I've no doubt that the true appeal of history is the pleasure of the story, the power to divert us. Not that my colleagues in their starched-collar self-importance would ever admit as much, preferring instead to distance themselves from their own children. When my tea finally came I tossed in two sugar cubes and watched them dissolve in the glass. After one more cigarette, I went to the restaurant.

I used to eat here two years ago, happy to have found a cozy, quiet, pleasant place. Behind a warm fogged-up window were stuffed grape leaves, *musakka,* as well as various other eggplant dishes, including a stew and a puree, all in a row on trays, each bathing in the same thick oil, as was a pile of half-melted meatballs, which called to mind so many water buffalo wallowing in mud to escape the summer heat. My appetite perked up. I ordered an eggplant *musakka,* a pilaf, and a plate of stew. When the waiter who was wearing socks and flip-flops proposed it, I said that, yes, I would have a beer, too.

I ate my food in a good mood, slowly savoring each bite, dipping my bread in the oil and drinking the beer. But suddenly I found myself thinking about my wife about to have a child with her new husband, and I became depressed. In our first few months of marriage, we had been careful not to have a child, to the point that it took all the fun out of things, since Selma wouldn't hear of contraceptive pills and devices. By the time we spoke about having a child a year later we discovered that it wouldn't be so easy, and for a long time, nothing materialized. One day Selma came to me and said it was time we consult a doctor, and in order to give me courage she said that she would go first. I objected, saying I wouldn't stand for those brutes called doctors getting involved in our private lives. I don't know whether Selma ever went or not. Maybe she did without telling me, but I didn't have a chance to think about this much, because we separated shortly afterward.

The waiter picked up the empty plates and carried them off. I asked what they had for dessert, and he said *kadayıf,* and I asked him to bring it. I also asked for another beer, telling him, it'll go well with *kadayıf,* won't it, and laughed. He didn't laugh, and I sat there thinking.

I remembered when I was with my mother and father in Kemah, in the east. There was still no Nilgün and no Metin. My mother was healthy and could manage the housework on her own. We were living in a two-story stone house; the steps used to be like ice, and so when I was hungry in the night I didn't dare go down to the kitchen all by myself, so I paid the price for my greediness with sleepless fantasies of what morsels there might be in the larder. The stone house had a little balcony, too; on cloudless cold winter nights, a pure-white meadow appeared between the mountains. When it got colder, we would hear the howling of the wolves, and it was said that they came down to the town at night, so hungry sometimes they would knock at the door, and so, it was said, we should never open up without asking who was there. One night my father even opened the door with a gun in hand. And in the spring, once, he went after a fox that had gotten in among the chicks with the same revolver. We didn't see the fox; we only heard the scratching and rattling noises he made. My mother said that crows were also known to make off with chicks. I thought what a pity it was I'd never seen that. Soon I realized that it was long since time for me to return to the archives.

When I started rooting around in the moldy papers again my spirits lifted immediately. I began to read at random. I had to laugh when I read how Yusuf, a debtor, finally paid what he owed, redeemed the donkey that he had left as guaranty, only to discover on the way home that the donkey had been lamed in its back right hoof, obliging the former debtor to go to court against his creditor, Hussein. For a moment I thought I had laughed only because of the two bottles of beer, but when I read the same story again, I laughed all the more. After that I would read whatever I happened on, regardless of whether or not I had read it before. I wasn't even bothering to take notes. As I perused one document after another, one page and the next, I found I was reading for the pure pleasure of it, enjoying every laugh. A little later I felt myself becoming excited; after the sensation had mostly passed, I realized it was like listening to a favorite piece of music after having had a few. My mind kept alighting on disjointed concern about my life as I tried to pay attention to the stories flowing by in front of me. A foundation director and a miller had fallen into dispute and appeared before the court reciting a whole pile of figures concerning the income and output of the mill. The court secretary wrote them all down carefully just as I did in my notebook. After I'd filled up a whole page with the figures—monthly and seasonal income, bushels of wheat and barley ground, the profit of years gone by—I looked at it all with a childish glee that propelled me on.

A ship carrying wheat had disappeared after docking in Kara-mürsel. It had never reached Istanbul nor had anyone shown up with news of its whereabouts. I decided that the ship had sunk somewhere on those rocks off Tuzla and that none of the crewmen knew how to swim. Then I read the trial transcript concerning Dursun's son Abdullah, who asked for the return of the four linens consigned to the dyers Kadri and Mehmet to be dyed, but I didn't write anything. I couldn't understand why Abdullah would want them back undyed. The pickler Ibrahim Sofu had sold three pickled cucumbers for one *akçe* on Shaban 19, 991 (September 7, 1583), a simple matter yet nevertheless one resulting in a complaint and court proceedings. Three days after this event, with no apparent connection, thirteen *akçe*'s worth of beef sold by Mehmet the butcher was found to be one hundred forty dirhams short, a grievance entered in the records and also in my notebook. I wondered what my colleagues on the faculty would think if they found this notebook; they couldn't possibly think that I had just made all this stuff up, which would really make them worry. If I could only find a good story, then they'd be completely astonished. My man Budak, who started out selling wine and climbed his way up, he'd be the ideal protagonist. I put my mind to thinking up a suitably grand title for such a story, a story I could fancy up with a heap of footnotes and document numbers: "A Prototype of the Nobility: Koca Budak of Gebze"! Not bad! If only it were Budak Pasha instead of just Budak, it would be even better. Perhaps he eventually became a pasha. Maybe I would write a paper explaining how he became a pasha, by way of sketching a general portrait of the first quarter of the sixteenth century. But when I thought about all the boring details I would have to include, my enthusiasm wilted; for a moment I thought I would weep, another effect of the beer, I thought, but surely its effect had worn off by then. Well, what could I do but keep reading.

I reread the arrest orders for the cavalry soldier Tahir, son of Mehmet, who had taken up banditry. I read the orders prescribing steps to be taken to prevent animals of the neighboring villages from grazing in the orchard of Ethem Pasha, and about Nurettin, thought to have died of the plague, but who, it was alleged, had actually been beaten to death by his wife's father. But I wrote down none of it. Instead I copied in full a long list of market prices. Then I read that Ömer's son Pir Ahmet promised in the presence of the attorney Sheikh Fethullah that he would pay his debt to Mehmet the *hamam* owner within eight days. Following that: the report of how Musa's son Hızır's mouth smelled of wine. I might have laughed had I drunk a little more beer. For a long while I continued reading through the court records very intently but without forming any particular thoughts or taking notes. I read as though I were looking for something, as though I were right on the heels of something. Finally I stopped when my eyes got tired, and I noticed that the sun was shining through the basement window.

Why did I become a historian? After my mother died in the spring, my father gave up his position as district administrator before he was eligible for a pension and settled in Cennethisar. I spent that summer there going through his books and walking in the gardens and along the seashore thinking about what I had read. I told people who asked if I was going to be a doctor that, yes, my grandfather was a doctor, too. But then just like that, I went off in the fall and signed up for history. How many are there like me who chose history for their occupation so willfully? Selma used to say that my foolish pride and the haughtiness inherent in my personality were the cause of idiocies I commit. But she wasn't displeased that I was a historian. I guess my father didn't like it; when he heard that I had registered for history he started drinking. Then again, he was already drinking anyway, something my grandmother would constantly scold him for. She herself wasn't too pleased with my chosen profession. When I thought of Grandmother, I thought of the house and Nilgün; it was nearly five. I no longer felt the effect of the beer. A little later when I could take no more pleasure in reading I got up and left without waiting for Riza.

15

Metin Goes Along for the Ride
and for Love

⚜

I popped the last bite of the watermelon into my mouth and got right up from the dining table.

"Where's this one going off to now without finishing his meal?" said Grandmother.

"Grandmother," said Nilgün, "he even finished his watermelon."

"Take the car if you want," said Faruk.

"If I need it, I'll come get it," I said.

"Don't feel obliged. I don't want you to be embarrassed driving my broken-down Anadol around here."

Nilgün laughed out loud. I didn't say anything. I went upstairs to get my key and my wallet, which gave me a feeling of superiority and security because it contained fourteen thousand liras, all the money I'd made working for a month in the summer heat. Giving a last buff to those moccasins I liked so much and throwing the green sweater my uncle had brought from London over my shoulders, I was on my way out the kitchen door when I saw Recep.

"Where are you going without eating your eggplant, boss?"

"I ate everything, even the watermelon."

"Bravo!"

Walking out the garden gate I could still hear Nilgün and Faruk laughing. They'll be at it all night long, I thought: one of them setting himself up for the other to laugh at and then a little later the other returning the favor, on and on like that, they'll sit under the dim light of the lamp for hours, deciding that the whole world is unjust, idiotic, and stupid while forgetting about all the stupid things they do, and if Nilgün hasn't gone to bed by the time Faruk has polished off a small bottle of *rakı,* he may start pouring his heart out to her about the wife he lost, so probably when I get back tonight I'll find him shitfaced at the table, and I'll wonder where a guy like that gets off giving me grief every time he lends me his crummy car. If you're so smart, how did you lose that smart, pretty wife of yours? Here they are sitting on a piece of land worth at least 5 million, but the plates they're eating off are all chipped, the knives and forks don't match, for a salt cellar they use an old medicine bottle the dwarf poked holes in with a rusty nail, while poor Grandmother, ninety years old, is spitting all over the place the entire time she eats and saying not a word . . . I walked all the way to Ceylan's and found her mother and father watching television, just like poor people with no other entertainment. So I went down to the shore looking for them and, sure enough, everybody from earlier in the day was there, with the sole exception of the gardener who watered the garden from morning till night and must have been handcuffed to the end of the hose. I sat and listened:

"In a little while when my parents go to bed we can watch a video."

"Oh, come on, you mean we are going to be stuck here all evening?"

"I want to dance," said Gülnur, swaying to some imaginary music.

"We were going to play poker," said Fikret.

"Let's go to Camlica and get tea."

"Fifty kilometers!"

"We could go to a Turkish movie and make fun of it."

As the lighthouse on the island blinked on and off in the distance I watched its reflection in the still water and I breathed in the scent of the jasmine and the girls' perfume that was hanging in the air. I thought about how I loved Ceylan, but some feeling I couldn't figure out kept her at a distance. Just as I'd planned all night long in bed, I knew I had to explain myself to her, but when I thought about it, this "me" that I was going to tell her about seemed like it never really existed. The thing I called me was like a box within a box; it was like there was always something else inside it, maybe if I kept looking I could finally find my real self and express it, but every new box I opened had, instead of a real, true Metin that I could show to Ceylan, just another box hiding him. Then I thought: Love makes a person deceitful, but I had also thought that believing I was in love would relieve me of always feeling two-faced. Oh, if this waiting would just end! But I knew that I wasn't even sure what I was waiting for. Just to calm myself down I decided to list, one by one, all my good points. It didn't do any good.

I caught up with the others, who had come to a decision. We got into the cars, making quite a racket, and went off to the disco at the hotel. There was no one there except for some stupid tourists. The others made fun of the tourists who had the whole world to take a vacation in and wound up coming to this ridiculous nowhere place.

We got out on the floor, and I danced with Ceylan, but nothing happened. She asked me to calculate twenty-seven times thirteen and then seventy-nine times eighty-one, and when I did it she laughed, but I could tell she wasn't impressed, and when the fast music started she said "I'm bored" and went to sit down. I went upstairs, and after groping along the silent carpeted corridors I found the amazingly clean toilet. When I saw myself in the mirror I thought, Goddamn it, all of this is because I believe I'm in love with a girl; I was disgusted with myself. Einstein probably wasn't like this when he was eighteen. John D. Rockefeller probably wasn't either. Then I took my time thinking how it would be when I was rich: I'd buy a newspaper in Turkey with the money I made in America, but I wouldn't drive it into the ground like our rich idiots, I'd get the hang of running a paper and live a life like Citizen Kane, I'd be kind of a mythic guy living by himself, but I'd also want to be president of the Fenerbahçe Club. When I was rich, I would forget all the grotesque stuff and pretensions that I hated about rich people, but thinking of Ceylan got me sidetracked. I smelled the place on my shirt where she had touched me when we were dancing. Coming out of the toilet, I met the others on the stairs, we were off to somewhere else, we got into the cars.

In Fikret's Alfa Romeo there were knobs, indicators, signals, gauges, and blinking colored lights, just like a cockpit. I was just staring at them when Turgay's car got really close, just before we got on the Istanbul–Ankara road. There someone decided the three cars should race as far as the Göztepe intersection. We zoomed beside the trucks and buses, under the pedestrian overpasses, past the gas stations, factories, coffeehouses, and people who'd stopped to watch us from the roadside, others getting some air on their balconies, repairmen, strikers, watermelon peddlers, and the guys running buffet stands and restaurants. Fikret kept honking the horn, especially when something exciting made everyone yell at once. At one red light, instead of braking Fikret dove into a side street barreling toward an Anadol at full speed, before pulling over to the side at the last second. "Jerk!" he said.

"We passed them," shouted Ceylan. "We passed all of them, step on it, Fikret!"

"Guys, I want to have fun, not die," said Zeynep.

"Why, do you want to get married?"

"This an Alfa Romeo. You have to know how to treat it right!"

We won the race and then turned to Suadiye and got onto Baghdad Avenue. I really like that street because it doesn't try to hide how disgusting it is; it openly proclaims that everything on it is fake! The repulsive marble of the apartment buildings, the ugly Plexiglas shop-windows, the hideous chandeliers hanging from the ceilings, the fluorescent glare in the pastry shops! I like all the disgusting things that are fine just being themselves. What's wrong with a little honest vulgarity? If I had a Mercedes I'd certainly try to pick up one of these girls on the sidewalk. But don't worry: I love you, Ceylan, sometimes I even love life! We parked the cars and went into another disco, one that doesn't say it on the door; it says CLUB, but anybody who gives them two hundred fifty liras at the door can get in.

Demis Roussos was singing, and I danced with Ceylan, but we didn't say much and it didn't feel right. She seemed bored, distracted, even sad, and as she stared right past me, as if she were by herself, at that moment, for some reason, I felt sorry for her and I thought how I could really love her.

"What are you thinking?" I said.

"Oh! Nothing!"

We danced a little more. I guess we both felt uncomfortable about the tension between us, because it was as if we were clinging to each other more to block it out than out of any enjoyment. But all these thoughts I had were just suspicions. A little later, the music that had turned out to be sappy more than sad ended, and a fast beat brought a new crowd fired up for fun onto the dance floor. Ceylan continued with them, but I sat down, and watching the fast dancers in the flashing colored lights, I thought: Look at them contorting themselves like stupid chickens! They're only doing it because that's what everybody does, not because it actually gives them any pleasure! When I dance, I know the stuff I'm doing is ridiculous, and it annoys me, so I tell myself that's the price I have to pay, unfortunately, to make this girl like me, then I think: It's okay, I'm joining in with these fools, but at the same time I'm not, so in the end I get the credit for being like them while at the same time I manage to be myself. There aren't a lot of people who can pull that off! Eventually, I got up and joined their silly dance, so no one would say I was sitting here all by myself playing the silent withdrawn teenage loner.

When we finally got up to go, Vedat and I pretended to pick

up the check or at least pay our share, but as we expected, Fikret wouldn't hear of it. Outside I saw that the others were tapping on the glass of Turgay's BMW and laughing: Hülya and Turan were asleep in each other's arms in the car! Zeynep let out a happy laugh full of admiration, as though she had special access to the love force.

"Well, they never even got out of the car!" she said.

I marveled that a boy and a girl my own age could wrap themselves in each other's arms and fall asleep like real lovers.

As we got on the Ankara road, Turgay's BMW stopped at the watermelon peddler on the corner. Turgay got out and said something to the guy under the gas lamp. The watermelon guy turned and looked at the three cars that were waiting. A little later Turgay called over to Fikret in his car:

"He says he doesn't have any."

"It's our fault," said Fikret. "We came with too many people."

"He won't sell us any?" said Gülnur. "What am I going to do now?"

"If you're willing to drink alcohol, we can get it somewhere."

"No way, I don't want to drink. Let's go to a pharmacy."

"What do you expect to get there? What do the others want to do?" asked Fikret.

Turgay went to the other car. He came back a little later. "They say we should get drinks," he said. He took a few steps, then stopped to say, "You know, they still haven't filled up the embankments."

"I gotcha," said Fikret.

We took to the road. Before we got to Maltepe they picked out a car with German plates and suitcases piled on the roof so that its rear was practically dragging along the road.

"And it's a Mercedes!" shouted Fikret. "Okay, guys!"

Fikret signaled to Turgay with his side lights, then slowed down and got behind him. We watched as Turgay's BMW first made to pass the Mercedes, but then instead of speeding up as a passing car would, stayed to its left, forcing the other driver toward the edge of the road until the Mercedes lurched side to side a little and, then, like it or not, had to let one of its wheels roll onto the shoulder, just to avoid hitting Turgay's BMW. Everybody laughed, saying the Mercedes was going like a crippled dog. Then Turgay hit the gas and took off, and when the Mercedes had righted itself, he called out to Fikret:

"Okay, your turn!"

"Not yet. Let him catch his breath."

There was only the driver in the Mercedes, some worker coming back from Germany, I figured. I didn't want to think about it beyond that.

"Absolutely do not look at him, guys!" said Fikret to us.

First he passed the Mercedes the way Turgay had done, then little by little moved over to the right. As the Mercedes started to blow his horn like crazy, the girls giggled, though they were probably a little afraid. When Fikret moved a little more to the right, and the guy from Germany's wheel lurched over the edge again, they burst out laughing.

"Did you see that guy's face?"

A little later, after we had zoomed on after Turgay, Vedat's car must have done the same maneuver, because we heard the Mercedes's hopeless angry horn sounding. We all met up at the next gas station, and they turned off their lights and hid. When the guy from Germany slowly passed by, they stomped their feet, laughing uncontrollably.

"But really I feel sorry for the poor guy," said Zeynep.

When they started reenacting their stunts and comparing notes to see who had riled up the guy from Germany most, I got fed up. I went to the station's canteen and ordered a bottle of wine, which I got them to open.

"You from Istanbul?" asked the clerk.

The interior of the canteen was brightly lit, like a jewelry-shop window. I don't know why but I felt like hanging around there a little, sitting and listening to the woman singing Turkish songs on his little radio, just to forget everything. Conflicting thoughts about love, evil, affection, and success, were going through my head, all jumbled together.

"Yes, I'm from Istanbul."

"Where are you all going like this?"

"We're just driving around!"

The guy shook his tired, sleepy head, knowingly. "Haa! With the girls . . . "

I seemed to be getting ready to say some things that could have been important, and he seemed ready to listen seriously, but the others started honking the horns outside. I ran and got in. Hey, where were you, they said, we won't be able to catch up because of you. I had thought the game was over, but it wasn't, not yet. We went full speed, and after Pendik we saw it again: the Mercedes slowly climbing the hill like a truck running out of gas. This time Turgay took the lead, closing in from the left and as he pushed the Mercedes to the right; Vedat bore down on its other side, after which we got behind it, so close we almost touched its bumper. He was caught in a vise that he could only escape by going faster than us. Eventually he tried to speed up, but he just couldn't break away. We kept up the chase, blasting our horns nonstop, our high beams right on the guy's neck. Then we opened the windows and blasted the radios, waving our arms out the sides, beating on the doors, whooping and singing along with the music. Things only got noisier as the panicked Mercedes stuck between us started honking desperately, and we went past I have no idea how many houses and factories and various neighborhoods in this crazy formation. Finally, when the guy from Germany got the idea to slow down, so that trucks and buses were getting jammed up behind us, we had to give him a last cheer and let him go. As we passed I turned to look him in the face, which I could just make out in the haze of his bright headlights: he didn't seem to see us anymore. And we'd made him forget about his life, his memories, and his future.

I didn't want to think of him anymore either, and I drank some of my wine.

We shot past the Cennethisar exit without even slowing down. The others seemed intent on squeezing past an Anadol with a ridiculous old husband and wife inside, but a little later they changed their minds. As they passed by the houses of ill repute beyond the gas station Fikret hit the horn and flashed the lights, but no one asked him why. After we went a little farther, Ceylan said, "Look what I'm going to do!"

When I turned around I saw Ceylan's bare legs sticking out the back window. Long and tanned, in the lights from the cars behind us, they looked poised and purposeful, like professional legs under the stage lights, sliding against each other as if probing for something in the air, as her feet, bare and pure white, twitched alertly against the wind. Gülnur pulled Ceylan by the shoulders and dragged her inside.

"You're drunk!"

"I'm not the least bit drunk," said Ceylan. She let out a happy laugh. "How much did I even drink! I'm just having so much fun!"

Then we were all quiet. We continued on that way for a long time, as though in a hurry to get from Istanbul to Ankara to carry out some important mission, on and on through the rundown holiday towns, past factories and olive and cherry groves, without saying a word and oblivious to the music still playing and for no reason blasting the horns as we passed trucks and buses, not even paying attention to them. I thought about Ceylan and how I could love her for the rest of my life just on account of what she had just done.

After we passed Hereke we stopped in a gas station, where we got some bad wine and sandwiches from the buffet. Eating on our feet, we mingled among the tired and timid passengers who had gotten off a bus. I saw Ceylan go over to the side of the road biting into her sandwich while her eyes followed the flow of vehicles, the way someone picnicking on a riverbank might absently watch the currents, and as I observed her I thought of my own future.

A little later I saw Fikret walk slowly over to Ceylan in the darkness. He offered her a cigarette and lit it. They started to talk: they weren't very far, but the noise of the traffic made it hard to hear what they were saying, and I was really curious. A little later this strange curiosity turned into a strange fear. I realized right away that I had to go over to them to beat the fear: but in the darkness, just like in dreams, I had this awful feeling of inferiority and shyness. But this loser feeling, like everything else, didn't last for long. A little later we got back into the cars and went off into the night without thinking about anything.

16

Grandmother Listens to the Night

When all that horrible hullabaloo lets up, when all that noise coming from the beach, the motorboats, the wailing kids, the drunken cursing, the songs, radios, and televisions, quiet down, and the last car goes screaming past, I slowly get up from my bed and stand just behind my shutters listening to the outdoors: nobody's there, they're all exhausted and have gone to sleep. Only the wind, occasionally the lapping waters of the sea, a rustling in the trees; sometimes there's a cricket nearby, a confused crow, or maybe a dog barking for no reason. So I slowly push the shutters open and listen to them, I listen to the silence for a long time. Then I think about how I've lived for ninety years, and I am horrified. A breeze coming up from the bushes where my shadow falls seems to be chilling my legs, and I take fright; should I go back and wrap myself in the warm darkness of my quilt? But I stay there a bit longer to feel the promise of the silence; I wait and wait, as though something is going to happen, as though someone has promised to come, as though the world could show me something new, but at last I close the shutters and go back to sit on the edge of my bed and listen to the clock tick past one twenty in the morning, and I think: Selâhattin was wrong about this, too: there's never anything new, nothing at all!

Every day is a new world, Fatma, he would say each morning. I wake before the sun comes up and I think how the sun will rise in a little while and everything will be brand-new and I myself will be renewed seeing new things I've never seen before, reading and learning until I look in a different way at all that I'd known, and I get so excited, Fatma, that I just want to leap out of bed and run to the garden to see how the sun will appear, how all the plants and insects will quiver and change at its appearance, then I want to run straight upstairs and write down everything I've seen, Fatma, why don't you feel like that, why don't you say something, what are you thinking? Look, look, Fatma, do you see the caterpillar, see what he does, one day he'll be a butterfly and take flight! Oh, a person should write down nothing but what he has seen and experienced, and then maybe I, too, could become a true man of science, like the Europeans, like Darwin, what an incredible fellow, but alas in the languor of the East a person can accomplish nothing. But why not? After all, I have eyes to observe and hands to perform experiments and, thank God, a mind that works better than anyone else's in this country, yes, Fatma, have you seen how the peaches bloom, if you ask me why they give off such a lovely scent, well, I have to wonder what is smell, what makes us sense it, Fatma, have you seen how the fig tree grows uncontrollably, I wonder how the ants signal one another, Fatma, have you ever noticed how the sea rises before the south wind blows and lowers again before the north wind comes, one must notice everything, observe it all, because only that way can science advance, only that way can we develop our minds; otherwise, we are no better than all those people who waste their hours sitting in the corners of cafés, who say *oh!* when the sky begins to thunder, then run mad with delight, like the devil fleeing two steps at a time, to get to their garden and stretch out on their backs and stare at the darkening clouds until they find themselves soaked to the bone..... I guessed that he was going to write about the clouds and that he was merely looking for his excuse to do so, because he used to say: When people realize that everything has its own reason for being, then they won't have room left in their heads for God, because the reason for flowers blooming and the chickens laying eggs and the sky thundering and rain falling isn't a divine command as they think, but what I describe in my encyclopedia. Then they'll realize that things are made by other things and absolutely nothing exists by the hand of God. They will see that even if he's there, that God, our science has taken out of his hands everything that he could possibly do, forcing him to content himself as a spectator. Tell me, Fatma, would you consider any being capable only of watching what goes on in this world to be a God? Yes, you are silent, and by your silence you attest that you, too, understand that there is no God anymore. One day, when they read my work, and they, too, realize this truth, what do you suppose will happen, are you listening to me?

No, I'm not listening to you, Selâhattin, but you're not speaking for me anyway: When they understand that nothing comes from the hand of God, then they'll see that everything is in their own hands; when they see that fear and valor, crime and punishment, idleness and action, good and evil are all in their own hands, well, what's going to happen, Fatma? He said this and suddenly got up and started pacing the floor and lecturing, as though he were at his desk instead of sitting behind all those emptied bottles on the dining table: Then they'll be as I was in my early years, frozen with fear, they won't believe their own thoughts, frightened to death at what passes through their own minds, then realizing that other people could be thinking the same things, they'll feel guilt followed by fear, imagining that at any time they could be strangled by their neighbor and, at that very moment, they'll hate me for having brought them to that point, but by then having no other recourse, desperate to free themselves from this terror, they'll come running to me, yes, they'll come to me, to my books, to my forty-eight-volume encyclopedia, they'll understand that henceforth the only real religion, the one true divinity, is to be found in these books of mine! Yes, why should I, Dr. Selâhattin, not take my rightful place in the twentieth century as the new God of all the Muslims? Because henceforth, science is our God, are you listening, Fatma?

No, because now I think that even to listen was a sin, because I had finished eating the potatoes and meatballs that Recep cooked for us and those tasteless leeks, and I'd put some of the dessert we call Noah's pudding in my bowl and gone off to the unheated little adjoining room. I sat there, with my legs clenched together against the cold, and slowly ate my dessert in little spoonfuls of pomegranate seeds, beans, chickpeas, dried figs, corn, dried black currants, with a little rosewater spread over it all, how nice, how lovely!

I'm not sleepy. I get up from the edge of my bed. I wouldn't mind a little pudding now. I go to the table and sit down: there's a bottle of cologne on it, not glass, but still transparent. When I first saw it yesterday at noon, I thought it was glass, but as soon as I touched it I realized it wasn't, and I was annoyed: What's this, I said, it's not even a glass bottle? Grandma, you can't find them anymore, said Nilgün, spreading it on my wrists, without even listening to my objections. You all might feel revived by something that comes from a plastic bottle, but not me. I didn't say that because they wouldn't understand. Your souls are all stillborn plastic! But if I'd said that they'd have probably laughed.

They laugh anyway, to pass the time and relieve their unease: These old people are so strange, they laugh, how are you, Grandmother, they laugh; do you know what a television is, they laugh, why don't you come down and sit with us, they laugh, what a nifty sewing machine, they laugh, it even has a pedal, they laugh, why do you take your cane into the bed with you when you lie down, they laugh, shall we take you for a ride in the car, Grandmother, they laugh; the embroidery on your nightie is so pretty, they laugh, why didn't you vote in the elections, they laugh, why are you always rummaging through your closet, they laugh. If I say why are you always laughing when you look at me, they laugh, again, laugh and say, we're not laughing, Grandmother, then they laugh again. Maybe it's because their father and grandfather spent their whole lives crying. It's all so boring.

Should I wake the dwarf and ask him for some Noah's pudding? If I tap on the floor with my cane, the sleeping runt will say, Madam, at *this* hour? And at this time of year? Put it out of your mind so you can have a nice sleep, tomorrow I'll make you some . . . If you're not going to take care of my needs, what are you here for? Get out! Then he'll go right off and find them: I put up with so much from your grandmother, so much! My point exactly! Why else would you still be here? Why didn't he clear out like his brother? Because, Madam, he is perfectly capable of saying, as you well know, Doğan Bey, God rest his soul, when he said, now, Recep, now, Ismail, take this money and use it as you see fit, I've had enough of feeling guilty about the sins of my mother and father, their crimes, take this money, Ismail, my dear brother, being clever, said, Fine and took it and built a house on that parcel on the top of the hill, the one we passed yesterday going to the cemetery, why do you pretend now that you don't know, Madam, as though it wasn't you who left one of us a cripple and the other a dwarf? Be still! I suddenly become afraid. He fools everybody. Everybody. My Doğan, because he was like an angel; what did you say to fool my baby and snatch that money from his hands, you wicked bastards; there's nothing more for you, my son: If you want, go look in my box, it's empty, thanks to your drunken father; Mother, please don't talk like that about my father, the devil take your money and the jewels, money's the source of all evil; give me the box and I'll throw it in the sea, no, I'll use it for something good, Mother, look, did you know I'm writing letters, I know the minister of agriculture, he was one class behind me at school, I'm preparing drafts of laws, I swear this time I'm really going to do something useful, Mother, okay, okay, keep the box, just don't hector me about my drinking. I get up from the table, go to my closet, take out the key, and open it, breathing in the cupboard scent. I had put it in the second drawer;

and when I open the second drawer, there it is. I sniff it without opening it and when I open it I sniff the empty box again and I remember my childhood.

It was springtime in Istanbul. I was a girl of fourteen, and the following afternoon we were to be going out. Ah, tell me, where will you be going? We're going to Şukru Pasha's, Father. You know his daughters, Türkân, Şükran, and Nigân, I have so much fun with them, we're always laughing; they play the piano, they can imitate anybody, they read poems to me and sometimes even translated foreign novels: I really like them. Fine, then, but it's really late now, so come on, let me see you go off to bed, Fatma. Okay, I'll go, I'll fall asleep thinking about going there tomorrow. My father closed the door, and the gust of air in its wake brought his scent to me, I thought of those things in my bed, and in the morning I awakened to discover a beautiful day from my bedside, as sweet as the scent from my box, but suddenly I was disgusted: Enough, you stupid box; I know how life is. Life pierced you and seared every corner, dear God, it tore you to pieces, you foolish girl! All of a sudden I got so angry that I almost threw the box out, but I held myself back; then how would I mark the time? Put it away, put it away, for surely a rainy day will come. This time I put it in the third drawer, I closed the closet, have I locked it, I check again, yes, I have. Then I go and lie down, staring at the ceiling. The ceiling is green. I know why I can't sleep. Because the car that comes after the last car still hasn't come. But the green paint is peeling. When he comes, I'll hear his footsteps and know he's gone to bed. The yellow shows through underneath. When I could believe that the whole world was mine, then I could go off into a sound sleep right under the yellow that's showing through the green. But now I can't sleep, I think of the colors, the day that he unraveled the mystery of the colors.

The secret of paints and colors is very simple, Fatma, said Selâhattin one day. He had turned Doğan's bicycle upside down on the dining table and on the back wheel had arranged a ring of seven colors to show me. Do you see, Fatma, there are seven, but let's see what happens to your seven colors as we spin the wheel. I looked on in astonishment and a little alarm as he gleefully started turning the pedal, and the seven colors started melting into one another, until the wheel turned white. At the evening meal, he proclaimed with pride that principle he would shortly discard: Fatma, I only write what I see with my own eyes, that's my rule; nothing I cannot confirm experimentally goes into my encyclopedia! But later he would forget how often he'd said these words, because he'd made the decision that life is short and his encyclopedia was long, and in the years just before he finally discovered death he would say: No one person has time to try everything, Fatma, it seems that the laboratory I set up in the laundry room was nothing but a youthful fancy, anyone who takes the whole treasury of knowledge that the Westerners produced and tries to reconfirm it in experiments is either a fool or an egoist, he would say, as though he knew that I thought, Well, you're both, Selâhattin. Then he would berate himself as if to fire up his spirits: Even the great Diderot couldn't finish his encyclopedia in seventeen years, Fatma, because he was an egoist, what need was there to argue with Voltaire and Rousseau, you idiot, they were at least as great as you, and if one can't accept that great men can think of things and discover them before he does, nothing will ever be completely finished. I'm a modest person, I accept that the Europeans found everything before we did and investigated it all down to the smallest detail. Isn't it ridiculous to look for and discover the same things all over again? To understand that a cubic centimeter of gold weighs 19.3 grams and that everything, people included, can be bought and sold, I don't need to use a scale and weigh it again or fill my pockets with gold and go bargain with the scoundrels of Istanbul, Fatma! Truths are truly discovered but once; the sky is blue in France, too, fig trees in New York bear fruit in August as well, and when the chicks come out of the eggs in our hatchery, I swear, Fatma, they come out the same day in China, and if steam drives an engine in London, it drives it here likewise; just as people everywhere are the same and equal, a republic is always the best government, and science is the basis of everything.

After Selâhattin had said these things he gave up having the ironmonger and stove maker in Gebze fashion strange machines and implements, and he ceased begging me for things to sell to the jeweler; he no longer passed his time pouring buckets of water into the compound tubes made out of stovepipes to see how a fountain works, playing the madman trying to find his peace by staring into the pool in the courtyard of the asylum; he gave up flying kites that got bedraggled in the rain and fell from the sky in an effort to show where electricity came from; and he ceased playing with magnifying glasses, windowpanes, funnels, pipes with smoke coming out the end, colored bottles, and binoculars. I caused you a lot of expense with all that foolishness, Fatma, he would say, you were right telling me it was all childishness, I'm sorry, imagining that we could add something to science with an amateur laboratory in the laundry room wasn't just a youthful fancy, but a juvenile idiocy stemming from my failure to understand the true grandeur of science, take that key, you and Recep, take those things, throw them in the sea, sell them if you can, do whatever you want. Yes, take those sketches as well, my insect specimens, the fish skeletons, those flowers and leaves I stupidly dried and pressed, those dead mice, bats, snakes, and frogs preserved in alcohol, pick those jars up, Fatma, oh God, what's there to be disgusted by or afraid of now, good, good, call Recep, I just want to get rid of all this nonsense, there's no room for my books anyway, it's better this way, because to think that sitting here in the East we can succeed at finding and discussing anything new is just foolishness. Those people have found everything, there's nothing left to add: it's as they say: nothing new under the sun! Fatma, look, don't you see, even that saying is nothing new, we learned that from them as well, the devil take it, do you understand, I don't have enough time left, I realize forty-eight volumes won't suffice, it would take fifty-four to gather all this material, but, on the other hand, I'm impatient for the masses to get their hands on this opus, it's so exhausting to do serious comprehensive work, but I have no right to condense it, Fatma, because, unfortunately, I can't content myself with mediocrity, like those common fools who reveal only the tip of a corner, a little shred of reality in their skimpy one-hundred-page books, and then puff themselves up and preen about it for years on end; Fatma, look at those essays by Abdullah Cevdet, simple fellow, I mean, is that all there is to reality, never mind he misunderstood De Passet, never even read Bonnesance, and on top of everything misused the word *fraternité,* but how can you correct these people and if you do who would understand, the fools, you have to explain everything reductively if these bumpkins are to understand, that's why I'm worn out, trying to insert proverbs and pithy sayings in my writings so that thickheaded brutes can follow them. Selâhattin was still carrying on in this way, when suddenly I heard the rumbling of the car, the one that always arrives after the last.

He stops in front of the garden gate. As the motor purrs, I hear the gate open: what kind of strange, awful music was that! Then they talk, and I listen.

"Tomorrow morning at Ceylan's, okay?" one of them shouts.

"Okay," Metin yells back.

Then the car starts up with painful screeches and grumbling and takes off. Metin comes into the garden, rattles the kitchen door as he enters the house, goes up the five steps to what Selâhattin called the dining room, and from there climbs the nineteen steps to the upstairs, and as he passes my door I think, Metin, Metin, let me call to him, come here, come, my darling, tell me, where were you, what's going on outside, what's out there in the world at this hour of night, come on, tell me, where did you go, what did you see, I'll say, give me a little distraction, liven me up, amuse me, but he is already in his room. By the time I count five he's undressed and thrown himself into bed with such force that the whole house shakes and, I swear, before I count five again, he's asleep, three, four, five, so, now he's fast asleep the way young people sleep, because when you're young you have such good sleep, didn't you, Fatma . . .

But I didn't sleep like that when I was fifteen. I was always waiting for things, for carriage rides that rocked us back and forth, for pianos to play, for my cousins to come, then for those who'd come to go back, for us to eat and while we were eating to be allowed to leave the table, and I thought of that deeper waiting for an end to all the other waiting, and how no one would ever know what it was we were waiting for in that wait. Now that ninety years have gone by, I understand that all those memories and waits have filled my mind the way sparkling water from hundreds of little faucets might fill a marble pool, and when in the silence of a soft summer night I draw nearer to the coolness of the pool, I see my reflection in the water, and I notice that I'm filled with my own self, and I want to puff and blow my image from the pool, so that nothing might tarnish the surface of that water, so pure and sparkling. I was such a light, graceful little girl . . .

Sometimes I wonder if a person could remain a little girl all her life. If she doesn't want to grow up and sink into sin and her only desire, like mine, is to remain a girl, she should be able to do that, but I wonder how. When I was still a child in Istanbul and I went to visit my friends, I heard the French novels translated into Turkish that Nigân, Türkân, and Şükran read one after the other: Christians have monasteries; if you don't want to be sullied by sin, you climb up into one and you wait; but as I listened to Nigân read that book, I thought it was a strange and ugly arrangement, all of them cooped up in there next to one another, like wretched lazy chickens refusing to lay eggs. Then when I thought of how it would be when they grew up and got old and shriveled I was disgusted: the Christian thing, the cross, idols, the crucifix; they'd rot inside cold stone walls like priests with black beards and red eyes! I didn't want anything like that. I wanted to remain just as I was without anybody seeing me.

No, I can't sleep! I'm staring at the ceiling in vain. I turn, get up slowly, walk over to the table, and look at the tray as though I were seeing it for the first time. The dwarf left peaches tonight and cherries. I take a cherry and put it in my mouth; it is like a huge ruby; I hold it between my teeth a little, then bite down and chew it slowly, wait for the juice and the taste to carry me off somewhere, but I waited for naught. Here I am, still. I spit out the pit and try another one, then a third, and three more, and as I look at the pits in my hand, I'm still here. By all evidence, this is going to be a long night.

17

Hasan Acquires Another Comb

✣

When I woke up, the sun had risen all the way up to my shoulder. The birds in the trees had already begun twittering, and so had my mother and father in the next room.

"What time did Hasan go to bed last night?" said my father.

"I don't know," said my mother. "I fell asleep . . . Do you want more bread?"

"No," said my father. "I'll be back at lunchtime to see if he's here."

Then they were silent, but the birds weren't: lying there, I listened to them and the rush of traffic to Istanbul. Then I got up to get Nilgün's comb from my pants pocket and got back into bed. Looking at the comb in the sunlight that came in the window, I stretched out a little and got to thinking. When I thought how this thing I held in my hand had been in the deepest corners of the forest of Nilgün's hair, I felt a little strange.

I silently climbed out the window, splashed my face with some water from the well, and I felt better: I'm no longer going to think the way I did in the middle of the night, that there's no way it can work out for me and Nilgün, that we live in different worlds. I went inside, put on my bathing suit, pants, and sneakers, put the comb in my pocket, but just as I was about to head out I heard a noise at the door. Good: my father was leaving, which meant that along with the tomatoes, cheese, and olives, breakfast wouldn't include a speech about how hard life is and how a high school diploma is so important. They were talking at the door.

"Tell him that if he doesn't sit down and study today . . . ," my father was saying.

"Well, he was studying last night," said my mother.

"I went out into the garden and looked in his window," my father said. "He was sitting at his desk, but he wasn't studying. It was clear his mind was somewhere else."

"He does study, he does!" said my mother.

"Well, he knows," said the lame lottery-ticket vendor, "that if he doesn't I'll give him to the barber as a helper."

Then I heard the unequal step of his two feet, one of them strong and one of them weak. When he had shambled off, *tak-takir, tak-takir,* I came down to the kitchen.

"Sit down," said my mother. "Why do you eat standing up?"

"I'm going out," I said. "It doesn't matter how much I study anyway. I heard Dad."

"Don't pay that any mind," she said. "Come sit down and have a proper meal! Should I make you some tea?"

She looked at me tenderly. All of a sudden I thought about how much I loved my mother and how much I didn't love my father. I felt sorry for her; it was because he used to beat her at one point that I didn't have any sisters or brothers. What was he punishing her for? But my mother was my sister, I thought: We weren't like mother and son but more like a sister and brother they'd forced to live with this crippled man and, as part of the punishment, they said, Okay, let's see you live on what he makes selling lottery tickets. True, our situation wasn't really bad, there were kids in my class a lot poorer than us, but we didn't even own a shop. If it weren't for the tomatoes, beans, peppers, and onions in the garden my sweet mother wouldn't have a cent for something to throw into the stew pot, not from what that cheapskate so-called lottery peddler brings in, and the both of us would probably starve. Just the thought of it made me want to explain to my mother everything about how this world works: how we were all the playthings of the great powers, the Communists, the materialists, the imperialists, and the rest, and how we were now reduced to begging for help from nations that used to be our servants. But she wouldn't understand: she just complains about her bad luck, but doesn't ask why it's that way.

She was still gazing at me, and I got annoyed.

"No, Mother," I said. "I'm going right away. I have things to do."

"Fine, son," she said. "You know best."

My sweet mother, so good hearted! But then . . .

"Just don't be gone long, come back and study before your father comes home for lunch," she added, but it doesn't matter.

Should I ask for money? I thought about it for a minute, but I didn't, I walked out and headed down the hill. She gave me fifty liras yesterday. Uncle Recep gave me twenty; I'd made two telephone calls, that was twenty there, and fifteen for a *lahmacun* leaves thirty-five liras. I pulled them out of my pocket and looked, yes, thirty-five liras, and I didn't even need logarithms or square roots to figure it out, but giving me what I need, that's not the aim of the people who left me behind, all those teachers and gentlemen: what they want is to show me up, make me grovel, grind me down until they've taught me submission and gotten me used to being happy with very little. I know that the day they see I've grown used to it, they'll be so pleased, and they'll declare with satisfaction, He's finally learned how it goes in life, but I'm not signing up for your life, gentlemen, I'll get a gun and teach you how it goes. They were passing by me quickly with their cars, going down the hill. It looked like there was a strike at the factory across the way. That irritated me, and I wanted to do something, I felt I should at least go to the Association, but I was afraid of being all alone there; what would happen if I went without Mustafa and Serdar? I thought: I could even go to the headquarters in Üsküdar on my own. Give me an important assignment, writing slogans on the walls and selling invitations, that isn't enough for me; I need something big, I said. The television and newspapers will talk about me one day, I thought.

When I got to the beach I looked through the fence. Nilgün wasn't there. I walked on a little and thought some more, then I started wandering the streets and did some more thinking. They were sitting on the balconies and in their little gardens, having breakfast, mothers, daughters, and sons; some of their gardens were so small and the tables so close to the road that I could count the olives on the plates. Suppose I gathered them all together on the beach—Line up, you slackers—and I stood on something and explained it all to them: Aren't you ashamed, aren't you ashamed. Fine, you're no longer afraid of hell, but don't you have a shred of conscience, poor wretched corrupt creatures, how can you live thinking about nothing but your own pleasure and the profits from your shops and factories, I don't understand, but now I'm going to show you. Fire! The machine guns *rat-ta-tat!* A shame they don't bring in historical films anymore. I'll do something to turn this dump upside down; they won't forget me.

I passed by Nilgün's house; there wasn't anybody there. What if I called on the phone and explained everything to them: You're dreaming! I went back to the beach, and she was still not there. A little later I saw Uncle Recep, carrying his string bag. When he saw me he changed course and came my way.

"What are you doing around here again?" he said.

"Nothing!" I said. "I worked hard yesterday, so I'm taking a little time off today."

"Okay, go on home, son," he said. "This is no place for you."

"Haa," I said. "I didn't spend the twenty liras you gave me yesterday. For twenty liras you can't get a notebook. I already have a fountain pen, so I don't want one of those. A notebook is fifty liras."

I stuck my hand in my pocket. I dug out his twenty liras and handed it back to him.

"I don't want it," he said. "I gave it to you so you would study. So you would study and make something of yourself."

"Making something of yourself isn't free," I said. "Even a notebook is fifty liras."

"Fine," he said. He took another thirty liras from his pocket and gave them to me. "But don't go off and smoke cigarettes!"

"If you think I'm going to smoke cigarettes I shouldn't take it," I said. Then, after a pause, I took it. "Thank you. Say hello to Metin's folks, to Nilgün and everybody. They're here, right? I have to go and study, English is really hard."

"It's hard all right!" said the dwarf. "Do you think life is easy?"

I walked on before he could start with the same crap I get from my father. When I looked back, he had continued the way he'd been headed, walking slowly, swaying from side to side. I felt sorry for him. Everybody holds the net bag from the top, but he holds it by the middle, so it doesn't drag on the ground, poor dwarf. . . . He said, What are you doing here? This is no place for you. They all say that. As though I might disturb the people here happily committing their sins, and seeing me would somehow ruin it for them. I walked on a little more so as not to meet up with the dwarf again, then I stopped, waited a little bit, and when I got back to the beach my heart started pounding: Nilgün had already been there for a while and was lying out on the sand. When did you get here? Just like yesterday she was looking at the book at the end of her arms without even moving her head. I watched in amazement.

"Hey!" somebody shouted. "You'll fall in!"

I was startled. I turned and looked. It was our Serdar.

"What's up, buddy?" he said. "What are you doing around here?"

"Nothing."

"Spying on the girls?"

"No," I said. "I've got something to do."

"Don't lie," he said. "You're staring at them like you're going to eat them. Isn't that rude? I'm going to tell Mustafa this evening, you'll see!"

"No," I said again. "There's somebody I know that I'm waiting for. What are you doing?"

"I'm going to the repair shop," he said. He showed me the bag in his hand. "Who is it that you know?"

"You don't know them."

"And you're not waiting for somebody you know," he said. "You're just staring at the girls—shameless. Well, which one is the one you know?"

"Fine," I said. "I'll show you which one, but don't let her know you're looking at her."

I showed him with the tip of my nose, and he looked.

"She's reading a book," he said. "So where do you know her from?"

"I know her from here."

I explained how a long time ago, before a single concrete house had been built, and our stone house was the only one on the hill, their strange old house stood, too, and also the little green shop in what's now the market. There wasn't anybody else around. The upper neighborhood didn't exist, there were no factories. Yenimahalle and Esentepe weren't there. None of these summer houses or the beach. In those days the train passed through gardens and orchards, not factories and store yards.

"Must have been pretty then?" he said, dreamily.

"It was pretty," I said. "When the cherries bloomed in the spring it was nothing like today. You could slip your hand in the water, if you didn't pull out a gray mullet it would be a sea bream that would swim right into your hand."

"You're a really good bullshitter!" he said. "Tell me at least why you're waiting for that girl."

"I was going to give her something," I said. "I have something of hers."

"What?"

I took it out and showed him the comb.

"It's just a cheap comb," he said. "Those people don't use combs like that. Let me see it!"

I handed it to him, so he could have a look at the quality and shut his yap, but, goddamn him, he started to bend it back and forth.

"So, what, are you in love with this girl?"

"No," I said. "Be careful, you'll break it."

"Ha! You're all red! So that means you're in love with this society girl."

"Stop bending it like that!" I said. "You're going to break it."

"Why?" he said and suddenly put the comb in his pocket and walked away. I ran after him.

"Okay, Serdar," I said. "Joke's finished." He didn't reply. "Knock it off, and give me that comb!"

He still didn't answer, but I kept at it. Just as we walked through the crowd at the entrance to the beach, he raised his voice, "You didn't give me anything, my friend! Now let me be! Have you no shame?"

Everyone was looking. I didn't say anything. I let him go on a little ways ahead and just followed him from a distance in silence. When there was no one around, I ran up and grabbed him by the arm and twisted it. He started to struggle but wouldn't submit, so I bent his arm straight upward, so he could really feel the pain.

"Aggh, you animal!" he shouted, dropping his tool kit. "Fine, I'll give it to you!"

He took the comb from his pocket and threw it on the ground.

"You don't understand anything. Retard Fox."

I felt like giving him one across the face, but what was the use? I turned around and walked to the beach. He cursed me from behind, then started shouting that I was in love with a society girl. I don't know if anybody passing by heard him, but I was embarrassed.

When I got back to the beach, Nilgün was gone. I was getting really upset, when I saw: No, look, her bag is still there. I took the comb out of my pocket and waited for her to come out of the water.

When she comes out, I'll go over, I think you dropped this comb,

Nilgün, I'll say, I found it on the road and brought it, don't you want it, or isn't it yours? She'll take it and thank me. It's nothing, I'll say, you don't even have to say thank you, you're thanking me now, but yesterday on the road you couldn't even bother saying hello, I'll say. She'll apologize. There's no need to apologize either, I'll say, I know you're a good person, I saw with my own eyes how you prayed with your grandmother in the cemetery. That's what I'll say, and when she asks what else I've been doing, I'll say that I got left behind in English and mathematics. Are you going to the university, if you know those subjects, well, maybe you could teach me, I'll say. Of course, she'll say. Come over to our house. In this way, maybe I'll get to visit her house, and nobody who sees how we sit and study at the same table would think of saying that these are people from two different worlds . . . Then I saw her in the crowd; she had come out of the water and was drying off. My feet wanted to race off! When she put on her yellow dress and took her bag and started to walk straight toward the gate, I left the beach and walked quickly to the shop. A little later I turned and looked around; I saw that Nilgün was coming behind me to the shop. Good. Going into the shop,

"Give me a Coca-Cola!" I said.

"Coming right up!" said the owner.

You'd have thought he did it just so Nilgün would find me hanging around the shop, but instead of just getting my Coke, the owner went over and started adding up the purchases of an old woman who was already there. When he finally got rid of the old woman, he opened my bottle and gave it to me together with a funny look. I grabbed the bottle went over to a corner of the shop and waited. Come on in, I'm just hanging around drinking from this bottle, what a surprise, I'll say, running into you here, hey, would you like to teach me English? I waited and waited, and when you came in, Nilgün, I didn't see you because I was lost in thought, looking at the bottle in my hand, and that's why I still haven't said hi to you. Fine, so you still haven't seen me, or you have seen me and you still are holding back on saying hello? I'm not looking anyway.

"Do you have a comb?" she said.

"What kind of comb?" said the shopkeeper.

Blood rushed to my face.

"Any comb," she said. "I've lost mine."

"I only have these!" said the shopkeeper. "Will they do?"

"Let me see!" you said.

Then there was a silence, and when I couldn't stand it anymore I turned and looked at you. I saw your face from the side: you're so beautiful! Your skin is like a child's skin, your nose is small, too.

"Fine!" you said. "I'll take one!"

But the shopkeeper didn't answer; at that point the old lady who had gone came back. So you were left waiting and looking around, and I got scared: maybe you would think that I was pretending I did not see you, so I spoke first.

"Hello."

You said, "Hello," to me, too.

But I got a flash of disappointment inside, because when you saw me your face didn't look happy but sort of annoyed; I saw that and I said, that meant you didn't like me, that meant I bored you. So I just stayed there like that, with the Coca-Cola in my hand. We were stuck standing there in the shop, like two complete strangers.

Then, She's right, I thought, she's right not even to want to make eye contact with me, because we belong to different worlds! Still I was surprised, surprised that a person couldn't even be bothered to say hello first, that they would look at you with such hostility for no reason at all: everything was money in this world, what a sewer, such nastiness! Damn it! I thought, I'll go study mathematics, okay, Dad, I'll go and sit down and study mathematics, and get my high school diploma, then throw it at your feet!

Nilgün bought a red comb, and I suddenly felt like I was going to cry, but I was even more surprised when she said:

"Oh, and a newspaper, *Cumhuriyet,* please!"

Amazing. I stared stupidly as she took the newspaper and went out the door without a care in the world, like some little kid who'd never even heard about evil and sin, and I suddenly ran after her.

"So you're reading a Communist newspaper!" I said.

"Excuse me?" said Nilgün, for a second looking at me not with hostility, more like she was just trying to understand something, and then when she'd understood it, she turned and went off without saying anything.

But I thought, I'm not going to let it go. She ought to explain herself, and I have some things to tell her, too. I was just about to go off after her, when I realized I still had that stupid Coca-Cola bottle in my hand. Goddamn it! I went back and paid for it, and I said to myself, Better wait for the change so he doesn't think something's up, and so I waited like an idiot, and the bastard took forever, maybe on purpose so I would lose you.

By the time I came out of the shop and looked, Nilgün was gone, must have even turned the corner. If I'd run after her I would have caught up, but I wasn't running, just walking fast, because people were looking, the stupid crowd going to the beach, going to the market, eating ice cream. I walked quickly up the hill, I went down, ran a few steps, then walked, then ran again when no one was looking, but when I turned the corner I saw that even if I kept running as fast as I could from there on, I couldn't catch up. So I walked as far as her gate and looked between the iron bars: she had gone into the house from the garden.

I sat down under the chestnut tree across the street to think for a while. It was terrifying to think about the Communists and the different disguises they could assume to trick some people. Then I got up, stuck my hands in my pockets, and was about to head back but: I still had the green comb in my pocket! I took it out and looked at it, I should break it, I said, but I couldn't bring myself to do it. There was a garbage can where the sidewalk started. And so, Nilgün, I tossed that green comb of yours into the bin. And I walked on without looking back. All the way to the shop. Because I'd thought of something.

Okay, how about a little chat, Mr. Shopkeeper. Didn't we tell you not to sell that newspaper? What do think your punishment should be, tell me! Maybe he'll have the courage to confess and say, I'm a Communist, that girl is a Communist, too, I sell that newspaper because I believe in it! Suddenly I felt very sorry for Nilgün because she was such a nice girl when she was little. By the time I went into the shop I was in a really bad mood.

"You again?" said the shopkeeper. "What do you want?"

I waited awhile because there were other customers. But the shopkeeper asked again, and the customers were looking at me.

"Me?" I said. "I want, uhh . . . I need a comb."

"Fine," he said. "You're the son of Ismail the lottery-ticket vendor, aren't you?" He pulled out the box of combs to show.

"That girl who was just here bought a red one. It's nice," he said.

"What girl?" I said. "I just want any old comb."

"Fine, fine," he said. "Just you pick whatever color you like."

"How much are you selling them for?"

He went to serve the other customers and left me in peace to look over the combs in the box one by one. I decided on a red one exactly the same color as yours, Nilgün. It was twenty-five liras. I left the shop thinking, Now we have the same color combs. Then I walked and walked until I came to the place where the sidewalk ended. The garbage can was still there, nobody was looking, and so I stuck my arm inside and pulled out the green comb, which you'd have never known had been sitting in a garbage can. Now there are two combs in my pocket, Nilgün, one actually yours, one the same as one that's yours! It felt good just to think about it. Then I thought that if one of these guys saw what I had done, if any of them had seen, they would both pity and mock me for being such an idiot. But I'm not going to keep from doing what I want just because those stupid morons might laugh at me! I'm a free man. And if I want I'll walk around in the streets thinking of you.

18

Faruk Needs to Find a Story

✤

It was nearly five o'clock. The sun had long since dipped toward the windows of the musty basement room. In a little while I'd collect my bag and go continue my search for the plague out in the open air. But I was a bit disoriented. Just a moment ago, it seemed that I was doing fine merely ambling through the documents with no particular purpose. Now I was beginning to suspect this odd success I'd been enjoying . . . A moment ago, history was a nebulous aggregate of millions of unrelated droplets that somehow managed to coalesce in my head. Perhaps, I mused, if I open my notebook and quickly read what I have been writing, I can recapture that feeling!

And so I read the results of an extraordinary inventory undertaken in six villages in the environs of Çayirova, Eskişehir, and Tuzla, these being among the fiefs of Minister Ismail Pasha and under the judges of Gebze; I read that Hızır lodged a complaint against Ibrahim, Abdulkadir, and their sons for burning down his home and pillaging his possessions; I read orders issued for the construction of a pier on the shore of Eskişehir; I read that a village worth seventeen *akçe* in the vicinity of Gebze, one formerly belong-

ing to Cavalryman Ali but taken from him when he failed to participate in a campaign and given to Habib, was now to be given to
someone else still, because it had been determined that this Habib
also had failed to take part in the campaign; I read that the servant
Isa, having absconded with thirty thousand *akçe,* a saddle, a horse,
two swords, and a shield belonging to his employer, Ahmed, took
refuge with someone named Ramazan, and Ahmed lodged a complaint against the man under Ramazan's protection; a certain Sinan
had died and a conflict over the estate resulted in one of his heirs,
Çelebioğlu Osman, demanding from the court a full inventory of
the deceased's possessions; I read the detailed testimony of Mustafa,
Yakup, and Hudaverdi to the effect that a stolen horse seized from
some thieves upon their arrest and placed in the brigadier's stable
was in fact the horse that had earlier been stolen from Suleyman,
the son of Gebzeli Dursun; and with that I felt my former euphoria
returning: the last quarter of the sixteenth century was once again
coming to life in my head, its multiplicity of events lodged there in
the folds of my brain without any links of causality among them.
Over lunch the image had occurred to me of an infinite worm gal-
axy stretching across empty space where there was no gravity, all the
events of that quarter century like so many worms squirming in the
void but unable to touch one another. I imagined my head as a large
walnut, and if one cracked it, he would see the worms hiding among
the folds of my brain!

But this renewed excitement did not last long, and again the galac-
tic haze dissipated and disappeared. My obstinate mind, following its
old habits, was making its customary demand of me: I had to find a
little story, to make up a convincing tale! The structure of our brain
probably has to change if we are ever to see and understand clearly,
not just history, but also the world and life itself. That passion for listening to stories leads us astray every time, dragging us off to a world
of fantasy, even as we continue to live in one of flesh and blood . . .

While I was eating lunch, I thought I had an answer for that as well. I was thinking of our Budak, whose story had been on my mind since yesterday. In the light of some things that I had read this morning it had taken on another dimension: I came to believe that Budak had found a way, who knows how, to be taken under the protective wing of a pasha in Istanbul. I was recalling other details gleaned from that book of my high school history teacher: they were all of a sort designed to win over lovers of stories, people who always try to make sense of the world by means of tales.

This got me thinking about a book I could write about sixteenth-century Gebze drawing on Budak's adventures, a book with no beginning and no end. The book would have only one principle: to encompass, with no attention to relative value or importance, every piece of information I could discover about Gebze and its environs in that century. In this way, meat prices and commercial misunderstandings, kidnappings of girls and revolts, wars and marriages, pashas and murders, would be arranged in a sensible and tolerant manner alongside one another, without connections, just as they appear in the archives. On all this I would superimpose Budak's story, not to give it any more importance than the other elements, but to offer at least one to people who insist on looking for stories in history books. Thus, my book would otherwise be a continuous feat of "representation." As I finished my lunch, and no doubt owing somewhat to the beers I had drunk, I got lost in the mists of this concept, a feeling almost like the excitement of studying that I had when I was young. I'll go into the Prime Ministry Archives, I said, I won't let a single document escape my eye, every single event will take its place, one by one. Someone reading my book from cover to cover will during those weeks and months end up able to glimpse that cloudlike mass of events that I managed to perceive while working here, and like me he'll murmur excitedly: This is history, this is history and life . . .

This crazy plan, which could consume thirty years of my life—no, all the rest of my days!—persisted in my mind's eye awhile longer, morphing according to every contingency, from the prime of life to dotage, failing eyesight, and nervous disease. I recoiled in horror at the thought of how many pages I'd have to write. Then as I began to feel that this vision, which had seemed so awesome, in fact reeked of deception and foolishness, it began to evaporate.

For one thing, I would be faced with a problem before even setting down on paper what I had planned to write. Whatever my intention, my text would have to begin somewhere. No matter how I wrote the events, they would have to be arranged in some kind of order. Whether I intended it or not, all of this would suggest some meaning to the reader. The more I determined to avoid this, the more flummoxed I became about where to start and how to proceed. Because the human mind, bound as it is to its accustomed ways, will always infer an order from every arrangement, a symbol from every event, to the degree that the reader himself will wind up stirring into the facts the story I'd wished to spare him. Then I thought in despair: There's no way to express history, or even life as it is, in words! The only solution would be to transform the structure of our brains: we'd have to change the nature of life in order to see life as it is! I wanted to formulate this notion better, but I couldn't find a way. I left the restaurant and came back here.

I thought about it all afternoon. Was there no way to write that book so as to provoke the desired reaction in readers? From time to time as I pondered it, I quickly reread the things I had written in my notebook, just to reignite the feeling I thought I wouldn't be able to explain to anyone.

While I was reading, I willed myself not to get absorbed in any particular story, just as I intended the book to be read: as a completely aimless stroll . . . A little while ago I thought that I had accomplished this, but now, as I said, I was suspicious of this peculiar success. And the sun even lower now, the time very nearly five o'clock, I was going to leave this musty basement without waiting for Riza and continue looking for the plague in the open air.

I got in the Anadol. I left the town where I had worked for three days in the archives completely deflated, as though departing a city where I had been forced to live for years as it slowly ate away at my insides. A little later I turned off from the Istanbul-Ankara road toward Gebze Station. I was going straight toward the Marmara through the olive groves and fig and cherry orchards. The station, which smelled of the republic and bureaucracy, was at one end of a meadow that stretched all the way to Tuzla. I thought that there must be the ruins of a caravanserai somewhere on this plain. I parked my car and went down the steps to the station.

Workers returning home, young people in blue jeans, aunties with head scarves, an old man nodding off on a bench, and a woman scolding her son were waiting for the train that would arrive from Istanbul before heading back the way it came. I was walking along the rail line, listening to the buzz of the electric wires and stepping over the switches. When I was little, I used to like to walk along the rail line. It was then I first saw the ruins, about twenty-five years ago, I guess. I was seven or eight years old. Recep was taking me around, supposedly to hunt. I had the air rifle my uncle had brought back for me from Germany, which could only wound a crow if you fired it from close by, but I was hardly a good shot! We had come as far as this meadow, Recep and I, gathering blackberries and walking along the creek. Suddenly a little wall sprung up in front of us, and then we saw some well-hewn stones spread out over a wide area. Five years later, when I could go around by myself without fear, I came and saw it again: I stopped and looked at just the wall and the stones, without trying to envision what they had been, not imagining anything other than what I saw. So there had been a creek, in a place near the railroad, then frogs, an open space, a meadow . . . How much of it was left? I looked around as I walked.

In a letter dated much later than the court records I'd found, there was mention of a caravanserai that had stood where the ruins were. The letter, written at the end of the nineteenth century, spoke with amazing sangfroid of certain deaths in the area, perhaps tied to the outbreak of a contagious disease. At that time I read the letter quickly and, in a moment of distraction, tossed it among the other papers without noting down its exact date or number. Of course, I would immediately regret having done that, and in an effort to find it again, I wound up turning everything upside down for an hour, but to no avail. By the time I returned to Istanbul my interest had been piqued even more.

As questions relating to this almost-mythical letter swirled through my head I finally found the creek: it was foul and had a rotten smell, but it was still able to host frogs. They weren't croaking; it seemed that they were dozing because of the poison and the muck, just sitting there like the particles of pitch on the grass and leaves. The livelier ones, hearing my footsteps, got into the water with an annoying languor. I saw a bend in the creek, which I remembered, along with the fig trees. Didn't there used to be more of them? Then the back wall of a factory disrupted everything, erasing my memories and returning me to the present.

If what I read in that letter could really point me toward things that once existed, that meant I could hope to hold on to my faith in "history" a few years longer. With this story of the plague I could destroy a host of historical "facts" just floating in the air without doubt as to their truth, like so many potted plants. In this way a whole crowd of credulous historians, realizing clearly that their work was in fact storytelling, would find the scales falling from their eyes, as I did. That day, I would be the only one ready to meet the ensuing institutional crisis, and through my writings and attack I'd hunt down these poor fools one by one. I stopped by the side of the railroad and tried to imagine in detail what would be a day of victory and grew a bit wistful. The truth was, I'd always envied my old professor Ibrahim, who spent twenty years of his life like a detective, researching the identities, whereabouts, and dates of those who, during the Ottoman Interregnum, proclaimed the sultanate and coined the first *akçe*.

The electric train appeared at one end of the station, loomed up before me, and passed by. I continued walking alongside the creek and the back walls of factories and little workshops on which political slogans had been scrawled in letters large enough for the train passengers to read them. Since, as I remembered quite well, this was where the creek started to move away from the railroad line, I should be able to find those hewn stones and remnants of the wall around there. The story must lie somewhere in the midst of those shanty houses, piles of garbage, tin drums, and fig trees, before you come to the gypsy tents along the road to Cennethisar. At my approach, the seagull observing me from atop the piles of garbage silently took to the air, opening like an umbrella in the wind, and spread out over the sea. I heard the engines of the buses lined up in the side court of the factory up ahead; those were the workers going back to Istanbul, slowly getting on the buses. Beyond the factory there's a bridge that goes over the train line and the creek; I saw piles of iron left to rust, tin cans, dilapidated houses whose roofs are covered with metal salvaged from these cans, children playing ball, and a horse with its colt; the horse must belong to the gypsies.

I turned back, but my feet were taking me to the same places. With the purposelessness of a cat that has forgotten what it's looking for, I walked toward the shanties, alongside the walls, between the railroad and the creek, over dead plants poisoned by chemical spills and brambles not yet dead; I saw the skull of a sheep and a bone from who-knows-what part of its skeleton, alongside a barbed-wire fence, and I kicked the bone and a tin can.

Maybe I could make things that didn't exist then look as though they belonged to that time. Then I saw the stupid chicken as big as an apartment house looking at me from farther down the plain: Chick Chicken was looking at me from a chicken farm's giant billboard supported by steel props. The image had obviously been copied from foreign magazines, with the chicken in short pants and suspenders, an attempt to make the Chick Chicken Farm seem modern.

I was approaching one of the shanties, thinking it might have been made out of stones pulled from the ruins of the caravanserai. In the back a little garden, an onion patch, laundry on the line, and some sort of sapling, but flimsy walls, made of crumbling, lifeless cement blocks from a time of factories, not the hard, chiseled old stones I was looking for. I stood there, staring vacantly at the shanty's wall and feeling that the things and period I sought were hiding somewhere; I lit a cigarette, and watched the smoking match fall to the ground, among dried branches, burnt grass, pieces of bottles, puppies running after their mothers, frayed lengths of rope, bottle caps, and a plastic clothespin broken in two. Someone had used a direction sign on the side of the railroad for target practice. I saw a fig tree and waited, staring at it, hoping it would remind me of something. In its shadow were unripe figs that had fallen from the branches, with flies continually landing and taking off the fruit. A little farther off two cows had their noses in the grass, grazing. When the gypsy's mare decided to make a little run I stood there watching in astonishment, but the mare stopped right away, even as the colt continued on, before it remembered its mother and came back. On the bank of the creek were shreds of paper among the shreds of tires, the bottles, and paint cans and an empty plastic bag. I felt that none of it had any real meaning. I also felt like having a drink, knowing I'd be heading back in a little bit. Two crows overhead went on and on, paying no attention to me. This was the huge meadow where Mehmet the Conqueror had died in 1481. In the back lot of a factory, there were enormous crates that had been emptied of the metal things inside them, which were melted down for sale. When I'm back home, I will read Evliya Çelebi. A stupid frog that had noticed me long after its friends launched himself into the muck of the polluted water. *Blup!* I'll talk to Nilgün. History? I'll explain it to her. Broken tiles had turned the earth red. A village woman was taking in the laundry in the garden of her shanty. I'll tell her history's nothing but a story. Where did you get that idea, she'll say. I stop and look at the sky. I can still feel the eyes of that chicken with the perplexed and modern expression on my back: cement blocks, bricks, crumbling walls with political slogans scrawled over them. Not a stone wall in sight! I started walking purposefully, as though I had just remembered something, and as another train went by, I looked at the abandoned construction materials, the planks, the leftover boards, no, it's not there, it's where the trees are, in the midst of the houses and the gardens, the rusty iron scraps, the plastic, the bone, the concrete, and the barbed wire.

19

Recep Serves the Quiet Dinner Table

They are sitting at the table, in the pale light of the lamp, eating hungrily. First Nilgün talks to Faruk, they laugh together, then Metin Bey gets up before even swallowing the last bite in his mouth, not even answering Madam with a nod when she asks where he's going, and leaves the others to keep up the conversation with her: How are you, Grandmother. And since there isn't anything that hasn't been said, they say, Come on, tomorrow let's take you for a ride in the car, they've built apartments everywhere, new houses, roads, bridges, let's go have a look at them, Grandmother, they say, but Madam is quiet, sometimes she mutters something, but they can't make out any words, since she is looking down at her napkin, as though finding fault with what she is chewing, as though she's astonished that they still haven't figured out their grandmother isn't capable of any reaction except disgust. At that point they realize, as I do, that it's better to be quiet, but then they forget and start annoying her again, before remembering that they shouldn't, and now they start to whisper among themselves.

"You're drinking a lot again, Faruk!" said Nilgün.

"What are you whispering about?" said Madam.

"Nothing," said Nilgün. "Why aren't you eating your eggplant, Grandmother? Recep baked it fresh tonight, didn't you, Recep?"

"Yes, miss," I said.

Madam frowned to show her disgust, and her face stayed that way, out of habit; the face of an old person who had forgotten why she was annoyed but determined never to forget that she was obliged to be . . . They fell quiet, and I was waiting two or three feet away, behind the table. No sound but that of the knives and forks under the pale light the sleepy moths kept circling: at that hour, the garden fell quiet too, a few crickets, some rustling trees, and in the distance, all summer long, on the other side of the garden wall, the holiday makers with their cars, ice cream, and the colored lamps hung on trees . . . In the winter they, too, would be gone, and the silent darkness of the trees on the other side of the walls would make my hair stand on end so I'd want to scream, but I can't, or I'd even like to talk to Madam, but she won't, so I'm quiet and I look at her wondering how a person can live like that without talking, and her hands creep slowly like spiders across the tabletop terrifying me. In the old days Doğan Bey kept silent, too, head bowed, intimidated, like a child; she would belittle him. Even longer ago, Selâhattin Bey, his thundering more feeble than intimidating, would spew his curses, as he struggled to fill his lungs with air . . . This country, this damn country! . . .

"Recep!"

She said she wanted fruit. I took away the dirty dishes and served the watermelon I had prepared for them. They ate it without speaking, then I went down to the kitchen to heat up some water for the washing up, before going back upstairs to find them still eating in silence. Maybe they finally understood that words are useless, or maybe they didn't want to waste their breath like people in the coffeehouses. But there are times when words can touch people, too, that I know. Somebody says hello, he listens to you tell about your life, then he tells you about his, and you listen to him, and in this way we each see our life through another's eyes. Nilgün ate the watermelon seeds, just like her mother.

Madam turned her head toward me: "Untie me!"

"Why don't you stay a little longer, Grandmother," Faruk Bey said.

"It's all right, Recep, I'll take her up . . . ," Nilgün was saying. But when Madam's napkin was untied, she stood up and leaned on me.

We went up the steps. At the ninth we rested.

"Faruk was drinking again, wasn't he?" she said.

"No, Madam," I said. "What gave you that idea?"

"Don't stick up for them," she said, and she raised her hand with the cane in it as if she were going to whip a naughty child, but not at me. Then we continued on our way.

"Eighteen, nineteen, thank goodness!" she said and went into her room; I put her to bed, and when I asked, she said she didn't want fruit.

"Close the door!"

Downstairs, Faruk Bey had taken out the bottle he had hidden and put it on the table, and they were talking.

"Strange thoughts are going through my mind," he said.

"Like the ones you tell me about every night?" said Nilgün.

"Yes, but I haven't told you everything!" said Faruk Bey.

"Fine, play your word games," said Nilgün.

Faruk Bey looked hurt. "I think my head is like a walnut with worms crawling around inside!" he finally said.

"What?" said Nilgün.

"Yes," said Faruk Bey. "I feel like I have worms crawling around in my brain."

I took the last of the dirty plates down to the kitchen and started washing up. These worms get into your intestines, Selâhattin Bey would tell us, if you eat raw meat, or go around barefoot, worms, you understand? We had just come from our village, we didn't understand. My mother had died. Doğan Bey felt sorry for us and brought us here: Recep, you help my mother with the housework; Ismail, you stay with him, downstairs, you can have this room, and eventually I'm going to do something for you both, why should you have to pay for the sins of those two? I kept quiet . . . Recep, would you also keep an eye on my father, he drinks a lot, okay? I was quiet again, I couldn't even say, Fine, Doğan Bey. Then he left us here and went off to the military. Madam kept complaining while I was learning about the kitchen, and every once in a while Selâhattin Bey would come in and ask, So, Recep, how is life in your village? Tell me, what do they do there? Is there a mosque, do you go to prayers? And in your opinion, how do earthquakes happen? What causes the seasons? Are you afraid of me, son, don't be afraid, I'm your father, how old are you, do you know, you don't even know your age, you're thirteen, your brother Ismail is twelve, I don't blame you for being afraid and holding your tongue, I wasn't able to take care of you, I know, I had to send you to the village, to those fools, but I was obliged to do it, I'm writing a long book, it contains all the knowledge of the world, have you ever heard of something called an encyclopedia? Ah, what a shame, but where would you have heard of such a thing, anyway, don't be scared, tell me, how did your mother die, what a good woman, she had the particular beauty of our people, did she tell you everything, she didn't? Fine, but if Fatma does anything mean to you, come up to my study and tell me, and don't be afraid. I wasn't afraid. I washed the dishes, I worked for forty years . . . I caught myself daydreaming. When I finished the dishes and put them away, I was tired, I took off my apron and sat down, Let me relax a little, I said, but then I remembered the coffee, so I got up and went outside to where they were. They were still talking.

"I don't understand how you can spend the whole day looking at things written down on documents in the archives, only to come home and spend the evening thinking about things that exist only in your mind!" said Nilgün.

"And what would you have me think about?" said Faruk Bey.

"Look at actual facts," said Nilgün. "At what's happening, at the causes . . . "

"Facts are written down on paper, too . . . "

"Sure they are, but they correspond to things in the real world, don't they?"

"They do."

"Well, that's what you should write!"

"But when I read these facts they're not in the outside world, they're inside my head. I have to write what's in my mind. And in my mind there are worms."

"That's crazy!" said Nilgün.

They couldn't agree. They fell quiet looking at the garden. They seemed a little sad, somehow pained, but at the same time perplexed. As though they were looking at their own thoughts and not seeing what they were actually looking at, not seeing the plants of the garden, the fig trees, and the hiding places of the crickets. But what can you see in thoughts? Pain, grief, hope, curiosity, longing, all those things stay with you to the end and your mind will wear itself out if you don't put something else in there, where did I hear that, your mind will be like two millstones with no grist between them. Then: you go crazy! Dr. Selâhattin was a perfectly ordinary doctor until he got involved in politics; he was exiled from Istanbul, he buried himself in books and went insane. What liars, old gossips, no, he wasn't crazy, I saw him with my own eyes, what wrong did he do except settling down to drink after dinner and occasionally overdoing it, otherwise he'd sit all day at his desk and write. Afterward once in a while he'd come and talk to me. The world is like the apple from that forbidden tree, he told me one day, it is only because you believe in lies and are afraid that you don't pick it and eat it; pick the fruit of the tree of knowledge and eat it, my son, look, I've picked it and I've become a free man, the whole world is yours for the taking, would you at least answer me? I was afraid and I remained quiet. I knew myself. And I was afraid of the devil . . . I got the idea to take a little walk, maybe go to the coffeehouse.

"What kind of worms," said Nilgün, by now exasperated.

"A whole load of unrelated facts. They won't stop squirming around my mind after all this reading and thinking."

"And you claim they are unrelated," said Nilgün.

"I can't establish relationships with any conviction," said Faruk. "Anyway I believe that they should arise naturally from the facts themselves, without my butting in, but it doesn't happen. As soon as I think I see a causal link, I immediately sense that this is something my own mind has just imposed. At that moment, events start to resemble horrible worms. They jump around between the folds of my brain as though they were hanging in the void . . . "

"Well, why do you think that's so?" said Nilgün.

"Perhaps I'm getting old."

They stopped talking. It seemed as though they were content to disagree with each other. When two people across from each other fall silent, that silence sometimes says more than if the two were talking. I sometimes think it would be nice to have a friend I could be silent with.

"Faruk Bey," I said. "I'm going to the coffeehouse. Do you want anything?"

"What's that?" he said. "No, no thanks, Recep."

I went down into the garden, I felt the coolness of the plants and as soon as I went out the gate I realized that I wasn't going to the coffeehouse. The Friday-night crowd would be there, and I couldn't face that again. I just kept walking and got beyond the coffeehouse without anyone seeing me, even Ismail, who was selling lottery tickets. Slipping past the lit-up windows I went out on the breakwater, which was deserted, and I sat down by the water, looking at the reflection of the colored lights strung up on the trees, adrift in thought. When I'd sat long enough, I went up the hill as far as the pharmacy: Kemal Bey was sitting behind his counter, gazing at the people across the way, relaxing and talking loudly as they had their sandwiches in the light of the buffet. He didn't see me. Better not disturb him! I came back home very quickly; without seeing anyone or saying hello to a soul. After I closed the garden gate behind me I saw them beyond the din and the trees, under the little pale lamp of the balcony: one was at the head of the table, the other had moved a little away from it, leaning back and balancing on a chair's rear legs, which could barely support the weight; brother and sister, perfectly still, as if afraid to make a move or a sound and maybe a little out of not wanting to arouse the accusing expression of the old woman who was lurking behind the open shutters upstairs. Then for a moment, as she closed the window, Madam's shadow appeared clearly; it seemed she had the cane in her hand, and then the shadow, cruel and pitiless, briefly fell on the garden. I silently climbed up the balcony steps.

"Sleep well!" I said. "I'm going to bed."

"Of course," said Nilgün. "You go to bed, Recep, I'll clean up the table tomorrow morning."

"Better not wait. It'll attract the cats," said Faruk. "Toward morning, they come right up to the house, never mind that I'm sitting here, the shameless things."

I went down to the kitchen, took some apricots from the cupboard, and some cherries left over from yesterday; I washed them and brought them upstairs arranged on a plate.

"Madam, your fruit."

She didn't say anything. I left it on the table and closed the door. I went downstairs and washed myself before going to my room. Sometimes I notice that I have a smell. I put on my pajamas, turned out the light, then quietly opened the window and got into bed; I waited for morning, with my head on the pillow.

I'll head out early and take a walk. I'll go to the market, maybe I'll see Hasan again, or somebody else, and we'll talk, maybe they'll listen to me! If only I were more of a talker! Then they would listen. Faruk Bey, I would say then, you drink too much. If you keep on like this, like your father, like your grandfather, God forbid, you'll

die from a bleeding stomach! It seems fresh to me: Rasim died, I'm
going to the funeral tomorrow; we'll go up the hill behind the coffin
in the noon heat. I'll see Ismail, Hello, brother, he'll say, why don't
you ever stop by? Always the same words! I remember when our
mother and my father, the father we had in the village, took Ismail
and me to the doctor. The doctor said that being a dwarf came from
being beaten at an early age, then he added, Make sure they get sunshine. Let the little one's leg get some sun, it might correct itself.
Fine, but what about his big brother, said my mother. I was listening
carefully. He's not going to change now, said the doctor. He'll always
be small, but have him take these pills, they might do some good.
I swallowed the pills, but they didn't do any good. I thought for a
little bit about Madam and her cane and her cruelty, but don't think
about it, Recep! Then I thought about that beautiful woman, the one
who every morning at nine thirty would come to the store, and later
I'd see her at the butcher's, too. I don't see her these days. Tall, thin,
dark haired! She smells nice, even at the butcher's. I wanted to talk
to her: Don't you have a manservant, my lady, you're doing your own
shopping, isn't your husband rich? How pretty she looks when she
watches the machine grind up the meat for her. My mother was raven
haired, too. My poor mother! And we turned out like this. Look at
me, still in this house. You're thinking too much: don't think, sleep.
I yawned, without a sound, and I was startled by the silence: strange!
Like winter nights. On winter nights when it's cold and I get scared I
tell myself a story. Try to think of one! Something from the newspaper? No, one of the stories my mother told: Once upon a time, there
was a sultan who had no children. I used to think, as my mother was
telling the story, didn't he even have children like us, this sultan? Oh,
the poor sultan, I felt sorry for him, and I loved my mother, Ismail,
and myself even more. Our room, our things . . . If only I had a book
like my mother's fables, if it had big letters, I would read and read, I
would fall asleep thinking about them.

20

Hasan Feels the Pressure of Peers

A fter dinner, when my father went off to the casino to sell his tickets, I left the house, too, without saying anything to my mother. When I got to the coffeehouse everyone was already there, including two new guys. Mustafa was explaining things to them. I sat down without drawing attention to myself and listened: So, said Mustafa, two superpowers, America and the Soviets, want to divide up the world, and that Jew Marx lies when he says that what makes the world go round is what he called the class struggle, it's nationalism and the most extreme nationalists are the Russians and the Europeans. Then he told them that the center of the world was the Middle East and the key to the Middle East was Turkey. It was the superpowers, he explained, that had started the argument over "Are you first a Muslim or a Turk?" using their agents to divide us. These agents are all around, they've infiltrated everywhere, he said, and unfortunately, they might even be among us. There was a nervous quiet for a little while, after which Mustafa told them how we used to be united and that unity terrified them to the point of throwing up blood, those treacherous, slanderous, imperialist Europeans, with their tales of

"Plants don't grow where the Turk has passed." I felt I could almost hear those hoof beats that made the Christians shudder on cold winter nights, but all of a sudden I got really annoyed, because one of those new fools who had just joined us piped up: "Okay, brother, but if we find oil, too, will we be like the Arabs and get rich and develop?"

As if everything's about money, everything's material! We are not fighting for money here, we are fighting for our spiritual salvation. Mustafa didn't lose his patience, he explained it all over again, but I didn't listen, I know these things, I'm not new anymore. I noticed a newspaper lying there, so I took it and started reading it, the want ads, too. Then Mustafa told them to come back when it was late. They gave him a salute to show that they had learned the need for absolute obedience and they left.

"Are you going out to write on the walls tonight?" I asked.

"We did them last night, where the hell were you?"

"I was at home," I said. "I was studying."

"You were studying?" said Serdar. "Or you were peeping in windows?"

He gave me a dirty smile. I don't pay attention to anything he says, but I worried Mustafa might take him seriously.

"I caught this guy down at the beach front this morning," said Serdar. "He was eyeing some girl. Some rich kid, he's in love with her. He stole her comb, too."

"He stole it?"

"Look, Serdar," I said. "Don't call me a thief, or you'll be sorry."

"Fine, so I suppose that girl gave you the comb?"

"Yes," I said. "Of course she did."

"Why should a girl like that give you her comb?"

"You wouldn't understand such things."

"He stole it!" he said. "He's in love, the fool, he stole it!"

I took the two combs out of my pocket. "Look," I said. "Today, she gave me another one. You still don't believe me?"

"Let me see," said Serdar.

"Take it," I said, holding out the red one. "I guess you learned this morning what will happen if you don't give it back!"

"This comb is totally different from the green comb," he said. "It isn't something that girl would ever use!"

"I saw her use it with my own eyes," I said. "She has one of these in her bag, too."

"Then she didn't give this one to you," he said.

"Why?" I said. "Couldn't she have bought two of the same comb?"

"The poor guy," said Serdar. "Love has taken control of his senses, he doesn't even know what he's saying."

"Don't you believe that I know her!" I shouted.

"Who is this girl?" Mustafa suddenly said.

I was taken aback and I thought, Mustafa's been listening.

"The guy's in love with some society girl," said Serdar.

"Really?" said Mustafa.

"It's a bad situation, brother," said Serdar.

"Who is this girl?" said Mustafa.

"Because he keeps on stealing the girl's combs," said Serdar.

"No!" I said. "She gave me this comb!"

"Why would she do that?" said Mustafa.

"I don't know," I said. "Probably just as a present."

"Who is this girl?" said Mustafa.

"You know, when she gave me this green comb," I said. "I wanted to give her a present in return, so I bought this red one. But as Serdar says, the red one isn't as nice as the other, it's not the same as the green comb."

"I thought she gave you both of them," said Serdar.

"Who is this girl, I'm asking you," shouted Mustafa.

"I know her from when we were little!" I said. "She's a year older than me!"

"She's the girl in the house where his uncle is the servant," said Serdar.

"Really?" said Mustafa. "Why didn't you say so?"

"Yes," I said. "My uncle works for them."

"So this rich girl just gives you a comb as a present for no reason?"

"Why not?" I said. "I told you: I know her."

"Are you a thief, you idiot!" Mustafa shouted.

Everybody heard him. I broke into a sweat; I hung my head down in front of me, wishing I were anywhere else. If I were at home now, nobody would be bothering me; I could go out to the garden, look at the mysterious lights on the silent ships going off to distant places.

"Well, are you a thief or not, answer us!"

"I'm not a thief at all," I said. Then I thought of something and, pretending to laugh a little, I said, "Okay, I'll tell you the truth! It was all a joke. Just to see what he'd say. I was joking with Serdar this morning, but he didn't get it. Yes, I bought the red comb from the shop. You can go and ask them in the shop if they have the same one. And this green comb is hers. She dropped it on the street, I found it, and I'm just waiting to give it back to her."

"Are you her servant, is that why you're waiting?"

"No," I said. "I'm her friend. When we were small—"

"The stupid guy's in love with a society girl," said Serdar.

"No," I said. "I'm not."

"If you're not, why are you hanging around her door?"

"If I take something that doesn't belong to me and then I don't return it to the owner, they'll call me a thief, that's why."

"This guy must think we're as stupid as he is," said Mustafa.

"So you see," said Serdar. "He's fallen really hard!"

"No!" I said.

"Quiet, you idiot!" Mustafa shouted. "He's not even ashamed. And I thought that this guy would amount to something. I was fooled when he came to me asking for something bigger to do and I thought that he was ready for more responsibility. In fact the whole time, he's been playing slave to some society girl."

"No!"

"You've been going around like a sleepwalker for days!" said

Mustafa. "While we were writing slogans last night, were you hanging around her house?"

"I wasn't."

"And you make us look bad with your thieving!" said Mustafa. "Enough already! Just get out of here!"

We were quiet for a bit. I wished I were at home right then, peacefully working on my mathematics.

"Look, this shameless guy is still sitting here!" said Mustafa. "I said I don't want him around anymore!"

I stared at them both.

"Why don't we just forget about it. We have more important things to worry about," said Serdar.

"No, get this guy out of my sight. I don't want to look at some society lover boy thief."

"Let it go. Look, he's shaking. I'll straighten him out. Just have a seat and relax, Mustafa."

"No!" he said. "I'm going."

And he really was.

"Come on, brother!" said Serdar. "Just sit down."

Mustafa was standing up, playing with his belt. I had an urge to get up and punch him. I'll kill him! I thought. But in the end, if you don't want to be alone, you have to learn to explain yourself, so others don't misunderstand you.

"There's no way I could be in love with her, Mustafa!" I said.

"You come tonight," Mustafa said to them. Then he turned to me. "You, don't show your face around here again. You don't know us, never saw us!"

I thought for a bit. Then I suddenly said "Stop!" and ignoring the trembling in my voice I said, "Just listen to me, Mustafa. And you'll understand."

"What?"

"I can't be in love with that girl," I said. "She's a Communist."

"What?"

"Yes!" I said. "I swear, I saw it with my own eyes."

"What did you see?"

"The newspaper. She was reading *Cumhuriyet*. She gets *Cumhuriyet* from the shop every day and reads it. Sit down, Mustafa, let me explain."

"Don't tell me you're in love with a Communist?" he said.

For a moment I thought he was going to hit me. If he did, then I would kill him.

"No," I said. "I don't fall in love with Communists. Until yesterday I still didn't know she was a Communist. Would you sit down, Mustafa, so I can explain?"

"I'm sitting down," he said. "But if you're lying it's going to end very badly for you."

Then I was quiet for a minute, and I asked if they could let me have a cigarette.

"So you've started smoking, too?" said Serdar.

"Just give the guy a cigarette!" said Mustafa and finally sat down.

Yasar gave me a cigarette but couldn't see how much my hand was shaking, because he lit the match. When I saw the three of them looking at me with great interest to see what I would say, I took a minute to puff and think.

"When I saw her in the cemetery she was praying," I said. "That's why I figured she couldn't be some society girl, because her head was covered and her hands were open to God, just like her grandmother's . . ."

"What's this guy saying?" said Serdar.

"Ssh!" Mustafa said. "What were you doing in the cemetery?"

"Sometimes people leave flowers there," I said. "My father says that if he puts a carnation in his lapel when he goes out at night, people in the casino buy more tickets. So he sends me there to look sometimes. So when I went there that morning, looking for flowers, I saw her next to her father's grave. Her head was covered and she had her hands lifted up to God."

"He's lying!" said Serdar. "I saw that girl on the beach this morning; she was totally naked."

"No, she wasn't, she had on a bathing suit," I said. "Besides, in the cemetery I couldn't have known what sort she was."

"Fine, so is the girl a Communist now?" said Mustafa. "Or are you just jerking us around?"

"No," I said. "She is. When I saw her praying there I was, all right, I admit it, a little confused. Because she wasn't like that when she was a kid. I'd known her since childhood. She wasn't bad, but she wasn't good either. You don't know them. Trying to figure it out, I got all confused, too. I was curious about what kind of person she is now. That's why I started to follow her . . ."

"No good bum!" said Mustafa.

"He's in love, that's it!" said Yasar.

"Quiet!" said Mustafa. "How did you learn she was a Communist?"

"Following her," I said. "Well, I wasn't actually following her at that point. By chance she came into the shop where I was drinking a Coca-Cola and she got a *Cumhuriyet*. That's how I realized."

"You understood just from that?" said Mustafa.

"No, not just from that," I said, and I was quiet for a second before continuing. "She goes and gets *Cumhuriyet* every morning and doesn't get any other paper. And then she no longer socializes with the other rich people here."

"She got *Cumhuriyet* every morning, and you were hiding this from us, because you were still in love and going after her, weren't you?"

"No," I said. "She got *Cumhuriyet* this morning."

"Don't lie, I can tell," said Mustafa. "You just said that she gets *Cumhuriyet* every morning."

"She goes to the shop every morning and gets something, but I saw this morning that what she gets is *Cumhuriyet*."

"This guy is lying," said Serdar.

"Another minute and I'm going to break his face," said Mustafa. "He went after this girl knowing full well that she's a Communist. So what's with these combs, then?"

"I am trying to tell you," I said. "She dropped one of them while

I was following her. I picked it up then. I didn't steal it, in other words . . . The other is my mother's comb, I swear."

"Why would you be carrying your mother's comb?"

I took another drag on my cigarette because I realized they had no intention of believing anything more I said.

"I'm talking to you!" he said.

"Fine," I said. "You don't believe me. But now, I swear, I'm telling the truth. No, this red comb isn't my mother's, it's true. I just said that because I was embarrassed. This red comb, she got it from the shop today."

"With the newspaper?"

"With the newspaper. You can ask the guy in the shop."

"And so, you mean, she gave you the comb?"

"After she left, I got one of the red combs for myself."

"Why?" shouted Mustafa,

"Why?" I said. "Don't you understand why?"

"I'm going to punch this guy in the mouth!" said Serdar.

If Mustafa hadn't been there I would have shown him. But Mustafa was still shouting.

"Because you're in love, you stupid idiot! You already knew she's a Communist. Are you a spy?"

Once again I thought, He's not going to believe anything I say from now on, and I kept quiet, but Mustafa continued shouting so much that I said, Let me try one more time to convince him that I'm not in love with a Communist anymore. I threw my cigarette on the floor and snuffed it out with my shoe, like a perfectly calm and sensible person. Then I took the red comb out of Serdar's hand, bent it back and forth, and said:

"If you found such a nice cheap comb for twenty-five liras you probably wouldn't pass up buying it either," I said.

"Goddamn you, you liar!" Mustafa howled.

At that point I decided that I was definitely just going to keep quiet. I don't have any intention of talking to you anymore, gentlemen, okay? Whether you want me around or not, either way, in just a few minutes, I'm going home. I'll sit down to my math, and one day soon, I'll go to headquarters in Üsküdar and ask for an important job: the guys in Cennethisar, I'll tell them, don't do anything except call one another spies, so give me something big to do! I can shoot anyone! For now, though, I'm just going to read my newspaper. I was halfway through it when I opened it and started reading again, ignoring all of them.

"What should we do now, my friends?" said Mustafa.

"Well, there's the shop that's still selling *Cumhuriyet*," said Serdar.

"No," said Mustafa. "I'm saying what should we do to this stupid Commie lover?"

"Forget it, Mustafa!" said Serdar. "Don't take it seriously, he's already shown remorse."

"Are you saying I should let him go and be devoured by the Communists?" shouted Mustafa. "And he'll run right off and tell the girl everything."

"Should we beat him up?" whispered Serdar.

"And what should we do about the Communist girl?" said Yasar.

"Let's do to her what they did to the girl in Üsküdar."

"And we have to teach the shopkeeper a good lesson!" said Serdar.

They continued to talk among themselves in whispers about what the Communists in Tuzla did to our guys and about me as if I were some retard and about how they'd hanged this girl from the rail of the Üsküdar boat when they caught her reading *Cumhuriyet,* but I stopped paying attention: I was reading my newspaper and I was thinking how I wasn't a professional licensed driver with experience, a telex operator with knowledge of English, a fabricator of aluminum shutters, a pharmacist's assistant with experience fitting eyeglasses, an electrical installer who has completed his military service, a sewing machine operator experienced in trouser welting. But, damn it, I'll still go to Istanbul, and one day, when I've done something big, yes, yes, I was thinking of that big job, and since I didn't know yet exactly what it would involve, I turned to the first page of the newspaper again, as though I would see my name and find the job I was meant to do there, but someone had torn a few sheets from the newspaper and it seemed to be missing page 1, or at least I was looking for it but I couldn't find it; and it was as if I had lost not part of the newspaper, but my whole future. I was trying to hide my hands so that they couldn't see I was trembling when Mustafa said loudly:

"I'm talking to you, you idiot! When does this girl go to the store?"

"After she goes to the beach."

"How do I know what time she goes to the beach?"

"She goes around nine, nine thirty."

"And this girl knows you, right?"

"Of course!" I said. "We say hello to each other."

"This retard! He's still proud of it."

"Yes," said Serdar. "That's why I said to forgive him."

"Listen to me!" Mustafa said. "Tomorrow at nine thirty I'll be there. You wait for me! You show me which shop it is! Let me see with my own eyes that the girl really buys *Cumhuriyet.*"

"She gets it every morning!" I said.

"Shut up!" he said. "If she buys it I'll give you a signal. Then you go and grab the newspaper out of her hands. You say that we don't allow Communists around here. Then you rip it up and throw it away. Got it?"

I didn't say anything.

"Good," he said. "Can't take any chances when it comes to these Communists, even with a fox. And tonight, you come out with us to write slogans. No going home!"

I wanted to kill Mustafa right there. But in the end, I figured, You'll only make more trouble for yourself, Hasan! I didn't say anything. Except I did ask for another cigarette. They gave it to me.

21

Metin Spins Out of Control

⚘

Cuneyt opened the window and was shouting into the darkness,
All teachers are maniacs, all the professors, and as he moaned,
Gülnur on the couch burst out laughing and said, He's high, he's flying, do you guys see this, but Cuneyt continued shouting, Faggots,
they completely fucked me up this year, bastards, what right do you
have messing around with my life, and Funda and Ceylan interrupted, saying, Ssshh, Cuneyt, what are you doing, look at the time,
it's three a.m., the neighbors, everybody's asleep, but Cuneyt kept at
it, saying, Leave me alone, sis, the neighbors and the teachers are in
on it together, and trying to take the joint from his hand, Ceylan said,
You're not getting this again, but Cuneyt wouldn't give it up and said,
Everybody's having some, but I'm the only one getting blamed, and
Funda, shouting to make herself heard above the awful music and
noise, said, Just be quiet, then, stop shouting, okay, and Cuneyt suddenly quieted down, as if he'd forgotten all his hatred and bitterness
in one instant, and began slowly rocking back and forth to the music
that was wailing in my ears; then they went out between the flashing
colored lights that Turan had strung up around the room to make it

look like a disco, and I looked at Ceylan, who didn't look upset, just beautiful, smiling a little, a little pained maybe, a little sad, God help me, I love this girl, I don't know what to do, am I going to wind up like those pimply young Turkish lovers who decide to get married as soon as they fall in love, like those lovelorn idiots at school, who show contempt for girls then sit down and write mushy love poems all night long in notebooks they hide from everyone, concealing their pathetic feelings so they can feel like a real man when they grope a girl the next morning, don't think about it, Metin, I hate all of them, I will never be like them, I'll be a heartless rich international playboy, pictured in the papers with the Countess de Roche-Whatever, and the next year, I'll live the life of a renowned Turkish physicist in America, *Time* magazine will catch us walking hand in hand in the Alps, me and Lady So-and-So, and when I come to Turkey on my private yacht to make a Blue Voyage, and you see me splashed across the front page of *Hürriyet* with my third wife—the beautiful only daughter of a Mexican oil tycoon—then, Ceylan, let's see if you don't say, I'm in love with Metin . . . Man, did I have a lot to drink! I looked at Ceylan again, and her beautiful face was looking stupid after just a couple of hits of hash, sitting among the others, stoned out of their minds, starting to howl, God, I even heard them ululate, and I don't know why, but I felt like howling along with them, and so I started to, at first just some weird animal noises coming out of my throat, and as I was making these hopeless noises Gülnur said, Metin, just be quiet, don't even pretend to be joining in, and showing me the joint in her hand, she said, You haven't even had any, and I laughed it off, as if it was all in fun, but then I said, gravely, I polished off a whole bottle of whiskey, okay, and I don't pass mine around from hand to hand, but she wasn't even listening and gave me a look as if to say, You wimp, why don't you smoke, have some consideration for Turan, why be such a drag on his last night before he goes off to the army, until finally I said, Okay, okay, and took the joint from her hand, and I looked your way, Ceylan, as if to say, See, I'm inhaling just like you, and Gülnur said, Yeah, that's it, and I took another drag before handing it back, but when Gülnur realized I was looking at you, she laughed out loud and said, Look, Metin, you're going to have to smoke a lot more to catch up with your girlfriend, and I was quiet and Gülnur said, Well, are you interested or aren't you, and I was quiet again, and Gülnur said, Metin, better move fast or Fikret will snag her from you, mark my words, and she made a gesture, as if to write them in the air with the glowing tip of her cigarette, and I was quiet again, and she said, Okay, where's Fikret, at which point I emptied my glass in one gulp and, on the pretext of going to refill it, I bolted out of there before something awful could happen, which made Gülnur burst out laughing again, and as I was looking for the bottle in the darkness, Zeynep suddenly appeared from I don't know where and wrapped herself around me, saying, Come on, let's dance, come on, Metin, this is such nice music, so I said, Fine, and as she embraced me I wanted to say, See, I don't just think about Ceylan from morning till night, look, here I am dancing with chubby Zeynep, but I had my fill very quickly, because she started right off giving me these dreamy eyes, like some contented cat that had just filled its belly, her idea of flirting, I guess, and as I was looking around for my exit, some of the others started patting my ass, when, damn it, somebody turned out the lights and they started yelling, Kiss, kiss, kiss, so I took the opportunity in the dark to push her away like a big hot pillow, and I'd just about broken free when I felt a real pillow hit me in the face, Fine, if that's the way you want to play, I said, and took a blind swing at someone in the darkness, which must have connected, because I heard Turgay moaning, but I kept going and made my way to the kitchen door, where Vedat, looking extremely messed up, said to me, Isn't this a beautiful thing, to which I answered, What's so beautiful, and in amazement he said, Don't you know, we just got engaged, and he put his hand affectionately on Sema's shoulder like a dutiful husband, saying, Isn't it great, man, and I said, It sure is, he said, It's a wonderful thing, we're engaged, aren't you going to congratulate us, and we embraced, and Sema looked as if she'd suddenly start bawling, and I didn't know what to say, but just as I was about to get away Vedat grabbed me for another embrace, and I was afraid that the English girl would see us and get the wrong idea, because in school, in the dorms, everybody was out to make everybody else out to be a homo, the sickos, they'd treat anybody without facial hair like one, but, thank God, I've got some hair, could even have a beard if I wanted, it wouldn't look bad either, even so, that bear Suleyman pinched me once on the ass, but I got him back, climbing on top of him one night when he was asleep and humiliating him in front of the whole dormitory, because if you don't stand up to them they'll crush you, just like they did to poor Cem, these animals, but in the end, what do you care, Metin, next year you're going to be in America, but there's still one year to go in this land of retards, and I'm telling you, Faruk and Nilgün, I thought, if I can't make it to America next year because there's no money, there's going to be hell to pay. Fortunately I finally found the kitchen: Hülya and Turan were there; Hülya had been crying, Turan had his bald head under the tap, when he saw me he straightened up and gave me a manly punch, and then when I said, Where the hell are the bottles and glasses, he said, The glasses are there, but he didn't show me anyplace, and when I said, Where, again, he said, Over there, again, and still he didn't show me where exactly and, finally, as I was opening and closing all the cabinets, Turan put his arms around Hülya and the two of them started to kiss passionately, biting each other with a force like pulling teeth, and I thought, We could be like that, Ceylan, and then they started to make kind of strange sounds, and Hülya managed to get her mouth away from Turan's, and then, all out of breath, she said, It'll go by quickly, just go and get it over with, but suddenly Turan got all angry and said, What do you know about military duty, men are the soldiers, and getting even more worked up, he pulled out of Hülya's arms, bellowing, Anyone who doesn't do his military duty isn't a man, and, planting another fist on me, this time my back, he said, Are you a man, are you a man, oh, and now you're even laughing, you're so sure of yourself, okay, come on, let's see if you measure up, let's see how much of a man you are, and as he put his hands on the buttons of his pants, Hülya said, What are you doing, Turan, please don't do that, Turan, and he said, Fine, I'm going in two days, but tomorrow night we'll have fun again just like tonight, okay, and Hülya said, Your father may have something to say about that, and Turan yelled, I have had it with that bum, I'll crap in his mouth, enough already, if you're a father know how to act like one, do I have to finish high school just because you say so, so you can just hustle me off to the military, what kind of father is that, so what if I'm not making anything of myself, okay, how about I just total your car, I swear, I'll take that Mercedes, Hülya, I swear I'll wrap it around a pole, let him figure it out, he said. Hülya was weeping, No, Turan, don't, please, she said, and Turan gave me one more punch before he, too, began swaying to the music coming from inside, as if he'd forgotten all of us, and slowly disappeared in the haze of strobe-lit hash smoke and music with Hülya running after him; as for me, I was finally making my drink when Turgay found me and he said to me Come on you come, too, we're going skinny-dipping, and I suddenly got excited and I said, Who is, who is, and he laughed and said, No girls, of course, and when he said *no Ceylan* I was taken aback and I thought of you, Ceylan, how did everybody figure out that I loved you, how did they realize that I don't think of anything but you anymore, Ceylan, where are you in all this smoke and music, why don't they at least open the windows, I looked and looked for you, and I didn't panic until I saw that you were dancing, and Fikret was with you, Calm down, Metin, don't make a big deal out of it, and I sat down somewhere like a guy who doesn't make a big deal out of things, when somebody put on a folk dance, the "Butcher's Air," I think, and since they all had been to too many middle-class weddings, they all got up and were going at it arm in arm, I had Ceylan on one arm, and when I stole a peek, of course, Fikret was on her other, and we started to turn, just as we would with our aunties at some distant relative's nuptials, and when the circle broke we became a long train, changing direction in the hall before one end went out into the garden, and then we all went out, and as we were going back in the other door, I felt Ceylan's beautiful hand on my shoulder, and I began thinking, What about the neighbors, and when the train entered the kitchen, we broke off, but Fikret kept going, leaving the two of us behind, Ceylan and me, and in the kitchen, where we saw that Sema was staring into the open refrigerator and crying, and we heard Vedat say, like a dutiful husband, Come on, dear, let me take you off home now, but Sema just kept on staring and crying, as though there were something in the fridge to cry about, and Vedat said, It's late, what will your mother say, and Sema was saying, I hate my mother, and now you're on her side, and when Vedat said, At least give me the knife, Sema suddenly let the knife in her hand drop to the floor, and at that point, I put my hand on your shoulder, as if it was perfectly natural that I'd be protecting you, Ceylan, and as I got you out of the kitchen you pressed up against me, and we went into the other room, yes, yes, the two of us together, everybody check this out, we went inside, everyone was shouting and jumping around, and then, just at my moment of triumph, because you had pressed up against me, Ceylan, you suddenly broke away and ran off, I don't know where, and I was left saying, Should I go after her, but then I looked and there I was next to Ceylan again, there we were dancing together, there I was holding her hand, and then I looked and she was gone again, but what difference does it make now, now everything is clear, I'm so happy I can hardly stand it, but suddenly I'm thinking that I'll never see you again and then I'm really scared, Ceylan, scared that for some reason I would never be able to make you love me, and I'm looking for you desperately, Ceylan, where are you, I love you, and I thought how when I was little everybody had a mother who kissed them when they came home in the evening, everyone but me, and I thought how I felt so lonely in the dormitory on weekends and how I hated myself and being lonely and how nobody at my aunt's house loved me, how everybody has money except me, and that's why I'll need to make some major discoveries but, Ceylan, who needs America, I don't have to overcome all these problems, we can live wherever you like, stay here if you want, Turkey isn't such a terrible place, there are nice stores opening all the time, one day this senseless street violence will end, too, and we'll have right here in Istanbul everything the shops carry in Europe and America, let's get married, I have a good head on my shoulders, at this very moment I have fourteen thousand liras in my pocket, none of these guys is carrying that kind of money, if you want, I'll work somewhere to get ahead, or if you want we can just agree that money isn't everything, can't we, Ceylan, where are you, you haven't left in Fikret's car, have you, but wait, there you are, sitting by yourself in the corner, my lonely little helpless pretty angel, what's happened, are your mother and father bothering you, too, you can tell me, I'm just sitting here next to her, and finally just to make conversation, as usual, the deadliest lines come flowing out, and I ask, Are you very tired, and you, taking the question seriously, say, Me, yes, I have a little headache, and since I can't think of anything else, I sit there silently for what feels like forever, and just as I'm about to lose it from the boredom and the music, Ceylan comes out with one of her happy laughs so full of life, and seeing my face looking stupider by the min- ute, she says, You're so sweet, Metin, tell me, what's twenty-seven times seventeen, and then furious with myself, I put my hand on your shoulder and then you bend your lovely head and it rests on my chest and I feel it there, the scent of your hair and your skin, in this unimaginable ecstasy, you say, There's no air in here, Metin, let's go outside for a bit, and we get up right away, my God, we're going out together, yes, good, away from all this awful noise, yes, together, and see, my hand is on your shoulder and we're pressing against each other, we're leaning on each other, like two hopeless lovers who by their affection save each other in this world full of ugliness, we've left it all behind, the terrible music and the crowd, and we're walking together through quiet empty streets, under the trees, looking at the colored lights of the nightclubs in the distance, we're talking like lov- ers who make everyone jealous, not just by their love, but by their deep friendship, their deep understanding of each other, and I'm say- ing to her how nice it is out in the fresh air, and Ceylan is saying how

she's not really that afraid of her mother and father, who's basically a
good man even if he's a little too Turkish, and I'm saying, Unfortunately, I never got to know mine well, because my mother and father
passed away, and Ceylan is saying how she wants to study journalism
and see the world, and she says, Don't look at me now, here we're
only out to have fun, we don't do anything, but that's not what I want
to be, I want to be like that woman, what is her name, that Italian
journalist, the one always interviewing famous people, she talks with
Kissinger or Anwar Sadat, yes, I know that to be like her you have to
be very sophisticated, but I can't read books from morning till night,
I have a right to live, too, because I passed all my classes this year, so
I want to have fun, not like that kid in our school, who read so much
he went nuts, they put him in the asylum, what do you say, Metin, but
I don't say anything, I'm just thinking that you're beautiful while
you're going on about your father, school, your friends, your future,
and what you think about Turkey and Europe and such things and,
when the dim light of the streetlamps filters through the leaves and
falls on your face, you're even more beautiful, and when you puff on
your cigarette with an anxious expression and toss back that curl on
your forehead, my God, just seeing you a person would want to have
a child with you, and suddenly I said to her, Let's go to the beach,
look how nice it is, there's no one around, it's so quiet, Ha, she said,
and off we went, and when we were walking on the sand Ceylan took
off her shoes and carried them in her hand all along the shore, with
her feet sparkling on the sand, those pretty little feet she carefully
dipped into the dark mysterious water as she talked, splashing the
water around, I couldn't see anything but those feet making little
waves in the water as she was talking about how she wanted to live
like a European, from then on not listening to me, but I was lost
anyway in the humid heat and the smell of the seaweed and of her
skin, then suddenly I ran into the water with my shoes still on and
put my arms around you, Ceylan, and she said, What are you doing,
I love you, I said, and I wanted to kiss her on the cheek, and she,
laughing at first, said, Metin, you're very drunk, but then I could tell

she got scared, so I pulled her to the shore and tried to pin her down, and as she was squirming under me on the sand, I tried to find her breasts and feel them, No, she said, no, no, Metin, what are you doing, have you gone crazy, you're drunk and I said, I love you, and she said, No way, and I kissed her neck and smelled her incredible smell, but when she pushed me again, I thought, What right does she have to treat me like that, so I worked my way on top of her again, lifted up her skirt, and there it was, under my legs, that unapproachable body I had imagined so long from a distance, and I unzipped my pants, and she was still saying no, pushing at me, why, Ceylan, why, one minute I love you so much and the next we're struggling like a cat and a dog, rolling on the sand, it's so stupid, everything is so hopeless, and you tell me again I'm drunk, fine, fine, I'm not some crude guy who can't take a hint, I'm stopping, but so what if we had, I was saying, I'm not some sex fiend, I really only wanted to kiss you a little, so you would know that I love you, but, okay, I got carried away, but I stopped, I let her pull her body out from under me, let my angry dick bury itself in the cold sand without finding relief, fine, I'm leaving you alone, I pull up my zipper and turn my face to the sky and stare vacantly at the stars, leave me alone, understood, go run off and tell your friends, Hey guys, be careful, that Metin is a weirdo, he attacked me, no-class slob, that much was obvious, absolutely no different from the creeps whose photos you see in the paper, my God, I could cry, I'll pack my bag and go back to Istanbul, this little Cennethisar adventure is over. If you want to sleep with a girl in Turkey, I guess you have to be a millionaire or marry, next year I'll be in America anyway, meanwhile giving lessons in mathematics and English to private high school students till the end of the summer, help for the mentally deficient at two hundred fifty liras an hour, and all summer long while I'm squirreling away money, staying in my aunt's hot, suffocating little house, back here, Fikret and Ceylan . . . I can't even think about it, it's so unfair, girls shouldn't be seduced by money but by cleverness, talent, and good looks, oh, just forget about it, Metin, it's not important, look at those stars, what could all those shining stars mean up there in the sky, people look at them and recite poems, and why do they do it, they claim they feel something mysterious, but they're just confused, and they call their confusion feeling, no, I know why they read poems, the whole point is to get women and make money, that's it, the fools, what counts is knowing how to use your head, and when I get to America the first thing I'll do is make some kind of very simple discovery in physics, something nobody has thought of, and immediately publish it in the *Annalen der Physik,* the journal that published Einstein's first discoveries, and after I get rich and famous overnight, the Turks will come begging me for the secrets and the formulas of all the rockets I've developed, Come on, please, won't you share with your fellow countrymen, so we can rain down some rockets on the heads of the Greeks, and then it's off to my villa, a bigger and better one than the one that billionaire Ertegun has in Bodrum, unfortunately, I don't have much time, I just come here once a year for a quick one-week visit, and by then, who knows, Fikret and Ceylan, maybe they'll be married, but where are you getting this from, there's nothing between them, Ceylan, where are you, maybe she ran off, I can see her panting while she tells the others all about it, but where is she now, I couldn't even lift up my head to look, I'm losing it, all alone out here on the sand, I have nobody, it's all your fault, whose parents leave their son alone like this, you could at least have left me a decent inheritance, then at least I would be like them with my money, but no, not a cent, not a dime, in the end all you left me was a fatso big brother and a big sister obsessed with politics, of course there's also the senile grandmother and the dwarf, not to mention the decrepit house they refuse to demolish, just you wait, I'll knock it down! I know why you never made any money, to make money you need courage and talent and guts, and I've got them, so I'll earn plenty, but still I feel sorry for you and for myself and how I have nobody, and as I was thinking of you and of my own loneliness, afraid I might start to cry, suddenly I heard Ceylan's voice: Are you crying, Metin, she said; she hadn't gone! Me? I said, Nooo, why would I cry, I said, Good, then, said Ceylan, that's what I thought, come get up, let's go back now, Metin, she said, Okay, okay, I said, I'm getting up, but I continued to lie there without budging, just looking stupidly at the stars, and Ceylan said again, Come on, get up, Metin, and when she put out her hand to help me me, I got up, though I could hardly stand, I was swaying back and forth, and I was looking at Ceylan, so this is the girl I just attacked, what a strange thing, she's smoking a cigarette as if nothing happened, so, to say something, I said, How are you, I'm fine, she said, I lost some buttons from my blouse, she said, but not in an angry way, and then I was ashamed, thinking what a warm, compassionate person she is, God, I was quiet for a little while, and then I said, Are you mad at me, I was really drunk, forgive me, I said, No, no, she said, I'm not mad, we were both pretty drunk, things happen, I know that's not your nature. I was stunned. What are you thinking, Ceylan, I said, and she said, Nothing, I'm not thinking anything, come on, let's go back, she said, and as we were turning to go she saw my wet shoes and she laughed, and I just wanted to put my arms around her again, I just don't understand anything, I thought, and then Ceylan said, We'd better pass by your place so you can go change those shoes, and I was even more stunned, and so we left the beach, without saying anything we walked and walked through the silent streets, breathing in the scents of honeysuckle, dried grass, and hot cement rising from cool dark gardens, and when we came to our garden gate, I was ashamed of how run-down the place was and a bit annoyed at those sleepyheads inside, when I saw that Grandmother's light was still on, then, on second look—oh, God—that my brother was in a stupor at the table on the balcony, where he was sitting in the darkness, and when his shadow moved, I figured he wasn't asleep, only leaning back in his chair at this hour of the night, or, rather, the morning, and I said, Let me introduce you, Ceylan, Faruk, my big brother, and they were pleased to meet, and catching a whiff of that disgusting stench of alcohol coming from my brother's mouth, I ran up the steps and madly changed my shoes and socks, so as not to leave them alone too long, but when I came downstairs Faruk had started:

Your moon appears step by step at night Naili
Is this not worth suffering worlds of pain

He was saying, Of course you understand, that it is Naili's seventeenth-century Ottoman poem, but after he'd recited it, the fatso looked so satisfied you'd have thought it was his own, and he started reciting again:

So intoxicated was I that I could not comprehend what was the world
Who am I, who is that the wine server, what is the elixir of dawn

Whose that is, I don't know, he said, it's from *Evliya's Travels,* said Ceylan smiling kindly at the unlidded Ottoman alcohol vat before her and ready to hear more when I said, Faruk, could I have the car keys, we're leaving, Sure, he said, on one condition, the lovely lady will answer one question for me, yes, I couldn't comprehend what was the world, please, could you tell us, Ceylan Hanım, it is Ceylan, isn't it, such a beautiful name, Ceylan, tell us please what then is the world, all these things around us, the trees and the sky and the stars and the empty bottles on the table before us, yes, what do you say, he said, and Ceylan looking at him with a sweet, familiar way, said nothing in words but with a look, You would know better than I do, and trying to change the subject so my drunken brother wouldn't get embarrassed, I said, Wow, Grandmother's light is still on, and for a moment we all turned and looked up, before I said, Come on, Ceylan, let's go, and we got into that piece of Plexiglas junk and as I started the engine, and as we pulled away from the garden that smelled of the graveyard, the decrepit old house, my stupefied fat brother, I wondered with a shudder what Ceylan must think of me, because she was surely saying, Only somebody with a house, car, and family like this would attack a girl on a deserted beach in the middle of the night, but please, no, Ceylan, I can explain everything, but there's no time, see, we're already nearly to Turan's, but no, you have to listen to me, and I veered off turning the car toward the hill, and when Ceylan asked where we were going, I said, Let's get a little air and she didn't protest, so off we went, and I repeated that I had to explain, but because I didn't know where to start, my foot started pressing on the gas, and as we zoom downhill, I'm thinking, and still I'm racking my brain when we get to the hill, and we head down and I still haven't started talking, but by now my foot is pressing down so hard that the Anadol begins to shudder, but Ceylan doesn't say anything, and going around the curve the rear wheels skid, but Ceylan still doesn't speak, and we came to the Istanbul–Ankara road, with vehicles coming and going, just to say something I said, Should we have some fun with one of them, and Ceylan said, Let's go back now, you're very drunk, and I thought, Okay, you want to get away from me, but at least listen for a little, I want to explain things to you, I'll tell you, you'll understand I'm a good person, even though I'm not rich, I know what people like you think, and the rules you live by, I'm just like any of you, Ceylan, but when I got ready to confess it all seemed horribly crude and insincere, and I couldn't think of anything else to do except to step on the gas, okay, then, at least see that I'm not some bastard, because people like that are afraid to die, and, look, I'm not afraid, I'm doing one hundred thirty in this crappy car. Are you afraid that we might die, and I stepped on the gas even more, and soon, when we start downhill, we'll fly off the road and be killed, and when my friends in the dormitory set up a poker tournament in my memory, they better use some of the money they win off the rich boys to buy a marble gravestone for me, and I pressed harder still, but Ceylan still was keeping quiet, and I thought that the end really was very near, when oh my God, I saw people strolling down the middle of the road as if they were walking on the seashore, so I slammed on the brake and the car came about like a boat and started to slide, so that we were coming right at them, and they all ran for cover, still holding some cans, and the car skidded on before entering a field where it smacked into something, and once the engine died we could hear the crickets. Ceylan, I said, are you all right, were you scared, and she said, No, but we almost ran over them, and they came running toward us, furious, and when I saw the paint cans in their hands, the kind for spraying slogans on the walls, I decided I better not get into something here with a bunch of terrorists, so I tried to restart the car, and luckily it worked on the second try, but as I was maneuvering to get back on the road, those three hoodlums came up to the car and started to curse at us, and I said, Lock your door, and one of those fools must have bumped into us because he cried out, and they all started to pound on the back of the car, but too late, you idiots, we were on the road and we were out of there, though not entirely, because up ahead, we saw there were still others writing on a wall:

Yeni Mahalle will be the graveyard of Communists

and

We will free the Slave Turks of Central Asia

Good for you, at least you're not Communists, but I didn't want to tangle with nationalists either, so we fled quickly, and I said, Were you afraid, and Ceylan said No, and I wanted to talk over what we'd just been through, but she was giving only one-word answers, so we were quiet on the road back, and when I finally parked the car in front of Turan's, Ceylan immediately jumped out and ran off, so I went to have a look, nothing much had happened to the car, if my brother had spent some of his monthly salary on changing the bald tires instead of blowing it all on bottles of *rakı,* we wouldn't have been in this fix in the first place. I went inside to find them all spread out, lounging in the armchairs, on the couches, on the floor, half passed out, wrecked, as if they were all waiting for something, like death. Meticulously taking the cherry pits from his mouth, Mehmet, as though it were the last meaningful action to be taken in the world, was concentrating on throwing them at Turgay's head, and Turgay, sprawled on the wet floor, was doggedly cursing each pit that hit him and sighing hopelessly, while Zeynep was asleep, Fafa was buried deep in a fashion magazine, her eyes looking frozen, and Hülya was planting kisses on Turan's head as he lay there snoring; the others were listening to Ceylan with a cigarette in her hand tell about our adventure, when, lifting her head from the magazine, Fafa said, Come on, the sun is coming up, come on, let's do something.

22

Hasan Does His Duty

❧

D id you get the license plate?" said Mustafa.
"It was a white Anadol," said Serdar. "I'd know it if I saw it again."

"Did you get a look at the people inside?"

"A girl and a guy," said Yasar.

"Could you see their faces?" said Mustafa.

Nobody said anything, so I didn't either; I had recognized Metin, but I couldn't tell: Were you the other one or not, Nilgün? You could have killed us, and at this hour of the morning! . . . But I refuse to think about it anymore. I'm continuing to do my job, writing slogans on the walls in huge letters, while Serdar, Mustafa, and the new guys just sit there smoking cigarettes and cursing. But look at me, I'm still at it, bravely writing what we nationalists will do if the Communists ever dare come around here: we'll make this place their grave!

"Okay, enough for now, gentlemen," Mustafa said after a little while. "We'll pick up again tomorrow night." He was quiet for a second and then said to me, "Good! You did a good job! But you'd better be there tomorrow morning! I want to see what you do to that girl . . . "

After everyone split up, I walked home reading the things we had written on the walls, and still wondering: Were you next to Metin in the car, Nilgün? Where could she have been coming from? Maybe her grandmother is sick. She was out trying to find medicine with Metin . . . Was that it? Anyway I'll ask you tomorrow morning.

It was light out now, but when I got home the lamp was still burning. Thanks, Dad. He'd locked the window and the door and was fast asleep, not in his bed, but all by himself on the couch again, and actually I felt sorry for him, my poor crippled dad. I tapped on the window.

He'd barely gotten up to let me in before he started to yell and scream, so much that I thought he was going to hit me again, but no, he only went on about life's hardships and the importance of a high school diploma; he never hits me when he's on these topics. As I listened I lowered my head, hoping he would quiet down, but it didn't do any good. I can't believe that after working all night, on top of everything else that has happened to me, I have to listen to you now: so I went inside, got a handful of cherries from the fridge, and I was eating them when suddenly, God, he tried to take a swipe at me, and though I pulled away quickly, he managed to nail my hand, sending pits and cherries all over the floor. He was still talking as I bent down to pick them up and when he realized I wasn't listening he started to plead: Son, son, why don't you study, etc. At that point I felt sorry for him again and a bit ashamed, but what was I supposed to do? Then he smacked me on my shoulder, and I got mad again.

"If you hit me once more I'm going to leave home," I said.

"Go on, get out!" he said. "Next time I'm not opening the window!"

"Fine," I said. "I earn my own money anyway."

"Don't lie!" he said. "What are you doing in the street at this hour?" When my mother came from inside, he said, "This one's running away from home! He's never coming back."

His voice trembled, the way it would when someone's about to cry, like the howl of a lonely old dog with no master. My mother signaled me to go inside, and I went in without saying anything. My father went on for a while, screaming and shouting, and when he stopped they talked. Finally, they turned out the lights and it was quiet.

As for me, with the sun already peeking at the edge of my window, I went to my bed without bothering to get undressed. I just lay down like that, looking at the ceiling, a crack in the ceiling that would drip when there was heavy rain, leaving a stain there. I used to think that stain on the ceiling looked like an eagle, like this old eagle with its wings spread that would come and carry me away while I slept, and then I would no longer be a boy but turned into a girl!

I'll go find her on the beach at nine thirty, I'll say, Hi, Nilgün, do you recognize me, but she still doesn't answer, Look you're sulking, I'll say. But we don't have a lot of time, because unfortunately we're in danger, I'll say, you misunderstood me, I can explain, and I'll tell her everything, how they want me to tell her off, to rip the newspaper from her hands and shred it to pieces, Please, Nilgün, let them see that they don't have to do any of this, I say all that, and then Nilgün can go over to Mustafa, who's watching us from nearby, she can tell him herself what kind of person she is, and Mustafa will get embarrassed and maybe then Nilgün will understand that I love her and maybe she won't get mad and maybe even be happy, because in life anything's possible, you never know . . .

I was still looking at the wings of the stain on the ceiling. Yes, I'd say an eagle, or sometimes a kite. Water would drip out of it. But not in the old days, because my father still hadn't built this room yet.

But back then I wasn't so ashamed that our house was small, that my father sold lottery tickets, and my uncle was a dwarf house servant. I can't say I wasn't ashamed at all, because we still didn't have a well, and when I used to go with my mother to the fountain I was afraid that you would see us, Nilgün, because you had started to go hunting with Metin, and at that time we were such good friends that, remember, it was in the fall, when the people in those Beşevler, the Five Houses that had just been built, each exactly like the others, before the vines had grown all over them, when the owners and everyone else had gone back to Istanbul, one day at the beginning of September, you were still here and you came to my house with Metin, Faruk's old air rifle on your shoulder, and you said, Let's go hunt crows, you were all sweaty because you had climbed up the hill, and my mother gave you water, clean water, in the new Paşabahçe shatterproof glasses, and you drank it with pleasure, Nilgün, but Metin didn't, maybe because he thought our glasses were dirty, or because he thought our water was, then my mother said, If you like, go pick some grapes, children, the vineyard wasn't ours, she said, to answer Metin's question, but never mind, it's our neighbor's, what's the problem, go and have some, she said, but the two of you wouldn't go, and when I offered to go and pick some and bring them to you, you said, No, because they're not ours, but at least you drank from our new glass, Nilgün, Metin wouldn't even do that, because we were poor and my mother wore a head scarf.

The sun climbed higher and I could hear the birds start chirping in the trees. I was thinking, What's Mustafa up to, is he in bed, did he go to sleep, or is he waiting, too?

Someday not too far in the future, maybe another fifteen years, not more, I'll be working in my office, at my factory, when my secretary—no, not some slave as in the West, more of an assistant, a good Muslim girl—comes in and says, There are some nationalist volunteers outside who'd like to see you, their names are Mustafa and Serdar, and I say, Let me finish my work, and then after that, I make them wait awhile, and when my work is done, I push the new automatic intercom button, and I say, I can see them now, show them in, then Mustafa and Serdar speak to me all embarrassed and uncomfortable, Of course, I understand, I say, you're asking for help, fine, I'll take 10 million invitations from you, but I'm not taking them because I'm against communism and atheism, it's that I feel sorry for you, because I have no fear of Communists, I'm honest, I've never cheated people in business, and every year I give my tithe and my poor tax without fail, I've made my workers junior partners, they like me because I'm a good man, why should they get involved with Communists and unions, they know as well as I do that this factory provides an income for all of us, they know that there's no difference between them and me, why don't you join us in breaking the fast at the *iftar* I'm giving for them tonight, I'm very close to them, there are seven thousand workers under me, and when I say that, Mustafa and Serdar would be so amazed, they'd realize then what kind of person I am!

I heard the familiar sound of Halil's garbage truck chugging up the hill. The birds became quiet. I saw an ant walking across the floor. Poor little ant! I stuck out my finger and touched it lightly on the back, and it was confused. There are creatures so much more powerful than you, you have no idea, you poor ant. You're running and running, and then I put my finger in front of you and you turn and run back the way you came. I played with it a little more, and finally, I felt sorry for it; I wanted to think of happy things and so I thought about that glorious day I always think about.

That day, as I switch from one telephone to another calling out orders, I take the last telephone receiver that's held out to me and I say, Hello, is that Tunceli, I say, that glorious day, hello, how is it there, Fine, Commander, says the gruff voice on the other end, we've cleaned the place out of all the bad elements, I thank him, and for the very last call I phone Kars, What's the situation there? Just about normal, sir, they say, we're about to finish off the atheists here, and I say, You've done a good job, thank you, and after hanging up, I enter the hall with a large entourage behind me, where thousands of delegates give me a standing ovation and I say, as the Nationalist's Operation Lightning comes to a conclusion, I have just learned that we have crushed the last nests of Kurdish Red resistance in Tunceli and in our border city of Kars. And just as I am saying that paradise is no longer just a dream, my friends, there is not a single Communist atheist left alive in Turkey, my aide whispers into my ear, and I say, Oh really? Okay, I'm coming, and after passing through endless marble corridors, each door with armed guards opening onto the next, I enter the last of the forty rooms, and in a brightly lit corner, I see you, tied to a chair, and when my aide says, She's just been caught, sir, they say she's the leader of all the Communists, I say, Untie her immediately, it's beneath us to tie a lady's hands up, so they untie you, and I say, Leave us alone, please, and my aide and the men click their heels together, salute, and when they close the doors behind them, I look at you, at age forty you're even more beautiful, a mature woman, and as I offer you a cigarette I say, Do you recognize me, Comrade Nilgün Hanım, and you say, Yes, a little embarrassed, I recognize you, and there's silence for a bit, and we stare at each other, and suddenly I say, We won, we won, and we didn't leave Turkey to you atheists, so now are you sorry? Yes, you say, I'm sorry, and when I see your fingers trembling as they reach out for the pack of cigarettes I'm offering you, I say, Relax, no harm will ever come to women or girls from me and my friends, please be calm, we are completely devoted to the Turkish traditions that have come down over thousands of years, so you don't have to be afraid, I say, I won't be the one deciding your punishment, it will be the court of history and the judgment of the nation, and you say, I'm sorry, I'm sorry, Hasan, and I reply, It's no use repenting when it's too late, and unfortunately I can't be swayed by my emotions to forgive you, because I have a responsibility to my nation before anything else, and suddenly I look and you've started to take off your clothes, Nilgün, you're undressing and coming on to me, just like those shameless, immoral women I saw in the sex films I secretly went to see in Pendik, oh my God, she's telling me she loves me, you're trying to turn me on, but I'm disgusted by you, and I become ice cold, and while you plead, I call the guards and say, Take this sad excuse for Catherine the Great out of my sight, I have no intention of falling victim the way Baltacı Mehmet Pasha did, my nation suffered plenty because of Baltacı's weakness for the czarina's charms, but those days are over, and as the guards are taking you away, I go into another room and maybe I cry, and just because they reduced a girl like you to such an awful state, maybe for that alone, I decide I'll be even harder on those Communists, but then I wipe away my tears and I comfort myself thinking, so, I've been suffering all these years for nothing, and as I go take part in the victory celebrations, maybe I completely forget about you from that day on.

I turned over and looked at the floor from the edge of the bed; the ant had disappeared. When did you get away? The sun was higher in the sky. Seeing I was late, I bolted out of bed. I stopped to get something to eat in the kitchen and then went out the window without anybody seeing me. The birds were in the branches again. Tahsin's family was lining up their cherry baskets on the edge of the road that goes up the hill. By the time I got to the beach, the guard and the ticket guy had come, but Nilgün still wasn't there. So I went over by the breakwater and looked at the yachts and feeling very sleepy still, I sat down.

I'll call her up in a little while, I thought: Hello, Nilgün, listen, you are in danger, don't come to the beach or the store today, I'll say, in fact, don't leave the house from now on. Who's this? An old friend! Then I'll hang up on her abruptly! Will she guess who it is? Will she understand that I love her, and only want to protect her from danger?

If there's one thing I know, it's that we have to be respectful toward women, we can't just be ripping newspapers out of their hand and tearing them up! Woman is a pitiful creature, it's not right to treat her badly. My mother, for example, is such a good woman! I don't like people who show them disrespect, guys who only think about going to bed with them, rich guys and materialistic bastards. I know that with women you have to show that you are polite and gentle: How are you, please—after you, if you're walking with a woman your feet should slow down by themselves at just the sight of a door, and without even thinking, your hand should reach out to open it for her, Please allow me, I know how to talk to ladies and girls. You want to smoke like us, even on the street? Fine, you can smoke, it's your right, too, I'm not some backward, I can swoop in to light your cigarette with my locomotive-shaped lighter and talk to you with ease, just as I would with a man or a classmate, perfectly comfortable, if I want, if I just make a little effort, I wouldn't even blush or stammer, and then they'll see what kind of a person I am, they'll be surprised and embarrassed that they had got me all wrong . . . can you imagine? Grabbing the paper and ripping it up! Maybe Mustafa wasn't serious.

I got fed up looking at the sea and the yachts, so I headed back to the beach. Mustafa must have said it just as a joke, because, after all, Mustafa knows that you can't treat girls badly. I did it to test you, Mustafa will say, to see if you'd learned that discipline means absolute obedience! There's no need to mistreat that girl you love, Hasan!

When I got to the beach I saw that Nilgün was there and was stretched out like always. I was so sleepy that I didn't even get excited. I looked at her like I was looking at a statue. Then I sat down, Nilgün, I'm waiting for you.

And maybe Mustafa won't even come, he might have forgotten the whole thing, or decided it was so unimportant, he'd just stay in bed. The crowd was racing to the beach: cars from Istanbul, mothers, fathers, and children with baskets and beach balls.

I thought, Maybe I just won't do it. I'm not that kind of person! But then they'll say that he couldn't even get the newspaper out of the Communist girl's hand, let alone rip it up! They may even say, Well, he used to be an nationalist, but now he's a Communist; watch out for that Hasan Karataş from Cennethisar, don't let him in your group! But I'm not afraid of being isolated, I'll do big things on my own, they'll see.

"Hey! Wake up, man!"

I was startled. It was Mustafa. I got right up.

"Did the girl come?" he said.

"Over there," I said. "With the blue bathing suit."

"The one reading the book?" he said, giving you a dirty look, Nilgün. "You know what to do!" he said then. "Which shop is it?"

I showed him, then I asked for a cigarette, which he gave me, before going off a little ways to a spot where he would watch and wait.

I lit the cigarette, and as I started waiting, too, my eyes were fixed on the burning tip: I'm not an idiot, Nilgün, I'll say, I have strong convictions, last night we were out writing slogans on the walls despite the danger, see, I still have paint on my hands!

"Ah, you're smoking cigarettes. It's bad for you. You're so young."

Uncle Recep, carrying his string bags.

"It's the first time," I said.

"Throw it away, and go back home, son!" he said. "What are you up to around here again?"

I threw the cigarette away just to get rid of him. "I have a friend I'm going to study with, I'm waiting for him," I said. And I didn't ask him for money.

"Your father's coming to the funeral, isn't he?" he said.

He stood there for a minute, then went off, swaying in a weird way, like single horse pulling a wagon uphill: *tick-tack, tick-tack.*

A little later I looked in Nilgün's direction. She was getting out of the water and coming this way. I went to tell Mustafa.

"I'm going to the shop," he said, "If she buys *Cumhuriyet* as you said, I'll come outside first and cough. You know what to do then, right?"

I didn't say anything.

"Pay attention; I'll give you the signal!" he said and went off.

I slipped into the side street and waited. Mustafa went into the shop. A little later, you went in, Nilgün. I got all nervous, so I decided, Let me tie my sneaker laces a little tighter, and as I did I realized my hands were trembling.

First Mustafa came out, looked my way, and coughed. Then Nilgün came out, the newspaper in her hand. I started to follow her. She was really walking quickly, her feet touching the ground the way a sparrow hops along before taking flight: If you think you can confuse me with those beautiful legs you're mistaken. We moved away from the crowd. I looked back, there was no one but Mustafa. When I got close, Nilgün heard me coming and turned around.

"Hello, Nilgün!" I said.

"Hello," she said, before she turned and continued on.

"Just a minute!" I said. "Can we talk a little?"

She kept on walking as if she hadn't heard. I ran after her. "Stop!" I said. "Why won't you talk to me?" No reply. "Or have you done something wrong that you're ashamed of?" No answer still, she kept on walking. "Can't we talk like two civilized people?" Still no answer. "Or don't you even recognize me, Nilgün?"

When she starts to walk faster, I realize that there's no point shouting after her, so I run up beside her. Now we're walking together like two friends, and I'm talking.

"Why are you running away?" I'm saying. "What did I do to you?" She's silent. "Did I do something wrong? Tell me." She doesn't say anything. "Tell me why you won't even open your mouth?" She still doesn't say anything. "Fine," I say. "I know why you won't talk, should I tell you?" She doesn't say anything, and now I'm getting mad. "You have a low opinion of me, don't you?" I said. "You take me for some who-knows-what! But you're wrong, girl, you're wrong, and now you're going to understand why!"

I said that, but I didn't do anything, because I felt so ashamed I could have screamed. Just then, I saw those two fancy young gentlemen coming along the other way.

I was waiting, hoping that these two snobs wearing jackets and ties in this heat wouldn't get involved in our business. I drew back a little, so that they wouldn't get the wrong idea, and when I looked again Nilgün was practically running. Since her house was off the next corner, I started to run too. Behind me, Mustafa started running, too. When I turned the corner there was Nilgün, arm in arm with the dwarf and the string bag dangling from his side. I stopped behind them, frozen.

Mustafa caught up. "Coward," he said. "I'll show you."

"No!" I said. "Tomorrow! I'll show them!"

"Tomorrow, huh?"

At that moment I thought, What if I just take a swing at Mustafa? He'd be lying there, knocked out. Then he'd see I'm no coward. I don't like anybody assuming they've got me figured out. I am a completely different guy from what you think, do you understand this? Once these fists start flying, I'm not me anymore; I get so angry that it's like stepping outside of myself and standing there watching all this anger, and then even I'm afraid of this other person. I guess Mustafa understood, because he couldn't say anything, because he understood. So we walked on in silence. Because you understood that otherwise you'd be sorry, too, didn't you?

In the shop, there was only the shopkeeper. When we asked for *Cumhuriyet,* he thought I meant we wanted one copy, so he gave it to me, but when I said we want all of them, he understood, and because, like Mustafa, he was afraid of me, he let us have them. There was no sign of a garbage can. So after I ripped up the papers I just scattered them around, wherever. I also pulled down the pictures of naked women the shopkeeper had in the window and ripped them up too, the sickening weekly porno magazines. So, it seems I'm the one who has to clean up all this filth! Even Mustafa was surprised by my anger.

"Fine, okay, okay, that's enough now!" he was saying. He got me out of the shop. "Come to the coffeehouse this evening!" he said. "And be here again tomorrow morning."

I didn't answer at first. But as he was going off I asked him for a cigarette. He gave it to me.

23

Fatma Refuses to Live with Sin

❖

After Recep took away my breakfast tray, he went to the market. When he came back he had someone with him. I realized from the footsteps, light as a feather, that it was Nilgün. She came upstairs, opened my door, and had a look at me: her hair was damp, she had gone swimming in the sea. After she left nobody else stopped by my room until noon. I could barely hear Faruk and Nilgün talking downstairs over all the noise coming from the beach. That's the paradise on earth you wanted, Selâhattin. I got up to close my windows and shutters and then waited to have my lunch so I could drift off into my afternoon nap. But Recep, who had gone to some fisherman's funeral, was late to bring it, and I had no wish to go downstairs. Finally he did come with my tray and shut my door behind him.

The afternoon nap, my mother used to say, is the best of all kinds of sleep. One has the best dreams after eating lunch. Yes. I would perspire a little at first and then relax until I felt light as a swallow. Afterward, we'd open the window to let out the stale air and let the fresh air in, together with the green branches of the trees in the garden in Nisantasi, and also to let my dreams escape, because I used to believe that my dreams continued on without me from wherever I left off with them. Maybe the same thing happens when we die, my thoughts floating around the room, inside the furniture, between the shutters closed tight, swirling around and brushing against my table and bed, over the walls and the ceiling, so that somebody slowly cracking open the door would think they saw the shadows of my memories: Shut the door, I don't want my memories tainted, don't poison them, just let my thoughts float in here like angels until Judgment Day, beneath my ceiling, in the hush of this house. But I knew what they'd do after I died: one of them, the littlest, actually, let it slip from his mouth once. This place has gotten so old, Grandmother, said Metin one time when he was eager to sin, let's have it knocked down, let's build an apartment house in its place.

You have to get beyond that ridiculous prohibition called sin, as I have, Selâhattin used to say, have some *rakı* with me, just a sip, aren't you at all curious, it does no harm, on the contrary it's useful, it stimulates the mind. God forbid! Fine, then just say it for me once, Fatma, that's all, and let the sin be on your husband, just say, "There is no God," say it, Fatma, come on. God forbid! Fine, then listen to this, the most important article in my encyclopedia: listen, I've just finished it in the new script. From the article on *bilgi*—knowledge—under the letter *B* in the Latin alphabet, listen: *The source of all knowledge is experimentation . . . nothing that is unproven by experimentation or that cannot be proved by experimentation can be deemed valid . . .* Here is the crux of all our scientific knowledge, this sentence, in an instant it lays aside the whole problem of the existence of God, because this is a problem that cannot be proven by experimentation, the ontological proof is merely so much scholastic blather, divinity is a concept only for metaphysicians to play with, there is, I'm afraid, no place for God in the world of apples and pears and Fatmas . . . ha, ha, ha! Do you understand, Fatma, your God is no more! I don't have the patience to wait until my encyclopedia is finished, I've made an inquiry with an Armenian printer, I'm going to have this article published right away on its own. And I'm calling Avram the jeweler again, for the same reason: I can't have the progress of knowledge subject to your possessive girlish whims, you'll have to give me a nice piece from your box, I swear, atheism and secularism will do the whole country good, and if those idiotic fanatics try to stop my article from being sold, I'll just go among the crowd at Sirkeci train station and hand it out to people myself. You'll see, they'll take it gratefully! Because I've spent years sifting through French books for these pearls and writing them in a language my people can understand. So you see, Fatma, what I'm really burning to know is not whether they'll read it, what I can't wait to see is what they'll be like after they've read it!

Thank goodness that no one, except maybe his dwarf, would ever read those disgusting lies, that description of hell that my poor devil-led fool of a husband had laid out with such joy. I was the only one to know the horror.

Seven months after Selâhattin discovered he was going to die and three months after he passed, my Doğan was in Kemah; it was in the middle of winter; I was all alone in the house with the dwarf: it was snowing that night, and I shivered at the thought of how the snow was sticking on his grave, and I felt a great need to get warm. I'd been sitting by myself in the room where I'd gone to escape the reeking wine fumes coming out of his mouth; the pale irritating light of the lamp hardly made me feel any better, and as the snow was hitting the window, I found I couldn't even cry. I went upstairs. Thinking it might be warmer in there, I went into his room, where I was never allowed while he was alive, the room from which I used to hear his footsteps endlessly, the pacing back and forth. I slowly pushed open the door and there, shamelessly scattered everywhere, obnoxiously strewn about, on the tables, the armchairs, in the pigeonholes of the desk, the drawers, atop the books, and stuffed inside them, all over the floor and the windowsills, were endless piles of papers, covered with writing. I opened the door of the big ugly stove and began to stuff them inside. I waited a little after throwing in the match before adding more papers, writings, newspapers; the stove swallowed them all up so nicely, Selâhattin, together with your sins!

As your sins went up in smoke I felt myself warming up. "The work to which I've devoted my entire life: my beloved sin!" Well, what did the devil write? In the course of ripping up those papers and burning them, I was able to make some things out: Republic—the form of government we require . . . there are various kinds of republics . . . in his book on the subject De Passet tells us . . . 1342 . . . the newspaper brings word that it was established in Ankara this week . . . Fine . . . But we must on no account allow it to become like these people . . . Compare Darwin's theory with the Koran and explain the superiority of science with simple analogies that even the idiots would understand . . . An earthquake is a geological phenomenon, the shaking of the earth's crust . . . Woman is the fulfillment of man . . . Women can be divided into two groups . . . The first is natural women, those who enjoy the pleasures and joys that nature has given to them, relaxed, without problems, without worries, who usually come from the people, from the lower class . . . like Rousseau's wife, whom he never married . . . a servant, who gave Rousseau six children . . . The second kind of woman: ill tempered, authoritarian, supposedly refined, who insists on persuading you to accept her preconceived notions, cold women with no empathy, like Marie Antoinette . . . This second kind is so lacking in empathy that many scientists and philosophers sought understanding and the warmth of love among women of the lower orders . . . Rousseau's maid, Goethe's baker's daughter, or Marx's household servant . . . He had a child by her also . . . Engels adopted it. Why be ashamed? . . . There are many more examples . . . And so, great men saw their lives poisoned by problems they never deserved, all on account of their cold unloving wives, and they exhausted themselves with nothing to show for it, never finishing their books . . . And those children that the law and society consider bastards are a separate grief! . . . I wonder if one could make a zeppelin in the exact shape of a stork with no screw propeller in the rear . . . The airplane is a weapon of war now . . . A twenty-two-year-old man called Lindbergh was able to fly across the Atlantic Ocean last week . . . All of the sultans were idiots . . . But

Resat the puppet of the Unionists was the biggest idiot of all . . . The fact that the lizards in our garden lose their tails in accordance with Darwin's theory without having read any Darwin should not be seen as a miracle but as a triumph of human thought! . . .

As I kept reading and throwing things into the mouth of the stove in disgust, I was getting nicely warm. I have no idea how much I had read, how much I'd thrown into the fire, when the door opened. It was the dwarf, only seventeen at the time but already bold enough to say: What are you doing, Madam, this isn't right. You be quiet! Please don't burn them. I said be quiet! Isn't what you're doing wrong? When he still wouldn't be quiet, I reached for my cane. Then he was silent. Are there any other papers you have hidden? Tell the truth, dwarf, is this all there is? He was silent. So that means you have hidden things, you're not his son, dwarf, you're his bastard, and you have no right to anything, do you understand, bring them quickly without another word! All right, then, where's my cane? As I walked toward him, the little sneak ran clattering down the stairs. He called up from below: I don't have anything, Madam, I swear, I didn't hide a thing! Fine! I let it go for the moment. Then in the middle of the night I burst in on him, got him out of bed, and sent him out while I looked in every nook and cranny of his strange-smelling room, even the tiny padding of the little child's bed he used. It was true, he had nothing.

But that didn't ease my fears entirely. He'd hidden something somewhere, there was some scrap of paper that had escaped my eye, and Doğan, very much his father's son, would look and find it and have it printed, because he was always asking: Mother, where are those things my father wrote? I'm sorry, what was that, my dear? You know, he was writing for years, where are all those papers, Mother? I can't hear you, my child. I'm talking about my father's half-finished encyclopedia, Mother. I'm sorry, I can't hear. Maybe it has some value, my father devoted his whole life to it, I really want to read those articles, Mother, please would you give it to me. I wish I could hear you better, my child. Maybe we can have it printed someplace, as my father had always wished, because, the anniversary of May 27 is coming up, and they say the military is going to stage another coup. After this coup there'll be another turn back to Kemalism, they say, at least we could get some pieces, the interesting parts of the encyclopedia, published. Why don't you get them out from wherever they are and give them to me, Mother! Oh, these ears of mine! Where are those papers, for God's sake, I look and look and I can't find them, and the books are missing, too, there's nothing but those weird instruments left in the laundry room! Oh, dear, can't hear a thing! Mother, what have you done with the books and papers, you didn't just throw them away? I was quiet. You couldn't have just burned them, could you, tell me you didn't? He started to cry. Eventually he found comfort in *rakı*. I'll be like my father, I'll take up writing, too, there's no choice, just look around you, everything is getting worse, something must be done about this dangerous decline, this mounting idiocy, they can't all be so base or stupid, there must be some good ones among them, Mother. I know the minister of agriculture from school, we were in love with the same girl, but we were good friends, he was one class behind me, but we were together on the track team, we both threw shot put, he was very fat, but he had a heart of gold, anyway I'm writing him a long report. And General So-and-So, second in command of the general staff, he was a captain when I was the assistant district commissioner in Zile, he's a good man, he only ever wanted to do some good for the country, I'll send him a copy of that report, too, you have no idea, Mother, of the injustices taking place . . . Fine, but why are they your responsibility, son? If we see things and do nothing, we are as guilty ourselves, that's why, Mother, I'm sitting down to write so at least I won't bear that blame . . . You're more pathetic than your father, and a worse coward! . . . I'm not, Mother, I'm not. If I were a coward, I'd join them, it's my turn to be governor, but I've had it up to here, have you any idea what they do to those poor villagers? I've never cared to know, my son! They've got them up in those forsaken corners of the mountains where, as they say, even the birds don't fly and the caravans don't pass . . . It was my father who taught me that simply bothering to know about it doesn't do a bit of good! They just leave them up there, with no teacher and no doctor . . . What a shame that I wasn't able to teach you what my dearly departed father taught me, Doğan! How once a year you could snatch the harvest from their hands at a cheap price . . . What a shame, son, that you didn't take after me at all . . . They just leave them, Mother, leave them to their sad fate in that awful darkness and forget about them. He would go on and on, even after I'd stopped listening and gone off to my room where I'd sit and think: How strange, it's as though some strange force had made them different from everyone else, for some reason not content simply to go back and forth in peace between work and hearth! Whatever being had made them this way must be enjoying a good laugh watching me in my torment! . . . It was three, but I still couldn't sleep, I could hear the hubbub from the beach. Then my mind turned to the dwarf and I shuddered.

What if he'd written to Doğan from the village and stirred his pity. Or maybe his father had told Doğan. But at that point Selâhattin thought of nothing but his writing. In the summer after he finished university Doğan started to ask about them over and over again: Why did Recep and Ismail leave, Mother? Then one day he went off. When he came back a week later, he had them with him; they were no longer children: a dwarf and a cripple, dressed in rags! Why did you bring them here from their village, son, what business do they have in our house, I said. You know why I brought them, Mother, he said, and put them both in the room where the dwarf is now. The cripple left when he got his greedy hands on the money from the diamond that he forced Doğan to sell, but he didn't go far: every year when we went to the cemetery they showed me his house on the hill road! I always wondered why the dwarf stayed. They said it was because he was ashamed, because he was afraid to go out among regular people. After Doğan left, I'd sometimes hear Selâhattin off in some corner talking to him: Tell me, son, Selâhattin would say, what was life like in the village, was it really hard for you, did they make you pray, tell me, do you believe in God, tell me, how did your mother die? She was such a good woman, she had the beauty of our people, but, unfortunately, I had to finish this encyclopedia. The dwarf would be silent, and when I couldn't bear it anymore, I'd run off to my room and try to forget, but I could never get it out of my mind: What a good woman, she had the beauty of our people, what a good woman she was!

No, Selâhattin, she was just a sinful woman and a servant. She and her husband fled their village because of a blood feud and came to Gebze, and when he went to the military, leaving her in the care of a fisherman, and the fisherman's boat overturned and he drowned, this one could be seen over there, by the ruins of the dock, wretched, snot nosed, ragged, living off who knows what. So when the cook from Gerede became high-handed with Selâhattin, saying things like You don't believe in God, but God will show you, Selâhattin got rid of him and brought this disgusting wretch into the house. What can we do, Fatma, it's become so difficult to find decent domestic help. I'll have nothing to do with it, I said, but she learned the housework quickly, and when she made her first stuffed grape leaves Selâhattin said, What a capable woman, Fatma, and I could see right then and there what was going to happen and I was full of disgust, thinking, How strange that my mother should have brought me into this world just to witness other people's crimes and sins.

On cold winter nights, when noxious fumes were rising up from the *rakı* well of his mouth, Selâhattin, thinking I was asleep, would creep slowly downstairs, where, in the room that is now the dwarf's, she would be waiting for him, my God such a shameful thing, he would walk back on tiptoe, but I would see him with loathing. Later in order to enjoy himself with her more comfortably and "in perfect freedom," to use the expression he employed so frequently in the encyclopedia, he built that little shack by the chicken coop; when, in the middle of the night, he would wander out of his study completely drunk and stumble over there, I would sit in my room, with my knitting in my hand, motionless, and horrified to think of what they were doing.

Things he couldn't make me do he was now forcing upon that

poor woman; to immerse her completely in sin he must have given
her drink, before making her . . . God forbid, Fatma, don't even think
of it! Sometimes, when I slipped out into the room overlooking the
chicken house and stared at the gloomy sinful lights of the shack, I
would murmur to myself: There, at this very moment, maybe he's
kissing his bastards, telling them how there is no God, maybe they're
all laughing and maybe . . . Don't think of that, Fatma, don't think of
it! Then I would go back to my room full of shame, take up the vest I
was knitting for Doğan, and wait for Selâhattin's return: I'd hear him
come out of the shack an hour later, and a little after that he would
be stumbling up the stairs, no longer even bothering to be quiet, I
would open the door of my room a crack, and from that little opening I would follow him with devilish curiosity, fear, and loathing
until he went back into his study.

Once, as he was tottering up the stairs, he paused for a moment:
just then, I saw him look straight at the crack in the door and into
my eyes, and I was so afraid, I wanted to shut the door and quietly
return to my room, but it was too late, because Selâhattin started to
shout: Why are you always poking your nose out from there, cowardly woman! Isn't it enough you know where I'm going and what
I'm doing, must you stand by the door every night? I wanted to shut
the door and get away, but I couldn't take my hand off the handle, as
though I would somehow be party to the sin if I let go! He shouted
some more: I'm not ashamed of anything, Fatma, not anything! I
have moved beyond all the foolishness of the East, the guilt and
the sins, Fatma, do you understand? You're watching me for nothing: I am proud of the things that you are pleased to condemn and
find revolting! Then, swaying back and forth, he went up a few more
steps and yelled at the door I still held open a finger's breadth: I'm
proud, too, of that woman and of the children she bore me . . . She's
a hardworking woman, honest, honorable, direct, and beautiful! She
doesn't live simply to avoid guilt and sins as you do, and she has no
intention of learning how to use a knife and fork to become refined!
Hear what I'm going to say, listen to me carefully! His voice wasn't

belittling now, it was persuasive, and I was listening, even as I held fast to the door handle between us: There's nothing to be ashamed of here, Fatma, nothing disgusting, no need to accuse anyone, you see, we're free! It's only others who would limit our freedom! There's no one here but us, Fatma, you know that, it's as if we're living on a desert island, like Robinson Crusoe, we've left that whole cursed thing called society behind in Istanbul, and we won't return until the day I can overturn the whole East with my encyclopedia. Now hear me: at this moment I am coming from that shack, but what reason is there to hide it, you know that I was there with the serving woman's children, my children, Recep and Ismail; I got them a stove from Gebze, but it hasn't done any good, they're freezing out there, Fatma, and I can no longer have them shivering in the cold just for the sake of your crazy notions of morality, are you listening to me?

I understood and I was frightened; I continued listening to what he said as he pounded on the door frame begging tearfully, and I remained silent. A little later, he went into his room weeping, and I was astonished to hear so soon afterward that deep, peaceful, drunken snoring of his, and I stayed up thinking until dawn. It was snowing. I was staring out the window. The next morning at breakfast he told me exactly what I had already guessed.

That woman was serving us, when suddenly, just as the dwarf does now, she went off, down to the kitchen, as if she'd had her fill of serving, and Selâhattin whispered, You call them bastards, but they're human beings like any others, he said in a voice so incredibly soft and polite, as if he were telling me some secret or pleading with me for something: The poor boys, they're shivering in that shack, and they're so little, one of them is just two, the other barely three, Fatma, I've made my decision, I'm going to settle them with their mother here in this house! That little room is too small now. I'll put them in the room next door. Don't forget, in the end they're my children. Please don't oppose this with your foolish beliefs! I listened and I said nothing. When I came down for lunch he said it again, this time in a loud, forceful voice, and he added: I can no longer have them sleeping on the floor wrapped in those rags for blankets . . . Tomorrow when I go do the monthly shopping in Gebze . . . So, I thought, he's going to Gebze tomorrow! Then in the afternoon I thought: Maybe at dinner he'll say that we're all going to sit together at the table from now on. Because doesn't he say that we're all equal? But he didn't say it. He drank his *rakı,* reminded me that he would be going to Gebze in the morning, and without pause rose from the table and went off. I ran upstairs right away and from the back room watched him from behind: March off, Satan, swaying over the snow sparkling in the moonlight toward the sinful light of the shack, tomorrow you'll see! I stared at the snowy garden with one eye on that dim light, so ugly, of the shack's lamp until he returned. When he did, this time he came to my room and said: Don't put too much faith in the fact that for the past two years the law would have required a court case for me to divorce you and that I couldn't have taken a second wife even if I'd wanted to! There's nothing left between us but that ridiculous contract called marriage, Fatma! Anyway, according to the conditions of that agreement, when we made it under Ottoman law, I could have divorced you anytime with just two words, or taken another wife as well, but I simply didn't feel the need. Do you understand? He went on talking some more, and I listened, until he said once more that he was going to Gebze in the morning and went off to bed.

But enough, Fatma, don't think anymore! I felt myself perspiring under the quilt. Then it occurred to me: Could the dwarf be telling them? Did you know that your grandmother used to come at us with that cane in her hand . . . !

I pulled the quilt over my head, but I still heard the noise from the beach, and I said to myself, Now I realize how nice those lonely winter nights were, when I had the silence of the night all to myself, when everything was stone still, I pressed my ear into the soft darkness of the pillow, I imagined that deep lonely silence of the world, as though it were coming from outside of time, the world was making itself known to me from under the pillow: Selâhattin went to Gebze the next day. The day of judgment seemed so far off back then! I was all by myself in the house. How far away they were, the bodies that didn't decay even in the tomb! As I'd decided, I picked up my cane, went downstairs and out into the snowy garden. Making tracks in the melting snow I walked quickly over to the nest of sin that devil called the shack. They were still far off, the bats, the rattlesnakes, the skeletons, so far away! I got to the shack, knocked at the door, waited a little, and the wretched simple woman, the foolish servant, opened the door. I pushed my way in, So these are your bastards, she even tried to restrain my hand! Please don't, *hanımefendi,* please don't, what wrong have the children done? Hit me instead of them, *hanımefendi,* what sin have they committed? Oh God, children, run, run! They couldn't run away! Rotten little bastards! They couldn't run away and I hit them and—What? You dare to raise your hand to me? So I hit their mother, too, and when she tried to hit me back I hit her even more, and in the end, Selâhattin, it was that woman you said was so hardworking and sturdy, she was the one who crumbled, not I! Then I looked around inside that disgusting nest of sin that you planted at the foot of the garden as I listened to the sounds of your bastards crying. Wooden spoons, tin knives, the chipped and broken dishes from my mother's sets, and look, Fatma, all those things that you thought were lost are here and in fine shape, the trunks serving as tables, rags, cloth remnants, stovepipes, bedding mats laid on the floor, newspaper stuffed under the door and window frames, oh God, what sickening piles of stained rags, heaps of paper, burnt matches, a broken table, scraps of wood in emptied tin cans, overturned old chairs, clothespins, empty *rakı* and wine bottles, bits of broken glass on the floor, dear God, and those bastards continuing to wail, I was sickened, and when Selâhattin returned that evening he shed a few tears, and ten days later he bundled them off to the village far away.

Fine, Fatma, as you wish, but what you did was inhuman, you broke the little one's leg, I don't know what you did to the big one, he's bruised all over and acts like he's suffered a stroke. I'll put up with all of this but only for the sake of my encyclopedia, sending them off this way, I've found a poor old man who is willing to adopt them in exchange for a goodly sum. I'll have to call Avram the jeweler again soon, well, what can we do, the price of our sins, okay, fine, fine, don't start that again, you've committed no sins, for the price of my sins, then, only from now on don't ask me why I drink so much, leave me in peace, you go work in your empty kitchen, I'm going upstairs to write the entry on infinity and clocks now, before you bring out any more of my demons, go lock yourself in your room, get into your cold bed, lie there all night like a little owl, staring at the ceiling, unable to sleep.

I'm still lying here and I still can't sleep. When night comes and I'm all alone, then I'll breathe in the scent of these things, taste them, touch them with my hand, and I'll think: The water, the pitcher, the keys, the handkerchief, the peach, the cologne, the plate, the table, the clock . . . They all sit there, just like me, all around me in the quiet emptiness, they creak, they rattle, in the silence of the night, they seem to be purifying themselves of sin, of guilt. It's then, at night, that time is truly time, and all the objects come closer to me, just as I come closer to myself.

24

Faruk and Nilgün See Everything
from Above

❧

In my dream, an old man in a cape was twirling around me and shouting, "Faruk, Faruk!" I gathered he was going to tell me the secret of history, but he was dragging things out to the point that I couldn't bear the anticipation anymore, and I woke up drenched in sweat. I could hear the noise from the beach now, the sounds of the cars and motorboats coming from over by the garden gate. The long afternoon nap had done no good: I was still exhausted.

I went downstairs and into the kitchen, and as I grabbed hold of the refrigerator door handle in my habitual way, I felt that same sense of anticipation, as if something would happen in my life, something, whatever it was, that would make me forget about the archives, those stories, and history. Opening the door, I looked into the fridge's gleaming interior as if peering into a jeweler's window: the sight of the pitchers, bottles in different colors, tomatoes, eggs, cherries, somehow beguiled me and made me forget my cares. But they also seemed to say: No, you can't be distracted by us anymore; you must find consolation by renouncing the pleasures of the world and cutting yourself off from it. And I wondered: Should I be like my grandfather, like my father, and abandon everything and shut myself up here, go every day to Gebze and sit at the desk devoting myself to a single work, a composition of millions of words, with no beginning and no end? Should I do all that not to change the world but merely to describe how things are?

The cool wind had picked up. The clouds had drawn closer, too. There was going to be a *lodos,* the strong southerly wind. Seeing Recep's closed shutters, I concluded he must be asleep in his room. Nilgün was sitting over by the chicken coop with her sandals off, pressing her bare feet against the earth. I wandered around in the garden for a bit, playing with the well and the pump a little, like a bored child, remembering my adolescence. When I started thinking about my wife again, I went upstairs, turned into my room, and randomly opened a volume of Evliya Çelebi's travels, reading whatever caught my eye.

He was telling of a trip through Western Anatolia in the mid-seventeenth century: he described Akhisar, the town of Marmara, then a small village, and the hot springs of the town. The waters of the hot spring coated a person's skin like wax and were supposed to be good for leprosy if one drank of them for forty days. Then I read how he'd had one of the pools repaired and cleaned, bathing in it with great pleasure. I reread this part and rather envied Evliya for being able to enjoy himself with no feeling of guilt or sin; I wished I could put myself in his place. He had the date of restoration inscribed on one of the columns around the pool. Later, he went through Gediz on horseback. He wrote of all these things without pause, in an easy and assured rhythm, with the relentless enthusiasm of a drummer striking his instrument in the *mehter* military band. I closed the book and thought about how he was able to do this, how he could match so nicely what he'd done with what he wrote and how he managed to see himself from the outside, as though looking at someone else. If I tried to do the same thing, for example, and tell my friend these things in a letter, it wouldn't be nearly as clear or as genial: I'd be intruding myself into things; my confused and guilty mind would cast a veil over the naked reality of everything. What I'd wind up doing and what I'd intended, the things as they are and my judgments of them, they would all get mixed up together, and no matter how painstakingly I pressed my nose against the surfaces of things, I'd never be able to establish as direct and true a relationship as Evliya had.

I opened the book and read some more, about the city of Turgutlu, the city of Nif, and Ulucaklı and a nice evening spent there: "We pitched our tents alongside an excellent spring, got ourselves a nice fat lamb, and without a worry or a care, we made kebabs and ate them." And so: pleasure and good cheer rendered as plain and simple as the natural world. The world is a place to be described and experienced as it is, usually with equanimity, occasionally with gusto or as something bittersweet; but it's not a place for finding fault or cause for anger while you're in it.

Maybe sly Evliya was only fooling his readers. Maybe he was actually someone not unlike me except he knew how to write well, an able liar: maybe he sees the trees and birds, houses and walls, no differently than I do, but he can trick you with his literary skill. I couldn't convince myself one way or the other, but after reading a little more, I decided this was no case of skill alone but rather of intuition and an open mind. Evliya's awareness of the world, the trees, houses, and people, was utterly different from ours. Then I wondered how this could be, how could Evliya's mind have developed this way. After I drink a lot and feel really sorry for myself, thinking about my wife, I sometimes call out desperately for someone or something, as if trapped in a nightmare that I can't wake up from and escape. It was with that sort of despair that I was now asking my question: Can't I be like him, can't I make my thoughts, the structure of my brain, like his? Couldn't I portray the world from start to finish with the same clarity as he does?

I closed the book and tossed it aside. I cheered myself by saying there was no reason I couldn't do it, or at least devote my life to this ideal with real determination. I could start as he did by describing the world and history from whatever point I first encountered each particular part of it. It would just be a matter of lining up the facts, as he does when he tells who had so many *akçe* in Manisa, so many fiefs, so many *timar* holdings, so many troops. All these details are just sitting in the archives anyway, waiting for me. I could transcribe those documents with the same ease that Evliya talked about buildings, traditions, and customs. And I could present them without inserting my own judgments at all, just as he does. I'd add only telling details, as when he tells us some mosque was covered with tiles or with lead. That way, my history would be nothing more than a seamless picture of things, just like Evliya's voluminous travels. Secure in this knowledge, I could interrupt my endless succession of facts once in a while, as he does, to acknowledge that there are other things in the world and so I'd write at the head of a page

Story

just to let my readers know that my narrative has otherwise been scrubbed clean of those pleasant tales typically offered for people who expect and enjoy them. If someone should bother someday to read my work, which will run significantly longer than Evliya Çelebi's six thousand pages, he would find there in black and white the whole cloudy mass of history exactly as it exists in my mind, and as in Evliya, natural things, like a tree, a bird, a pebble, will give the reader to feel that behind each description is an equally natural reality. In this way I'll free myself at last from the strange worms of history that I feel wandering through the folds of my brain. On that day of liberation, perhaps I'll finally go swim in the sea with as much pleasure as Evliya found in his pool.

A car was obnoxiously blowing its horn. I quickly got up from the bed and went downstairs and out into the garden. The wind had picked up, the clouds were closer: rain was on the way. I lit a cigarette, walked across the garden, and found myself out on the street walking. Yes, show me now whatever you have to show me, all you walls, windows, cars, balconies, and people cooking on them, beach balls, sandals, inflatable life preservers, flip-flops, bottles, suntan lotions, boxes, shirts, towels, bags, legs, skirts, women, men, children, bugs, show me, show me your dismal faces . . . I want to press my nose up against every surface and lose myself, forget myself staring anew at the neon lights, at the Plexiglas billboards, at the political slogans, at the televisions, at the corners of shops, at the pictures in the newspaper, at the tawdry advertisements.

A sailboat slowly making its way toward the jetty to escape the southerly wind was gently rocking back and forth in the waves that were not yet big. As it swayed, it seemed unaware of the subconscious that was tossing it about: happy boat! I walked toward the coffeehouse. It was crowded, and outside, the corners of the tablecloths were flapping in the wind, but thanks to the rubber clips put on the edges of the tables, the mothers and fathers and little ones could enjoy their tea and soda pop in peace. Offshore, they were having a hard time taking down the sail, now full of the wind. The white canvas resisted with the fluttering despair of a pigeon's wing, but to no avail: in the end, they managed to lower it. If I put aside this game called history, what would it matter? Should I sit and have a tea? There was no empty table outside, but going over to the window I could see men playing cards within and empty tables. The card players studied their hands, then put them down as though they had wearied themselves doing this and now needed to relax. One of them picked up the cards he'd laid down and shuffled them. As I absently watched him shuffling, I thought of something. Yes, yes, a deck of cards could solve everything!

On my way home I was thinking like this:

I'll take all those crimes and robberies, wars and villagers, generals and crooks, that are asleep in the silence of the archives and write each of them down, one by one, on slips of paper the size of playing cards. Then I'll shuffle that awesome deck consisting of hundreds—no, millions—of cards, just as you shuffle a deck of playing cards, but, of course, with much more difficulty, perhaps using special machines, like those lottery machines in front of notaries, and I'll place them in the hands of my readers! And I'll tell them: None of these has any connection with any other, preceding or following, front or back, cause or effect. Come, young reader, this is life and history, read it as you will. Everything that exists is in here, it all simply exists, but there's no story binding it together. Then the disappointed young reader will ask: No story at all? At that point, appreciating his point of view, I'll say, You're right, at this age you do need a story to explain everything just so you can live in peace, otherwise you'd come unhinged. And with that, as if slipping a joker into my deck of millions of cards, I'd write

Story

and begin to gather together the cards in a way that tells a tale. But no sooner have I done that than the young reader peppers me with questions: But what's the meaning of all of this? What does it add up to? To what conclusion are you leading me? What should we believe? What's right, what's wrong? What is life? What should I do?

As I passed by the beach, the sun went in behind the clouds, and the whole mass of people covering the sand suddenly had no purpose for being there. I tried to imagine them stretched out not on the sand but on a glacier, their business being not to sunbathe but rather to warm up the ice sheet, the way hens brood on their eggs. I recognized my intention: to break the chain of causality, to free myself of the moral imperative of necessity. If what they were lying on were ice instead of sand, I could recover my innocence; under such freedom I could do anything, anything was possible if one's imagination was free. I walked on.

The sun came out again. I went to the store and asked for three bottles of beer. While the clerk was putting the beer into a brown paper bag, I tried to find a resemblance between another customer—a short ugly old man with a big forehead who was waiting there—and Edward G. Robinson. The amazing thing was he really did look like him, from the pointy noise to the little teeth and the mole on his cheek. But he also had the big head, and there was a mustache. So, to ask the question that was central to the hopeless social sciences of a non-Western country: How does the physical construct we have before us differ from the original of which it is a poor copy? The answer could be a bald head and a mustache or, equally, it could be democracy and industry. I came eye to eye with the fake Edward G. Robinson. Suddenly he said what he felt: Sir, do you know how hard it is for me to spend my whole life as a pale copy of someone else! My wife and children look at the real Edward G. Robinson and then criticize me for the ways in which I don't look enough like him, as though it were my fault. Is it a crime to resemble him somewhat, for God's sake, tell me, can't a person just be himself, if that guy hadn't been a famous actor what would have happened, what fault could they have found with me then? I thought, and I told him that they'd have just found some other famous original and criticized your inadequate resemblance to him. Yes, of course, you're right, sir, tell me, are you a sociologist or something, or perhaps a professor? An associate professor, actually! Then the aged Edward G. Robinson slowly picked up his cheese and left. I took my bottles; I, too, had had enough for now.

At home, I put the beers in the fridge, but the devil got to me as I was closing the door, and I poured myself a glass of *rakı,* having it on an empty stomach as though it were medicine, and I went to find Nilgün. She was waiting for me so we could go out. Her hair and the pages of her book were fluttering in the wind. I said there was nothing to see in the neighborhood, so we decided to take the car. I went upstairs for the keys, getting my notebook, too, then I picked up the *rakı* bottle, a bottle of water, and some beers from the kitchen, not forgetting the opener. When she saw what I was bringing, Nilgün ran off and got the radio. The car started up with a whine and cough. We made our way slowly through the crowd coming from the beach, and, as we left the neighborhood toward the open spaces, a bolt of lightning flashed very far off. The elegant thunder clap came much later.

"Where should we go?" I said after a while. "To your caravan-serai with the plague," said Nilgün. "*Nights of Plague and Nights of Paradise*," I muttered. "Is that a novel you're reading?" said Nilgün in astonishment. "Do you know," I said, suddenly more animated, "this whole idea of the plague is getting to me more and more. Last night I remembered having read somewhere that it was plague which allowed Cortez to defeat the Aztecs and take Mexico City with such a small army. When plague broke out in the city, the Aztecs decided that God must be on the side of Cortez." "That's great," said Nilgün. "Now, just uncover our plague, connect it with some other events, and you'll be on your way." "But what if there is no such thing." "Then you won't be!" "And what do I do then?" "You'll do what you've always done, keep tinkering with history." "I'm afraid I won't be able to do that anymore." "Why do you refuse to believe you could be a good historian?" "Because I know that people can't be anything in Turkey." "Nonsense." "Yes, you better learn that now, that's how this country is. Give me some of the *rakı*." "Oh no, you don't! Look how pretty it is here. Cows and everything. Auntie Cennet's cows." "Cows!" I bleated. "I'm surrounded by them every day!" "Seriously, aren't you just looking for an excuse to give up on yourself?" said Nilgün. "Exactly, so pass the *rakı*!" "But why give up like that?" said Nilgün. "Isn't that a waste? A man like you?" "Lots of people give up. What's so wasteful about my case?" "Well, sir, for one thing you've spent much more time studying than they have!" Nilgün said in a teasing voice. "You actually want to say that seriously, but you don't dare, am I right?" "Actually, yes," said Nilgün, this time with conviction. "Why should a person give up on himself for noth-ing?" "It's not for nothing," I said. "When I give up on myself I'll be happy. I'll be myself then." "But you are yourself now," said Nilgün, with a slight hesitation. "Where are you going?" "Up there," I said, suddenly getting enthusiastic. "Up where?" she said. "Wherever we can have the best view of everything. All of it together . . ." "All of what?" "Maybe if I can see everything at once . . ." "Maybe what?" said Nilgün, but I was pensively unresponsive.

Silently, we went up the hill, passing Ismail's house. I turned onto the Darıca Road, going by the cemetery, and then took the old dirt road that ran behind the cement factory, and we swayed back and forth as the car rumbled up the road that had been left rutted by the rain. When we got to the top it had started to sprinkle. I turned the nose of the car toward the view, stopped, and, like the young people who came here from Cennethisar in the middle of the night to kiss, we gazed at the view: the shore that twisted and turned as far as Tuzla, the factories, vacation villages, the campsites of bank employees, the olive groves fast disappearing, the cherry trees, the agricultural college, the meadow where Mehmet the Conqueror died, the barge on the sea, the trees, houses, shadows, all were being swallowed up by the rain that was gradually advancing on us from Tuzla Point. We saw the quivering white trace of the thunderstorm on the sea. I filled my glass with the remains of the *rakı* bottle and drank up.

"You'll ruin your stomach!" said Nilgün. "Why do you think my wife left me?" I said. There was a brief silence; then Nilgün said carefully, reluctantly, "I thought the decision was mutual." "No, she just left me." "No." "Actually, yes," I said. "Hey, look at the rain!" "I don't understand." "Don't understand what? The rain? If you drank you'd understand more. Why don't you drink? Maybe you consider it a sign of defeat?" "No, I don't think like that." "Yes, you do, I know what you think. So I'm surrendering, so what?" "But you haven't even declared a war yet," said Nilgün. "I'm surrendering because I can't stand living with two souls. Do you ever feel that way: sometimes I think I'm two people. But I've made up my mind, I'm not going to do it anymore. I'm going to be one person, one whole, completely healthy person. I love the carpet commercials on television, and those for refrigerators overflowing with food, I love my students who raise their hands during exams and ask, Professor, can we start from the second question? I love the magazine supplements of the newspapers, guys who hug one another when they drink, the ads for night schools and sausage that you see inside buses. Do you understand?" "A little," said Nilgün in a melancholy way. "The sky looks bad, doesn't it?" "Yes . . . " "Well, I'm drunk." "You couldn't be drunk on what you've had." So I opened one of the bottles of beer, and as I drank from it I said, "Well, what do you think looking down at everything from up here?" "You can't see everything . . . ," said Nilgün seeming cheerful now. "What if you could? I remember a passage from *The Praise of Folly:* if someone were to go to the moon and look down at the earth and see everything happening all at once, what would he think?" "Maybe he would think it was all confusion." "Yes," I said, and suddenly I recalled, " 'This matter of the imagination seems confused as well . . . ' " "What's that from?" "It's a poem of Nedim's from the early eighteenth century!" I said. "His capping off a *ghazal* of Nesati's. It just stuck in my mind." "Recite a little more!" "I don't remember any more. At the moment, however, I'm rereading Evliya's travels. Why do you suppose we're not more like him?" "What do you mean?" "Well, this majestic poet and a singular soul, he manages to be himself. I can't do it. Can you?" "I guess I haven't really thought about it enough," said Nilgün. "Oh," I said. "So cautious. You're terrified to take one step outside of your books, you can't help but keep the faith, like my colleagues . . . Look, the rain's made the factory disappear. What a strange place this world is." "What do you mean?" "I don't know . . . Am I boring you?" "Not at all." "We should have brought Recep along." "He wouldn't have come." "Right, he'd be embarrassed." "I really like Recep," said Nilgün. "Chops!" "What?" "That's the sneaky dwarf in one of Dickens's novels . . ." "Faruk, you are really cruel." "Yesterday he was trying to ask me about some historical event in Üsküdar, I think." "What did he ask?" "I didn't really give him a chance to ask! Look what he showed me today!" "You really are cruel." "A list that our grandfather wrote." "Our grandfather?" I reached in and pulled it out of my notebook. "Where'd you get that?" "I told you, Recep gave it to me!" I said and began to read aloud. " 'Knowledge, hats, pictures, commerce, submarines . . . ' " "I don't get it." "List of things lacking in our poor Turkey." "You know Recep's nephew Hasan?" "No." "I think that Hasan has been following me, Faruk." "Shall I continue with the list?" "I'm telling you he's following me." "Why should he be following you? Let's see, 'submarines, a bourgeoisie, the art of painting, steam power, chess, a zoo . . . ' " "I just don't get it." "You never even go out—how could he be following you . . . 'factories, professors, discipline.' Pretty funny, isn't it?" "Every time I come back from the beach this Hasan is behind me." "Maybe he wants to be friends." "Yes, that's what he said." "Well, that explains it . . . Our grandfather had given this matter some real thought, all those years ago, let's see, 'zoo, factories, professors'—well, I think we have enough professors by now—'mathematics, principles, sidewalk,' and then he wrote with a different pen 'the fear of death' and 'the awareness of nothingness' and 'liberty.' " "That's enough, Faruk." "Maybe he's in love with you." "Something like that, I suppose." "Now, here's his list of the things we have an excess of: 'men, villagers, bureaucrats, Muslims, soldiers, women, children.' " "Those don't seem funny to me." " 'Coffee, laziness, arrogance, bribery, sleepiness, fear, porters . . . minarets, honor, cats, dogs, guests, family and friends, bedbugs, oaths, beggars . . .' " "Enough!" " 'Garlic, onions, servants, shopkeepers'—certainly too many of all of those—'little shops, imams . . .' " "You're making this up." "I'm not. Take a look." "It's in the old script." "Recep showed this to me today, read it, he said our grandfather gave it to him." "Why would he have given it to him?" "I don't know." "Look at the rain! Is that an airplane I hear?" "Yes!" "In this weather!" "The plane is such an incredible thing!" "Yes!" "Imagine we were in that plane right now." "It would probably crash. Faruk, let's go back, I've had enough." "My wife always used to say that. First, tell me what you think of me." "What I think of you? I love you very much, Faruk." "Besides that." "I wish you wouldn't drink so much." "And?" "And why are you like this, my wonderful sweet brother?" "Like what?" "I want you to be happy!" "You think I'm no fun? Wait, let me entertain you. Where's my notebook? Hand it here! Listen: 'Butcher Halil's twenty-one *akçe*'s worth of beef were weighed and came out one hundred twenty dirhems short.' The date, the thirteenth of Zilhicce 1023, so that's, let's see,

January fourteenth 1615." "But what does it mean?" "The meaning is very clear: 'The servant Isa robbed his master Ahmet of thirty thousand *akçe,* a saddle, a horse, two swords, and a shield, then took refuge with someone named Ramazan.'" "Very interesting! Maybe you should turn on the windshield wipers." "Interesting? What's interesting about it?" "It makes me glad that these things intrigue you, but please, dear brother, don't drink so much." "Nilgün, would you like to come stay with me?" "What?" "Not in this car, at my house, I'm very serious now, instead of living with our aunt in Istanbul, Nilgün, come stay with me. There's a huge empty room and I'm all alone." There was a silence. "Thank you, it is a good idea," said Nilgün. "Well?" "I'm just wondering if my aunt and her family would think it was rude." "Okay," I said. "Let's go back." I turned on the ignition and started the windshield wipers.

25

Metin Pushes His Luck and His Car

⚜

Because everyone had had such a good time the night before, they decided that the best thing would be to do it again, and that's how we wound up hanging around Turan's a second night. But when everyone started complaining about having to listen to the same music, too, Funda started pushing Ceylan to go home and get her best of Elvis album to liven things up.

"In this rain?"

"I have my car, Ceylan," I said cautiously.

And so Ceylan and I, just the two of us, left the house, and that drowsy, cranky bunch slowly being poisoned by the boredom of the awful music, and we headed off in my brother's old Anadol. We sailed along saying nothing as the raindrops dripped off the leaves, the wet, dark road suddenly appeared in the light of the old car's dim headlamps, and the rusty windshield wipers kept up their sad whispering. When we stopped in front of Ceylan's house, I waited as she leaped out toward the door and followed her orange skirt, which was dazzling even in the gloomy rain. Then when the lights in the house went on, I tried to imagine Ceylan going from room to room and what she was doing there. What a strange thing love is! A little later Ceylan came running out with the record in her hand and got into the car.

"I had a fight with my mother!" she said. " 'Where do you think you are going at *this* hour!' " she said, mimicking her mother.

We were silent again, until I drove right past Turan's house without even slowing. Ceylan asked, nervously, even suspiciously, "Where are we going?"

"I'm getting tired of those guys! Let's go for a spin, okay, Ceylan? I'm really bored, and it would be nice to get some air!"

"Okay, but not a long one, they're waiting."

I went slowly through the back streets, totally pleased with myself. When I saw the pale lights from the little houses of those decent, ordinary folks peering out from their windows or from their little balconies at the trees to see whether the rain was letting up, I thought, Oh, what a fool I am to believe that we could be like this, that we could get married, that we could even have children. But when it came time to go back, I pulled another childish move and instead of heading toward Turan's, I left the neighborhood and started speeding up the hill.

"What are you doing?" she asked.

I didn't answer or even turn my head, but just kept going, my eyes glued to the road, like a good race driver. Then, even though she would know it was a lie, I said that we had to get gas.

"No, let's go back now!" she said. "They're waiting for us."

"I just want to be alone for a little bit so we can talk, Ceylan."

"About what?" she said sternly.

"What do you think about what happened last night?"

"I don't think anything! Things like that happen, we were both drunk."

"Is that all you've got to say?" I said resentfully as I pressed down harder on the gas.

"Come on, Metin, let's go back. It's rude."

"I'll never forget last night!" Cringing at the cheesiness of my own words.

"Well, you drank a lot, it'd be better if you didn't drink so much again!"

"No, not because of that!" I couldn't help taking her hand, which was resting on the seat cushion. Her little hand was burning hot, but she didn't pull it back as I had feared. So I said, "I love you," feeling very ashamed.

"Let's go back!"

I squeezed her hand tighter and thought of my mother, whom I can barely remember, and as I tried to put my arms around Ceylan, she screamed.

"Look out!"

A pair of mercilessly powerful lights was in my eyes, coming straight at us, so I pulled sharply to the right. A long truck passed like a train with a huge roar, blaring its horrible shrill horn. Since I had forgotten to step on the clutch while leaning on the brake, the old Anadol shuddered to a halt as the engine stalled. And then I couldn't hear anything but the song of the crickets.

"Were you afraid?" I said.

"No. Let's go right back, it's getting late!"

I turned the ignition key, but the motor wouldn't start. I tried it again, but still no luck. I got out of the car and tried to get it going with a push, but that didn't work either. Working myself into a sweat, I finally managed to push it onto the flat road. Then I got in, turned off the lights to save the battery, and let the old Anadol slide quickly and silently down the long hill.

As the tires sped up, they made a nice sound on the wet asphalt, and we went gliding downhill like a ship setting sail in the black darkness of the open sea. A few times I said, Let me try the motor, but it still didn't work. When a bolt of lightning struck somewhere in the distance, in the bright yellow light that filled the sky we could see people writing slogans on the walls. After that I didn't use the brake at all, even as we made the curve, and with the momentum from the hill we were able to glide all the way down to the train bridge and after that very slowly as far as the gas station on the Ankara highway. At the gas station I got out of the car and went into the office. Leaning over the table, I woke up the attendant and told him the engine wouldn't start and the clutch seemed to be broken. I asked if there was anybody who knew about Anadols.

"It doesn't have to be somebody for Anadols," the attendant said. "Just wait a minute!"

In a Mobil oil ad that was on the wall, the model holding a can of gasoline looked incredibly like Ceylan. I returned to the car stupefied.

"I love you, Ceylan!"

She was angrily smoking a cigarette. "We're late!"

"I said I love you."

We must have just been staring emptily at each another. When I couldn't take it anymore, I made as if I'd forgotten something, got out of the car, and quickly walked off. I found a dark corner, not too far, and just watched from a distance. In the dim light of the irritating neon sign blinking overhead, the cigarette smoker was only a shadow. I continued sweating as I saw the red tip of the cigarette flare up every few seconds. I must have stayed there like that for almost half an hour, watching her and feeling like a low-class sneak. Then I went to a stand a little ways down the road and bought a chocolate, the brand you see advertised most on television. Finally, I went back to the car and sat down next to her.

"Where were you? I was worried," she said. "We're terribly late. They'll be wondering what happened."

"Look, I got you a present."

"Oh, hazelnut! I don't like that one."

I told her I loved her; she didn't react; I tried again, then let my head fall on the hand she had in her lap. And from there I was able to quickly kiss her nervous fidgeting hand a few times, and then, as if I were afraid of something getting away from me, I took her hand in mine. After kissing it some more I lifted my head up so I could get some fresh air, and so that I might not drown in the despair I felt engulfing me.

"People are watching!" she said.

I retreated for the moment and went over to watch a family of laborers returning from Germany for the summer. They'd stopped for gas, but the light above the pumps must have been broken, because it just kept blinking on and off. I really didn't want to, but my feet carried me back to resume the same pointless idiocy inside the car.

"I love you!"

"Oh, come on, Metin, let's go back!"

"Let's just stay a little longer, Ceylan, please!"

"If you really loved me, you wouldn't hold me hostage out here in the middle of nowhere!"

I was trying to think of something to say that would seem more meaningful, but when you get down to it, words aren't very useful at baring our souls, they're just something else we hide behind. As I was looking around helplessly, I saw something in the backseat: a notebook. Faruk must have left it there. I started flipping through it in the neon light, and then I showed it to Ceylan, trying to keep her from exploding out of boredom or anger or both. She read a few lines, gritting her teeth, before suddenly throwing it into the backseat of the car, exasperated. When the guy finally came to repair the car, I got out to help him push it to where he could see better, and in that harsh light I saw Ceylan's cold empty face.

Later, after the mechanic and I had checked the engine, and he'd gone off to buy a part, I looked again and saw Ceylan still had the same cold and bored look on her face. I walked away from the broken Anadol in the rain, which had started again, full of confusing thoughts about love and cursing all those poets and singers who glorify this disastrous and destructive emotion. But then I remembered that there was something about this terrible feeling that made people put up with it and even enjoy it. Even so, I couldn't take Ceylan's resentful look, so I slid under the car with the mechanic while he was working. There, in the dirty greasy darkness, covered by the old car, I felt Ceylan just fifty centimeters above me and yet very far away. Eventually, the engine turned over, and from where I was I could see Ceylan's lovely feet and long beautiful legs getting out of the car. Her red high heels carried her first a few steps to the left, and then changed course and took her to the right, before she got really annoyed and, finally figuring out where she meant to go, headed there in angry determination.

When her orange skirt and broad back finally entered my field of vision I realized she had gone into the office. I quickly slid out from under the car and, telling the guy to "make it snappy!" ran after her. Inside, Ceylan was eyeing the telephone on the desk, and the attendant sitting there, still sleepy, was eyeing Ceylan.

"That's okay, Ceylan!" I shouted. "I'll call them."

"Did you just think of that now?" she said. "We're very late. They'll be worried, who knows what they'll be thinking . . . It's two in the morning . . . " She was going on, but, thank God, the sleepy attendant went outside because a car had pulled up to the pumps, and I was spared further humiliation as I opened the directory and immediately found Turan's family. As I was dialing, Ceylan was saying, "You're really inconsiderate!"

Then I told her again that I loved her and, without thinking, added, with conviction, "I want to marry you!" but nothing I could say made a difference anymore; it was amazing how much Ceylan looked like that woman in the poster she was standing next to, except that Ceylan was scowling, so angry she couldn't even look at me, only the telephone in my hand. I don't know what unsettled me more, the hatred on her face or her magical resemblance to the Mobil oil woman, but anyway I was ready for the worst.

After just a couple of rings, someone answered. I recognized Fikret's voice right away. "Is that you?" I said. "I'm calling so you don't worry about us!" At the same time, I was wondering what he was doing answering the phone at Turan's with so many other people there. "Who's there?" Fikret abruptly asked. "It's me, Metin!" "You,

I got, but who's there with you?" "Ceylan!" I said, taken aback. For a second I even thought the two of them were playing some gag on me, but Ceylan's face was expressionless: she only kept asking, "Who's on the line?" Fikret said, "I thought you were dropping Ceylan off at her house!" "Well," I said, "actually we're here together, at the gas station, but we're fine, don't worry. Okay, I've got to go now!" "Who is that, who are you talking to," Ceylan asked. "Will you please give me the phone?"

But I wouldn't give it to her and kept trying to answer Fikret's annoying questions. "What are we doing at the gas station?" I said. "A minor repair," and I quickly added: "But we're on our way back, Okay? So, bye!" But Ceylan, now yelling so she would be heard on the other end, said, "Stop, stop, don't hang up, who is it?" Just as I was about to get off the line, Fikret said in a cold, unpleasant voice, "It seems Ceylan wants to speak to me!" I reluctantly handed the receiver to Ceylan and went out into the gloomy rain.

After walking a short way, I turned and looked back at the bright room where among the shelves, ads, and Mobil oil cans, Ceylan had come to life and was still eagerly talking on the phone while twisting the end of her hair, and I thought how I would forget about all this when I was in America, but then realized I didn't want to go anymore. As Ceylan shifted her weight from one beautiful leg to the other, impatient as a stranded child, I muttered to myself, She is more beautiful than any girl I've ever met, and I stood there in the rain like a schoolboy, helpless and resigned as he awaits the punishment being decided for him. Soon Ceylan hung up the phone and came outside, completely happy.

"Fikret's on his way!"

"But I'm the one who loves you!"

I ran over to the car and started yelling at the mechanic, telling him that if he got the car started right now I'd give him all the money I had on me.

"I'll get it started," he said. "But this clutch will give out on the road again!"

"No, it won't. Just get it running!"

After he fiddled around for a while, the guy told me to try the starter. I got into the car gleefully, but it wouldn't turn over. After he'd fiddled a little more, the mechanic told me to try it again, but still no luck. And after this routine was repeated a few more times my anger and frustration got to the point where I lost it.

"Ceylan, please don't leave me."

"Settle down, you're having a fit," said Ceylan.

When Fikret's Alfa Romeo arrived at the gas station a little later, I pulled myself together and got out of the car.

"Come on, let's just get out of here, Fikret!" said Ceylan.

"What's wrong with the old car?" said Fikret.

"It's working now," I said. "I'll be in Cennethisar before you. I'll even race you, if you want!"

"Fine," said Fikret. "Let's race."

Ceylan went and sat in Fikret's Alfa Romeo. I hit the starter hard, and thank goodness the car worked. I gave the kid a one-thousand-lira note, then I gave him another one. We lined the two cars up at the starting line. "Be careful, Fikret," said Ceylan. "Metin's nerves are shot."

"Up to Turan's! On your mark, get set . . . ," Fikret said.

When he said "go" the Anadol roared and shot off like an arrow and was responding just fine as I pressed the gas all the way down to the floor, but since Fikret had just slightly jumped the gun he was already in the lead, but that was okay, because I was blowing my horn and shining my brights on the back of his neck and staying right on his tail, even with this lousy Anadol, because I was not going to leave you alone with him, Ceylan! When we went over the bridge I got closer still, not slowing down at the turn at the top of the hill, but actually stepping on it even more, because, though it might be a ridiculous thought, I knew now that, to get a girl like you, I had to be willing to stare death in the eye, even though it was so unfair, you in that coward's car, look, Ceylan, when he takes the turn, he hits the brakes, I see the red taillights, but when I try to pass, he plays an even dirtier trick and won't let me by, My God, I was saying to myself, I've got no luck, when suddenly I was completely thrown for a loop, because first he downshifted and then, when he hit the gas, that Alfa Romeo really took off, like a rocket, climbing up the hill at incredible speed, the little red lights getting smaller and smaller until, in about two minutes, they had disappeared from view. I was pushing the gas all the way down, but my car was like a quick horse forced to pull a load uphill, skidding in the ruts, gasping for air; it soon started whining, until the rear wheels once again began to disregard the engine, because of the damn clutch, and so when I turned it off so that at least it wouldn't overheat, I wound up stuck there, halfway up the hill, all alone like an idiot. Just me and the stupid crickets again!

I tried a few times to restart the engine, but I soon realized that the only thing to do was to push the car to the top of the hill so it could coast down the other side, all the way to Cennethisar. At least the rain was letting up as I started to push, but that barely mattered, because I was drenched in sweat and trying to ignore my aching back, but when it started to sprinkle again, and the pain became unbearable, I pulled the hand brake and kicked the car in disgust. I saw another car coming uphill, but it just passed right by me, blowing its horn, ignoring the pathetic hand I'd raised for help. The sky began to rumble off in the distance, so I resumed pushing; by now the strain in my guts was bringing tears to my eyes.

When I looked back and saw how little progress I had made for all this anguish, I lost it, and I began to run along the road, as the rain got heavier, I took a shortcut through the cherry orchard and the vineyards, but I got bogged down in all that mud, swallowed by the pitch-black darkness! A little later, I was bent over gasping from pain, wondering if my spleen had burst, my feet covered with mud, when I heard the growls of the dogs trying to scare me off the property, and since they were getting really close I turned back. I got in the car again so as not to get any wetter than I already was, and as I sat there, with my head pressed against the wheel, I thought: But I love you.

Eventually, I saw three guys coming down the hill, so I jumped out eagerly to ask them for help. But as the dark shadows got closer and I got a look at them, I immediately regretted leaving the car. The biggest had a can of paint in his hand, the second had a mustache, the other was wearing some kind of jacket.

"What are you doing here in the dark of night?" said the one with the mustache.

"My car broke down. Will you give me a hand, please?"

"What, do you think we're horses, or maybe your father's servant? Just push it down the hill."

"Just a minute, just a minute!" said the one with the jacket. "I recognize you now, my good man, don't you remember, this morning you almost ran us over!"

"What? Was that you! I am terribly sorry, brother!"

The one with the jacket spoke in a simpering female voice that was supposed to be me: "Oh, gee, I'm sorry, sweetie, I guess I almost ran you over this morning! I guess it's a good thing I didn't!"

"Let's get out of here," said the one with the mustache.

"No, I think I'm staying here with our friend," said the one with the jacket. He went and sat in the car. "Come on, guys, you too."

After a moment's hesitation, the one with the mustache and the one carrying the spray can got in the backseat. I sat behind the wheel, next to the one with the jacket. The rain was really starting to come down.

"We're not bothering you, I hope, sweetheart?" said the one with the jacket.

I smiled cooperatively.

"Good! I like this one, he knows how to take a joke, he's okay, this one! So what's your name?"

I told him.

"Pleased to meet you, Metin Bey. I'm Serdar, this is Mustafa, and this retard we call Fox. His real name is Hasan."

"You're going to go too far again, just watch it!" said Hasan.

"What do you mean?" said Serdar. "Of course we must introduce ourselves. Isn't that so, Metin Bey?"

He held out his hand. When I stuck mine out he squeezed it with all his might. When I couldn't take it anymore, I squeezed his back, out of desperation, and finally he let my hand go.

"Good for you! You're a strong one, but not as strong as I am!"

"So what school do you go to?" said Mustafa.

"The American High School."

"Ah, the society school?" said Serdar. "Our Fox here is in love with one of your society types."

"Don't start again," said Hasan.

"Wait a sec! Maybe he can show you the way. He's one of them. Isn't that so? Why are you laughing?"

"I'm not!" I said.

"I know why you're laughing," said Serdar. "You're making fun of this poor guy because he's in love with a rich girl. Isn't that so, creep?"

"You were laughing, too," I said, confused.

Serdar shouted, "I can laugh. I'm his friend, I don't look down on him, but you do. What's with you, you son of a bitch, haven't you ever been in love?"

He ranted some more, and when I didn't say anything he got even angrier and started to root around in the car. He opened the glove compartment, read the insurance papers in a loud official voice, laughing as if they were completely hilarious, and when he learned that the car wasn't mine but my brother's, he fixed me with this stare of contempt and said:

"So, what do you think you're doing with these cars and these girls in the middle of the night, huh?"

I didn't answer him. I just grinned at him like some pathetic low-life.

"These guys have no shame! But you do all right for yourselves! Tell me, was that one with you last night your sweetheart?"

"No," I said nervously. "She wasn't."

"Don't lie," said Serdar.

"My sister!" I said. "My grandmother's sick, we were out trying to find medicine."

"You couldn't just go to the pharmacy on the hill road, across from the beach?"

"It was closed."

"It's open every night, you liar! But maybe you knew that that pharmacist is a Communist!"

"I didn't know."

"What do you know except how to go around with society girls?"

"Do you know who we are?" said Mustafa.

"I know," I said. "You're Idealists!"

"Good!" said Mustafa. "Do you know what we're all about, do you know that?"

"Nationalism and things like that."

"What does 'and things like that' mean?"

"This boy's probably not even a Turk!" said Serdar. "Are you a real Turk, man, your father, your mother, are they real Turks?"

"I'm a Turk!"

"Then what's this?" He showed the record that Ceylan had forgotten. Serdar spelled out "Best of Elvis."

"It's a record," I said.

"Don't be a wiseass, I see right through you. What's this faggot record doing in a Turk's car?"

"I'm not interested in that stuff. My sister left that record in the car."

"So, in other words, you don't go to discos or places like that?" said Serdar.

"Not very often!"

"Are you against communism?" said Mustafa.

"I am!"

"Tell me why you're against it."

"Well, you know . . ."

"Noo . . . I don't know anything. You tell us, and we'll learn . . . "

"Our friend seems like he's shy," said Serdar. "He's keeping quiet . . . "

"Are you a coward?" said Mustafa.

"I don't think so."

"He doesn't think so! If you're not a coward, why aren't you fighting the Communists that you say you're against?"

"I never got a chance," I said. "You're the first Idealists I've met."

"Well, how do you find us?" said Serdar. "Do you like us?"

"I do."

"You're one of us, then. What do you say we come look for you tomorrow night and take you along with us?"

"Sure, come and get me . . . "

"Quiet, you lying coward. As soon as you get away from us you'll go to the police, won't you?"

"Calm down, Serdar," said Mustafa. "He's not a bad kid! Look, I'll bet he'll even take some invitations from us!"

"We're sponsoring an evening in the Sports and Exhibition Palace in Istanbul. Would you consider doing us the honor?" said Serdar.

"I'll come!" I said. "How much is it?"

"Look at this, now. Now, did anybody say anything about money?"

"It's okay, Serdar. If he wants to buy them himself, let the kid pay for them. It'll be a help."

The one called Serdar asked with a fawning voice, "How many would you like, sir?"

"Five hundred liras' worth."

I was quickly pulling a five-hundred-lira note out of my wallet.

"Hey, is that snakeskin, that wallet?" said Mustafa.

"No!" I held out the five hundred liras anxiously. Serdar didn't take the money. "May I see the snakeskin?"

"It's not snakeskin, I said!"

"Give it to me and let me take a look at that wallet."

I handed over the wallet full of the money I had collected working in the summer heat for over a month.

"Right you are!" said Serdar. "It's not snakeskin, this wallet, you fooled us."

"Let me have a look, I can tell," said Mustafa. He took the wallet and went through it. "Do you need this address book? No, you don't, you know so many people, and they all have phones, don't they? . . . Somebody who knows so many people doesn't have to carry around an ID card to identify himself. So I'm just taking your ID card and, wait a minute . . . twelve thousand liras. Does your father give you this kind of money?"

"No, I earned it myself," I said. "I give English and math lessons."

"Look, Fox, just the guy for you!" said Serdar. "Would you give him a math lesson? For free, of course . . ."

"I will," I said and then I understood which Hasan the Hasan they called Fox was.

"Good!" said Mustafa. "Anyway, I've decided that you are a good kid. With these twelve thousand liras you can buy all together twenty-four invitations. You can give them out to your friends."

"At least leave me a thousand liras," I said.

"Complaining? Careful or you'll start pissing me off!" Serdar shouted.

"No, he's not complaining. You're giving us the twelve thousand liras of your own free will, right?" said Mustafa.

"We're talking to you, you bastard!"

"Easy, Serdar!"

"Okay," said Serdar, "now next, what's this for?" He opened Faruk's notebook, which he found in the backseat, and began to read from it. " 'A village valued at seventeen thousand *akçe* in the vicinity of Gebze being formerly possessed by Sipahi Ali was, upon his failure to participate in the campaign, thereby taken from him and given to Habib.' What is this, you can't even read it! 'The complaint of Veli against Mahmut who did not pay the value of the mule he had purchased from him . . . ' "

"What is all this stuff?" said Mustafa.

"My brother's a historian."

"Poor guy!" said Serdar.

"Come on, let's go, the rain's letting up," said Mustafa.

"At least give me my ID back," I said.

"What does 'at least' mean, prick!" said Serdar. "Did we do anything bad to you?" Then he stuck his head inside the car, looking for something bad to do. He saw "Best of Elvis" and said, "I'm borrowing this too, okay?" He took Faruk's notebook as well. "If you drive a little slower from now on, maybe you won't confuse everybody with one of your father's servants. Pathetic little creep!"

He slammed the door and went off with the others. When I figured they were a good ways off, I got out of the car and started to push the Anadol up the hill.

26

Hasan Tries to Return the Record
and the Notebook

❖

We gave that guy a good lesson!" said Serdar.

"You go too far sometimes," said Mustafa. "What if he goes to the police?"

"He won't," said Serdar. "Didn't you see, he's a total coward?"

"Why did you have to take the record and the notebook?" said Mustafa.

That's when I saw it, Nilgün: Serdar had taken the record you'd left in the car, and Faruk's notebook, too. When we got to the neighborhood down below he stopped under the streetlight and looked at the cover.

"I took it because it makes me sick that he thinks everybody is his father's servant!" he said.

"That wasn't a good idea," said Mustafa. "You got him mad for no reason."

"If you want," I said, "give me the record, and I'll take it back to the car."

"God, what kind of idiot is this guy!" said Serdar.

"Look," said Mustafa. "You do not call this guy an idiot, a retard, or a fox in front of anybody ever again."

Serdar was quiet. We walked downhill without saying anything. I thought how with that twelve thousand liras in Mustafa's pocket I could buy the knife I saw in Pendik, the one with the mother-of-pearl handle, and a pair of leather shoes with rubber soles for winter. If I kicked in a little more, I could even get a gun. They stopped when we came to the coffeehouse.

"Okay," said Mustafa. "Time to split up."

"Aren't we going to tag some more walls?" I said.

"It's going to rain again, we'll get wet," said Mustafa. "You keep the paint and brushes tonight, Hasan. Okay?"

So it was time for those two to go down to their houses and for me to turn around and climb up the hill, but first: twelve thousand liras three ways, that's four thousand liras. Not bad. And if I got Nilgün's record and the notebook, too . . .

"What's the matter?" said Mustafa. "Something on your mind?" Then, finally, acting as if he had just thought of something, he said, "Oh, here, Hasan, cigarettes and matches for you, so you can smoke."

I wasn't going to take them, but he gave me such a look that I did.

"Aren't you going to thank me?" he said.

"Thank you."

They turned and as I watched them walk away, I was thinking again: there's a lot I could get with four thousand liras! As they passed through the pool of light in front of the bakery and disappeared in the darkness, I shouted out, "Mustafa!"

I heard their footsteps stop, and he called out: "What's up?"

I paused before I ran over to them.

"So, can I take that record and the notebook, Mustafa?" I said, out of breath.

"What are you going to do?" said Serdar. "Are you really going to take them back to the guy?"

"I don't want anything else," I said. "Just give them to me, and that'll be enough."

"Give them to him," said Mustafa.

As he was handing me the book and record, Serdar said, "Are you some kind of idiot?" with an expression that said he was actually wondering.

"What did I say?" said Mustafa. "Look, Hasan, we decided to use the twelve thousand liras to cover expenses; don't misunderstand. It doesn't come to very much for each of us anyway. But, here, take five hundred as your share, if you want."

"That's okay," I said. "It should all go to the Association, it should all be for the cause. I don't want anything for myself."

"But you're taking the record!" shouted Serdar.

At that point, I got confused, so I took the five hundred he said was my share and put it in my pocket.

"Happy?" said Serdar. "Now that's it for you out of this twelve thousand. I hope you won't be telling anyone about it."

"He won't tell," said Mustafa. "He's not as stupid as you think. He's very sharp, in fact, he just doesn't show it. Look how he came back to get his share of the money."

"Little sneak!" said Serdar.

"Okay, let's get out of here," said Mustafa.

I stayed there for a little while watching them go. They were obviously making fun of me. When they had disappeared, I lit a cigarette and went up the hill, with the paint and brushes in one hand and the record and notebook in the other. I'll go to the beach tomorrow morning, I said, and if Mustafa shows up he can see I'm keeping an eye on the girl, and if he doesn't, I'll tell him tomorrow night, Mustafa, I was on the job, but you didn't come, and that way he'll realize that I know what discipline means: goddamn them all!

A little ways up the hill, the sound of Metin yelling gave me a fright, he was somewhere out there in the darkness just ahead, all by himself, cursing furiously. As I got closer, taking silent steps on the wet asphalt, it sounded like someone pounding on a plastic gas can, but actually Metin was kicking his car. He was like an angry horseman whipping a stubborn nag, but the Plexiglas beast didn't respond, and so he beat it all the more. I had a weird thought: I could go give Metin a pounding, too! Then I thought of other violent things, hurricanes, people dying, earthquakes. I put down what I was carrying and imagined jumping him: So, you don't even recognize me? How could you just forget who I am? I guess some people are important, you recognize them, you'd know them even from a distance, everything going on in their lives, all the details, but others you can't be bothered to recognize, they live out their whole lives and you don't even notice. One day, you won't be able to help but recognize me!

Eventually, I left the poor jerk so he could go on kicking his car. I was going up through the muddy orchard so that he wouldn't see me, when I realized what was going on. I'd thought he was fuming because of the money he'd lost and that piece-of-junk car that wouldn't start, but it turned out there was a girl to blame, because he kept repeating that word for women who sell their flesh. Sometimes that word frightens me, women like that are scary, and I'd rather not think about them, so I went on my way.

Maybe you're the one he's talking about, Nilgün, I thought, but then maybe it's somebody else. What a nasty word! Women scare me sometimes. They are like things you just can't understand, with dark thoughts you can never know, some parts of them are so horrifying, and disaster is waiting for you if you fall for them. They're a little like death that way, except dressed like a prostitute that stands there smiling at you with a blue ribbon in her hair! . . . The sky turned yellow in the distance, and I started to worry about lightning. Clouds, dark storms, shadows I don't understand! Sometimes it's as if we're all slaves of someone we don't even know, sometimes we stand there, trying to fight back, but then there's fear, of thunderbolts, lightning, of unknown distant disasters that will come upon us! At those moments, I tell myself it's enough just to live in the peaceful light of our house, without fighting back or knowing anything. I'm so terrified of sin! Like my poor father, the lottery seller.

It had started to sprinkle again when I noticed the light was still on in the house. Getting close I looked into the window, and I saw that not only was my father still up but my mother was as well. I wondered what that cripple could be saying about me to my poor mother to keep her from sleeping. The grocer must have told him what happened today. The fat slob just couldn't wait. Ismail, he must have said, your son came to the shop this morning, he ripped up the newspapers and magazines and threw them all over the place, threatening people, who knows what sort he's hanging around with, he's gone berserk! What do I owe you, my father would have said, the lottery-ticket seller who can only think of things in terms of money, and he probably wound up paying for those horrible newspapers. But not for nothing, no: he'd be planning to take it out of my hide in the evening, assuming he could find me, of course. Maybe that was why I couldn't make up my mind whether to go inside or not. I just stayed there watching my mother and father through the window, and when it started to rain again, I left the paints, Nilgün's record, and Faruk's notebook on the sill of my closed window, and, sheltered under the eaves, I stared at the downpour. When the gutters that my father had attached himself could no longer keep up with the flow of the water, I crept back toward the window and saw my poor mother running around inside with plastic laundry tubs and cooking pots trying to catch the leaks in the ceiling. When she remembered the one in my room, the one that made the eagle with its wings spread over the bed, she ran in there, turned on the light, and folded up the quilt.

Later, when the rain stopped, I realized that I wasn't thinking about them or anybody else, but only about you, Nilgün! No doubt, you were lying in your bed, maybe the sound of the rain had awakened you, and you were gazing out the window at this moment, lost in thought, startled now and then by a clap of thunder. In the morning when the rain had stopped and the sun came out, you'd head to the beach, and I'd be waiting for you and finally you'd see me, we would talk and I'd tell you everything. Ah, life, I love you!

If a person believes, he can become a completely different person. There are so many possibilities: distant countries, their endless rail lines, the forests of Africa, the Sahara, the white deserts, frozen

lakes, the pelicans in geography books, charging lions, the water buffalo I saw on television, the hyenas that corner them and rip them
to pieces, the elephants in movies, India, the American Indians, the
Chinese, the stars, intergalactic wars, all wars, history, our history,
the thundering beat of the war drums and the fear in the heart of the
infidels who heard them: yes, a person could become someone completely different. We are not slaves: I free myself of all fears, rules,
all borders, marching on to my goal, waving the flag: sabers, knives,
guns, power! I am somebody different, not held down by my past, I
have no more memories, from now on there is only a future for me.
Memories are for slaves, to lull them. Let them sleep!

I was feasting on these thoughts, but then knowing I wouldn't
have the strength to just forget everybody, I picked up the notebook
from the windowsill, the record, too, and walking into the darkness,
I could already see the end of this night. The water was streaming
downhill; the air smelled of rain. Let me take one more look at the
neighborhood down below, I said, one last view of the lights, the
well-kept artificial gardens, the smooth soulless concrete; while
there was no one under the streetlights, I'd look one more time at
those sinful streets, where no one had a care or a worry. And I'd take
one last peek at one of those windows, a window I'd never see again
until the day of victory. Maybe, I thought, you're not asleep, Nilgün,
and you're looking out the window at the rain, and when a bolt of
lightning strikes and in a flash everything's blue, then maybe you'll
see me, planted there in this terrible rain, soaking wet, in the middle
of the night, at your window. But in the end, remembering about
the watchmen, I didn't go: Son, they'd say to me, what are you doing
around here at this hour, come on, this is no place for you! Okay,
okay, I'm going!

I turned back and headed toward my house, all sleepy, as if going
through some strange neighborhood. My mother and father still
had the light on. A poor, pathetic light! They didn't see me, and as
I crossed the field and started to go downhill I was startled again:
Metin was still there in the dark, cursing and pushing his car. I

stopped and watched him from a distance, like someone observing strange people in some foreign country where he had just set foot for the first time, curious but a little afraid, an enjoyable feeling. Then I thought I heard him crying, some broken sound, and you couldn't help but pity him if you heard it. I remembered our friendship as children, and forgetting that these people lived to accuse others, I went over to help him.

"Who's that?"

"It's me," I said. "Metin, you didn't recognize me back there, it's me, Hasan!"

"I did eventually!" he said. "Did you bring the money back?"

"I'm all by myself!" I said. "Do you want the money back?"

"You stole my twelve thousand liras! Don't you realize that?"

I didn't say anything. We were quiet for a while.

Then he shouted, "Where are you? Come out where I can see your face!"

I left the record and the notebook in a dry place and went over to him.

"Aren't you going to bring the money back?" he said. "Come out here!"

As I got close I saw his sweaty unhappy face; we just looked at each other.

"No," I said. "I don't have your money!"

"Then why did you come?"

"I heard you crying just now."

"You heard wrong," he said. "I'm just tired . . . why did you come here?"

"We were such good friends when we were kids!" I said. I quickly added before he said anything: "Metin, if you want I'll help you!"

"Why would you do that?" he said at first. Then a second later, he said, "Fine. Help me push, then!"

I pushed. After a minute, as the car budged from where it was and started moving uphill, I think I was gladder than he was. It was a strange feeling, Nilgün. But then when I saw what a short way we'd gone I got discouraged.

"What's the matter?" said Metin, pulling the hand brake.

"Stop! Let me rest a little."

"Come on," he said. "I'm late."

I put my back into it again, but we still didn't get very far. It was more like moving a boulder than something with wheels! I stopped for a second, and I was going to say, Let me rest again, when he released the brake. I pushed so the car wouldn't roll backward, but then I stopped.

"What's wrong?" he said. "Why aren't you pushing?"

"Why aren't *you* pushing?" I said.

"I don't have any strength left!"

"Where are you going at this hour?"

He didn't answer. He just looked at his watch and cursed. He started pushing the car with me, but we didn't get anywhere, because while we were pushing the car uphill, it seemed the car was pushing us downhill, and we were just stuck in place. We both tried harder and managed to go a few feet, but by then I'd had it. When the rain started again, I got in the car. Metin came and sat next to me.

"What are you doing?" he said. "We've got to keep going."

"You can go there tomorrow!" I said. "Let's talk a little now."

"What are we going to talk about?"

"What a peculiar night," I said after a while. "Are you afraid of lightning?"

"No, I'm not afraid," he said. "Come on, let's try again."

"I'm not afraid either!" I said. "But when you think about it, it's pretty terrifying stuff, you know what I mean?"

He didn't say anything.

"Want a cigarette?" I said. I took out the pack and offered it to him.

"I don't smoke!" he said. "Come on, let's push a little."

We got out, pushed it as far as we could, and when we were good and soaked, we got back inside. I asked him again where he had to get to, but he answered with another question: why did those guys call me Fox?

"Oh, it's stupid!" I said. "They're maniacs, if you want to know the truth."

"You hang around with them," he said. "You joined in with them to rob me."

I thought about telling him everything then—should I tell him the whole story?—but it was as if I didn't know the story, not because it wasn't all in my head, but because I didn't know where to start. Because once I'd found the beginning, I'd feel obliged to go and punish the ones who were to blame in the first place, and since I had no desire to get blood on my hands, it seemed as if I really didn't want to remember who started this, even though I knew that's what I had to do, but I'll tell you all about it tomorrow morning, Nilgün. But why wait till then? If Metin and I could just push this Anadol to the top of the hill, we could coast down the other side together as far as your house, and Metin would wake you up and then, while you listened to me in your white nightgown in the darkness, I could tell you without delay about the great danger you were in: They think you're a Communist, my beloved, come on, let's run away, let's go, they're everywhere, and they're so powerful, but there's got to be somewhere in the world we can live in peace, I'm sure there is . . .

"Come on, push!"

We pushed and pushed in the rain. After a while he gave up, but I kept at it until I couldn't do it anymore, and when I stopped, too, Metin was staring accusingly. I went and sat in a spot where I thought I would not get wet.

"You say they're maniacs," he said, "but you hang around with them. It wasn't just those two that took that money from me, it was all three of you."

"I don't answer to anybody!" I said. "And I didn't take a cent of that twelve thousand liras, Metin! I swear."

When he gave me that severe look that said he didn't believe me, I wanted to grab him by the neck and strangle him. The key was there in the ignition. If I knew how to drive! There were so many roads in the world, so many countries, cities, seas, out there in the distance.

"Go on, push!"

I threw my back into it again, out in the pouring rain, but Metin wasn't pushing, just standing there with his hands on his hips, observing like a gentleman. When I ran out of steam, he couldn't even bother to pull the hand brake.

I practically shouted to make myself heard in the rain: "I'm tired!"

"No!" he said. "You can still push some more."

"I'm letting go!" I shouted. "It's going to slide back!"

"Fine, who can I ask about that money?"

"Are you saying if I don't push you're going to go to the police?"

When he didn't answer, I pushed with all I had, until I thought my back would break. Finally he put on the hand brake. I was completely soaked. Just as I lit up a cigarette the whole earth and sky blazed with an awesome brightness, and I was terrified to see lightning fall right there at the tip of my nose.

"That scared you, huh?" said Metin.

"It landed right there!" I said.

"It landed way over there, maybe all the way out at sea, what are you afraid of."

"I don't want to push anymore."

"Why?" he said. "Because you got scared? It won't come that close again. Don't they teach you in school?"

"I'm going home," I said.

"Fine, what about my twelve thousand liras."

"I said I didn't take it!"

"You can tell it to the police tomorrow."

Tucking my head between my shoulders to protect my neck from the rain, I began to push again, not even looking up, until I realized that we were nearly at the top, and my heart was glad. Metin got out of the car now, but unlike before he wasn't even pretending to push with me, only once in a while contributing a "Come on, that's it" word of encouragement.

Finally I stopped, thinking, I'm not his father's servant.

And he said: "No, you can't stop now! What is it, a matter of money? Do you want me to pay you? I'll give you whatever you want. Just please keep pushing, Hasan."

I got back at it only because we were very near the top. But when I couldn't stand the pain in my back, and I paused to give my poor heart a little blood and my lungs a little breath, he started to whine again. "I'll give you a thousand liras!" he said. So I pushed with all the strength I had left. And the next time I had to stop, he said, "Okay, two thousand liras!" I was thinking, I don't know how you're going to pay that after our guys cleaned you out, but I didn't say it. When we finally got to the top he was so angry and impatient that he was no longer paying any attention to me. I thought that in a minute he might start kicking the car again, but he did something strange and frightening: he turned his face to the rain, cursing the dark sky, as if aiming his anger at the Almighty. I was afraid even to think it, so I pushed the car to the other edge as the sky rumbled just above the hilltop and everything flashed bright blue again, with the incredible blue rain streaming off my hair and forehead right into my mouth. I closed my eyes not to see the lightning flashes coming more and more frequently, and with my head pulled in between my shoulders, I turned my face toward the earth and started pushing like a blind slave, a pathetic creature who had forgotten his every thought, so no one could accuse me or punish me, with my head bowed down, see, and I don't even know about guilt and sin. I felt a strange happiness as the car picked up speed. Metin got back in behind the wheel, still cursing and howling out the open window, like that old wagon driver who gets so angry at his horse, he winds up cursing Him as well. As though it wasn't He who made the sky rumble! Who are you anyway? I won't take part in anybody's blasphemies. I stopped; I was not pushing anymore.

But the car still glided on for a while all by itself. As it slowly pulled away, it was like watching some terrifying ship silently slip its moorings. The rain had let up, too. And as I looked at the car going off by itself it occurred to me that God was separating the two of us in order to spare me the punishment He would deliver, but a little farther on the car stopped. The sky lit up in a flash, and I saw Metin get out.

"Where are you?" he bellowed. "Come here, you have to push it!"

I didn't budge.

"Thief!" he shouted into the darkness. "Shameless thief. Run away, go ahead, run!"

I stood where I was for a minute, shivering from the cold. Then I ran over to his side.

"Aren't you afraid of God?" I shouted.

"If you are, why do you steal?" he shouted.

"I am!" I said. "But you, you look up at Him and curse. You'll be punished one day."

"Ignorant fool!" he said. "You were afraid of the lightning just now, weren't you? A little lightning, and you're afraid of every tree's shadow, the cemetery, the rain and the storm, aren't you? At your age! What grade are you in? Ignoramus! Let me tell you: there is no God! Neither here nor in the West. Got it? Now, come on, push this thing. I tell you I'll give you two thousand liras."

"Where are you going to go?" I said. "To your house?"

"I'll take you, too," he said, "or wherever you want to go, if this car would just slide down the hill!"

I pushed, Nilgün. He got into the car, still cursing, but not in anger, now more like the wagon driver, out of habit.

As the car started moving a little faster, I thought how the incline of the hill would soon become steep, and then the car would be going nicely on its own, which made me think: Poor Metin, he is just as sick and tired of everything as I am! I'll get in the car, and he'll turn on the heat, and we'll warm up. Then we'll pick you up and go off somewhere far away, maybe to another country . . . When the car started to go down the hill, the motor didn't make a sound, and all you could hear was the strange whisper of the tires on the wet asphalt. At that point I ran and caught up to him to jump into the car, but the door was locked.

"Open up!" I said. "Open it, Metin, the door is locked! Open it and take me, too! Will you stop!" But he seemed not to hear me. I ran next to him as far as I could, pounding on the window, gasping as if I were drowning, but before you knew it, that hunk of plastic had passed me by and was gone. I continued running after it still, shouting, but it didn't stop, and Metin wouldn't stop it. I kept on after the car as the headlights softly illuminated the gardens and orchards, and it swayed and swerved around the turns, all the way down until it was lost to sight. Then I stopped and stared.

My teeth were chattering at the cold. I realized: Your record, Nilgün, I left it there, all the way on the other side of the hill. I turned around and ran back the way I came, hoping it would warm me up, but it was no use, because my shirt was sticking to my body. My feet were trudging through little streams of water. When I got to where I thought I had left the record and I couldn't find it, I started to run around frantically. I shivered when the sky rumbled and lit up, not because I was afraid but because I was cold. When I was out of breath I could feel the pain in my back again. All that running, bending down, and standing up, shivering, and searching, but there was no record.

I forget now how many times I ran up and down that hill until I found the record a little after the sun came up. Just as I felt myself about to faint from exhaustion and the cold, I realized that one of the shadows that I'd been sure wasn't what I was looking for was in fact the stupid record and notebook, and it seemed as if somebody was playing a dirty trick on me, hiding things for the pleasure of watching me crawl around like a slave. I felt like digging the heel of my shoe into that idiotic American cover on the "Best of Elvis" and saying, To hell with all of them! But it had turned to mush from the rain anyway. So I didn't crush it, I'll bring it to you!

Halil's garbage truck was the first vehicle to climb the hill; the beautiful rosy light of the rising sun was behind it. Leaving the main road, I went into the orchard and came out onto the cemetery road, which I followed to the end of the wall until I got onto the goat path I used to take with my mother when I was little. There was a favorite hiding place of mine here, among the almond and fig trees.

I gathered sticks and branches, though it was hard to find any dry ones. So I pulled a few pages out of Faruk's stupid notebook, and I was able to start a fire. No one would see the hazy blue smoke that rose up. I took off my shirt and pants, just about walked into the fire in my sneakers and stood there. It felt good to warm up. I looked at my body with pleasure, naked in the red flames: I'm not afraid of anything! My dick hanging above the flames; I looked at how it hung there. It was like looking at some other man's body: tanned by the sun, strong like steel, taut like an archer's bow! I thought: I'm a man, I can do anything, you've been warned! It seemed that even if the hair on my legs caught fire, nothing could happen to me. In a little while I stepped away from the fire to feed the flames, and as I was looking around for branches and brush, a cool wind blew and made my butt shiver, and I thought: I'm not a woman that I should be afraid. After the flames roared back to life and I stepped back into the fire, I thought of all the things I was capable of, and more, of death, fear, fire, foreign countries, weapons, wretched souls, slaves, the flag, the nation, the devil, hell.

Then I held the mushy cardboard record sleeve to the flames and dried it out. I dried my clothes, too, and put them on, before finding a dry corner in which to stretch out.

I fell asleep right away. When I woke up I knew I had been dreaming but I couldn't remember what the dream was about. Something hot, I guess. The sun was high in the sky. I jumped up and started running. It might be too late!

As I raced down the hill past our house with your record in my hand, the Sunday beach crowd whizzed past me in their disgusting cars. Nobody seemed to be at the house, neither my mother nor my father. Anyway, they had pulled the curtains. Tahsin's family was busy gathering the cherries before they could get all wormy after the rain. When I got down into the neighborhood I broke the five hundred liras; all the stores were open around here on Sundays. I asked for tea and toast, and while I ate I took the combs out of my pocket to look at them: one green and one red. God sees everything.

I would tell her the whole story, not holding back anything. You'll realize what kind of man I am, Nilgün. You'll say, You are not like the others, I'm not afraid. Take a look at me, will you, I can do what I like, I have the rest of the five hundred liras in my pocket, I'm my own master, a gentleman. You there, going to the beach, with your inflatable balls, your bags, and weird sandals on your feet, you with your husbands and children beside you! You look, but you don't see, you think, but you don't know! They don't realize who I am, they don't know who I'm going to be, because they're worse than blind, this disgusting crowd, going to the beach, seeking pleasure! If I'm the one who has to straighten all of them out, so be it. Look at me: I have a factory! A whip in my hand! I'm a gentleman.

Looking through the barbed wire at the beach, I didn't see you in the crowd, Nilgün. Mustafa hadn't shown up either.

So I left the beach, heading toward your house. A gentleman is calling, the dwarf will say, he'd like to see you, Nilgün Hanım. Really, a proper gentleman, you say, very well then, Recep Efendi, show him into the salon, I'll be right there. As I walked I kept looking around on the chance you had already left the house, but our paths didn't cross, my lady. When I got to your garden gate, there was no sign of the car, and I preferred to forget who had pushed it uphill in the rain all night, like an idiot and a blind slave. Where was the Anadol? I passed through the gate, but being a gentleman and not wishing to disturb anyone, I didn't go over to the main entrance up the stairs but out back to the kitchen door. I recognized the shadow of the fig, the stones of the wall. Like a dream.

I knocked on the kitchen door, waited a little: Are you the servant of the house, Recep Efendi, I'll say, this record and this green comb,

I believe, belong to a young lady who lives here, I used to know her somewhat, but anyway, that's not important now, I've only come to drop these off, I have no other purpose. After a while, I knocked again; still no answer: Uncle Recep must have gone to the market, he wasn't at home. Maybe nobody was home! As in a dream, yes! My hair stood on end!

When I pushed on the handle, the door slowly opened. I went into the kitchen silent as a cat. I knew that smell of cooking oil. I didn't see anyone, and because I had my sneakers on, nobody heard me climbing up the stairs that twisted upward beside the large earthenware water jar. I felt like a ghost haunting someone's dream, and I was thinking it was because I hadn't really slept, but when I smelled the cooking oil, I thought, So this is what such houses smell like inside, like a real house! I'm really here.

When I got upstairs, I slowly opened one of the doors. Looking inside, I recognized that disgusting shape right away: Metin asleep with the sheet over his head! I thought how he owed me two thousand liras and how he had said there was no God. I could strangle him and nobody would know. But then I thought for a second: they'd find my fingerprints. So I quietly shut the door and went in the open door of the room on the other side of the hall.

I realized from the bottle on the table and the huge pair of pants thrown on the unmade bed: this was Faruk's room. I got right out of there, and when, without thinking first, I opened the next door, I shuddered because it seemed to me I saw my father on the wall. How strange: my father with a beard; he seemed to be staring out of the frame at me in anger and disappointment, as if saying, Oh, what a shame, you're a total idiot. I was very nervous at that moment. But when I heard the old woman's voice with the rattle in it, I understood who the picture on the wall and the room belonged to.

"Who's that?"

I froze, but when I saw her completely wrinkled face and huge ears buried in the crumpled sheets, I shut the door right away.

"Recep, is that you, Recep?"

I silently ran down the hall to the last room, and as I waited trembling by the door I heard that voice again.

"Recep, is that you? I'm talking to you, Recep, answer me!"

I went right in, and suddenly I was astonished, Nilgün, my lady, to find myself in the room that was obviously yours! I pulled back the covers from the empty bed and breathed in your scent, then hurriedly made it up again when I heard that ancient voice still calling, as if to keep me from moving on to your closet.

"Who's there? Who's there, Recep?"

I took your nightie out from under the pillow and gave it a sniff. It smelled of lavender and Nilgün. Then after I'd folded it up to look as if I hadn't smelled it, tucking it back under the pillow, I thought, Why don't I just leave the record and the combs here? Yes, right on your bed, Nilgün, is where I should leave them. When you find the combs you'll understand: how I've been following you for so many days, how I love you. But I didn't leave them, because I had the thought that that would mean everything was finished. Then I decided, let me end it, but it was too late.

"Recep, I'm talking to you, Recep!"

I had to leave the room immediately, because I understood from the heavy rattling that the grandmother must be trying to get out of bed. As I twisted quickly down the spiral stairs I heard her door open behind me and a cane pounding on the carpet hard enough to put a hole in it.

"Recep, I'm talking to you, Recep."

I turned around and went into the kitchen, stopping just as I was about to fly out the door. I can't go without doing something . . . There was a pot over a low flame on the stove. I turned the knob until the flame shot all the way up. I did the same with the other knob and went out thinking, I should have done more.

Telling myself not to pay any attention to anybody, I walked quickly, and when I came to the beach, just as I thought, this time through the barbed wire I saw you, Nilgün Hanımefendi, there in the crowd. Let me give you the record and comb and put an end to all this! I'm not afraid of anyone. She was drying off. She must have just come out of the water. Mustafa still hadn't come.

I waited a little before going to the shop. There were other customers.

"Give me a *Cumhuriyet*," I said.

"Sorry!" said the shopkeeper with a deep red face. "We don't sell it anymore."

I didn't say anything. After a little while, Nilgün Hanımefendi, you came in from the beach and asked, as you did every morning, "A *Cumhuriyet*, please."

But again the shopkeeper said, "Sorry. We don't sell it anymore."

"Why?" said Nilgün. "You had it yesterday."

The shopkeeper indicated me with the tip of his nose, and you looked at me: we looked at each other. Did you understand at that moment? Did you understand the kind of man I am? Now, I thought, I can explain everything to you patiently and without rushing, like a gentleman. I went outside, and with the record and the comb at the ready, I waited. A little later you came out, too. Now I'll explain, and you'll understand everything.

"Can we talk a little?" I said.

She stopped and looked at me for a second with surprise, oh, that beautiful face! I thought she was going to say something, but she just walked away as if she had seen the devil. I ran after her, not even thinking about who might be around.

"Please stop, Nilgün!" I said. "Listen to me for once!"

She stopped. When I saw her face up close I was even more astonished. What a strange color were her eyes!

"Fine," she said. "Tell me what you have to say right now."

It was as if I had forgotten everything: nothing came to mind, as if we had just met and had nothing to say.

"This record is yours, isn't it?" I said. I held it out to her, but she didn't even look at it!

"No," she said. "It's not."

"It's yours, this record is yours, Nilgün! Take a good look. You can't tell because it's a little sooty! It got wet and I had to dry it."

She bent her head down and looked. "No, this isn't mine!" she said. "You must have me confused with somebody else."

And off she went again. I ran after her and grabbed her arm.

"Let go!" she yelled.

"Why do you all lie to me?"

"Let go!"

"Why are you running away from me? You can't even say hello! Can you tell me what harm I've ever done you? If it hadn't been for me, do you know what they would have done to you by now?"

"They who?"

"How can you lie to my face? As if you have no idea. Do you or do you not read *Cumhuriyet*?"

Instead of giving me a straight answer, she cast her eyes hopelessly around, as if looking for somebody who might help her. Still holding her by the arm, I made a last attempt, gentle and polite as I could.

"I love you, do you know that?"

Suddenly she slipped out of my grip and tried to run off, but halfheartedly, as if she didn't really believe she could get away. I ran two steps after her, and like a cat reaching for a wounded mouse, I firmly but kindly grabbed her wrists, so delicate, in the middle of the crowd. Stop a minute. It was easier than I could have imagined. She was shaking. I wanted to kiss her, but being a gentleman, I wasn't going to take advantage of her now just because she realized what she had done wrong. I know how to control myself. Look, nobody in this crowd is rushing to help you, because they know you're in the wrong. So, tell me, little lady, why were you running away from me, tell me, what were you and the others all scheming about in secret, say it so that everybody in the crowd can hear, so that nobody can misunderstand and accuse me of being involved in anything. I was wondering if Mustafa was anywhere near. Then just as I was waiting to hear what she would say, so that once and for all everyone would stop making up things about me, and this endless nightmare would finally be over, she suddenly started shrieking:

"You crazy fascist, leave me alone!"

And by that she confessed that she was in fact working together with the others. At first I was really surprised, but then I recognized it was my job to give her the punishment she deserved, and so right then and there I started hitting her again and again.

27

Recep Takes Nilgün Back Home

❦

When I realized that the girl lying there was Nilgün and that it was Hasan who'd beaten her and run off, I let go of my net bags full of groceries and ran and ran until I got to her.

"Are you all right, my girl?"

She was bent over, like a sleeper in bed, with her head in her hands and turned toward the pavement, trembling.

"Nilgün, Nilgün," I said, holding her by her shoulders.

She was still crying softly. People came out of all the corners where they had hidden and began to crowd around us, curious, timid heads leaning out over the shoulders of those standing in front of them, trying to get a better look and say something, some shouting themselves hoarse with concern. Seeing them all around her, she seemed embarrassed and reached out to me for help to stand up. I saw her bleeding face, and I told her, "Lean on me, dear girl, lean."

She got up on her feet, leaning on me, and I gave her my hand-kerchief.

"There's a taxi," I said. "Let's get out of here."

The crowd cleared the way for us to pass. As we were getting into the taxi, somebody ran up with my grocery bags and Nilgün's bag. Another kid said, "Wait, this is hers," and gave her a record.

"To the hospital?" said the driver. "Istanbul?"

"I want to go home!" said Nilgün.

"At least let's stop by the pharmacy!" I said.

She remained quiet the whole way there, still trembling, and every once in a while giving a blank and indifferent look at the handkerchief she was dabbing her eye with to see whether she was still bleeding.

"Hold your head like this!" I said, pulling back her hair.

Once again it wasn't Kemal Bey in the pharmacy, but his beautiful wife, listening to the radio.

When the woman saw Nilgün, she let out a scream. Then she began to rush around the shop as she peppered us with questions, but Nilgün just sat there in silence. Finally Kemal Bey's wife was silent, too, and went to work cleaning the cuts on Nilgün's face with cotton and medicine. I couldn't look.

"Kemal Bey's not around?"

"I'm the pharmacist!" his wife said. "What would he do? He's upstairs. Oh, sweetheart, why did they do this to you?"

Just then the door opened, and in came Kemal Bey. He paused for a moment, and then, looking as if he had always expected something like this would happen, he said, "What happened?"

"They beat me," said Nilgün.

"My God, what have we come to?" said the lady pharmacist.

"Who is 'we'?" said Kemal Bey.

"Whoever did this . . . ," said his wife.

"Hasan," murmured Nilgün. "He belongs to a nationalist gang."

"Just be quiet now, you, quiet," said the woman.

But Kemal Bey heard the word and seemed angered. Looking around he reached toward the radio and yelled at his wife, "Why do you always have this thing turned all the way up?"

With the radio turned off, the shop suddenly seemed empty, and then pain and shame and guilt flooded in.

"Don't turn it off," said Nilgün. "Could you turn it back on?"

Kemal Bey did as she asked, and we didn't speak while the lady finished her task.

"Now straight to the hospital!" she said. "God forbid, there could be internal bleeding."

"Is my brother at the house, Recep?" said Nilgün.

"Faruk? No," I said. "He took his car for repairs."

"Just get into a taxi and go," said the woman. "Do you have money, Recep?"

"I'll give you some," said Kemal Bey.

"No," said Nilgün. "I want to go home now." She groaned as she stood up.

"Wait," said the woman. "Let me give you a shot for the pain."

When Nilgün didn't say no, and the pharmacist took her to the back of the shop, Kemal Bey and I were quiet. He was looking out the window at the view he looked at all night long: the window of the snack bar across the street, the Coca-Cola sign, the lamb and the gyro sandwiches. To break the silence, I said, "I came on Monday evening and got aspirin. They said you were asleep. You'd been fishing in the morning."

"It's everywhere," he said. "No matter where you go, it grabs you by the collar."

"What?"

"Politics."

"I don't know," I said.

Then we looked outside for a bit more. The crowd was going down to the beach. When we heard footsteps, I turned and saw Nilgün returning: one of her eyes was half shut and both of her cheeks were completely purple. Kemal Bey's wife said again that we had to go to the hospital, but Nilgün didn't want to, and the wife insisted, telling her husband, "Call a taxi," and then Nilgün said No very forcefully. She took her bag. "We'll walk; it'll do me good. Besides it's just a short way to the house."

While the husband and wife were still talking, I gathered my groceries and Nilgün's bag and took her by the arm. She leaned on me easily, as if she had done it many times, like some family custom.

As we opened the door to leave, and the little bell rang, Kemal Bey said, "So, are you a leftist?"

Nilgün nodded yes, and he said, "How did they know?"

"From the newspaper I bought at the store!"

"Oh!" said Kemal, with a look of relief, but then seemed embarrassed, especially when his beautiful wife said:

"I told you not to buy it every day."

"Be quiet, you!" he said, as if he was done with being embarrassed.

Nilgün and I went outside into the sunshine. We got across the main avenue without anyone noticing us and entered the little street on the other side; we walked past the gardens and the balconies with the colorful bathing suits and towels hanging off them. There were still some people having breakfast, but they paid no attention to us. A teenager on a bicycle stopped to stare, but I think it was because I was a dwarf, not because Nilgün was hurt; I could tell by the look. Then a little girl with swim flippers walked passed us like a duck, and it made Nilgün laugh.

"When I laugh it hurts here," she said, pointing at her side, and laughed some more. "Didn't you think that was funny, Recep? You're always so serious, wearing a tie the way humorless men do. Why don't you laugh for once?"

When I forced myself to laugh, she said, "Look, you even have teeth!" and I got embarrassed and started laughing for real. But then we fell silent, and her tears and trembling started again.

"Don't cry, my dear. Come on, don't."

"I'm such a fool, a stupid, foolish kid . . ."

I started to stroke her hair, but then it occurred to me that a person would want to cry in privacy. So I turned away and looked at the street. A child was watching with curiosity and fear from the balcony across the way. He'll think I made her cry, I thought. When Nilgün stopped she asked for her sunglasses. She put them on and said, "Am I beautiful?" and before I could answer, she said, "Was my mother beautiful? What was my mother like, Recep?"

"You are beautiful, and your mother was beautiful, too."

"What was my mother like?"

"A good woman," I said.

"Good in what way?"

She didn't ask anything from anyone, she wasn't a burden to anyone, as though she didn't know why she was alive; like a shadow, like a cat, Madam would say, following her husband around. But she also knew how to laugh, a big laugh, dazzling like the sun, but openhearted. Good, yes: a person wouldn't be afraid of her.

"Good like you," I said.

"Am I good?"

"Of course."

"What was I like when I was little?"

You used to play so nicely in the garden. You two little ones. Faruk was too old to join in. You'd run around under trees; you were full of curiosity. Then *he* would come out of the house and join you. You didn't make any difference between him and yourselves. I remember once when I was listening from the kitchen window: "Let's play hide-and-seek. Okay, who will be it? You pick, sister." And you went "Eeny, meeny, miny, moe," and Hasan interrupted you, saying, "Do you know French, Nilgün?" And you gave him a tender smile.

"You were like that even as a child," I said.

"Like what, what do you mean?"

Then when dinner was ready I would call upstairs from inside. "Madam, it's ready," I would say, and she would open the window and call out, "Nilgün, Metin, come to dinner! Where are you? They've gone off somewhere again, Recep, where are they?" And I would say, "They're over there, Madam, by the fig tree," and she would cast her eyes around, and then suddenly seeing you through the leaves she would shout, "Oh, with Hasan again! Recep, how many times have I told you not to let that child in here, why does he come here, let him go sit in his father's house," and as Madam carried on, the other shutter would open, too, and Doğan Bey would stick his head out of the room where his father had sat working for years, and he would say, "What's the matter, Mother? What's the harm if they play together?" And Madam would answer him: "Don't interfere, just go sit like your father in your room and write down your idiocies, you're completely unaware, of course, but if these children spend all their time with the children of the servants . . ."

And Doğan Bey would cut her off, saying, "What's the harm, Mother? They're just playing nicely, like sister and brothers."

"Recep, it's like pulling teeth to get anything out of you."

"Excuse me?"

"I asked about my childhood."

"You and your brother Metin played together very nicely."

"Brother?" Madam would say, "God forbid! Where did that slander come from? These children have only one brother, who's making up this gossip that I should have to answer it at eighty years of age?" I would listen and be quiet. Then when each of them went back inside and shut the window I'd go outside and call you in for dinner, and as you went upstairs, he would skulk in some corner alone.

"We played with Hasan, too!" said Nilgün.

"Yes!"

"Do you remember?"

And while you were all upstairs eating—your grandmother, Doğan Bey, you, and Metin, and Faruk, who would appear at the last minute—I would find him in whatever corner he was hiding and say, Psst! Hasan, are you hungry, my boy, okay, then, come and have something. He would follow me, silent and scared, and I'd sit him on my little stool and set in front of him the tray that I still eat from to this day. Then I would go upstairs and bring down the meatball plate, the salad, beans that were just sitting there, as well as the peaches and cherries that even Faruk couldn't finish, and give him some, and as he ate I asked: What's your father been doing, Hasan? *Nothing, just the lottery.* How's that foot of his, is it giving him much trouble? *I don't know.* And how are you, my boy, when do you start going to school? *I don't know.* Why, it's next year, isn't it, son? He would be quiet and look at me fearfully, as if he'd never seen me before. And after Doğan Bey died and he started school, I'd ask him: What grade will you be in this summer, Hasan? He would be quiet. Third, isn't it? Eventually, you'll study and grow up to be a great man! Then what will you do?

Nilgün suddenly staggered on my arm.

"What is it?" I said. "Should we sit down?"

"My side hurts," she said.

"Should we get a taxi?"

She didn't reply, so we walked on. We came out onto the main avenue again and passed between the cars parked on the seashore and the Sunday crowd out from Istanbul. As we went in the garden gate I looked and saw that the car was there.

"My brother's here," said Nilgün.

"Good," I said. "You should go to the hospital in Istanbul right away."

We went in the kitchen door. I was surprised to see I had left the gas on, and one of two burners was lit. It gave me such a fright, and I immediately turned it off. Then I took Nilgün upstairs. Faruk Bey wasn't there. I set Nilgün down on the couch and was just putting a pillow behind her back when I heard her call from her room.

"I'm here, Madam, I'm here, I'm coming," I said. I placed a pillow behind Nilgün's head as well. "Are you okay?" I said. "I'll send Faruk Bey right now."

Madam had come out of her room and was planted at the top of the stairs, with her cane in hand.

"Where were you?" she said.

"I was at the market, you know . . . ," I said.

"And where are you going now?"

"Please just give me a moment," I said. "If you go into your room, I'll be right there."

I knocked on Faruk Bey's door, but there was no reply, and so I opened it, and without looking I went inside. Faruk Bey was stretched out on his bed reading.

"They were able to fix the car in two shakes," he said. "I don't see why Metin got stuck on the road all night."

"Nilgün Hanım is downstairs," I said. "She's waiting for you."

"Me? Why?"

"Recep," Madam called out. "What are you doing there?"

"Please," I said. "Would you just go downstairs, Faruk Bey?"

He seemed a little taken aback and stared me in the face for a moment. Then he put down his book and got up from the bed.

"Why are you standing here, Madam?" I said. "Take my arm and let me put you back in bed. You'll catch cold here. And you're tired."

"Sneak!" she said. "You're telling another one of your lies. Where did Faruk just go off to?"

I went into Madam's room through the open door and straightened out her bedclothes.

"What are you looking for there?" she said. "Don't disturb things."

"I'm airing it out, Madam," I said. "I'm not disturbing anything. See for yourself. Come, lie down in your bed," I said as I opened the shutters.

She lay down, pulled the quilt up to her chin like a small child, and, as though she had forgotten for a second, forgotten to be annoyed and mean, she asked with childish curiosity, "What was there at the market? What did you see?"

I went over and took her pillow and puffed it up.

"There wasn't anything," I said. "They have nothing nice anymore."

"Contrary dwarf!" she said. "I know that perfectly well. That's not what I'm asking you anyway . . . "

"I got fresh fruit; do you want me to bring you some?" I said.

She was silent, back to her normal self. I pulled her door closed and went downstairs, where Faruk and Nilgün had been talking all this time.

28

Faruk Watches a Belly Dancer

ᴥ

After she told me about the lady pharmacist and her husband and how she limped home leaning on Recep, I wanted to hear more about how she felt. It was as though she read my mind.

"It's nothing, Faruk," she said. "Like getting a vaccination. Afterward, I was only angry at myself. Because I couldn't manage that idiot . . ."

"You think he's actually an idiot?"

"When he was little he wasn't like that, he was a good kid," she said. "This year, I started to get the impression that he was foolish and a simpleton. But now I realize that I just let things spin out of control. I shouldn't have snapped at him. I must have been yelling, even though nobody ran over to help."

"What do you make of that?"

"I don't know. Why are you so interested in the morbid details, Faruk?"

"Because I'm like that," I said.

"No, you're not," she said. "You're just pretending to be. You've convinced yourself there is no hope, and for no good reason."

"Is that so? Well, then enlighten me please: what is this thing you call hope?"

She thought a little. "It's the thing that keeps a person on his feet, so he doesn't simply die. As children we wonder, What would happen if I died . . . When I used to think about it, I enjoyed feeling very rebellious. But that fun doesn't last. The trouble is that if you indulge this curiosity too much, it just becomes unbearable."

"But it's not curiosity," I said. "It's simply envy. When you think about how things will be after you're gone, you're realizing that people will enjoy themselves, be happy, forgetting all about you and going on with their pleasant lives."

"No," she said. "Deep down, you are simply curious. You're pretending not to feel this thing that keeps people from dying, but in fact you do feel it."

"No!" I said, getting annoyed. "I'm simply not curious, and that's that."

"Okay, then," she said, with a strangely serene confidence, "what keeps sending you to the archives to read all those words in books? You're acting as if you don't even know."

"What else am I supposed to do, just hang around here?" I said.

I still hated myself for harboring hypocrisies inside, but it's hard to hide from the recognition of someone who knows you well. One can only claim self-understanding to a certain point, and beyond that one is babbling, whether one knows it or not. It was an oddly liberating thought while it lasted.

When Recep came into the room, I said, "Come on, Nilgün! I'm taking you to the hospital."

"Ooff!" she said, like a child. "I don't want to."

"Don't be foolish! The pharmacist was right. What if there's bleeding?" said Recep.

"It wasn't even the man who is the pharmacist, it was only his wife! I feel fine, there's not going to be any bleeding."

I tried to get a bit of my own back by suggesting that in this case she was not the best judge of what she was truly feeling, but after some careful reasoning, I realized I was losing the argument: Nilgün was getting sleepy. She stretched out on the couch on which she'd been leaning her head, and closing her eyes, she said, "Faruk, why don't you tell me a bit of history? Read to me from your notebook."

"So, you think that will put you to sleep?"

She smiled mischievously, like a little girl settling in to hear a story, and as she lay there, I happily ran off, thinking I knew just the story for her, but when I went up to my room the notebook wasn't in my bag. I looked in the drawers, the closet, the suitcase, then searched the other rooms, even Grandmother's, but I couldn't find it. It occurred to me that in my drunken state I might have left it in the backseat of the car, but it wasn't there either. By the time I was going back upstairs to check the rooms again, Nilgün was fast asleep. Seeing Recep draw near, I felt guilty not to have taken charge of the situation, and so I went out to the garden. I installed myself on the dainty chaise longue where Nilgün had spent the entire week reading books, and just sat there.

I thought about the university corridors, the city traffic, white short-sleeved shirts, the hot, humid summer, lunches in the heavy air . . . Back home, I'd find water dripping from taps, though I'd taken care to shut them tight, the rooms would smell of dust and books, and in the metal fridge, a pale, petrified stick of margarine with a taste of plastic would still be waiting. The empty room, it seemed, would still be empty! I had the urge to drink, to sleep. Then I thought: This sort of thing happens to the best of us! I got up and crept in quietly to see Nilgün sleeping. Recep came in.

"Take her to the hospital, Faruk Bey!" he said.

"Let's not wake her up!" I said.

"Not wake her up?" He shrugged his shoulders and went down to the kitchen. I went out again and sat down by the chicken coop where the chickens had come out to take in the sun. Finally, Metin got up, still sleepy, but his eyes wide with curiosity. Nilgün told him what happened, and he told her how they took twelve thousand liras from him last night. When I asked what he was doing out there all by himself at that hour, he fell silent.

"Say, you didn't happen to see my notebook in the car, did you? I can't find it anywhere," I said.

"No, I didn't see it!"

He was curious about how we'd managed to get the car into the repair shop. I said that it started right up after Recep and I pushed it for a bit, but he seemed not to believe it, and so he ran off and asked Recep. When Recep said the same thing, Metin cursed his luck. He asked whether anybody had gone to the police. But I, gesturing to the effect that there was a bit much going on for us to file a police report, told him nobody had gone and went inside to repeat the warning to Nilgün about hemorrhaging and the possibility of death, though without using that word, wishing only to do my duty and impress upon her a sense of urgency without causing panic.

"I don't want to go to the hospital now," she said. "Maybe after dinner."

Since Grandmother hadn't come down, I was able to relax and drink during the meal and generally ignore Recep's efforts to make us feel irresponsible. By the end of the meal, I even had an irksome thought: If Nilgün hadn't called Hasan a fascist maniac maybe none of this would have happened. Then as I was sitting there, my mind drifted to something I'd once read about in the paper: somewhere on the Bosphorus, probably Tarabya, one of those municipal buses, full of passengers, had fallen into the sea at midnight. I felt, at that moment, as if I were in that bus, as if we had all fallen to the bottom of the sea, and because the lights inside the bus still worked, everybody was looking at the windows in panic, as the shadow of death, which seemed oddly alluring somehow, poured in through them.

After dinner, I asked Nilgün about the hospital again, but she said that she wouldn't go. So I went up to my room, lay down on my bed, and opened Evliya Çelebi's travels. I must have fallen asleep reading. When I woke up a full three hours later, it felt as if an invisible elephant was kneeling on me, pinning down my arms and legs. It seemed that if I just closed my eyes I would go right back to sleep, but I resisted the beautiful dreamy feeling and got up. I stood stupidly in the middle of the room for a while: What is the thing we call time? I went back downstairs.

Nilgün had woken up, too. "I always wanted to be sick this way," she said. "So I could lie in bed and read whatever I want without any guilt."

She was reading *Fathers and Sons* for the second time. The intensity of a bookworm who wants to shut out all of life's little distractions. She seemed content, and I didn't have the heart to invoke the specter of death again.

I went upstairs and wandered the rooms vacantly, looking for my notebook. I kept trying to remember whether I had managed to jot down in it some ideas about the plague that had occurred to me. I went down to the garden and out to the street. There wasn't a trace of yesterday's activity on the main avenue or on the beach. The sand was wet, the sun was not warm, and the Marmara was still, dirty, and colorless. Folded up, the pale umbrellas had a melancholy look. I walked to the coffeehouse at the head of the breakwater, among the parked cars that would keep emitting all the heat they'd absorbed from the sun until the very end of the day. I saw an old friend from the neighborhood: he was all grown up and married; he even had his wife and kids with him. We chatted a bit.

When they ran into Recep on Monday night, the old friend Sitri had told his wife that I was one of the oldest fixtures around here. He asked about Selma, but I didn't tell him that we had split up. Then he reminisced about our youthful escapades: how we went out in rowboats and drank until dawn, things like that. He asked me who else was around from the old gang, what were they up to, and filled me in on what he knew. He had seen Şevket and Orhan's mother, who said they would be coming next week. Şevket had gotten married; Orhan's supposedly writing a novel. He asked if I had any kids, moved on to how things were at the university, and then got to the political violence: apparently, they had attacked a girl here this morning, though there didn't seem to be a suspect. In broad daylight, with everybody standing around. Finally saying we should get together in Istanbul, he pulled out a business card from his pocket and held it out to me. As I read it, he deflated the claim printed on the card: Well, not really a factory, he said, it's more of a workshop (they made plastic basins, buckets, baskets).

I stopped at the shop on the way home and picked up a bottle of *rakı*. When I walked in, I said "Hospital?" to Nilgün before I sat down to drink. Nilgün replied with a stubborn, "Nope." Recep heard her, too, but still looked accusingly at me. Maybe that's why I didn't feel I could ask him to make me a snack, which I went and made for myself in the kitchen. Then I sat down and tried to clear my head so that the words and images I'd been collecting could flow freely through my mind and possibly take shape so I could do some writing. When it got dark, and Recep brought Grandmother downstairs, I hid my bottle. Metin did not hesitate to put it back on the table and have a few himself. Grandmother was muttering her complaints softly, like prayers. Finally, Recep brought her back upstairs.

"Let's go back to Istanbul now, right away!" Metin said.

"But weren't you supposed to stay until the middle of the summer? What about all your friends?" said Nilgün.

"I just can't take it here anymore," said Metin. "You stay if you want, Faruk. Just give me the car keys, and let me take Nilgün."

"You don't have a license," said Nilgün.

"Don't you understand? You've got to go," said Metin. "What if something happens? Faruk's not about to do anything. I can certainly drive."

"You're as drunk as he is," said Nilgün. "Let's at least stay the night."

Having put Grandmother to bed, Recep came down and was clearing the table.

"Well, if that's the way you feel, I'm not just going to waste the evening," Metin said. He went upstairs, and a little later he came down with his hair combed and wearing fresh clothes, and he left without a word to anyone. We could still smell his aftershave when he got to the garden gate.

"What's with him?" said Nilgün.

I recited a slightly modified verse from Fuzuli in reply:

> *He's in love with a new rose, a truly lovely sight*
> *And every drop of red he has makes him want to fight*

There was a magical silence in the garden, deeper and darker than the silence after the rain. I got to my feet.

"Yes, go for a little walk, Faruk, it'll do you good," said Nilgün.

I hadn't been thinking of that, but I went for a walk.

As I went out the garden gate, I was thinking about my wife and also about how the Ottoman poets sought out the experience of pain. I wondered whether the classical poets just recited their poems spontaneously or spent hours and hours composing and correcting them. The streets were deserted in the Sunday-evening way, the coffeehouses and clubs were half empty, too; some of the colored lights hung in the trees had blown out, probably owing to the powerful storm yesterday. The muddy tracks of bicycles that had gone in and out of puddles on the street corners left meaningless arcs on the sidewalk. I swayed along as far as the hotel, entering it through the revolving door, led like a dog who smells his way to the kitchen. Above the waiters' padding on the silent carpets, I made out the source of the music and followed it downstairs. I opened a door: drunken tourists, men and women, at tables, with bottles in front of them, wearing fezzes and yelling at one another. It was one of those "Anatolian nights" prepared for foreign travelers on their last night in Turkey. A pathetic orchestra was churning out metallic-sounding tunes at high volume. The belly dancing had not yet begun. I took a table behind the crowd and ordered *rakı*.

Later I heard the clanging of the cymbals, I saw the tanned flesh of the belly dancer undulating at the edge of the spotlight making its way around the semidarkness, and the shimmering jewelry caught my eye: light seemed to beam out from her bottom and the tips of her breasts. I got excited.

I was on my feet. The waiter brought a second glass. The dancer was playing at being the objectified Oriental woman. As the spotlight traveled around between the tables, I looked at the faces of the German women tourists; they weren't astonished, though perhaps they wanted to be, smiling as what they had come for gradually materialized, and as they looked at the dancer, I could sense their satisfaction at thinking how they themselves weren't "like that," the comforting thought of imagining themselves equal to their men; I felt that they saw all of us as being "like that," to be looked down on for their own reassurance, a feeling such as housewives enjoy when they order the servants around!

I wanted to break up this unwholesome spectacle, but I knew I wasn't going to do a thing: I was enjoying the feeling of defeat and mental confusion.

The music grew harsher as a drum whose amplifier was hidden in some corner drowned out the other musicians; the dancer turned her back to the tables and shook her ass with the nervous energy of an overheated hand anxiously fanning itself. I realized that there was a kind of challenge meant by this when she brandished her breasts proudly under our noses, a feeling confirmed when the spotlight revealed an unexpected expression of triumph and confidence on her face. I was myself reassured: You see, it's not so easy to cow us: we can still do some things; we're still on our feet.

At that moment, the dancer was all defiance, making those looks from the tourist women taking uneasy sips from their drinks every now and then, their anthropological scrutiny, seem completely ridiculous. Meanwhile, most of the male tourists in their fezzes had let themselves go; they were no longer looking at a woman "like that"; they were relaxed, disarmed of their superiority, humbled as they would be in the presence of a "respectable" woman.

I felt a strange contentment. The body of the dancer, past her prime but full of action, got me all excited. It was as though we were all waking up from sleep. As I beheld the tanned flesh around her sweaty navel, I felt that I could do just about anything, and I murmured: Let me go right back home, take Nilgün to the hospital, and then give myself over to history without so much fuss about it. There was no reason I couldn't if I would only believe that stories had their truth, flesh-and-blood experiences that actually happened.

The dancer, as though wanting to prolong the belittling she had begun, made her way through the crowd, and taking by the hand certain ones who'd caught her eye, drew them out onto the dance floor. My God! She was forcing them to belly dance! The German men at first were jiggling slowly back and forth, their arms making incompetent little gestures, shooting flustered looks to their friends, but somehow never losing the conviction that they had the right to enjoy themselves.

Eventually, the dancer did what I most dreaded. She masterfully selected the stupidest and seemingly most pliant German and began to strip him. As the fat German removed his shirt, smiling at his friends, clumsily playing along with his version of a belly dance, I lowered my head, unable to take it anymore. At that moment, I wished my whole consciousness could be erased. I wanted to escape from my own awareness, to wander freely in a world outside my mind, but understanding now that I would always be two people, I realized that I'd never be able to let go.

29

Grandmother Receives Visitors
in the Night

It's well after midnight, but I can still hear them moving about: what could they be doing down there, why don't they go to sleep and leave me the silent night? I get out of bed, walk over to the window, and look down: Recep's light is still on, lighting up the garden: what are you doing there, dwarf? It's frightening! He's so sneaky, that one: every once in a while I catch him giving me a look, and I realize he notices everything about me, watching the smallest gesture, how I move my hands and my arms, I know he's plotting something in that big head of his. It's as if they now want to poison my nights too, pollute even my thoughts—it's frightening just to think of it! I remember one night when Selâhattin had come to my room, so I couldn't bury myself in my own thoughts, in the innocence of my childhood, and purify myself of the daily filth; it terrifies me still to think of it, I shiver as if feeling a chill: he told me that he had discovered death. Thinking about it again now, I become even more afraid and pull back from the darkness of the window; reeling in my shadow that fell in the garden, I quickly go back to my bed, get under my quilt, and remember:

It was four months before he died: a north wind blowing outside whistled through the cracks in the window. I had gone to my room, stretched out in bed, but between the endless creaking of Selâhattin's footsteps back and forth in his room and the storm slapping the shutter open and closed, I couldn't sleep a wink. Then I heard footsteps approaching, and I was scared! When the door suddenly opened, my heart came into my mouth, as I realized that he had, for the first time in years, come to my room! He stood there for a while, planted on the threshold: "I can't sleep, Fatma!" As though he weren't drunk, as though I hadn't seen how much he had at dinner! But I didn't say anything. He came in swaying, his eyes blazing like fire. "I can't sleep, Fatma, because I've made a terrible discovery. Tonight you'll listen to me. I won't give you permission to take your knitting and go into the other room. I've discovered something so horrifying I have to tell someone!" The dwarf is downstairs, Selâhattin, I thought, and he loves to listen to you, but I didn't say anything, because his face looked very strange, and he suddenly whispered: "I've discovered death, Fatma, nobody here is aware of it, I'm the first to find it in the East! Just a short while ago, tonight." He paused for a minute, as though truly frightened of his discovery, but he wasn't slurring his words. "Listen, Fatma! After so many months' delay, I finally finished with the letter *O,* and naturally having reached the letter *O,* I eventually had to write the article about *olüm,* death, as you know." I knew only because he'd spoken of nothing else at breakfast, lunch, and dinner. "But I just couldn't write it, I'd been pacing up and down in my room for days and asking myself, Why aren't you writing? Because I was simply going to take it like the other articles from existing articles in other languages, thinking, of course, I had nothing to add to what they thought and wrote, but still I was inexplicably unable to begin writing this article . . ." He laughed for a bit. "Maybe I was paralyzed by the thought of my own death approaching and how I'm nearly seventy and still I haven't been able to finish my encyclopedia—is that what you're thinking?" I didn't say any-thing. "No, Fatma, it's not like that, I haven't finished all the things I mean to do, but I am still young enough! What's more, I feel myself completely revitalized by this discovery: there are so many things to be done in its wake that it wouldn't be enough time even if I lived another hundred years!" He suddenly shouted: "Everything, every event, every life, has taken on a whole new meaning! After a whole week pacing up and down in my room without writing a single word, two hours ago, for the first time in the East, a pair of eyes opened to the fear of Nothingness, Fatma. I know you don't understand but listen and you will." I listened to him, not because I wanted to under-stand but because I couldn't do anything else, and he had started walking up and down, as if he were in his own room. "For a week I've been pacing the floor of my room thinking about death and wondering why they give it so much space in their encyclopedias and books, even ignoring its prevalence in their works of art. In the West there are thousands of books simply about death. I was thinking, Why do they elevate such a simple subject, which I intended to deal with quite briefly in my encyclopedia. I expected to write something like this: 'Death is the failure of an organism!' Then, after a short medical explanation, I was going to discredit, one by one, all the notions about death in legends and sacred books, merrily showing once again how all these scriptures were cribbed from one another, and then describe the comical assortment of funeral ceremonies and traditions that had developed among the world's different peoples. It might seem I wanted to keep things brief because of my anxiousness to finish the encyclopedia once and for all, but that's not the real reason: I didn't understand what death was until two hours ago, because, like a typical Easterner, I didn't place any importance on it, Fatma. Two hours ago I noticed the thing that I had overlooked for so many years while looking at the photos of dead people in the newspaper. It's an awful thing! Listen! I was reading that the Ger-mans had proceeded to attack Kharkiv this time, but that isn't impor-tant! Two hours ago, as I looked absently at the dead in the newspaper, with the same fearlessness I had acquired looking at cadavers at the medical faculty forty years ago, a sudden flash came into my head, a pure terror, like a sledgehammer coming down on my skull, and I thought: Nothingness! There is something called Nothingness, and these poor war dead now have fallen into its dark well. It's a terrible feeling, Fatma: since there is no such thing as God and heaven and hell, there's only one thing after death, only what we call Nothingness. Now, I don't expect that you'll understand right away. Nobody in the East is aware of this. And that's why we've been oppressed for hundreds, thousands of years, but let me not get ahead of myself, I'll explain it to you very slowly, just so I don't have to bear the burden of this discovery all by myself tonight!" He was making nervous gestures with his arms and hands the way he had done when he was young. "Because in one instant I understood why: why we are the way we are and why they are the way they are. I understood why the East is the East and why the West is the West, I swear I understand, Fatma, please, I'm begging you, please listen carefully to me now, and you'll understand, too." He went on speaking to me as though he didn't realize that I hadn't listened to him for forty years. He talked as he did in the early days, with conviction and care, in the sweet, affectionate voice of a foolish old teacher trying to reason with a small child, but he only managed to sound agitated and sinful: "Now listen carefully, Fatma! Don't get annoyed, okay? We say there is no God, how many times have I said this, because his existence cannot be proven by experiment; so, therefore, all religions predicated on the existence of God are no more than empty poetic babbling. It follows that the heaven and hell they babble about also don't exist. You follow me, don't you? If there's no life after death, the lives of those who die disappear altogether. There remains of them absolutely nothing. Now, let's look at this situation from the dead person's point of view: where is the person who died, the person who was alive before death? I'm not talking about the body: where at this point is his awareness, feeling, his mind? Nowhere. It doesn't exist. You see, Fatma, it's where there isn't anything, buried in what I call Nothingness; it neither sees nor is seen anymore. What a strange, horrifying thought! When I try to summon it my hair stands on end! You try it, too, Fatma, think of something with absolutely nothing inside, no sound, no color, no smell, no touch, nothing, something that had no individuality and no place of its own in the void, think of that, Fatma; you can't possibly envision something that occupies no space in the air, remains invisible, and can't be heard, can you? This is the thing that they call death. Are you afraid now, Fatma? While the corpses of our dead are rotting in the nauseating and icy silence of the earth, while the bodies of the war dead, with holes the size of my fist in them, their shattered skulls and brains splattered on the earth, their oozing eyes and their ripped bloody mouths decaying among the concrete ruins, what about their consciousness? Ah, that is buried in the bottomless depths of Nothingness; as they topple down an unfathomable abyss head over heels toward eternity, they are like blind men unaware of what is happening to them. And so I don't want to die, when death comes to mind I want to fight, dear God, what an unnerving thing, to know you will just be lost in the darkness, never, ever to emerge and never to feel anything: we'll all sink into Nothingness, Fatma. Aren't you afraid, don't you want to resist? I won't leave you tonight until you've awakened that rebellious fear of death inside yourself! Listen: There is no heaven, there is no hell. No God, nobody watching and supporting or punishing and forgiving you; after death, you'll descend into this lonely nothingness like a stone going to the bottom of a dark sea. As your corpse decays in the cold ground, your skull and your mouth will fill with earth just like a flowerpot, your flesh will break up into pieces and fall away like dried manure, your skeleton will become dust, like pieces of coal; you'll enter this disgusting swamp that will make you decay down to the last strand of hair, with no right even to hope of coming back again, until you've completely disappeared, all alone in the pitiless icy mud of Nothingness, Fatma, do you understand?"

I lifted my head from the pillow in terror and looked around the room. The same old world, the world that still exists, only my room and my furniture were sound asleep. I was in a sweat. I wanted to see someone, to talk to someone, to touch them. Then I heard the rattling around downstairs and I was curious. It was 3:00 a.m. I quickly got up and ran to the window: Recep's light was still on. The sneaky dwarf, the servant's bastard! I thought of that cold winter night, their miserable hovel, the overturned chairs, broken windows and plates, the disgusting rags. Where's my cane? I took it and banged it on the floor, and then I banged it again. I called out.

"Recep, Recep, quick, come up here!"

I went outside my room, over to the top of the stairs.

"Recep, Recep, I'm speaking to you, where are you?"

From there I could see shadows down below, dancing on the wall: I know you're there. I yelled again and finally saw a familiar silhouette.

"I'm coming, Madam, I'm coming," and the shadow grew smaller until the dwarf appeared. "What's the matter!" he said. "What do you need?"

He wasn't coming up.

"Why aren't you asleep at this hour?" I said. "What are you doing down there?"

"Nothing," he said. "We're just sitting around."

"At this hour?" I said. "Don't lie, I always know. What are you telling them down there?"

"I'm not telling them anything. What's wrong? Have you been thinking about things again? Don't think about them! If you can't sleep, pick up your newspaper, go through your closet, see if your clothes are in order, eat some fruit, just don't start thinking about those things all over again!"

"You let me worry about it!" I said. "Tell them to come upstairs."

"There's only Nilgün Hanım," he said. "Faruk Bey and Metin aren't here."

"Not here? Bring me down, let me see. What have you told them?"

"What would you expect me to tell them, Madam? I don't under-stand!"

As he made his way upstairs, I thought he was coming to help me, but he went into my room.

"Don't make a mess of things," I said. "What are you doing?"

The dwarf was just standing there, looking. I came in behind him, and suddenly he turned around and took me by the arm; it surprised me, but all right. Holding me, he brought me over to the bed: he tucked me in, spreading the warm quilt over me, so I felt like a little girl again, innocent, and I forgot about everything.

As I lay there he said on the way out, "You took only one bite out of your peach. These are the best peaches, but you don't like them. Shall I bring up an apricot?"

When I didn't answer, he left, and I was there alone: with the same ceiling overhead, the same floor under the bedposts, the same water in the pitcher, and the same glass, brush, cologne, plate, and clock resting on the same table, I stretched out in my bed, thinking, How strange it is, this thing we call time, and with that I took fright, realizing that I would again be thinking about what Selâhattin had discovered that night. The devil continued on his way:

"Can you reckon the enormity of this discovery, Fatma? Tonight, I've identified the invisible line dividing them and us! No, East and West aren't separated by clothing, machines, houses, furniture, prophets, and governments. All of these are mere consequences; what separates us from them is that simple little truth: they have discovered the bottomless pit of Nothingness, whereas as we remain unaware of this terrible truth. To think that this inconceivable gulf is all due to this tiny discovery makes my head spin! How could it be that for a thousand years not a single person in the East has thought of it. If you think of all the time and the lives that have been lost under this misconception, even you can see, Fatma, the dimensions of what it has cost us. Still, I have faith in the future! Because, now, tonight, I have taken the first step, crossing the line that could have been crossed at any time for centuries now; tonight, I, Selâhattin Darvinoğlu, have become the first in the East to discover death! Why are you staring blankly. Of course, because only someone who truly comprehends darkness can truly see the light, only someone who comprehends death knows the meaning of existence. I think of death, therefore I exist. No! Because actually, those insensible Easterners also exist, you and your knitting exist, too, only none of you knows a thing about death! So to be perfectly accurate, I should say: I think of death, therefore I'm a Westerner! I suppose that makes me the first person of the East to become one! Do you understand, Fatma?" I didn't answer, and he shouted, "Dear God, you're as blind as all the others!" Then he staggered two steps toward the window half weeping, and for a moment I had the very strange impression that he would open it and jump out into the storm, flap his wings and for a little while remain aloft on the joy of his discovery until, realizing the truth, he fell to the ground and died. But Selâhattin stayed inside the room and only looked out from the closed dark windows in hatred and despair as though he could see the whole country and what he called the East. "Poor blind creatures! They're asleep. They've gone to bed, wrapped in their quilts, buried in the tranquil sleep of their idiocy, snoring away. The whole East just sleeps! Slaves! I will teach them about death and deliver them from this slavery. But first I'll free you, Fatma, listen to me, understand and tell me that you're afraid of death!" And so he started to beg, just as he had when he tried to get me to say that there is no God, twisting words and bending my fingers back as he listed what he called the proofs: I didn't believe. When he got fed up and stopped talking, he sat on the chair in front of me, staring aimlessly at the table as the wind continued to slap the shutters against the house. He looked at the clock on the wall next to me with a start, and it scared me, too, because I imagined he had seen a scorpion or a snake, but then he shouted: "We have to catch up! Faster!" Taking the clock from the wall and throwing it on my bed, which was still made up, he continued shouting: "Between us and them, there's maybe a thousand years difference, but we have to catch up, Fatma, so I can't delay in publishing this article and setting our poor people right. Poor fools! They live out their days in blind contentment, without the slightest doubt about anything, unaware that they have only this life! I'll bring them all to their knees with the fear of death! They'll get to learn their true nature; they'll learn a proper fear of themselves, and a proper disgust! Have you ever seen a Muslim with an honest self-loathing, have you ever met an Easterner capable of being disgusted with himself? They ask nothing of themselves, they bow their heads without even knowing to what, and they view anyone who seeks anything more as either perverted or crazy! I'm going to teach them to fear not solitude but death, Fatma. Then they'll actually prefer the deep anguish of loneliness to the foolish peace of mind bestowed by the crowd! Then they'll see they don't have to place themselves at the center of the universe! Then they'll no longer take pride in remaining exactly the same people all their lives, but instead they'll feel ashamed; they'll question themselves and not in the eyes of God but according to their own lights! This is all going to happen, Fatma, I'm going to wake them from that peaceful foolish dream that's lasted for thousands of years!" Eventually, he quieted down, as though exhausted by his own rage. I was waiting for him to leave me to the solitude of the night so that I could go back to a nice sleep.

When the noise downstairs reached my ears again, I lifted my head from the warmth of my pillow. I could hear the dwarf shuffling around the house as if he were inside my own head. What are you doing, dwarf, what are you telling them? I heard the bang of the garden gate, and I was frightened when I recognized the footsteps in the garden: Metin! Where were you at this hour? I heard him rattling the kitchen door open, but he didn't come upstairs. I thought: They're down there, they're all down there, and the dwarf is telling them everything. I shuddered and said, Where's my cane, I'll catch them all in the act, but I didn't get out of my bed. I heard his footsteps coming up the stairs. Metin knocked and came into my room. "How are you, Grandmother?" he said. How odd! "Are you okay?" I didn't answer,

I didn't look at him. "Everything's fine, Grandmother, nothing to worry about, nothing's going to happen to you." Then I understood: drunk! Like his grandfather! I squeezed my eyes shut. "Don't go to sleep, Grandmother! I have something I want to say to you!" Don't tell me! "Don't go to sleep now!" I'm sleeping and I feel my soft bed beneath me. "Let's knock this old house down, Grandmother!" I knew it. "Let's knock the house down and have them build a nice big apartment building in its place. The developer will let us have half of it. It would be good for all of us. You don't know what's going on." Right, I don't know anything! "We all need money, Grandmother! The way things are going, soon we won't be able to cover the kitchen expenses for this place." Our kitchen, I was thinking: When I was little our kitchen smelled of cloves and cinnamon. "If we don't do something soon, you and Recep will just starve here. The others can't face up to this stuff, Grandmother. Faruk's drunk every day now. Nilgün is a Communist, did you know that?" I smelled the scent of cinnamon; I didn't know, but I knew that if you want to be loved it's better not to know it all. "Please, won't you answer me! This is for your own good! Don't you hear me?" I don't hear you, because I'm not here, I'm asleep and I remember: we boiled jam, drank lemonade, ate sherbet. "Answer me, Grandmother, please, answer me!" Then I paid a visit to Şükrü Pasha's daughters: Hello, Türkân, Şükran, Nigân, hello! "Don't you want that? Wouldn't it be better to live in a nice new heated apartment than to be cold and hungry in this decrepit old house?" He comes over to the edge of the bed and rocks the headboard with the brass balls to get my attention. "Wake *up,* Grandmother, come on, open your eyes, answer me!" I'm not opening them, and still the bed is rocking: Then we got in the horse carriage to pay our visit. *Tiki-taka, tiki-taka.* "They're convinced that you don't want to tear down this house! But they need money, too. Why do you think Faruk's wife left him? People don't care about anything but money anymore, Grandmother!" He won't stop rocking the bed. *Tiki-taka,* the carriage rocked along. The sweeping horse-tails . . . "Grandmother, answer me . . ." They brushed away the flies. "If you don't answer me, I won't let you sleep!" I remembered, I remembered, I remembered. "I need money, too, more than any of them, do you understand? Because I"—my God, he sat down on the edge of the bed—"I just can't be happy as they are with so little. I hate this country of idiots! I want to go to America. I need money. Do you understand?" His mouth reeked of alcohol, and turning my head in disgust I understood. "Now, Grandmother, all you have to do is tell me that you want this, too, and I'll tell the rest. Say, yes, Grandmother!" I didn't say it. "Why won't you say it? Because you're hanging on to your memories? We'll move all your furniture into the new apartment! Your wardrobe, your trunks, your sewing machine, your dishes, we'll take it all. Grandmother, you'll be happy, too, do you understand?" What I understood was how beautiful the winter nights were when no one was around: when the silence of the night was mine alone, as I lay there with everything completely still! "We'll hang that picture of Grandfather that's on the wall now. Your room will be exactly the same as this one. Come on, please, give me an answer!" I didn't! I was afraid when I felt his cold hand on my shoulder. His weepy voice came close, he was begging with his alcoholic breath, and I remembered: There's no paradise, there's no hell, your corpse will stay there all alone in the icy darkness of the earth. Your eyes will fill with earth, the maggots will eat away your insides, your flesh will decay. "Grandmother, I'm begging!" Ants will run around in your brain, slugs will crawl through your lungs, worms will writhe inside of your heart. "Why are you still alive when my mother and father are dead?" he said at a point of despair. "Is that right?" I thought, They've tricked him, too. The dwarf downstairs is telling them everything! He didn't say anything else. He was crying, and at one point, I thought his hand was going for my throat! I thought of my own grave, seeing him stretch out on the edge of my bed, still crying. I was filled with disgust. Hard as it is for me to get out of my bed, I managed it. I put on my slippers and grabbing my cane made my way out of the room and stopped to call down from the top of the stairs.

"Recep, Recep, come up here, quick!"

30

Recep Tries to Take Care of Everyone

❧

When I heard Madam call out, I jumped up right away from where Nilgün and I were sitting. I found Madam at the top of the stairs.

"Hurry up, Recep!" she was shouting. "What's going on in this house? Tell me this instant!"

"Nothing," I said, out of breath.

"Nothing, you say! This one's gone completely insane. Take a look!"

With the tip of her cane, she pointed inside her room, as though there were a dead mouse there. Metin was lying facedown on her bed, his face buried in the embroidered pillow, sobbing and heaving.

"He was going to kill me!" said Madam. "What's going on in this house, Recep? Don't think you can keep things from me."

"Nothing," I said. "Metin Bey, is this any way to carry on, come on, get up."

" 'Nothing,' you say. Someone put him up to this. Take me downstairs now!"

"Metin had a little too much to drink, Madam! That's all. He's young, he drinks, but he's not used to it. So you see what happened. Weren't his father and his grandfather just like this?"

"That's enough out of you!" she said.

"Come on, Metin Bey!" I said. "Come, let me put you in your own bed!"

As he dragged himself to his feet, he paused to look at his grandfather's portrait on the wall. When I got him into his own room he looked like he was about to cry again.

"Why did they die so young? Would you tell me why, Recep?"

As I was helping him out of his clothes so he could get to bed, I started to explain to him about God's will when he suddenly pushed me away.

"Never mind, I can do it myself. God? You stupid dwarf!" But instead of getting undressed he pulled something out of his suitcase, and he announced in a funny voice that he was going to the bathroom. I heard Madam calling.

"Take me downstairs, Recep. I want to see for myself what's going on."

"There's nothing going on, Madam," I said. "Nilgün Hanım is reading, Faruk Bey's gone out."

"Where would he go at this hour? What did you tell them? I want the truth!"

"It is the truth, Madam. Come, let me put you to bed," I said, leading the way into her room.

"Don't tell me there isn't something going on in this house. And don't go into my room and disturb things!" she said, following me in.

"Come on, Madam, get into your bed, before you exhaust yourself," I said. Then hearing Metin cry out, I was frightened and ran into the hallway immediately.

Metin was downstairs, staggering like a drunk, cradling his arm. "Oh, Recep, look, look what happened!" he said looking tenderly, like a child, at the blood dripping from his wrist. There was a cut, but not a deep one, thank God, more of a scratch. Suddenly his fear and my presence reminded him of everyday life, and he seemed regretful.

"Do you think the pharmacy is still open now?" he said.

"It is," I said. "But let me press some cotton on that first, Metin Bey!" And as I was about to go fetch it, Nilgün called over to us without lifting her head from the book.

"What's going on?"

"Nothing!" said Metin. "I cut my hand."

He was pressing on the cut with the cotton I'd brought him when Nilgün came over for a look.

"It's not your hand, it's your wrist," she said. "But it doesn't look bad. How did you manage that?"

"It isn't bad, is it?" said Metin.

"What else is in that closet, Recep?" said Nilgün, curious about the place where I kept the cotton.

"So, you agree, it's nothing, right?" said Metin. "But I better go to the pharmacy anyway."

"Oh, just odds and ends, *küçükhanım*," I said.

"Not any of my father's or my grandfather's old papers? I've always wanted a look at what they were writing."

I held my tongue for a moment, but then I just came out with it, I don't know why: "Miss, they were writing that there is no God."

This amused Nilgün. A pretty smile came to her face. "And how do you know?" she said. "I suppose they told you?"

I closed the closet. When I heard Madam calling again, I went upstairs to put her back into bed again and assure her that there was absolutely nothing going on she had to worry about. She asked me to change the water in her pitcher. By the time I'd brought her fresh water up and come back down, Nilgün was coughing again. Then I heard some noise at the kitchen door. It was Faruk Bey having trouble getting in.

"It wasn't locked," I said as I opened the door for him.

"Every light in the house is on," he said, blowing strong *rakı* vapors into my face. "What's happened?"

"We're waiting for you, Faruk Bey," I said.

"What's it got to do with me?" he said. "Why didn't you take a taxi to Istanbul? I just went to see some belly dancing."

"If you're wondering about Nilgün Hanım, she's fine," I said.

"She is?" he said, a little surprised, and then he said, "I knew she'd be. She's fine, isn't she?"

"Yes. Aren't you going to come inside?"

First, he turned, looking into the darkness at the dim lamp on the other side of the garden gate, as though he wanted to go out there one last time. Then he came in, opened the icebox, and pulled out the bottle. He took two sudden steps backward, as though the weight of the bottle in his hand had made him lose his balance, and collapsed into my chair. He was gasping, like someone with asthma.

"You're destroying yourself, Faruk Bey," I said. "Nobody drinks this much."

"I know," he said, hugging the bottle the way a little girl might hold her doll.

"Shall I make you some soup? I've got bouillon."

By the time I brought the soup Metin had returned with a thin little piece of tape on his wrist.

"The pharmacist asked about you, Nilgün!" he said. "She couldn't believe it when she heard you didn't go to the hospital."

"Yes," said Faruk. "It's not too late. We can still go."

"Relax, nothing's going to happen," said Nilgün. "Where were you this evening?"

"I went to see the belly-dance show, together with all the idiotic tourists in their fezzes."

"Was it good?" said Nilgün, cheerfully.

He didn't answer, only saying, "I wonder what could have happened to my notebook? I had some really good notes in it."

"Look at you," said Metin. "You're practically asleep, and now because of you—"

"Because of me? Look, Metin, do you want to go back to Istanbul? But here or there, I don't see what difference it makes for you!"

"You're both drunk. Nobody's in any condition to drive any-where," said Nilgün.

"I can drive fine!" Metin shouted.

"No, we're just going to stay here tonight, the three of us together, the way it used to be," said Nilgün.

"How did it used to be?" Faruk said. "It's just another story!" He was quiet for a moment, then he added, "Stories are just stories, they have no rhyme or reason . . ."

"That's not true! I tell you every time. There is a reason for them."

"For God's sake. You really never tire of repeating yourself."

"That's enough!" said Metin.

"I wonder what we'd be like if we'd been born to a Western fam-ily," said Faruk. "A French family, for example! Would Metin be happy then, I wonder?"

"No," said Nilgün, with a teasing smile. "He wants America."

"Is that true, Metin?"

"I said quiet!" said Metin. "I'm trying to sleep."

"Metin Bey, don't sleep there," I said. "You'll catch a cold."

"You stay out of it."

"Should I bring you some soup, too?"

"Fine, bring it!" said Metin with a sigh.

When I came back upstairs from the kitchen, Faruk Bey was stretched out, too, on the other couch. He was staring at the ceiling as he chatted with Nilgün, and they were both laughing. Metin was looking at a record he was holding.

"This is great!" said Nilgün. "Just like being in the dorm."

I started to say, "Don't you think you should all go upstairs and get to bed," when I heard Madam call out.

It took me awhile to calm her and get her back into bed. She still wanted to go downstairs; I gave her a peach. By the time I'd finally closed her door and returned to the others, Faruk Bey was fast asleep, making a strange rasping noise that came from deep inside, like some old person who had been through too much.

"What time is it?" whispered Nilgün.

"It's three thirty," I said. "Are you going to sleep here, too?"

"Yes."

So I went upstairs, and from their rooms, one by one, I collected their bedclothes and brought them downstairs. Nilgün thanked me. I covered Faruk Bey, too.

"I don't want it," said Metin, still looking blankly at the cover of the record in his hand, as though he were watching television. When I got close I saw it was the record from the morning. "Turn out the lights," he said.

Since Nilgün didn't say anything I went over and turned out the single bulb that was hanging from the ceiling, but I could still see them. The raw light of the streetlamp was shining in through the shutters and striking the bodies of the three of them lying there, revealing Faruk Bey in his troubled, defeated sleep but also reminding me that so long as there is even a little light and the world isn't in total darkness, a person mustn't be frightened. Then I heard the sharp and insistent chirping of a cricket, not in the garden, but very close by, and it was almost as if I wanted to be afraid, but I couldn't be. As I continued watching, and every once in a while one of them stirred slightly from that sleep of the three of them in the same room under the quilt of the darkness and the steady, peaceful snoring, I thought, It must be beautiful to be like this. Because like this, even though you're asleep, even on a cold winter night, you're not shivering all alone! It's as if your mother or father or both of them are in the room upstairs or the one next door, listening to you rustle, waiting for you, and this thought alone is enough to let you lose yourself in the soft goose down of sleep. It was then I thought of Hasan and how he must be shivering alone now. How could you have done it, my boy? Why? I watched their forms move slightly, and I thought, I'll sit here until morning, knowing I should be afraid but feeling unable to be.

"Recep, are you still there?" said Nilgün.

"Yes, little lady?"

"Why didn't you go to bed?"

"I was just going to."

"Go lie down, Recep. There's nothing wrong with me."

I went to the kitchen and drank some milk and ate some yogurt before finally going to bed, but I didn't fall asleep right away. Turning in my bed, I thought about how the three of them, siblings, were asleep up there together in the same room, then death came to mind, then Selâhattin before he died. Oh, my son, he said, what a shame I couldn't see to an education for you and Ismail. It was of course partly my fault: that imbecile they brought you to in the village and passed off to you as your father, he let you rot in ignorance. I closed my eyes when Fatma sent you there, he said, I was weak, I didn't want to cross her while she was still paying the expenses for my important scientific studies, the bread you eat is from her, too, and the pain you suffer, he said, but still I was heartbroken that those idiots in the village brainwashed you with fear. Unfortunately, I am no longer able to raise you up to be free men who think for themselves and make their own decisions, it's too late, not just because the tree is bent when it's young, as they say, but also because I now have one foot in the grave, and it's not enough that I educate and save just one or two boys anymore when there are millions of poor Muslims chained in the dungeons of darkness, millions of poor benighted slaves waiting for the light of my book! Time is so short! Good-bye, my poor thing, my silent child, let me at least give you some final advice, listen to me, Recep: be open-minded and free, and only trust to your own intelligence, do you understand? I was silent, hanging my head, and I thought: Words! Pluck the fruit of knowledge from the tree in paradise, Recep, take it without fear, maybe you will writhe in pain, but you'll be free, and when everyone is free the true paradise will be established, the real paradise on this earth where you will have nothing to fear. Words, I was thinking, a bunch of sounds, that are said and then vanish into the air . . . I fell asleep thinking of them.

Long after sunrise, I woke up to the sound of someone tapping on my window. It was Ismail. I opened the door right away. We gave each other a look full of fear and guilt. "Hasan hasn't been here, has he?" he said in a tearful voice.

"No," I said. "Come inside, Ismail."

He came into the kitchen and stood there carefully, as if he were afraid of breaking something. We were silent for a bit.

"Did you hear what he did, Recep?" he said.

I didn't say anything but went inside and took off my pajamas, and as I was putting on my shirt and pants, I heard him saying, as if to himself: "I let him do everything he wanted. He didn't want to be a helper in the barbershop. Fine, I said, then study. But he wouldn't study either. Then I find out he's going around with these national-ists, people saw them, they said they go all the way to Pendik, they collect money by force from the shopkeepers!"

Then he fell silent. I thought he was going to cry, but when I returned to the kitchen he wasn't crying. "What are they saying?" he said. "The people upstairs. How's Nilgün?"

"Last night she said, 'I'm fine,' now she's sleeping," I said. "But they didn't take her to the hospital. They should have taken her."

Ismail seemed pleased. "Maybe it wasn't so bad that they had to go to the hospital," he said. "Maybe he didn't hit her that much."

"I saw it, Ismail," I said. "I saw how he beat her!"

He slumped down on the little stool, ashamed, and again I thought he would cry, but he just sat there. A little later, when I heard movement upstairs, I put the water on for tea and went up to Madam.

"Good morning," I said. "Do you want to have breakfast down-stairs or here?" I opened the shutter.

"Here," she said. "Call them in, let me see them."

"They're all asleep," I said, but when I went downstairs I saw that Nilgün was up, and in a red dress, and when I asked, she said, "I'm fine, Recep. Nothing wrong with me."

But her face didn't say that. One eye was completely closed, the cuts had scabs on them, and they seemed to be more swollen and had turned purple.

"You're going straight to the hospital!" I said.

"Is my brother up yet?"

I went downstairs. Ismail was still sitting where I'd left him. I brewed the tea. A little later he said, "The gendarmes came to the house yesterday. Don't hide him, they said. Why should I hide him, I said, I'll punish him before the state does, I said." He was quiet, waiting for me to say something. "What are they saying?" he said. When he got no answer he lit a cigarette. "Where will I find him?" I was cutting bread to make toast. "He has friends, they say he goes to the coffeehouse," he said. "He did this to be like them. He doesn't know anything!" I felt that he was looking at me as I kept cutting the bread.

When I went upstairs Faruk was awake, too, and talking. Nilgün was happily listening.

"That's how I found myself in the arms of the muse of history!" Faruk Bey was saying. "She was hugging me like a motherly aunt: 'So, now, I'll tell you the secret of history.'"

Nilgün giggled.

Faruk continued, "But what a dream! I woke up, but it wasn't really like waking up. You know how you want to wake up, but you feel yourself in the abyss of sleep. Look, I found this thing crushed in my pocket!"

"Ohh," said Nilgün. "A fez!"

"The tourists were wearing them at the belly-dancing show last night, but I have no idea how it got into my pocket. How did it even fit in there?"

"Should I give you your breakfast right away?" I said.

"Yes, Recep," they said.

Knowing they would want to get back to Istanbul before the mob of vendors and the heavy traffic, I went down to the kitchen, put the bread on the stove, and boiled some eggs. I was bringing the tray up when Ismail said, "Maybe you know, Recep. You spend your life in this kitchen, but maybe you know more than anybody. More than me, for sure!"

I thought for a second. "I know as much as you do, Ismail!" I said. I told him I had seen the boy smoking. Ismail looked surprised, as if he had been betrayed. Then, sounding more hopeful, he said, "Where would he go? Someday he'll turn up again. And with all that's been going on around here every day, so many people dying, they will forget about this." I didn't answer but went upstairs.

"They're up, Madam." I said. "They're waiting for you downstairs. Come, why don't you go down and have breakfast with them on their last day."

"I told you to call them!" she said. "I have things to say. I don't want them falling for your lies."

I went downstairs without saying a word. I was setting the table. Faruk and Nilgün were laughing together. Metin, who was now up, too, was sitting silently. When I went down to the kitchen, Ismail said, "Hasan hasn't been home for two nights. Did you know?"

"I didn't know," I said. "Was he out on the night it rained, too?"

"Out," he said. "The roof was leaking, the water was carrying everything in the house away. We sat there the whole night and waited, but he never came."

"When the rain started he must have ducked inside somewhere and stayed there," I said.

He eyed me carefully, saying, "And you're sure he didn't come here?"

"He never came here, Ismail!" I said, even though the gas that someone had left on did cross my mind. I took the tea, toast, and eggs upstairs.

"Do you want milk, Nilgün Hanım?"

"No," she said.

I wish I had just boiled the milk and put it in front of her. I went down to the kitchen, "Come on, Ismail," I said. "Why don't you drink your tea?" I put a breakfast service in front of him and cut some bread. I took Madam's tray upstairs.

"Why aren't they coming up?" said Madam. "Didn't you tell them that I asked for them?"

"I told them, Madam . . . They're having their breakfast now. But before they go, they'll come up and kiss your hand, of course."

She lifted her head from the pillow with a quick cunning movement. "What did you tell them last night?" she said. "Tell me now, I don't want any lies!"

"I have no idea what it is you want me to tell you!" I left her tray and went downstairs.

"If I could at least find my notebook," said Faruk Bey.

"Where was the last place you saw it?"

"In the car. Then Metin took the car, but he didn't see it."

"You didn't see it?" said Nilgün.

They both looked at Metin, who was sitting there like a child who had just been slapped but forbidden to cry: he had bread in his hand, but he sat there just staring at it for a long time,

"Metin, we're talking to you!" Nilgün shouted.

"I didn't see your notebook!"

Downstairs, Ismail had lit up another cigarette. I sat down to have my breakfast with the bread he'd left. Ismail and I didn't talk; we were just looking out the open door, at the garden and the patch of earth where the sparrows walked about. The sun was shining in, burning our helpless hands.

"When are they going to draw the lottery, Ismail?"

"They did it last night!" he said. We heard a long roar. Nevzat's motorcycle passing by. Then he said, "I should go."

"Stay," I said. "Where are you going? When they leave we can talk." He sat down. I went upstairs.

Faruk Bey had finished his breakfast and was smoking a cigarette. "Be nice to Grandmother now, Recep! We'll give you a call every now and then. And we'll come out again for sure before the end of the summer."

"You are always welcome."

"And if, God forbid, something should happen, be sure to call. If you need anything . . . But you're not used to using the phone, are you?"

"You're going to the hospital first, aren't you?" I said. "Before you go, let me give you another tea."

When I carried up the tea from downstairs, Nilgün and Faruk were chattering away again.

"Did I tell you about the deck of cards theory?" Faruk was saying.

"You did," said Nilgün. "You also said that your head was like a walnut and that if somebody cracked it open they would see the worms of history crawling around in its folds. Remember, I said that it was crazy. But still I think your stories are entertaining."

"That's just it. Stories are good for a laugh but not much else."

"That's not true at all," said Nilgün. "Everything has its cause and effect. Even what happened to me didn't happen for nothing."

"But wars, riots, plunder, rapes?"

"None of them happens by chance."

"Swindlers, plagues, merchants, disputes . . . "

"You know as well as I do that each of them has a reason."

"Do I?" Faruk asked. "Seems to me they just make for better or worse yarns and nothing more!"

"I'm feeling a little nauseated," said Nilgün.

"Let's go now," said Metin.

"Why don't you stay here, Metin?" said Faruk. "You were going swimming. What'll you do in Istanbul? Why not stay?"

"Because while you two don't give any thought to where money comes from, I've got to earn some!" said Metin. "I'll be tutoring kids at my aunt's house all summer long, for two hundred fifty liras an hour. Okay?"

"You frighten me sometimes," said Faruk.

I went down to the kitchen, trying to think of something that would settle Nilgün's stomach. Ismail stood up. "I'm going," he said. "Hasan will come home eventually, won't he, Recep?"

I considered that question for a moment before saying, "He will come! Wherever he goes, he'll come back, but don't leave yet, Ismail, sit down!"

He didn't sit down. "What are they saying upstairs?" he said. "Should I go up and apologize?"

That took me by surprise, and I thought about it. I started to say,

Sit, Ismail, don't go, when I heard a familiar noise from upstairs. Madam's cane pounding on the floor. "Do you remember that?"

We stopped for a moment and looked up. Then Ismail sat down. She rapped a few times on the floor, as though it were Ismail's head. Then we heard that faint, weak, but tireless old voice.

"Recep, Recep, what's going on down there?"

I went upstairs.

"There's nothing wrong, Madam. They're coming upstairs now," I said as I was leading her back to her bed. I wondered whether I should take the bags down to the car now and save some time. Finally I grabbed Nilgün's suitcase and slowly carried it down. I thought that seeing me she might ask why I had brought it down so soon, but at the sight of her stretched out on the couch I realized I had forgotten about her upset stomach. I was blaming myself for not remembering the one thing I meant not to forget, when suddenly she started throwing up. I froze with the suitcase still in my hand as Metin and Faruk just stared in astonishment. Then, without making a sound, Nilgün turned her head to one side: when I saw what was coming out of her mouth I thought of eggs, I don't know why. I ran back down to the kitchen to find something to soothe her stomach. I was thinking, It's because, like a fool, I didn't give her milk this morning, it's my fault. Then I found myself gazing foolishly at Ismail, who was saying something, until I remembered what was going on above and ran back there. When I got upstairs again, Nilgün was dead. They didn't say that she had died; I realized it when I saw her, but I didn't say the word either. We all looked guiltily at her green face and her slack, darkened mouth, her face like that of a young girl who was just trying to relax after we had inconsiderately worn her out. Ten minutes later, Kemal Bey's pharmacist wife, whom Metin had gone to get in the car, said the word. And she said two others, "cerebral hemorrhage," which sounded final. Still, for a long time we stared at Nilgün with hope, thinking she might yet get up and start walking.

31

Hasan Goes His Way

I lifted the empty paint can and waited silently for the hedgehog to poke his stupid nose out from inside his spines so I could have a little fun. But he didn't do it. Must have got wise to me. After I'd waited a little longer, I got bored, so I carefully picked up the hedgehog by one of his spines and held him up in the air. When I suddenly let go, he plopped to the ground on his back, helpless. Feeling the pain now, huh? This dumb animal is really pathetic, I feel sorry for you, hedgehog, but I've had enough of you.

It was seven thirty, I'd been hiding here all day, with no entertainment for six hours but this hedgehog I found in the middle of the night. My mother and I would always know them right away from the rustling noise they made, and when you lit a match in front of its eyes in the darkness, it would get startled and freeze there, the fool! You could put a pail over it and keep it captive until morning. They had mostly disappeared now, just this one was left: the last startled hedgehog! But I've had enough of you. As I was lighting a cigarette I thought I might set it on fire, not just the hedgehog, but everything around here, the cherry orchards, the last of the olive trees, everything. It would be a proper farewell to all of you, but I thought, It's not worth it. I turned the hedgehog upright with my foot. Go on, do whatever you want. I'm just going to go off now with my cigarette, trying to forget how hungry I am.

First, let me gather my stuff together, I said. I'd set down my cigarette pack with seven cigarettes left in it, along with the two combs, my matches, and the paint can next to the stupid hedgehog, but I held on to Faruk's notebook just for a look, because even if it was of no use to me, they wouldn't be so suspicious of somebody carrying a notebook, assuming of course they thought it was even worth it to come after me. Before leaving, I said, Let me take one last look at this old spot of mine between the almond and the fig trees, I used to come here when I was little, too, when I was bored at home, bored with everything. I looked for the last time, and I was off.

After I'd crossed the goat path, I said, This time let me take a look from far away at my house and the neighborhood down below. Fine, Dad, good-bye, on the day I come back in triumph—anyway, who knows, you might have read about it in the papers—you'll understand then how wrongly you treated me; I'm not meant to be a simple barber. Good-bye, Mom: maybe the first thing I'll do is free you from that stingy lottery dealer. Then I looked at the rich, meaningless walls and roofs of those houses of sinners. I can't see your house from here, Nilgün; anyway, you've probably already called the police; good-bye, for now.

I didn't mean to stop at the cemetery, my path just took me that way, and as I passed through among the tombstones, I was reading one, when I noticed their names: GÜL and DOĞAN and SELÂHATTIN DARVINOĞLU, it said, MAY THEY REST IN PEACE. And suddenly I felt, for some reason, very alone, guilty, and hopeless; I walked on quickly, afraid I might start to cry.

Worried somebody might see, that some jerk would point me out or turn me in or something, I didn't take the highway on which they race back to Istanbul on Monday morning to cheat one another; instead I went through the orchards and fields. The crows, gathered in the branches of the sweet cherry and the morello trees, made a guilty exit and flew away as I approached. Dad, did you know that even Atatürk and his sister chased away crows once? Last night I screwed up my courage and went to see what was going on at our house; when I looked in the window, all the lamps were lit and nobody was running around saying, Turn them off, it's a sin, and my father was sitting there with his head in his hands so you couldn't tell whether he was crying or muttering to himself. I said to myself, Somebody must have told them what happened, maybe the gendarmes came. When the image of my father like that appeared before my eyes again, I felt sorry for him, I almost began to feel guilty.

I didn't go by the lower neighborhood, because there was a pack of worthless bums hanging out there, watching everybody pass, trying to figure out what they were up to. I went off the paved road, right where Metin's car got stuck last night, and straight down through the vegetable gardens. When I reached the train track, I walked the length of the Agricultural School toward the station. If it had been up to my father and if the entrance exam hadn't asked questions about stuff we were never taught, I would have been put in this Agricultural School, because it was close to home, and I would have graduated next year with a gardener's diploma. But when you have a diploma, they don't call you a gardener, they say, "civil servant," yes, a civil servant, because you wear a tie, but, if you ask me, you're just a gardener wearing a tie. They have classes in the summer too. You see them when the bell rings, running over to kiss the teacher's ass so they can show you in a laboratory what a tomato seed looks like. Pathetic zit faces! Anyway, seeing them, I was really glad that girl crossed my path, because if she hadn't brought all this upon me, I might have been willing to become a gardener with a tie or a barber with his own shop. Of course to get to be a barber from being an apprentice, I'd have to spend at least ten years smelling not just my father's breath but the barber's as well. These things took time!

In front of the cable factory, a bunch of workers were waiting together by the red-and-white guardrail that went up and down so that cars couldn't cross when the train was passing, except they didn't enter that way but quietly through the little side door, punching in at the guard shack, where the watchmen looked them over like prison inmates. The factory was completely surrounded by barbed wire. Yes, what they called a modern factory was basically a prison, and for the pleasure of the machines, the lives of the poor slaves were consumed from eight in the morning until five in the evening. If my father had only had a connection, he would have instantly forgotten about my studies and gotten me a place among these workers, and while I fretted about spending all my years in this prison at some machine, he would have been happy, telling himself "My son is set for life."

I looked at some empty barrels on which our guys had written what we do to Communists. Then I watched some freight that a crane was lifting from a ship at the factory's dock. What a huge load! Its movements in the air were so strange! Who knew where this ship would go now, once it had delivered its cargo. I wanted to watch the ship a bit longer, but then, seeing the workers coming from across the way, I didn't want them to think I was some kind of worthless bum. Just because these guys had some connection by which to get themselves a job, I couldn't have them thinking they were better than me. Anyway, there wasn't much difference between us; their hair was combed and their clothes were clean. If I didn't have mud on my sneakers you wouldn't even know that I was out of a job.

I had forgotten about the fountain here. First, I had a really good drink of water, which hurt my empty stomach, but still it was good. Then I managed to clean my sneakers, and as I was getting the red mud of this godforsaken place, the disgusting filth of the past, off my feet, somebody came by.

"Could I get in and have a drink there, brother?" he said.

I stepped back. He must have been a worker, considering he was wearing a jacket in this heat. He took it off, folded it neatly, and laid it to the side. Then instead of drinking water, he started to flush out his nose and gargle. I got it: if you were really smart, you could not only find a job, but you could take somebody's turn by asking if you could have a drink and then wash your snot out. I wondered if he had graduated from middle school. I could see a wallet in the pocket of his jacket. While he was still blowing his nose, I got mad, so I grabbed the wallet out of his jacket and stuck it in my back pocket. I had it tucked away, and he was still blowing his nose. A little later, just to make me feel good, he pretended to take a sip of water.

"Okay, buddy, that's enough," I said. "I have work to do, too."

He stepped back. Then he said, "Thanks!" out of breath. He took his jacket and put it on. He didn't notice anything amiss. As I calmly washed off my sneakers he went off toward the factory. I didn't even watch him go. By the time I had removed most of the mud he was gone from sight. I went off quickly in the other direction, straight toward the station. The crickets had started up on account of the heat. A train came in behind me, people packed like sardines, heading to work on Monday morning, and they stared at me as it passed by. I figured I'd let this one go by and wait for the next one.

I walked the station platform with the notebook in my hand, trying to seem lost in thought like everybody else with something to do. I didn't even look at the two gendarmes on patrol. I headed straight to the snack bar.

"Three cheese toasts!" I said.

A hand reached out into the window and took three pieces of yellow cheese that were hanging there and put them into rolls. They hang the cheese slices in the window like that so you think that the sandwiches have a lot of cheese in them. You're very clever, aren't you, and because you think you're smarter than I am, you think you've got it made. But what if I'm not the idiot you think I am; what if I'm smarter than you are, and I mess up your little schemes. Then I had an idea.

"Let me have a razor blade and some glue," I said, laying one hundred liras on the marble countertop of the snack bar.

I picked up the change and my purchases and left. Again, I didn't look at the gendarmes. The restrooms in these stations are at the end of the platform. They smelled like shit. I fastened the latch on the door from the inside and proceeded to go through the wallet I'd put in my back pocket. Our clever worker had one one-thousand-lira bill, two five hundreds, and so, together with the change, that made two thousand five liras. In the other compartment of the wallet there was identification, as I expected—a social security card. Given name: Ibrahim. Family name: Şener. Father's name: Fevzi. Mother's name: Kamer, Trabzon, Sürmene, etc. Perfect. I read all of it a few times and memorized it. Then I took out my student ID and, leaning against the wall, carefully cut out my picture with the razor. With the edge of my fingernail I scraped off the cardboard backing from the picture. Then I took Ibrahim Şener's picture off the social security card, and when I'd glued my picture in its place, I became Ibrahim Şener. So far it was easy. I put Ibrahim Şener's social security card back in the wallet and put the wallet in my pocket. Then I left the restroom and walked back to the snack stand.

My toasts were ready. I ate with pleasure, since I had put nothing in my stomach for a whole day except for cherries and unripe garden tomatoes. I drank an *ayran,* too, and looked to see what else I could eat, since my pocket was full of money. There were cookies, chocolate, but none of it caught my eye. So I asked for another toast and told him I wanted it well done, but the guy didn't say anything. Leaning against the counter, I turned a little toward the station, I felt good, not worried about anything. Only once did I turn toward the fountain to see if anyone was coming along the train tracks, but there was nobody. He thought he was so smart, our clever worker, but he still hadn't figured out that I had made off with his wallet. Maybe he did realize it was gone but couldn't imagine that I would have taken it. When my toast was ready, I asked for a newspaper.

"Hürriyet."

They had put a bench there, so I sat down without attracting anyone's attention and read while I ate my sandwich.

First, I looked to see how many people had been killed yesterday. In Kars, in Izmir, in Antalya, in Balgat, in Ankara . . . I skipped over

Istanbul and looked at the end. We'd lost twelve, they'd lost sixteen people. Then I looked at the ones from Istanbul, nothing there, not even the name of Izmit. Then, anxiously, I looked at the section I was really afraid of; I read quickly, but there was no Nilgün Darvinoğlu among the injured. I read through all the names again, but in fact she wasn't there. Maybe this newspaper missed her, I thought, so I went and got a *Milliyet*. She wasn't among their list of injured either. Anyway, they listed the injured, but not usually the ones who did it. It's not important: if I'd wanted to see my name in the newspaper, I would have become either a prostitute or a football player.

Then I absentmindedly folded up the newspapers, went inside, over to the ticket booth; I knew right away where I was going.

"One for Üsküdar," I said.

"The train doesn't go to Üsküdar!" said the obnoxious ticket agent. "The last stop is Haydarpasha."

"I know, I know!" I said. "Give me a Haydarpasha."

He still didn't give me the ticket. Goddamn you. This time:

"Regular or student?" he said.

"I'm not a student anymore!" I said. "My name is Ibrahim Şener."

"What do I care what your name is!" he said, but he must have got scared when he saw my face, because he shut up and gave me the ticket.

I was ticked off. I'm not afraid of anyone. I went outside and looked up and down the track, but there was nothing coming or going. Some other smart alecks were sitting on the bench where I had been sitting. I thought of going over and making them get up, saying I was just sitting here, but it didn't seem worth it right now, the whole crowd waiting for the train might have ganged up on me. As I looked around to see if there was anyplace else to sit, I suddenly got scared: the gendarmes were looking at me.

"Buddy, do you have the time?" said one of them.

"Me?" I said. "Yeah, I have the time."

"What time is it?"

"Time?" I said. "It's five after eight."

They didn't say anything, just went off talking together. I kept on walking, but where was I going? Anyway I spotted an empty bench, so I sat down. Then like the people going to work, I lit my cigarette and opened my newspaper and concentrated on my reading. After finishing with the domestic news, I read the international news as well, paying close attention, like some important guy with a wife, kids, and responsibilities, interests to look after; I said to myself, If Brezhnev and Carter have secretly agreed to carve up Turkey, nothing could stop them. I was saying, Maybe they are the ones who sent the pope to Turkey, too, when somebody sat next to me, and I got scared.

I looked at him from the corner of my eye, without lowering my paper. He had huge, wrinkled hands, thick fingers, resting in a tired way on pants that were even more worn than mine. I looked at his face and understood: he was a poor old worker, sagging from work. I felt sorry for him. In a few years, assuming you don't die, you'll retire, and your life will have been for nothing. But he seemed completely unaware, not complaining, just staring at the people on the other side of the tracks, pretty cheerful, actually. Then I thought, Is he up to something, maybe he and they are in on this together, maybe all of them, everybody waiting in the station, are just playing with me. I shivered. But then the old worker let out such a yawn that I realized he was just a complete fool. What am I afraid of? They should be afraid of me! When I thought of that, I relaxed.

At that point it occurred to me that I could tell him everything, this old guy, maybe he even knew my father from somewhere—my dad really gets around—that's right, I'm the son of that crippled lottery-ticket seller, and now I'm going off to Istanbul. To Üsküdar! I could even tell him about Nilgün and about our guys and what they thought of me, But look, that newspaper you're holding has nothing about it yet, you know, sometimes it seems to me that all of this, all our country's sorrows, are on account of some bastards who just enjoy playing with us, but one day I'm going to do something, I'm going to take the fun out of their games. I don't know yet what it is that

I'm going to do, but you're all going to be amazed, you understand? This newspaper here will write all about it then, these fools waiting for the train, happy because they have a job to go to every morning, who ignore everything that's going on, they will understand then, they'll be shocked, they'll even be afraid of me, and they'll think, We didn't know all this, everything, was so pointless, and we had no idea. When that day comes, the television will talk about me, too, not just the newspapers, they'll understand, you'll all understand.

The train was coming; I folded the newspaper carefully and calmly got to my feet. Then I took a look at Faruk's notebook filled with his handwriting, even read a little! What nonsense! *History is for slaves, stories for people who are half asleep, fables for stupid children; history is for fools, pathetic creatures, cowards!* I couldn't even be bothered to rip it up. I just threw it into the trash bin next to the bench. Then, just like people who don't think about the things they do, just like everybody, I dropped my cigarette butt casually on the ground, and I crushed it without thinking, just the way you do. The doors of the cars opened: hundreds of faces looking out at me. They go off to work in the morning, they come home from work at night, so they can go back to work in the morning and come home at night again, poor jerks, they don't know, they don't know! But they'll learn! I'll teach them, but not just yet, I thought; for now, okay, I'll be like one of you who has a job to go to in the morning, look, I'm just like all of you, I'm getting on the crowded train, I'm joining you.

The inside of the car crawling with people was humid and hot. Watch out for me from now on! Be afraid!

32

Fatma Finds Consolation
in Holding a Book

❖

I was lying in my bed waiting for them. I was waiting with my head resting on the pillow, thinking that when they came to kiss my hand before going back to Istanbul, we would talk, I would say things, and they would listen to me, when all that noise coming from downstairs suddenly stopped. I couldn't hear footsteps going from one room to the other, I couldn't hear the rattling when they shut the doors and opened the windows, I could hear nothing of those conversations echoing on the stairs and the ceiling, and I was afraid.

I got up from the bed, took my cane, and tapped on the floor a few times, but the sneaky dwarf pretended not to hear me. After tapping the cane a few more times, I thought maybe I could shame him in front of the others, because he couldn't well pretend not to hear me if they did, so I slowly got out of my room, and from the top of the stairs I started again:

"Recep, Recep, quick, come upstairs."

But there was not a sound downstairs.

What a strange, frightening thing this silence is. I quickly went back to my room, my legs went wobbly as I pushed open the shutters and looked down to the garden: somebody was running frantically to the car, it was Metin, and when he got in and took off, dear God, I was full of anxious confusion. I stayed there thinking the worst, but not for long, because very soon, he rushed back and to my surprise a woman got out of the car with him and they went inside together. When I saw the bag in her hand and her long scarf, I recognized the woman: it was the lady pharmacist, who, when they think I'm sick, comes with that huge bag, more suitable for a man to carry, and chats sweetly to coax me into letting her stick me with her poison needles: Fatma Hanım, you have a fever, it's a needless strain on your heart, let me give you a shot of penicillin, just relax, why are you afraid, why, you're a doctor's wife yourself, and everyone here only wants the best for you. Those were the words that would most arouse my suspicion, and in the end, after I'd cried a little, they would give up and let me be with my temperature, and then I would think: They want to poison your body because they couldn't poison your mind, Fatma, be careful.

I was careful, waiting in fear. But nothing happened. The footsteps I was expecting never came up the stairs; nothing broke the silence downstairs. After waiting a little longer, I heard some noises coming from the kitchen door, and I ran to the window again. The pharmacy woman with her bag was going, this time by herself: this pretty lady, rather young and lively, was walking in an odd way in the garden, and as I was watching her, just a few steps before the garden gate she stopped to pull something from her bag and, setting the bag down, unfolded a big handkerchief, and she started to cry, wiping her nose with it. I felt such pity for the pretty woman, tell me, what did they say to you, tell me, but she collected herself, and after wiping her eyes one last time, she took up her bag again and left. As she was going out the garden gate she turned for a second to look at the house, but she didn't see me.

Out of curiosity, I just stayed on there at the window. When I couldn't stand it anymore I got furious at them, go now, begone from my thoughts, and leave me alone! But they still didn't come, and there was not a peep from downstairs. I went over to my bed. Don't worry, Fatma, soon enough that unpleasant noise will start up again, in just a little while, that wild hilarity, so inconsiderate. I got into my bed and thought: They'll be up in a little while, after they galumph up the stairs, Faruk, Nilgün, and Metin will come into my room, and I'll feel that familiar mixture of irritation and jealousy and peace of mind as they bend down to kiss my hand and I am reminded: what strange hair they have—not from our side! We're going, Grandmother, we're going, they'll say, but we'll come again soon. Grandmother, you're looking really well, you'll be fine, just take good care of yourself, don't make us worry, okay, we're going. Then there'll be silence for a moment and I'll watch as they stare at me: attentively, lovingly, pityingly, and with a strange kind of gladness. That's when I'll know they're thinking about my death, and how death might even suit me, and because I have no use for their pity, I may even try to make some kind of joke then, as long as they don't annoy me by telling me to be more tolerant. Perhaps I'll say, Would anyone like a taste of this cane to remember me by, or Mind your manners, children, or I'll take you by the ears and nail you to the wall, but it was really no use, these wisecracks wouldn't so much as make them smile, and after a moment of not reacting, they'd take their cue to mouth the same life-less empty words of farewell that they've memorized:

"Well, we're going, Grandmother, whom do you want to say hello to in Istanbul?"

No matter how many times I hear it, somehow this question always stirs my feelings, as if I wasn't expecting it. I'll remember Istanbul, which I left seventy years ago, it's a pity actually because I know they're up to the necks in sin there, just wallowing in it, but still, sometimes I'm just curious. On cold winter nights, especially when the dwarf hasn't lit the stove properly, and I'm chilled to the bone, even I would like, just for a while, to be there with them, in a cheerful room, well lit and warm, I dream of that, but, no, I'll have none of their sinfulness! In the end, if I just can't banish that warm

and cheerful room from my mind, I'll get out of my bed, open my
closet, and take out the box where I keep them all, together with
the broken sewing-machine needles and bobbins and the old electric bills, right beside my jewelry box, I'll take them out and look
at them: Oh, what a pity, you've all died, they announced it to the
whole world afterward, and I clipped them out of the newspapers
and kept them, look: Death notice, Semiha Esen, daughter of the late
Halil Cemil Bey, former general director of the administration of the
sugar factories; Death notice, member of our Administrative Coun-
cil (they should have been glad of that least), Murruvet Hanımefendi;
and the stupidest one of all: Death notice, Nihal Abla, only child
of Adnan Bey, one of the old moneyed people, of course I remember, look, you married a tobacco merchant, had three children and,
God bless them, eleven grandchildren, but you really loved Behlul,
while he was in love with that immoral Bihter, don't even think of
it, Fatma, look there's this last one, it must be ten years now: Death
notice, Nigân Işıkcı Hanımefendi, daughter of the late Şükrü Pasha,
minister of foundations and ambassador to France, sister of the late
Türkân and Şükran, ooh, Nigân, when I read that you have gone
back to God, standing here alone in the middle of the room, I realize that I have nobody left in Istanbul and I think, You all endured
that hell Selâhattin described in his encyclopedia and that he wished
more than anything to descend upon the earth, you all sank into the
ugly sins of Istanbul, to die and be buried among concrete apartment
houses, factory smokestacks, plastic smells, and sewer pipes—just
awful! When I think of this I feel the strange peace of a little pang
of fear, and I go back to bed seeking the warmth of the quilt on the
cold winter night, and tired by thoughts, I want to sleep, to forget. I
have no one to say hello to in Istanbul.

Let them come and ask anyway, this time I'll give them the
answer straight off without being surprised and stirred, but there's
still not a sound downstairs. I got out of my bed, looked at the clock
on the table: ten in the morning! Where were they? I went and stuck
my head out the window; the car was sitting there where Metin had

left it, and it was then I realized: I couldn't even hear the noise of the cricket that hadn't budged from where it had been sitting outside the kitchen door for weeks: I'm afraid of silence! Then I thought about the pharmacist lady who had come a little while ago—what could she have wanted? —and then again about what the dwarf could be telling them. I went straight out of room to the top of the stairs and knocked with my cane on the floor:

"Recep, Recep, come up here right away!"

But this time I knew that he wasn't going to come, that I was tapping with my cane on the floor for nothing and straining my old voice to no end, but I called out anyway, and as I did I had a strange feeling and I shivered: as though they had all gone without telling me and they were never going to come back, they'd left, and I was there in the house all alone! It was a frightening thought, and to forget it I called out downstairs again, but only to have that strange feeling all the more. As though there was no one left in the world, not a bird, not a shameless dog, not so much as an insect to remind us with its buzzing about the heat and the time of day: time had stopped, and only I remained, with my panicked voice calling out again downstairs for nothing, and my cane knocking again and again on the floor, and still it seemed there was no one to hear me: only empty armchairs, tables slowly accumulating dust, closed doors, hopeless furniture that creaked all on its own, death as you described it, Selâhattin! My God, I was scared, thinking that my thoughts would freeze like the furniture, that I would become as colorless and odorless as a piece of ice, stuck here for eternity never to feel anything. Then I suddenly thought of going downstairs to reunite with time and motion, and so I forced myself, making it to the fourth step down, before I got dizzy. I stopped in fear: There are still fifteen steps, you can't make it, Fatma, you'll fall! Slowly, anxiously, I went back up the steps, turning my back to that terrifying silence, hoping to lift my spirits and to forget: They'll come along now to kiss your hand, Fatma, don't worry.

When I got to my door I was no longer afraid, but I wasn't in good spirits either: Selâhattin's picture on the wall was giving me a frightening look, but I couldn't feel anything, as though now I had lost the senses of smell, of taste, and of touch. I took seven more little steps, got to my bed, sat on the edge, not letting myself go until I'd managed to lean back against the headboard, and from there, as I stared at the carpet, I thought of how useless were these endlessly recurring thoughts of mine, and I was annoyed: I was trapped in the void with only my pointless thoughts. Then I stretched out on the bed, and as my head touched the pillow, I thought, Is it time, are they coming now, are they coming through the door to kiss my hand, good-bye, Grandmother, good-bye, but still there was not the slightest sound from the stairs or down below, and because I was afraid of worrying, I told myself I was not yet ready for this ceremony, it would have to wait as I prepared myself, cutting time into equal pieces, like an orange, just as I did on silent lonely winter nights. So I pulled my quilt up over myself and waited.

While I was waiting I knew I would find something to brood about. But what? I wanted my mind to reveal itself to me like a glove turned inside out: So that's what you're really like, Fatma, I'd tell myself in the end, the exterior form that the mirror shows is the opposite of what I'm like inside! Let me be astonished, let me forget, let me wonder: it's my exterior that they come time and again to look at, the thing they bring downstairs for dinner and whose hand they'll kiss in a little while; sometimes I wonder what my interior actually is. A heart that goes pitter-patter and thoughts that glide by like little paper boats on flowing water, and what else? A strange thing! Sometimes lying there between sleep and wakefulness, I confuse them, and I marvel with a sweet excitement: it's as though my outside has become my inside and my inside my outside, and in the dark I can't figure out which one I am. My hand reaches out like a silent cat and turns on the light, I touch the cold iron bars of the bed, but the cold iron only leaves me in a cold winter night: where am I? Sometimes you can't even tell anymore. If a person can live in the same house for seventy years and still be confused, then this thing that we call life, and imagine we have used up, must be such a strange and incomprehensible thing that no one can even know what their own life is. You stand there waiting and on it goes from place to place, no one knows why, and as it goes, you have many thoughts about where it's been and where it's headed; then just as you speak these strange thoughts, which aren't right or wrong, and lead to no conclusion, you look, and the journey ends here, Fatma, okay, this is where you get off! First one foot, then the other, I get out of the carriage. I take two steps, then step back and look at the carriage. Was this the thing that brought us here, swaying all the way? Well, I guess that was it. So at the end that's how I'll think: that was it, it wasn't the most pleasant trip, I didn't understand a thing, but I still want to start it all over again. But one is not allowed! Come on, they say, we're here now, on the other side, you can't get back on again. And as the driver snaps his whip and the carriage draws away I want to cry, looking at it from behind: So that means I can't start again, Mother, there's no next time! But in my rebellious way I think that people have to be able to start over, just as I believed that a little girl has to be able to stay an innocent child her whole life long if she wants to, and that's when I remember Nigân, Türkân, and Şükran and the books they read and that trip back I took with my mother and I am cheered up, in a bittersweet way.

That morning my mother took me to Şükrü Pasha's, and before turning me over to them, she said in the carriage as she did every time, Look, Fatma, when I come to pick you up in the evening, please don't start to cry again, or this will be the last time, but I quickly forgot what my mother had said as I played all day with Nigân, Türkân, and Şükran, admiring them, thinking how much smarter and prettier than I they were, because they played the piano so beautifully and could mimic not only the lame driver but even their father, and him so perfectly that I was startled and only dared to laugh along with them much later; in the afternoon they recited poems, and having gone to France, they knew French, but later, they'd pull out novels translated into Turkish and read from them, passing the book from hand to hand, and it was so nice just to listen that when I suddenly saw my mother in front of me, I began to cry, realizing that it was time to go home, and though my mother would give me a very stern look, I still wouldn't remember what she had told me that morning in the carriage, and besides I wasn't crying just because it was time to go home but also because my mother had given me such a stern look, so that Şükran, Nigân, and Türkân's mother felt sorry for me and said, Girls, bring her some candy, and as my mother said, Madam, I'm so embarrassed, their mother insisted it was nothing, and Nigân brought the candy in the silver bowl, and as everybody looked on waiting for me to stop crying, I didn't reach out and take one, but rather said, That's not what I want, to which they answered, But what is it that you want, and my mother replied, That's enough now, Fatma, but I, gathering all my courage, said, I want that book, but because, through my tears, I couldn't even say which one, Şükran asked her mother to let her bring them all, and then, as my mother said, Madam, I don't believe she can read these books and besides she doesn't even like to read, I was glancing at the covers of the books out of the corner of my eye, *The Count of Monte Cristo,* Xavier de Montépin, and Paul de Kock were there, but the one I wanted was *Robinson Crusoe,* which they'd read to me after lunch, and when I asked for it, my mother was so ashamed, but their mother, said, Fine, my girl, you can borrow it, but don't lose it, it's Şükrü Pasha's, and then I was quiet and I left quietly, sitting in the carriage with the book in my hand.

As I sat across from her on the way home, I was afraid to look at my mother's face: my eyes red from crying stayed on the road behind us and on the windows of Şükrü Pasha's villa, which I could still see, until my mother suddenly burst out, calling me spoiled child. Obviously that wasn't enough, a little later she added that I would not be going back to Şükrü Pasha's mansion next week. Looking at my mother's face, I thought about how she had just said this to make me cry, because words like those had made me cry before, but I didn't this time. I felt a strange contentment and peace of mind, an easy feeling inside me, whose reason I understood only much later, as I thought and thought about it, lying in my bed: much later on, I decided that the pleasure came from that book I was holding, from looking at the cover and remembering how Nigân, Türkân, and Şükran, one after the other, had read to me from it that day; I didn't follow everything, it seemed like a confusing book to me, but still I was able to gather some of what was going on: an Englishman lived for years alone on a desert island because his ship had sunk, no, not entirely alone, actually he had a servant whom he had discovered years later, but still it was very strange. It was very strange to think of someone living for years all by himself, without seeing another soul, but as the carriage swayed back and forth, I knew that it wasn't this thought that filled me with peace, I knew it was something else. True, my mother was no longer furrowing her brows at me, but even better, I was facing backward, as I liked to do, not looking forward with the driver; and though Şükrü Pasha's mansion was no longer to be seen, I had before my eyes the road and the memory of this day, which was so lovely to contemplate. But the thing that pleased me above all was the feeling that once back home, because of the book in my hand, I might be able to relive those delightfully confusing moments now past. At home, my impatient eye would perhaps travel aimlessly through the incomprehensible pages of the book, but as it wandered and wandered, I would remember bits and pieces of the things we did at Şükrü Pasha's house, where I wouldn't be going next week. Because, as I would always tell myself so many years later, lying here in my bed: You can't start out again in life, that's a carriage ride you only take once, but with a book in your hand, no matter how confusing and perplexing it might be, once you've finished it, you can always go back to the beginning; if you like, you can read it through again, in order to figure out what you couldn't understand before, in order to understand life, isn't that so, Fatma?

ALSO BY ORHAN PAMUK

"Deeply human and engaging. . . . [Pamuk] has
become one of the essential writers that both East
and West can gratefully claim as their own."
—Pico Iyer, The New York Times

THE BLACK BOOK

Galip is a lawyer living in Istanbul. His wife, Rüya, has
disappeared. Could she have left him for her ex-husband or Celâl,
a popular newspaper columnist? But Celâl, too, seems to have
vanished. When Galip begins to investigate, he finds himself assuming the enviable Celâl's identity, wearing his clothes,
answering his phone calls, even writing his columns. Galip
pursues every clue, but the nature of the mystery keeps
changing, and when he receives a death threat, he begins to fear
the worst. With its cascade of beguiling stories about Istanbul,
The Black Book is a brilliantly unconventional mystery, and a
provocative meditation on identity.

Fiction

ISTANBUL

A shimmering evocation, by turns intimate and panoramic,
of one of the world's great cities, by its foremost writer. Orhan
Pamuk was born in Istanbul and still lives in the family apartment building where his mother first held him in her arms. His
portrait of his city is thus also a self-portrait, refracted by memory and the melancholy—or *hüzün*—that all *Istanbullus* share:
the sadness that comes of living amid the ruins of a lost
empire. With cinematic fluidity, Pamuk moves from his glam-
orous, unhappy parents to the gorgeous, decrepit mansions
overlooking the Bosphorus; from the dawning of his self-
consciousness to the writers and painters—both Turkish and foreign—who would shape his consciousness of his city. Like Joyce's
Dublin and Borges's Buenos Aires, Pamuk's *Istanbul* is a triumphant encounter of place and sensibility, beautifully written and
immensely moving.

Travel/Memoir

THE MUSEUM OF INNOCENCE

It is 1975, a perfect spring in Istanbul. Kemal and Sibel, children of two prominent families, are about to become engaged. But when Kemal encounters Füsun, a beautiful shopgirl and a distant relation, he becomes enthralled. And once they violate the code of virginity, a rift begins to open between Kemal and the world of the Westernized Istanbul bourgeoisie. In his pursuit of Füsun over the next eight years, Kemal becomes a compulsive collector of objects that chronicle his lovelorn progress—amassing a museum that is both a map of a society and of his heart.

Fiction/Literature

MY NAME IS RED

The Sultan has commissioned a cadre of the most acclaimed artists in the land to create a great book celebrating the glories of his realm. Their task: to illuminate the work in the European style. But because figurative art can be deemed an affront to Islam, this commission is a dangerous proposition indeed. And when one of the chosen miniaturists disappears, the only clue to the mystery lies in the half-finished illuminations themselves. Part fantasy and part philosophical puzzle, *My Name Is Red* is a kaleidoscopic journey into the intersection of art, religion, love, sex, and power.

Fiction/Literature

THE NAIVE AND SENTIMENTAL NOVELIST

In this fascinating set of essays, based on the talks he delivered at Harvard University as part of the distinguished Norton Lecture series, Pamuk presents a comprehensive and provocative theory of the novel and the experience of reading. Drawing on Friedrich Schiller's famous distinction between "naïve" writers—those who write spontaneously—and "sentimental" writers—those who are reflective and aware—Pamuk reveals two unique ways of processing and composing the written word. He takes us through his own literary journey and the beloved novels of his youth to describe the singular experience of reading. Unique, nuanced, and passionate, this book will be beloved by readers and writers alike.

Literature/Essays

THE NEW LIFE

"I read a book one day, and my whole life was changed." With these words, the protagonist of Orhan Pamuk's fiendishly engaging novel is launched into a world of hypnotic texts and (literally) Byzantine conspiracies that whirl across the steppes and forlorn frontier towns of Turkey. Through the simple act of reading a book, a young student is uprooted from his old life and identity. Within days he has fallen in love with the luminous and elusive Janan; witnessed the attempted assassination of a rival suitor; and forsaken his family to travel aimlessly through a nocturnal landscape of travelers' cafes and apocalyptic bus wrecks. As imagined by Pamuk, the result is a wondrous marriage of the intellectual thriller and high romance.

Fiction/Literature

OTHER COLORS

In the three decades that Nobel Prize–winning author Orhan Pamuk has devoted himself to writing fiction, he has also produced scores of witty, moving, and provocative essays and articles. In this collection, Pamuk engages the work of Nabokov, Kundera, Rushdie, and Vargas Llosa, among others, and he discusses his own books and writing process. We also learn how he lives, as he recounts his successful struggle to quit smoking, describes his relationship with his daughter, and reflects on the controversy he has attracted in recent years. Here is a thoughtful compilation of a brilliant novelist's best nonfiction, offering different perspectives on his lifelong obsessions with loneliness, contentment, and the books and cities that have shaped his experience.

Literature/Essays

SNOW

An exiled poet named Ka returns to Turkey and travels to the city of Kars. His ostensible purpose is to report on a wave of suicides among religious girls forbidden to wear their head scarves. But Ka is also drawn by his memories of the radiant Ipek, now recently divorced. Amid snowfall and universal suspicion, Ka finds himself pursued by figures ranging from Ipek's ex-husband to a charismatic terrorist. A lost gift returns with ecstatic suddenness. A theatrical evening climaxes in a massacre. And finding God may be the prelude to losing everything else.

Fiction/Literature

THE WHITE CASTLE

In the seventeenth century, a young Italian scholar sailing from Venice to Naples is taken prisoner and delivered to Constantinople. There he falls into the custody of a scholar known as Hoja—"master"—a man who is his exact double. In the years that follow, the slave instructs his master in Western science and technology, from medicine to pyrotechnics. But Hoja wants to know more: why he and his captive are the persons they are and whether, given knowledge of each other's most intimate secrets, they could actually exchange identities. *The White Castle* is a colorful and intricately patterned triumph of the imagination.

Fiction/Literature